mixed

mixed

An Anthology of
Short Fiction on the Multiracial Experience

Edited by **Chandra Prasad**

Introduction by **Rebecca Walker**

W. W. Norton & Company
New York London

Manufacturing by Courier Westford
Book design by Judith Stagnitto Abbate / Abbate Design
Production manager: Anna Oler

Library of Congress Cataloging-in-Publication Data

Mixed : an anthology of short fiction on the multiracial experience / edited by
Chandra Prasad ; introduction by Rebecca Walker.
p. cm.
ISBN-13: 978-0-393-32786-1 (pbk.)
ISBN-10: 0-393-32786-8 (pbk.)
1. Short stories, American—Minority authors. 2. American fiction—21st century.
3. Difference (Psychology)—Fiction. 4. Race—Fiction. 5. Racially mixed people—Fiction.
I. Prasad, Chandra.

PS647.E85M59 2006
813'.01083552—dc22

2006009080

W. W. Norton & Company, Inc., 500 Fifth Avenue, New York, N.Y. 10110
www.wwnorton.com

W. W. Norton & Company Ltd., Castle House, 75/76 Wells Street, London W1T 3QT

1 2 3 4 5 6 7 8 9 0

Contents

Foreword

Chandra Prasad

The year after graduating from college, while living in Washington, D.C., I started to tally the number of strangers who would stop me and ask me what I am—Mexican, Pakistani, Greek, Lebanese? The list went on. The perpetual questioning wasn't annoying so much as amusing. For by then, in my early twenties, I was used to being asked about my background, and understood that such inquiries generally arose not from idle curiosity, but from deeper, murkier issues of identity and belonging. My younger brother, Ravi, who has a quirky sense of humor and looks like he could have come from anywhere, likes to make a game of the what-are-you grilling. He gives a different answer each time, then studies the person's reaction. Often Ravi is met with the warmth of familiarity—"Ah, so you *are* from the old country!" Other times it's nonchalance, or the faint bristle of aversion.

All of us, whether we're conscious of it or not, compartmentalize people so that we can more readily place them along the continuum of what is personally comprehensible. The government compartmentalizes too. It was only in 2000 that the U.S. Census finally allowed citizens to check off as many racial categories as are applicable—"White," "Black," "American Indian," "Asian Indian," etc. Previously, Americans were allowed to check off only one, leaving multiracial people invisible and unaccounted for.

Now that the mixed identity has become a matter of public discourse, so too have some of its intricacies. Because multiracial people are united only by the fact that they are not easily bracketed, the experience of being mixed is not a singular one. But there is some commonality among multiracial people: being the physical proof of an increasingly global society, acting as the solder between various communities, straddling cultural expectations. For some, the challenges are much more formidable. Within the American foster care system, for example, mixed-race children represent a rapidly growing segment. Multiracial adolescents stand a greater risk of depression and substance abuse, according to a recent study published in the *American Journal of Public Health*. And against life-threatening diseases that require bone marrow transplants, mixed-race people—given their highly specific ethnic makeup—face steep odds of finding a match, reports the Mavin Foundation.

Fortunately, a greater awareness of multiracial people is keeping pace with this group's exploding population (the United States alone currently counts over twenty million multiracial inhabitants). Dozens of books, websites, and community organizations devoted to multiracial issues are flourishing. Mixed-race stars are now mainstays of music, movies, and professional sports. In publishing, too, multiracial authors are offering some of the most deft, insightful, and well-received prose around. I'm proud that so many of these authors have chosen to contribute to this anthology.

What's vital about *Mixed* is its timeliness and its ability to welcome all readers into its fold. The literature here is by and about multiracial persons, but the feelings it evokes are universal, whether it be the determination and desperation of Peter Ho Davies's minotaur, the determination of Emily Raboteau's plucky young hero, or the jolting panic of Wayde Compton's drug-addled university student.

Ultimately, I hope *Mixed* will help readers to explore a new, hybridized world; to ask sticky questions; to refuse easy answers. My quietest, grandest dream, though, is that this book will blur boundaries—or better yet, expose how illusory most boundaries are in the first place.

Acknowledgments

Many people and organizations believed in this book from the beginning. To these I offer my sincerest thanks, and especially to my agent, Rosalie Siegel, Amy Cherry and the dedicated staff at W. W. Norton, Radha and Sue Prasad, Raman and Ravi Prasad, and the Mavin Foundation, which inspires me and countless others. Thanks to my husband, Basil Petrov, for seeing humor and optimism in just about everything. Lastly, I am enormously grateful to *Mixed*'s contributors, all of whom understood the importance of getting this book published, and made good on their promise to deliver outstanding fiction.

Introduction

Rebecca Walker

When I wrote *Black, White, and Jewish* six years ago, there were very few books that plumbed the depths of the mixed race experience. I knew of only one, *The Color of Water* by James McBride, that managed to (mostly) escape the trope of the tragic mulatto. This moving account of growing up the black son of a white mother so captured the heart of America that even today, almost ten years after it was published, people ask wistfully if I have read it. Deservedly, *Water* stayed on the *New York Times* best-seller list for over two years.

Black, White, and Jewish did not stay on the *New York Times* best-seller list for two years (although it did hit number 36 on the extended list for a couple of weeks), and I have often wondered why it didn't do even remotely as well as *Water*. Not in an insecure writer way, though like every other writer I know I've had my moments. But more in terms of what the discrepancy says about America and how mixed race people are or are not incorporated into our collective image of the American Family.

Which multiracial narrative fits our ethos of triumph over great odds? Which reaffirms our hopeful belief that our country really is a place everyone can call home?

Water is a story of self-discovery told through the lens of the author's deep reverence for his self-sacrificing white mother. Unlike many multiracial people, McBride had the luxury of cultural cohesion. Because his mother pretended to be African American, he always thought of himself as Black. At least in part because of this initial wholeness, the outcome of McBride's journey is uplifting and transcendent rather than fragmented and heartbreaking. Indeed, we come away from the memoir with the wonderful notion that God is the color of water, and so our true color as human beings is clear, and not this other nonsense that breaks our world to pieces.

My book came to a similar conclusion, minus a few dollops of uplift. At the end of 247 pages and 18 years I am still torn between camps, somewhat adrift on the sea of American race relations. I have accepted that there are no easy answers and that in addition to love and hope, I carry profound rage and sorrow in my mixed race knapsack. Where McBride was able, God bless him, to overcome, I still had some questions. And the display of that, my heart and mind ripped open and aching on the page, was shocking and cathartic. It was far more reminiscent of the LA riots than the successful melting pot in which much of America likes to think it lives.

Which is why I turned to the short stories in this collection with interest. I was keen to find out if there had been a shift in the American psyche. Certainly, there are more self-identified multiracial people in America than ever before, some twenty million and counting. And if Alicia Keys, Keanu Reeves, Jessica Alba, and Vin Diesel are any indication, mixed people are more visible and successful as a result. Add in our heavyweight symbolic status—we're the poster children for globalism, hybridization, humanism, and a dozen other cultural products predicated on transcending boundaries—and you can't help but conclude: It's more than cool to be mixed, it's downright relevant.

Would I then read two dozen stories about the privilege of being biracial and the joys of calling two cultures home? Would the lingering questions in *Black, White, and Jewish* be eclipsed by a water-colored mixed race generation that had finally surpassed the "caught between two worlds" existence? And if so, would the book be embraced by a wider audience? Would it, like *Water*, also cross over and out of the mixed race ghetto, indicating that Americans are closer to embracing our multiracial citizenry than folding them into some "don't ask, don't tell" social engineering project?

I mean, really, it's 2006. My white, Jewish sister is in love with an African American man and my father worries because he knows from experience it's not easy. Should I tell her otherwise?

Just what is the state of the mulatto nation?

Well, if this collection is any indication, the mulatto nation is still rife with pathos. Even though a few of these short stories suggest the possibility of looking at our plight with an eye toward the glass half full, we're far from arrived. Emotional cruelty, rape, abduction, and excommunication punctuate these pages like poison. Broken friendships, destroyed marriages, and devastated families haunt the space that's left, while alienation, guilt, and especially anger lurk furtively in the subtext. Apparently, even though it's hip to be mixed, it still doesn't feel very good.

While we may play dress up on TV, in real life mixed people are more likely to find ourselves in potentially lethal situations with untrustworthy and inappropriate bedfellows. We are still asked to choose between different races and cultures. Still ridiculed for our approximation of a discrete cultural blend all our own. Still not trusted because of our inability or unwillingness to readily take a side. Still hated for our belief that there is life beyond racial categories.

Speaking from experience, I can attest that a lifetime of being thought of as a traitor and misfit, a poser and malcontent, takes a toll. The pity of those who view mixed race people as morbidly lost wears on the psyche. The opportunism of those who prey upon our plasticity and profit from our fifteen minutes of cultural currency is depressing. The bitterness of the race-war recruiters who shake their heads at us in disgust is demoralizing. We put on a good face, because that's what we do, we soothe opposing factions in order to survive, but underneath it all, there's quite a bit of something else brewing, and it ain't pretty.

Which seems about right. How could it be otherwise when the culture at large is enthralled with futuristic postrace scenarios and stirring stories of transracial redemption? If we can't acknowledge how pissed we are, how downright beat up we often feel, we will never make it to mental health, never mind social parity. Acts of cultural contortion and psychic mutilation will be our constant companions, all the way to the bank. As a dear friend likes to say when speaking of emotional wounds that are hard to face, "We've been in an accident, honey. The only thing to do is find the hospital."

But what and where is our hospital? How can we come to terms with our experience and its aftermath in a way that might actually bring us some relief? After all, the problem of the tragic mulatto is not that she is tragic, but that the presentation of her tragedy suggests no exit.

Fortunately, there are a few potent remedies in this collection, and by all means I prescribe them. Steal the lawn jockeys in your neighborhood and paint them white (resist racism), reconnect with once alienated monoracial friends who now have biracial babies (forge alliances where you can), call up the one person you're absolutely certain loved you (seek unconditional love), make lifelong pacts of connection with other multiracial people (surround yourself with people who just might understand the set of dynamics you call your life), and perhaps most important, reevaluate the very notion of race. Ask yourself if alleged racial differences exist in the objective or subjective field. Who, exactly, is it that draws the lines and assigns the opposing sets of adjectives? We might think we know who did it first, but who is doing it now, today, at this very moment. Who will do it tomorrow?

(Free your mind.)

This last prescription is especially important because mixed race people can become morbidly obsessed with race, both because everyone else is and because it is the place of our deepest wound. We carry an internal brokenness as a result of our experiences betwixt and between, and if we aren't careful we end up hoarding and polishing it like gold, as if the brokenness is the true indicator of who we really are. As if racial incoherence is the axis upon which our very existence revolves.

I didn't really understand the extent to which I identified with an unhealthy sense of fragmentation until four or five years ago. I was having lunch with a friend, and we were talking about our favorite writers, and our favorite lines of our favorite writers. My friend quoted Shakespeare and Marguerite Duras, and I quoted, with great emotion and emphasis, Zora Neale Hurston. He said, "Love is not love which alters when it alteration finds," and I said, "Put me down easy, Janie, I'm a cracked plate." The look on his face, a mixture of surprise, sympathy, and sadness, gave me pause, and after a few seconds I knew he was right. I'd read thousands of books, dozens of plays, and what line did I internalize and turn into my own, private mantra? By identifying so deeply with the sentiment, I had reified my own brokenness, again and again.

But not one of us has ever been a cracked plate. We have only held the fractured projections of others, innocently imbibing harmful judgments that were not our own. This mindless absorption of the negative mythologies of others is a source of great misery in our lives. I fear this habitual self-sabotage much more than garden-variety racism, for it has the power to destroy from within that which outwardly, physically, cannot be denied. Namely, that multiracial people exist, that we call all categories into question, and that, if we can survive this internal battle, we embody a different tomorrow. But if we remain mesmerized by the idea of ourselves as eternally broken, we all but guarantee the loss of our lives as fully functional, whole human beings.

I rarely think about being mixed these days, other than to notice the effect it has on others and to consider the assumed implications of it in a racially charged situation. When I do contemplate my mixedness, it is like visiting an old friend, familiar, but no longer involved in the day-to-day goings-on of my life. I have found and fortified the person beneath the projection; I have become the director of the movie and not just the passive screen. I can't say it's been easy, but I can say that when I saw an opportunity to exit the tragedy, I am extremely glad I took it.

DAVID FENTON

Rebecca Walker was named by *Time* magazine as one of fifty influential American leaders under forty. She is the author of the award-winning, international best-seller *Black, White, and Jewish: Autobiography of a Shifting Self* and the editor of two groundbreaking anthologies, *What Makes a Man: 22 Writers Imagine the Future* and *To Be Real: Telling the Truth and Changing the Face of Feminism*. She has written for many publications, including *Essence*, *Harper's*, *Glamour*, *Spin*, *Vibe*, and *Buddhadharma*, and her work is widely anthologized. She divides her time between New York City and northern California.

mixed

MARION ETTLINGER

Ruth Ozeki

Ruth Ozeki is a writer and filmmaker. She is the author of *My Year of Meats* and *All Over Creation*, both award-winning novels, national bestsellers, and *New York Times* Notable Books in 1998 and 2003, respectively. She was born in New Haven, Connecticut. Since 2001, she has been living in British Columbia, Canada.

The Anthropologists' Kids

There used to be this joke at Yale, that in order to get tenure in the Anthropology Department you had to have an Oriental wife. Mostly it was the Oriental wives who told this joke and found it funny, but everyone knew there was truth in it. After the war, many of the tenured anthropologists had married Asian women, and if you included all the graduate students and untenured teaching staff—the assistants, associates, and adjuncts who, by accident or design, had mimicked the marital predilections of the senior faculty—their numbers achieved some statistical significance.

The anthropologists were all white guys.

They were tall white guys with stooped shoulders and sun-burned necks that they protected from the rays with folded kerchiefs. Their skin, turned leathery from years in the field, had the crosshatched texture of plucked chickens. Their thin, sand-colored hair was matted with sweat, and it stuck to their high receding foreheads when they took off their pith helmets. Some of them worked for the CIA.

I'm just kidding. They didn't really wear pith helmets, at least not at home. At home, in New Haven, our dads wore tweed jackets with fraying cuffs and patches on the elbows and missing buttons, which their wives, our moms, deftly repaired with quick Asian fingers, muttering all the while in their various tongues.

Our moms were indeed various. They were Japanese and Korean and Burmese. They were Filipina and Fujianese, Mandarin and Malay. Some of them had been students. Others worked as secretaries or linguistic informants for their husbands. A few had Ph.D.s and taught. All of them knew how to catalogue and file. Here is something else they had in common: they were all considerably shorter than their husbands.

Anthropology Department parties were exotic affairs, tribal gatherings much envied by other faculties at Yale. When a Political Science or Mathematics professor was invited to dinner, or graduate students from Econ or English Lit infiltrated one of our cocktail parties, they stood out like sore thumbs, made instantly conspicuous by their tall, blond wives. In the days before cheap ethnic cuisine, before sushi and pad thai and shwarmas and falafels became available on every street corner in New Haven, these departmental outsiders came to sample our anthropological fare. They came to eat our roasted meat on skewers, to dip their shrimp chips into our strange sauces. Because when an Oriental wife cooked even something as mundane as meat loaf, you could be sure it had a hidden kick to it, something peppery and piquant.

Our mothers were narrow and neat. They wore sheathlike shifts with small stand-up collars and cap sleeves. They wore cat-eye glasses that accentuated the up-turned slant of their eyes. They had dark hair that they kept bobbed and cropped and curled with chemical permanent waves in an Occidental style. They held their bodies as carefully as they held their drinks, never spilling a drop. They were quick, bright, and birdlike, in comparison with our slow-moving, long-limbed, observant fathers. We, their dusky half-breed children, slipped amongst their adult legs like eels in sea grass. We fed from the circulating trays and ogled our guests, those exotic non-anthropological Others. We snapped up shrimp toasts and small dumplings, trying to avoid the sharp eyes and pinching fingers of our mothers, who could scold us in so many languages and didn't hesitate to do so.

My best friend in the department was a girl named Fatima, who was half Filipina. Her mother was a Moro, from Mindanao, and Fatima used to tell everyone that she was a cannibal. No one messed with Fatima, except for me. She and I were always trying to one-up each other, shuffling through our ancestors' ethnographic traits and hurling exoticisms down onto the table like baseball trading cards.

"My grandpa had a samurai sword," I told her once. "He could have cut your grandpa up into little pieces."

She stared at me and shook her head. "Nah," she said. "My grandpa woulda ate your grandpa for breakfast and digested him and pooped him out again before lunch."

What could you say to that?

I was named Joji after my Japanese grandfather, but everyone called me Georgie, or Georgie-boy, which I hated. Fatima had an American name too, which was Norma, but as the son of an anthropologist, I was drawn to authenticity and insisted on using her Muslim name when we were together. She let me, as long as I promised not to call her that in school. She told me that in the Philippines she had always been just Fatima, but when she came here the kids in school called her Fatty. She wasn't fat at all, in fact she was tiny; still it bothered her just the same. That was before America toughened her up.

Her mom couldn't drive, and my mom had a job at the museum, so after school we used to hang around the Anthropology Department building and wait for our dads to finish teaching so they could drive us home. The Department was located at 51 Hillhouse Avenue, next to the president's mansion. It was housed in an old, wooden folly of a building, bristling with turrets and arches and pinnacles and dentil molding. It's brown now, but back then it was painted a dark yellow color that always looked faded, and it had a huge, heavy pair of oaken doors, which, until I was seven, I didn't have the strength to open by myself.

Inside, a wide staircase led up the middle of the building, with a swooping banister that we could slide down when classes were over and no one was watching. In the winter we used to play in one of the empty seminar rooms or in my dad's office. The secretaries gave us scrap paper to draw on, and sometimes, if we begged them, they let us help run the mimeograph machine. We loved the smell of the purple ink. You could get high on it.

In early summer, when the weather turned hot and the New Haven air grew as thick and muggy as a rain forest, we used to sit on the splintery wooden steps that led up to the department building and talk. The large casement windows in the downstairs class-rooms were kept open in the heat, and we could hear our dads inside, droning on about kinship systems or totemism or sexual taboos. When we got bored, we played hopscotch or bounced our Superballs on the sidewalk in front of the Department. There was one particular spot of pavement that sounded hollow and there-fore, we speculated, must contain something hidden or lost: a vast store of untold treasure; votive statuary in solid gold; jewel-encrusted amulets; exquisite trinkets and baubles. Being anthro-pologists' kids, we knew all about these things.

"It's right under here," I told Fatima, bouncing. "Can you hear it?"

Beneath the thin skin of sidewalk, the cavity resounded. If we could only reach it and uncover its riches, we would be so cel-ebrated! Our fathers would run from their classrooms, trailed by their graduate students. They would shake their heads and marvel—*But they're just children!*—while our mothers would smile, knowingly.

"Yes," Fatima said. "How are we going to get it out?"

Fatima had an annoying tendency to get mired in practicalities, but she had a point. This, however, was my area of expertise, since my dad was more into the archeological side of anthropology, whereas hers leaned more toward the cultural.

"We have to launch an expedition," I told her. "We have to secure funding. We'll apply for a grant. We'll hire graduate students to do the digging."

I pictured the moment when the square of pavement would be lifted like a lid to reveal not just the treasure but an entire ancient world below—a world where boys like me were princes, lying under canopies on silken divans with ropes of gold draped around our necks, while slaves with palm fronds fanned our languid bodies.

Fatima looked skeptical. "What if there's no treasure?"

"There's treasure. Just listen." I bounced my Superball on the adjacent concrete and the sound was solid and dense. Then I tried the spot in question, which echoed. "See?"

"What if it's just a hole?"

I wanted to hit her. "It's not," I said. I found a stick and crouched and dug into a crumbling patch of cement, uprooting a tuft of grass that had withered in the heat. "It's filled with stuff, I promise."

Fatima watched me. "You know," she said, "even just one diamond, if it was big enough, could be worth millions of dollars."

I considered this possibility. "I'm sure there's at least two," I told her. It was my hole. I could afford to be generous.

"Well, even if there is treasure, we can't keep it," she said.

"We won't. We'll sell it."

And I knew exactly how I would spend my millions. I would buy the *Adventures in Chemistry!* set that I'd seen in the toy department at Malley's. The deluxe edition had a picture on the box of this earnest-looking blue-eyed boy in shorts with a blond cowlick. I wanted to be him, and if I couldn't be him, then I wanted his chemistry set. It came with forty-nine different chemicals, and test tubes that you could display on a rack, and a booklet with over fifteen hundred experiments that would teach the young chemist everything from nuclear physics and atomic energy to glass blowing. I was going to turn my bedroom into a lab and learn how to blow things up. I was going to make a fortune inventing enormous Superballs that would bounce me to the moon. I was going to concoct a special potion that would make me as fair as the chemistry boy, or as dark and beautiful as Fatima.

She shook her head. "You can't," she said.

"Why not?"

" 'Cause you have to make the treasure available to science, so that other people can study it and benefit. You have to donate it to a museum or something."

She was right, of course, but her high-minded principles were cramping my infinite chemical potentiality and I resented her for that. Without the sale of at least one large diamond I would never be able to buy the deluxe edition of *Adventures in Chemistry!*, and without it, my world contracted abruptly.

"We won't tell them," I said. "We'll turn over most of the stuff but just keep one gem each. . . ."

Fatima frowned and pushed forward her lower lip, which I'd always admired for its plumpness and purplish tinge. "It's wrong to keep secrets," she said. Fatima was a bit square, which could get on a person's nerves. "They'd find out, and then we'd be in trouble."

"So what? We'd be rich. It wouldn't matter."

I was always the bold one. I was the boy, after all, and almost twelve, a full year older than she was. And my dad was the chairman of the department, and her dad didn't even have tenure. Usually I could make Fatima do what I said, but not always.

. . .

The day the two men in suits showed up at the Department, we were in the supply room on the second floor, sniffing Magic Markers and stealing chalk. I'd read about how to make invisible ink using lemon juice and candles, and we were going to make a secret map leading to our treasure, but first we had to mark the spot on the sidewalk with an X, which was why we needed the chalk. The Magic Markers had nothing to do with our plan, only that the acrid smell made us light-headed and caused us to stay in the closet a lot longer than we needed to. Just as we were about to come out, we heard the creak of the staircase and the sound of footsteps on the treads. We ducked back inside, leaving the door open just a crack. Crouched in the dark, we watched the flat-cropped tops of their heads come into view as they climbed the broad staircase. Then, a moment later, we noticed the suits.

Suits like these were signifiers. With the exception of some of the younger faculty who had taken to wearing turtlenecks because it was 1969, most of the anthropologists wore coats and neckties to the office. These outfits of our fathers could hardly be called suits, however, since rarely did the jackets and trousers match. But these two men were different. They matched. Nobody in our tribe dressed like this.

It was a subtle thing, the semiotics of these suits that enabled Fatima and me to read danger. Most conspicuous were the color and texture, a sleek, gunmetal gray, with a brand new sheen that was most definitely not anthropological. Then there was the matter of the fabric of the jackets, which was identical to the trousers, and which displayed a conspicuous absence of fraying at the cuffs and the equally significant presence of freshly pressed creases.

There were other telltale signs, too, which marked these men as outsiders as clearly as ritual scarification or a facial tattoo: the bristling military haircuts; the subdued neckties, neatly tucked inside their jackets; the jackets that were properly buttoned. They carried folded raincoats over their arms and slim briefcases that shut properly and weren't spilling over with ungraded papers. They did not wear cardigan sweaters. They hadn't forgotten to shave.

"They must be spies!" I whispered to Fatima, as they passed our closet. "Or assassins. Come on!"

Fatima clung to my shirt. "We can't!"

"We can," I told her, gravely. "We must."

I slipped out of the closet and followed, staying close to the wall where the worn floorboards were less likely to creak and give away our position. I could hear the men moving down the hallway toward my father's office, and even their footsteps sounded different—not a distracted professorial shuffling, but rather a purposeful striding.

Fatima, my shadow, was right behind me. We ducked behind a filing cabinet in the small conference room adjacent to my father's office and watched as the men came to a full stop in front of his door. They glanced at each other, and then they knocked. I heard my dad's muffled voice reply, and I knew that they had caught him in the bathroom. My dad hated being chairman of the department because people were always catching him in the bathroom. People were always dropping in right before classes were about to start, or phoning him just as we were about to sit down for dinner. And sure enough, when he came to the door he had a smudge of toothpaste in the corner of his mouth. I wanted to tell him about it so he could wipe it away, but one of the men had started talking in a low voice that I couldn't hear, and then my dad stepped back and I heard him sigh and say, "Of course. Come in. But I have a class starting in a few minutes."

I watched those two neat men cross in front of my rumpled father. The door clicked shut behind them, and the sound made me shiver. Just then Dorothy, the departmental secretary, came up the stairs with a stack of mail. She spotted us lurking and shooed us downstairs and out the door.

G*eemen!*" my mother said that night. Her lip curled and her mouth expelled the syllables, as though they were something horribly bitter. She deposited a loaded dinner plate in front of my dad.

"Well, yes," my dad said, looking up at her. "So you see why I couldn't exactly send them packing . . ."

My mom didn't reply, just turned her back, which meant she certainly did not see at all.

Dinner that night was beef teriyaki, which was one of my favorites. I waited until she finished serving and sat down. "What's a geemen?" I asked.

"Eat," she told me, picking up her chopsticks.

I took a bite, barely noticing, and swallowed. "What's a geemen?"

My dad cleared his throat. "Government men," he said. "G stands for government."

My mother snorted. "You mean gangster, more like it."

"Michi . . ."

"It's true," she stated.

I waited, but she didn't continue. "Are they really gangsters?" I asked.

"Of course not," my dad said. "They work for the Central Intelligence Agency, which is a part of the federal government."

"Intelligence?" my mother said, but it wasn't a question. She put down her chopsticks. "They steal," she said. "They kidnap. Just like gangsters."

My father didn't reply. Married to an Oriental, he had learned a thing or two about silence.

"You know it's true," my mother told him, then she turned to me. "They stole your Grandpa Joji's store. They kidnapped us and took us to the desert. They made us live in a horse stall. We lost everything."

But I'd heard the story a million times. She turned back to my father. "I hope you told them to get lost."

"Well," my dad cleared his throat. "In a manner of speaking . . ."

My mother pursed her lips and made a sound with her nose, which indicated her feelings for my father's manner of speaking.

"It's not that simple, Michi," my dad said, defensively. "I told them that none of our men would be interested. I can only hope they got the message."

"Good," my mother said. "Good riddance."

My dad hesitated. "They wanted to talk to Manny."

My mom looked up. "Why Manny?"

Manuel Estrada was Fatima's dad. He was a white guy, but different. He was short. And Hispanic. His jackets were just a little bit nattier, like he had tried too hard. "Did he do something wrong?" I asked.

"Of course not," Dad said. He took another bite of teriyaki and paused to chew. He was a very thorough chewer. I thought the conversation was over, but then he turned to my mom. "Things are heating up again in his part of the world."

The men of anthropology had the world pretty much divided up and covered. Manny's part of the world was the Philippines.

"Are they going to kidnap him?" I asked. If they were going to kidnap him, I had to warn Fatima.

"Of course not."

"Are they going to assassinate him?" It wasn't such a far-fetched idea. Martin Luther King and Robert Kennedy had both been assassinated the previous year.

"Don't be silly, George," my father said.

"Poor Manny," my mother said. "Are you going to give him tenure or not?"

"It's not up to me, Michi. You know that."

"Poor Samira," my mom said.

The Peabody Museum of Natural History is the big neo-Gothic building with steep pinnacles and vaulted windows on Whitney Avenue, right around the corner from the Anthropology Department. My mom worked there, cataloguing for the curator, and Fatima and I liked to hang out in the gift shop, where they sold small polished stones that we would slip into our pockets when the cashier wasn't looking. There were two matching silver rings inlaid with mother-of-pearl that we coveted too, but they were locked up in the display case by the register. I decided that when I sold my diamond, I would buy us those rings, and then maybe Fatima would marry me, not immediately of course, but somewhere down the road.

I had grown up in the museum. The Great Hall of Dinosaurs was as familiar to me as my own living room, and I had even helped to paint the base under the towering brontosaurus skeleton. Now that I was older, I was colonizing less-populated corners of the cavernous old building. Cutting through the Ages of Man, I would lead Fatima past the dioramas where Native American Indians crouched in perpetuity next to teepees, weaving baskets for eternity and skinning elk with crude stone tools. We climbed up the stairs, ignoring the Birds of the Connecticut Valley, and headed instead to where the living reptiles were kept. There are no live animals at the Peabody now, but back then they kept a few, tucked away on the very top floor. There, amidst the snake tanks, I was teaching Fatima how to fox trot.

I was taking ballroom dancing at the Lawn Club once a week. It was my mother's idea. She thought boys needed to be civilized and that dance classes would do the trick. Although I sensed he didn't quite agree, my father just kept quiet. I didn't mind. Unlike my dad, I liked dancing, and I was good at it. The teacher,

Mr. Porter, was tall and probably gay, although we didn't know it at the time. He was so tall that when he demonstrated a dance step with the girls, they would have to stretch their arms way over their heads to reach his shoulder, lifting their minidresses up the backs of their thighs until sometimes you could even see their underpants. The boys liked that. They sat on the sidelines and laughed and tried to push each other off the folding chairs. I wasn't that interested in girls, except for Fatima, but I liked the boxes of chocolates with creamy centers that you could win if you did the steps right. I would save my chocolates and share them with Fatima at the museum. We would stick our tongues right into the creamy centers. Fatima didn't take dance lessons. She said she didn't want to, but I think it was more that she wasn't allowed, either because of her mother's religion or because she was so dark. The Lawn Club was that kind of place in those days.

Box-stepping Fatima past the asps and the thick constrictors, I would tell her about dance class and who'd had to waltz with Mr. Porter. We would circle the cobra that hung from its stump, then tango down to Minerals and Gems, where the halls were narrow and black lights made the hard crystals glitter. There, in the darkness, I would share chocolates with her and show her how to do things. In front of the feldspar, I taught her to suck the inside of her arm hard enough to leave a hickey. Next to the long shafts of tourmaline, I taught her how to kiss. Fatima was really dark, and I was always amazed, holding her wrist and twisting it, to see how pale the underside was in comparison. In the dim, ultraviolet light, she glowed like alabaster, and in my childish, inchoate way, I desired to bring blood to the surface of her skin, to mark her with my lips. Maybe we're all a little cannibal at heart.

The day after the dinner conversation with my parents, I met Fatima in the gift shop of the Peabody after school. We didn't linger. I grabbed her hand and dragged her up the old stone stairs to the deserted top floor. Without so much as a curtsy or a bow, I took her in my arms, danced her down the Hall of Gems, and told her what I'd heard about the G-men.

"They want to kidnap your dad," I whispered into her ear. "Things are heating up in his part of the world."

I felt Fatima stumble. I pressed my hand into the small of her back and held her tighter.

"They may even want to assassinate him."

I thought for sure she would argue with me, but to my surprise she made a little whimpering noise instead, as though she might start to cry. I gave her a gentle push, steering her deeper into the darkness.

"We have to save him."

My breath tangled in her hair and felt hot against my lips. Her little fingers gripped my shoulder as I danced her toward the wall. We came to a stop against the glass of a display case. Backlit against the ultraviolet, with the rocks and minerals sparkling behind her, she looked beautiful and mysterious. Her black hair veiled her face. Her eyes brimmed with tears and glinted like agates. I lifted the wing of her hair and kissed her. Her mouth was soft and wet and strangely compliant, and somehow this enraged me. I longed for her resistance. I kissed her again, harder, aware now of the edge of her tooth, the ridgeline of her jaw. My tongue was a primitive tool, a blunt rock or a sharpened stick, useful to pry her open. She struggled. I clamped my hands against her narrow skull to hold her in place. I heard a strangled noise, her voice, a cry of protest, but I ignored it. I knew I was pushing too far. I should have stopped. I should have listened to her, I should have respected her wishes, but I didn't, and so she bit off my tongue.

Luckily, she severed just the tip of it. The pain was blinding, a searing whiteness that exploded like shrapnel in my face. I stepped back, shoving her away from me. Hot blood filled my mouth. She stared in horror, then her hand flew to her lips. I watched her through the haze of pain as she spit, then looked down at the little nub of flesh cupped in her palm. Not knowing what to do with it, she held it out to me.

"Here," she said.

It looked like a very small piece of bloody chewing gum. Speechless, I reached for it. She tipped my tongue into the palm of my hand, and that was when I fainted.

F atima never told anyone what really happened, and neither did I. Later I learned that she had run downstairs to the basement and the museum archives where my mother was filing. Fatima's mouth was red with blood, so of course my mom, having no way of knowing that the blood was mine, thought she had been horribly injured. Somehow Fatima convinced her otherwise, then she led my mom in a mad dash up the many flights of stairs because the ancient elevator was too slow. They found me on the floor beside the tourmalines and crystals, deathly pale beneath the black light that drained all color from my face. The gem stones glittered. The blood spilled from my mouth, inky in the ultraviolet. My mother must have screamed then, because I came to and opened my eyes. An image of her face, as white as a vampire, fluttered briefly into my consciousness, before I lost it again.

The next thing I remember was lying on a bed in the hospital, under the light, with my mouth prised open, jaw clamped, and a doctor leaning over me, attempting to stitch the tip of my tongue back onto its root. They had found the little nub, clutched in my fist on the way to the emergency room. Once again, Fatima had led them to it. In the midst of all the chaos and commotion, she reached over and took my wrist and pried opened my fingers, one by one. Then she tugged on my mom's sleeve to show her.

"It's his tongue," she whispered.

They say that mouth wounds heal quickly, but still it took several weeks. My mother let me stay home from school for the first little while, and she fed me rice puddings and Japanese egg custard and bright cherry Jello with disks of pale banana suspended inside. It soon became clear that the damage to the anterior portion of my tongue was permanent, although not terribly severe. I lost some of my ability to taste sweetness, and I still speak with a slight lisp. But I shouldn't complain. That I have a tongue at all is due to Fatima's kindness. That I almost lost it was certainly not her fault.

My mother never questioned the explanation I provided. At first, on account of the injury, I couldn't say much of anything at all, and by the time I could talk again, I'd concocted a story about tripping and falling and knocking my jaw against the display case. But I could tell by the way my mother looked at me, askance, from behind her cat-eye glasses, that she had her suspicions. She was wondering how my blood had ended up on Fatima. In Fatima's mouth. She never confided her suspicions to my father, however. These were matters that our mothers handled on their own.

"Where's your little friend?" my dad would ask me in the months that followed, when he noticed me skulking around the Anthropology Department corridors alone. I would shrug my shoulders and play dumb. He would pat my head absentmindedly and shamble off. That's one thing about anthropologists—they never notice what is happening right underneath their noses.

When I could eat again, I returned to school and quickly understood that Fatima was avoiding me. She wouldn't talk to me. She wouldn't even catch my eye. Our mothers had come to a decision, either by direct consultation or some other form of inscrutable telepathic consensus, to end our friendship. Samira was very strict, and I knew Fatima would obey the maternal dictum without protest. My great fear was that she might be obeying out of preference as well.

Desperate to win her back, I considered my options and finally came up with a plan. If her father was in danger, I would protect him. I would keep an eye on him, shadow his every move, and when the G-men jumped him, I would be there to save his life. There would be a fight of some sort—this part was still hazy in my mind—but in the end, due to my cleverness and the righteousness of my cause, I would prevail. Manny and my father would clap my shoulder and shake my hand. Samira would weep with gratitude at my bravery, and my mother would too, and together they would humbly apologize for their sly interferences and false aspersions. But best of all, Fatima would be mine again.

The minute school was out, I ran down to Hillhouse Avenue and began the stakeout. Mostly it was pretty boring. Professor Manny Estrada spent his afternoons either in class teaching, or in his office seeing students. Since he was in line for tenure, he attended department and committee meetings regularly. I used those times as opportunities to scope out the surrounding areas, figuring the hit men wouldn't try to take him out in front of a roomful of anthropologists. There wasn't much out of the ordinary to discover, though. Once I thought I spotted the two of them, lurking in their suits by the Kline Biology Tower, but when I got closer, they had vanished.

Then, one day, I was outside Professor Estrada's office helping Dorothy with the mimeograph machine, when I heard his phone ring. He spoke for a while, and although I couldn't make out what he was saying, I could tell that he was in a hurry and was keeping his voice low. I heard him hang up, then a few minutes later he emerged from his office, locking his door behind him. Making up some excuse or another, I left Dorothy holding a sheaf of fragrant, wet stencils and ran after him.

When I got to the sidewalk, Professor Estrada had turned left and was heading toward Science Hill. He crossed Sachem and climbed, cutting through Kline Biology, where I thought I'd seen the two G-men lurking. From there he proceeded on toward the Wright Nuclear Labs. He didn't see me following. He never looked behind him, nor to the left or to the right. He just kept walking straight ahead, his head ducked and body angled forward as though he were walking into a stiff wind.

I trailed him to the parking lot behind the Electron Accelerator, where he stopped. Then, without warning, he turned back in my direction. I ducked behind an old Studebaker that was parked nearby. I rested my forehead on the big cool chrome fender. My heart was pounding. My tongue throbbed and tasted of metal. I waited for a moment, then I stood slowly and peered around the tail fin.

Across the parking lot, I could see a car pull up, and Professor Estrada leaned down and started talking to someone through the window. I was pretty sure it was the G-men. I could tell from the car, a sleek black Ford with a profile that meant business. Still, I needed to be certain. Like a crab, I scuttled closer, moving down the row of parked cars, keeping low to the ground. As I approached, I could hear the smooth purr of the Ford's engine and the murmur of voices. I stopped once again and gathered my courage, and then lifted my head over the hood of a VW. Professor Estrada was still leaning down and talking, blocking my view, but I could just make out that there were two men, sitting in the car. The tinted glass of the driver's window was rolled partway down, and I could see that the men were wearing matching mirrored sunglasses. Professor Estrada looked hot in his tweed jacket, which was unusually rumpled, and for a moment he seemed genuinely anthropological. He took a step back away from the car, then leaned forward again and shook hands with the driver. The black Ford moved silently away. Professor Estrada watched. When the car pulled out onto Whitney Avenue and merged into traffic, his shoulders slumped. He ran his hands through his hair, only he held them there a little too long so that it looked like he was clutching his head on either side to keep it from rolling off his shoulders.

That night at dinner, I waited until my mom had served us and sat down, and my father had taken his first bite—if I recall it was beef in black bean sauce, which was one of his favorites—and then I broached the subject.

"I saw the G-men down by the Atom Smasher," I said.

Dad put his chopsticks down and wiped his mouth. "They're not G-men, George."

"But mom said . . ."

"Just because your mother tells you stories, you mustn't go around imagining things. That was then, and this is now."

"I'm not imagining!" I cried. "I saw them in the parking lot. They were in a black car." I hesitated for a moment. "They were talking to Fatima's dad."

Dad looked at me hard across the table. "Are you sure?"

I nodded. "They were talking, and then he shook hands with them, and then they drove away." I waited for my dad to take in this information, then I added, "Does this mean that they're not going to assassinate him?"

Dad looked startled. "Where on earth did you get that idea?"

"You said things were heating up in his part of the world. You said they wanted to talk to him."

"So I did." His face looked pained.

"What were you doing in the parking lot?" my mother demanded. "You were supposed to be at your father's office doing your homework."

"I thought Professor Estrada was in trouble. I was trying to save his life."

"Oh, for goodness sake," my mother said. The two of them fell silent, and for a while there was just the sound of chewing. Them my mother looked at my father. "You don't think Manny . . . ?"

Dad shrugged. "Let's hope not."

"Poor Samira," Mom said.

P rofessor Estrada didn't get tenure. Dad told us at dinner, several weeks later. I don't remember what we were eating that night. Leftovers, probably. Mom was a great fan of leftovers. When Dad broke the news, she pursed her lips, and I could see her shoulders tighten.

"He's going back to the Philippines," Dad said. "He's taking the family."

My heart sank.

"He's found the funding for his fieldwork," Dad added.

"Funding?" Mom said. "Hah!" But it wasn't funny.

Dad shrugged. "He does need to be in the field, you know."

My mother pressed her lips together.

"Michi, it's his choice. There was nothing I could do."

Mom stared at her plate.

"They'll be OK," Dad said. "Manny's a survivor."

"I'm not worried about Manny," Mom said.

A s usual, Mom's intuition was right. Manny survived. So did Samira. Fatima went to university, until she dropped out and joined the Moro Islamic Liberation Front. She was killed in an uprising in 1987. I heard the news from Dorothy, who had retired by then but still kept up with former departmental members. She used to stop by 51 Hillhouse from time to time to check up on things, and she happened to be there when I was home for a visit and had come by to pick up my dad. Dorothy had always had a soft spot for Manny Estrada.

"I never understood why your father and the others didn't give him tenure," Dorothy said to me. "He was such a charming young man, so outgoing, and his little girl was a darling."

She looked up at my face, then seeing my stricken expression, she reached out and patted my hand. "You two were good friends, weren't you, dear?"

The Estradas had moved away as soon as the semester ended, and the month before they left had been a bad one. Fatima continued to avoid me, refusing even to meet my eye in the corridor between classes, and traveling en masse with her classmates like a quick shiny fish in the middle of a migrating school. I was desperate to talk to her, to apologize and explain, but she never gave me the chance. In the afternoons, her mother would be waiting for her on the sidewalk in front of the school where the other mothers pulled up in their station wagons. Samira always wore a longish coat and a headscarf, and she and Fatima would walk to the corner and wait there for the public bus, never raising their eyes from the ground in front of them.

Right around that time, some of the kids in school started bullying me. They would encircle me and chant:

> *Georgie Porgie puddin' & pie*
> *Kissed the girls and made them cry . . .*

It certainly wasn't the first time I'd heard this rhyme—with a name like Joji, you come to expect it—but this was different. The first time they chanted it, I felt my blood surge and my face start to burn, certain that Fatima had told them what had happened at the Peabody. Thinking about it now, I'm sure it was my newly acquired lisp that made me the butt of my classmates' teasing. The lisp gave my speech a fey quality, which the children read as both signifier and cliché. But at the time I was overwhelmed with fury, and I blamed Fatima both for my shame and for the vileness of her betrayal. After that, I avoided her too. I stopped trying to talk to her. I stopped talking to anyone.

> *When the boys came out to play,*
> *Georgie Porgie ran away . . .*

On the last day of school, I hid in a classroom and watched Fatima go, and I didn't even say good-bye.

We did communicate one last time. Although we never again spoke, I wrote her a letter. I was in graduate school, doing a doctorate in Post-Colonialist Studies. I was thinking a lot about my childhood and what it was like growing up in the Anthropology Department at Yale, and of course I thought of Fatima. I tracked her down through Dorothy, which wasn't hard since Professor Estrada had gone on to get tenure at the University of Manila and to chair the department there. I addressed the letter to Fatima in care of her father. I figured that as an anthropologist married to an Oriental wife, Professor

Estrada had probably been sheltered from most of what had transpired so many years ago, and the chances were good that he would pass my letter on to his daughter. A few months, maybe half a year later, I got a letter back.

"Dear Joji," Fatima wrote. "Thank you for your letter and your apology. I don't remember dancing with you in the Peabody Museum, and I certainly don't remember anything about a kiss. Maybe it happened. I don't know. What I do recall is the decadence of American children, how spoiled they were, how greedy and how cruel. I remember that you, in particular, were obsessed with treasure and material gain. I was interested to hear about your paper on *Manichean Allegory and the Polarization of Gender and Identity*. Now I have a question for you: Why are you Americans so obsessed with your identities? Why don't you know who you are? We know who you are. The rest of the world knows exactly who you are. . . ."

Harsh, but somewhat accurate. *Dear Fatima*, I wrote. *Here in America, we are what we own.* But I quickly realized that this was an overly simplistic analysis, and I never finished the letter.

Still, she was right about one thing: I was obsessed with treasure. I still have in my possession three little plastic treasure chests, the size of sugar cubes, which I must have gotten from the dentist to hold my baby teeth as they fell out. The chests were cheap things, made in Hong Kong, in garish colors, and I was surprised to come across them many years later when I was cleaning out the New Haven house after my parents died. They were in the back of an old junk drawer, under a tangle of string and wire twist-ties, covered in dust. I fished them out and lined them up in front of me on the counter. Seeing them there, blue, yellow, and pink, all in a row, I remembered how precious they had once seemed. Their little covers were attached by flimsy plastic hinges. I picked up the blue one and pried it open with my fingernail. Inside was a pearly molar with a brittle, brownish root, which must have been mine, only I didn't remember. The next chest, the yellow one, held a nervous ball of mercury, which I did recall.

Those were the days of better living through chemistry, and words like "toxicity" hadn't yet entered our lexicon. My mother let me keep the mercury after I apologized for breaking the thermometer, and I used to play with it like a quick, silvery pet.

The third chest, the pink one, contained a bedraggled, dried out thing that I could not identify at first. I tipped it into my palm and studied it. It was the size and shape of a bullet, but light and covered with what looked like silver fur. Turning it over, I saw that it was pussy willow, and suddenly I remembered.

It was the first time I met Fatima. I was with a bunch of kids, playing on the slope in back of the Divinity School. I don't remember why I was there, but the other kids were mostly white, so it couldn't have been an anthropological gathering. Fatima was there, and she stood out like me. She was just a little thing, recently arrived from the Philippines, and I had never seen her before, but I recognized that her face, like mine, bore the telltale traces of hybridity. It seemed she was being looked after by one of the older girls, and she had to go to the bathroom. She was begging the girl to take her inside, but the girl was busy talking to her friends, and she told Fatima to go behind a bush.

"I can't," Fatima whimpered, pressing her knees together.

"Sure you can," the girl said, smirking at her friends. "Just pull down your pants and squat. Isn't that how you do it at your house?"

"No," Fatima said, "We sit down. I have to sit down."

"Oh, honestly!" the girl exclaimed. She rolled her eyes and shook her head. Her friends snickered. The girl grinned. "Listen, Fatima. You see those pussy willows over there?" She pointed to a bush growing by the wrought iron gate. "All you have to do is find a nice fat one of those and stick it up your nose. You'll never have to go to the bathroom again."

"Really?"

"I promise," the girl said, solemnly.

The others nodded in wide-eyed agreement. Fatima hesitated, then she limped quickly toward the bush.

I was watching the whole thing from the swings, not far from the pussy willows. Being a boy, it had never before occurred to me what it must be like to be a little girl, playing outside, and suddenly have to go. It meant interrupting everything and running inside with the other kids knowing why, so instead you held it and held it until you were about to burst. In light of all that, I could see how the older girl's alternative might seem attractive, and I was curious to see if it would work. And at first it was funny, watching little Fatima go cross-eyed with concentration as she plucked a soft, gray pussy willow and fitted it into her nostril. The big girls all started to laugh—*Oh my god, she's really doing it!*— and Fatima looked up, and I could see the elation infuse her face. She had succeeded, finally, in joining in the fun, and the pleasure in this small accomplishment distracted her momentarily from the pain and pressure in her bladder.

"I think it's working," she said, proudly, and that's when she inhaled.

Up shot the catkin like a sleek silver bullet, lodging itself high up in her nasal passage, and it wouldn't come out no matter how forcefully she exhaled. The shafts of fur were pointing in the wrong direction. So the first time I spoke to Fatima, she had pee'd in her pants, and she was running around in little circles, snorting like a spooked pony. The big girls hadn't quite realized what had happened. They were sitting on the picnic table, still cracking up. So I walked over and took Fatima's hand and led her away from the Divinity School, down St. Ronan Street, across the parking lot by the Atom Smasher, up and over Science Hill, past the Peabody Museum to 51 Hillhouse Avenue. There, I brought her sobbing up the broad stairs of the Anthropology Department to my father's office.

My dad was sitting at his desk, grading papers. "Oh my," he exclaimed, softly, dropping his pencil and coming around to kneel in front of us. "What have we here?" It was a reasonable question. Even for a trained anthropologist, it would have been a challenge to determine through mere observation that the damp little girl weeping before him had a pussy willow stuck up her nose, never mind deduce how it had gotten there.

"Aren't you Manny Estrada's daughter?" he asked, pulling out his handkerchief and gently wiping her tear-streaked face.

She gulped and nodded, and then I explained what had happened. My father frowned. Without saying another word, he pocketed his keys, scooped Fatima up in his arms, and drove us to the emergency room. He carried her straight up to the admitting desk and spoke to the nurse, and Fatima was quickly whisked away. By the time she was led back out again, both Manny and Samira had arrived. They were newcomers to Yale, baffled and helpless. Manny clasped my dad's hand and thanked him over and over for his kindness. Samira scolded Fatima, then hugged her, then scolded her again. Fatima gazed at me with eyes as dark and wet as a fawn's.

"I'm proud of you," my dad said later on, tucking me under his arm as we drove home that evening. We sat side by side on the broad bench seat of the Pontiac. "You should always help other people. That's what we do."

I nodded, listening to his words. I remember feeling unsure, wondering who he meant by "we." Did he mean we, anthropologists? We, our family, in our Pontiac sedan? We, Americans? I didn't quite understand, but it didn't matter. Sitting up tall, next to my dad, I clutched my new treasure in my hand and knew that he was right.

Earlier on, just when we were leaving the hospital, Fatima had sidled over to me. She still smelled faintly of pee.

"Here," she said in a small voice, holding out her hand.

I looked down, and noticed for the first time the darkness of her skin and how white the underside of her arm looked in comparison. Her palm was pink and damp, and centered in the middle was the bedraggled silver catkin.

"You can have it," she whispered, and I took it. I heard the tremor in her voice, saw the tears of gratitude in her eyes, and experienced a sudden surge of power. In that moment, I felt immensely proud, as if somehow, as a result of the exchange, we would be friends forever.

The setting for "The Anthropologists' Kids" is somewhat autobiographical, although I've taken many fictional liberties in my depiction of this world, and certainly everything that happens in the story is imaginary. I grew up as a faculty brat at Yale in the 1960s, the daughter of a Japanese linguist mother and a Caucasian anthropologist father (although to clarify, my mom didn't actually teach at Yale, since Yale wasn't hiring full-time women faculty back then). It was true that a great many white Yale anthropology professors did have Oriental wives, and as the child of one such union, I was always aware that I was different. We called ourselves "half" (in Japanese, "ha-fu"), and thusly described, I must have felt somewhat diminished, divided, and estranged from myself. I clearly recall feeling as though one half of me was always studying the other, which I suppose it was. As a half-Asian, half-Anthropologist kid, I was genetically predisposed to ethnographic introspection—although the same is true for many writers. I've gone on to use the metaphor of being "half" or "mixed" in all my writing and filmmaking. Most of my protagonists have been hybrid, non-native, or exotic. Most of my stories straddle worlds and genres. I like to mix things up: comedy and tragedy; irony and innocence; truth and fiction. And speaking of which, I should clarify one last point. I said that the events in the story are imaginary, and it's true, they are. Except for the part about the CIA. The CIA is not imaginary. It is real, and there really were CIA agents prowling the halls of the Anthropology Department at Yale back then. When you think about it, anthropologists make ideal operatives. They have the linguistic skills, the cultural knowledge, and perfect cover stories. So you can understand why CIA agents would have been lurking in the halls of academia back then. I'd be willing to bet they still are.

Lucinda Roy

Lucinda Roy is the author of the novels *Lady Moses* and *The Hotel Alleluia*, and two poetry collections. *Lady Moses* was selected for Barnes & Noble's Discover Great New Writers Series. Roy is an Alumni Distinguished Professor at Virginia Tech, where she codirects the Creative Writing program. She is of Jamaican and British descent, and her work has appeared in the United Kingdom, the West Indies, and the United States.

Effigies

The first thing Professor Samuel Bernard Monroe saw that morning was the cloud. A large skylight was positioned over his king-sized bed, so the cloud was directly above his head. Oddly, it was pasted to a pretty blue sky. When the final curl of charcoal-colored cloud had disappeared from view, Sam sat bolt upright in bed like a revived corpse and called out, "Come back!" His voice was scarred with loss. He had no idea why he'd called out like that, to a cloud of all things! He had no idea what he meant.

Embarrassed by his uncharacteristic outburst, Dr. Samuel

B. Monroe, Irving L. Jones Distinguished Professor of Africana Studies, looked around his bedroom as furtively as a burglar. He fancied he heard the echo of his cry ricocheting off the olive walls of his bedroom. Fortunately, there was no one else there to hear it. Sam hadn't slept with anyone since he'd been seduced by a grad student when he'd delivered a keynote address at UNC last year. The room was his, permeated by the smells that gave him comfort—his fabric softener, his orange tea.

Sam rubbed his eyes so roughly that the sockets hurt. He soon put two and two together. He must have been half awake. In fact, wasn't that the very same cloud he'd seen in his dreams? The one that chased him to Main Hall and up the wide steps of the Student Union? The one that had followed him into the bathroom on the third floor of Cochran Hall, then changed into a flock of ugly, screeching birds?

Sam knew exactly what the problem was: the little red pills he'd been taking to help prevent acid reflux. There wasn't a cloud in the sky anymore. Likely never had been. He swung his heavy, six-foot-three-inch frame out of bed and shoved his feet into the threadbare, down-at-heel slippers that had appalled his ex-wife but which he held onto just to spite her.

In the master bathroom, Sam peered at his reflection in the mirror. Unlike the facial hair of most black men he knew, his own beard grew at a rapid rate. Overnight, the lower half of his face was pitted with stubble. Carly used to tell him he resembled a partial eclipse in the morning. He wore a thick black mustache, graying now, distinguished. He didn't want a beard; it would detract from the hair on his head. Because of his hair, Carly had called him Samson instead of Samuel when they'd first met— threatened to "do a Delilah on him"—shave it all off one day when he was sleeping. He hadn't told her he'd kill her if she did. It wasn't the kind of thing you said to a woman on a first date.

If Sam had a great love in his life apart from his work and the academy, it was his hair. It gave him credence as a man of color. So light skinned he could pass for white, Sam had been obliged to cultivate an aura of ethnicity if he wanted to be taken seriously by the white establishment. Although he was biracial (his father was Ibo from Nigeria, his mother Irish), Sam had inherited barely a trace of Africa in his countenance. But his hair told a different story. His hair resembled that of Frederick Douglass—untamable, almost immovable in the strongest wind, so thick he had to wet it before he could get a comb through it, so gravity defying that it sprang upright when he removed his hat. Sam knew that he owed his hair a debt of gratitude; it had granted him passage into his race in a way that nothing else could have. His hair was his passport, his weapon, a winner of arguments, a diadem. He swore to himself that if he ever had to have chemotherapy, he'd have his hair cut off and fashioned into a wig before it fell out.

At various times during adolescence, Sam had submitted to his mother's wishes and had his hair cut. But as soon as Afros took hold in his neighborhood, he'd refused to let a white woman tell him what to do with his own head. Once, in a fit of anger, he'd waved his metal pick in his mother's face and told her he'd stab her if she came any closer with those scissors. Ever since the sixties, Sam had been trimming his hair himself, but no more than an inch or so. Eventually, it grew past his shoulders. Then, when he reached the age of twenty-six, the same year he got his doctorate, it stopped growing. It seemed like a sign at the time. He'd blossomed into manhood; he and his hair had arrived.

Several times, Sam had been asked (always by white women) to donate his hair to charitable organizations. In the summer of '83, for example, he'd been accosted outside the Smithsonian by a balding woman in a pink bouclé suit, who pleaded with him to cut it and sell it to her. "That head of hair is too beautiful to waste," she'd said. "I'll give you a thousand dollars for it." "Madam," he'd said, in his politest, most civil tone, "I'd no more cut off my hair than I'd allow you to cut off my dick." In the wake of her little scream, he'd walked away. He'd learned early that there were some white people who hated you if you had something they coveted. The worst of them were willing to tear it out by the roots.

Sam turned around suddenly. He thought he saw a shadow with outstretched arms come up behind him. He jumped back as if he'd seen a ghost. The jerky movement caused him to nick his jaw with the razor. He yelped in pain. It was a deep cut. He swore and dabbed at it with a washcloth. His bright red blood on the white cloth made him think of hospitals. Hospitals put him in mind of his mother and what they'd done to her. But he couldn't possibly care for his mother himself—not when he was delivering keynotes, teaching one course a semester, and turning out a book every five years or so. Neither his half-brothers nor his stepsister wanted to take responsibility for the old woman when senility had set in. So they'd pooled their money (or rather, they matched his contribution because, as they kept reminding him, he earned three or four times what they did combined) and committed her to a nursing facility in New Jersey. Recently—probably because of those damn red pills—he'd been visited by his mother in his nightmares. She appeared like some wizened old witch from *Macbeth*, her gnarled finger jabbing at his temple. She told him he looked like a hobo and threatened to cut off his hair. Her fingers turned to scissors and she sliced at him like Edward Scissorhands. As he remembered this, Sam realized that it was her shadow he'd caught sight of in the mirror—not her *shadow*, no. Her negative. Yes—that was it. It was as though his Irish mother's image were a negative of itself—her pale skin coal black, her white hair darker than his had been when he was younger. He shuddered. What was the matter with him today? He was going nuts.

Sam shaved more carefully after that. He couldn't let his imagination get the better of him. After more than eighteen years as an authority on race, he was someone who didn't succumb to much of anything. When he'd woken up in '87 to find himself quoted by the senator from Massachusetts who'd used his theory of Obligatory Homogeneity to decry the state of higher education, Sam had been anointed into the fold of a select few men of color. Sam spoke with patience and a slight condescension to other men (mostly white) who wanted to fathom the mystery of race. Sam Monroe wasn't someone who was afraid of his own shadow.

It didn't take Sam long to realize that, at a time of black male scarcity, there was nothing more potent than an articulate black scholar. When he spoke, presidents of the various institutions that had wooed him to their campuses inclined their heads slightly—reverently, he liked to think—and nodded in agreement. He wasn't one of those mealymouthed brothers who never said boo to a goose, nor was he at the other extreme—an activist type who deliberately stirred up trouble. He'd chosen to take up a position in between these two extremes: he was vocal when appropriate, discreet when necessary, cautiously optimistic about the fate of Blackness in America, suitably deferential to all women of color (the only people he feared), and scrupulously well prepared. If you were prepared, you could survive; no one could ambush you with questions you couldn't answer. He studied academic protocol so that he never, ever made a fool of himself.

By five P.M. that evening, when Sam sat up on the platform with the other panelists in Main Hall, he'd forgotten all about the incidents of the morning. He was in his element, surrounded by colleagues who admired him, a few of whom he admired in return, trying to grapple with an outbreak of racism on campus that had shocked the white people and come as no surprise to everyone else. The auditorium was nearly two hundred years old. High windows ran along one side; the afternoon sun streamed in, making dust motes visible and polishing the linseed oil in the framed paintings of past presidents and rectors. Outside one of the windows was a massive oak tree. Its branches were filling with leaves. The fecundity of the season gave Sam profound joy.

He looked around at the people in the hall. Must be well over two hundred faculty and several dozen graduate students. Sam had gotten to know many of the faculty and administrators pretty well over the past seven years. Two of them—Dean Richard Farley, ruddy cheeked and boyish, and his coconspirator Jim

McFadden, an associate dean who prided himself on his political machinations and close friendship with the rector of the Board of Regents—were sitting in the front row. The pair had worked hard to woo Sam from UCLA. Sam smiled at his friends, and they smiled back broadly. The upper administration was out in force. Next to the dean was the indomitable president, Bill Trenchard; and beside him was Lance Beckly, CFO. The recent spate of incidents had been a PR nightmare for a university that was witnessing a startling decline in African-American enrollment; they needed to turn things around fast.

The panel had been Sam's idea—bring the community together, hash out a few things. Sam felt wise and magnanimous as he sat on the platform in the middle of the other panelists. He knew he was precisely where he wanted to be at this stage in his career. He'd spoken well. As usual, the applause he'd received had been more enthusiastic than the applause that greeted the other panelists. He was satisfied.

It was time for the audience to make comments and ask questions. A woman approached the microphone that was placed in the center aisle some twenty or thirty feet from the stage. Sam didn't recognize her at first because she wore a woolen hat which she ripped from her head as she walked toward them. As soon as her scalp was revealed, however, Sam recognized his nemesis. Sheraye Agness Underwood (Agness with a double "s" like the hiss of a snake) stood at the microphone ready to strike. Her black eyes were scrunched up into meanness, and each one of her pointy little braids jabbed at him as if he were prostrate on a grill and her head was a fork.

The J. P. Atkinson Visiting Professor of Women's Studies, whose tome on gender roles in African-American families had made a splash four years before, had a permanent position at Williams College. Sam hadn't realized that she was visiting for the entire year. In fact, he'd thought they'd rid themselves of her several months before. He'd been especially friendly to her at the Christmas reception, thinking it would be the last time he'd have to make the effort. Contentious, opinionated, vicious, disarmingly clever, and as well prepared as he himself was, Sheraye was a formidable enemy. Of course none of the other faculty knew they were enemies. In fact, in the spirit of the pact that existed among most African-American academicians, he'd tried to defend her ludicrous statements to others. Sam knew that Sheraye wasn't fooled by the gestures of courtesy he adopted in her presence. She knew just how hot his hatred was of her. To Sam's alarm, his hatred seemed to excite her. Her eyes sparkled more intensely around him, and her body became more animated. At a party soon after she'd descended upon them, he'd even imagined that she might be attracted to him. But when he'd made his move, she'd stunned him with the cruelty of her response. He'd expected some kind of come-on, something playful and a little lewd. She'd been knocking back the Chardonnay and giving him coquettish grins all evening. He'd strained to hear her above the noise of the other guests. She'd giggled like a girl, pulled his face to her mouth, then whispered in his ear. "I don't believe in interracial dating, Sam." The comment had been utterly demeaning. She was accusing him of being white, telling him he'd sold out. He'd avoided her like the plague after that.

Sam set his face into a rigid smile and pointed it in her direction. She began to speak. Sam heard his ex-wife Carly in her accusatory tone. Sheraye reminded him of Carly: tall, confident, brash, attractive (for a Women's Studies scholar), and lethal. Her p's popped when she spat her poison into the microphone.

Carly had evolved into feminism during year three of their marriage. At first his young wife had admired him. But as she read books by women like Sheraye, she began to cast him in the role of the oppressor. The more she read—books he'd introduced her to, ironically enough—the more she despised him. "You're a pompous ass, you know that, Sam?" she'd said one evening, out of the blue. *The Women of Brewster Place* lay on the table beside her. He blamed Gloria Naylor for his wife's sudden vitriol, and he blamed himself for urging her to continue her pursuit of her master's degree. Her words had stung him because they were said without rancor—simply as a matter of fact. She'd filed for divorce two years later. Carly wanted children, Sam didn't. He'd told her that when he'd married her, but women have convenient memories. She'd written about him in an article she published later in a feminist magazine. He was disguised, of course, but everyone who knew them understood who was being referenced in the passages on black male chauvinism. Last year, at the Conference on Tolerance in New Orleans, Sam had found time to visit an old woman in the French Quarter who made a little effigy of his ex-wife and invited him to stick pins into it. He'd skewered every orifice with the kind of passion he usually reserved for debates on NPR. The effigy looked like a photo he'd seen in a medical journal of a fetal twin that had grown inside a normal twin and been excised from the boy's stomach during adolescence. The nightmare fetus had brown, leathery skin, long hair, and shocking malformations. The thing was long dead but thriving; not sentient but blossoming as a vile growth inside the stomach of the boy.

Naturally the skewering hadn't worked—had the opposite effect, in fact. Carly had just had another book accepted by Doubleday. She was engaged to John Gregson, the renowned African-American scientist. To top it all off, she was bearing Gregson's male twins. Her yearning to lactate was about to be fulfilled. Sam was tempted to call the witch doctor and demand a refund.

Up until the moment when Sheraye opened her mouth, the conversation had been lively and constructive. The perpetrators would be found and punished. The "n" word could not be tolerated, especially not when it was written in all caps. The shock suffered by President Trenchard when he'd discovered the graffiti etched into the hood of his Mercedes was matched by his bewilderment. No one was whiter than Bill Trenchard. He was related to British aristocracy, so he'd been white his whole life and then some. He assumed it was a case of wrongful identity. "Whomsoever these hooligans meant to target," he said, his crisp British accent filling the auditorium, "it was the institution they violated when they carved their appalling word into my vehicle." To underscore his outrage, he said the word "vehicle" with a pronounced "h."

Sam noticed that President Trenchard shuffled uneasily in his seat when Sheraye walked up to the microphone. Sheraye Underwood was a visitor, a guest. This was an internal affair. Most of those in the room wore gray pants. Sheraye didn't. Sheraye was dressed in red.

When Sam managed to pull himself together, he realized he had his mouth open. It wasn't distinguished for a distinguished professor to have his mouth open in public. It was fishlike. He tried to close it. It was very difficult because his tongue seemed to have swollen freakishly inside his mouth. Sheraye had begun by asking the panelists why they hadn't thought to include a woman (presumably her) on their panel. The panelists looked at each other, seemingly for the first time. Granted, none of them were women, their expressions said, but three of the five were minorities. Sam took it upon himself—a move he soon deeply regretted—to apologize for the oversight. Sheraye looked him up and down. Even her braids were sneering at him.

"Dr. Monroe," she said, "may I ask if you yourself are the owner of a Mercedes Benz, E-class?" Her thick braids gestured at him as rudely as middle fingers.

The audience got very quiet. Sam knew immediately what she was trying to infer. *He'd* been the target, not Trenchard. For some reason, the thought had never occurred to him. For once, he was unprepared.

"I-I sold it," Sam stammered.

"To whom?" she asked.

"I didn't sell it to *Bill!*" Sam protested, much too loudly. The microphone screeched in protest. Sam felt a flock of crows gather in a storm cloud above his head.

"I didn't say you did," she shot back.

Another of the panelists, Dr. Lyle Weir from Biology, leapt to Sam's defense.

"What are you suggesting—Dr. Underwood, isn't it? That our esteemed colleague was, in fact, the target of racial hatred? That this was a personal rather than a random attack? If so, we should rally round him with renewed fervor."

"I don't know whose car they thought they were vandalizing," she said. Her voice was a clear bell sounding its way up to the stage where they sat like rows of ducks waiting for her to take aim and fire. "But I'm sorry that there are professors at this institution whose racial identity is, perhaps—how can I put it?—*compromised* in some way. Perhaps the perpetrators were being ironic."

Sam was the only one who seemed to understand what she was getting at. She was accusing him once again of being an Uncle Tom. She was trying to humiliate him in front of his colleagues.

Weir asked her pointedly if she had a question. It was the only cue she needed. She launched into a five-minute lecture, telling them what they needed to do to improve the campus climate, citing statistics Sam hadn't known about the campus even though he'd been there for years, running rings around several of the panelists' arguments, and eliciting laughter from the audience who, increasingly, appeared dazzled by her wit. She sat down to energetic applause. At least a dozen graduate students and faculty members stood up and cheered. Weir, the silly old bastard who prided himself on his perspicacity, had been seduced along with the rest. "What we need," Weir proclaimed, his face shining like a beacon, "is a task force to examine all these incidents, a fresh perspective. Perhaps Dr. Underwood could head it up. What do you think, Sam? Someone from the outside? Shake us all up a bit?"

That was the moment when Sam's jaw had dropped open. He sat there for what seemed like several seconds before forcing his mouth shut and nodding. It was settled. He'd been caught by an opponent who was more prepared than he had been.

Sam rushed out of the auditorium as soon as the session was over, almost shoving Jim McFadden to one side in his distress. Out of the corner of his eye, Sam saw Sheraye gossiping with the president. She was telling him something confidential—leaning into him coquettishly so that she could plunge her fangs into his flesh.

The call the next morning was vindication. President Trenchard wished to see him. Sam knew what he was going to ask. In the cold light of day, Bill had seen through Sheraye Underwood. He wanted to invite Sam to head up the task force. As he shaved, careful to avoid the gash in his cheek, Sam decided to serve on the task force even if it meant including Sheraye Underwood. As chair, he could undermine her comments at every turn, turn her into an object of ridicule.

Sam stepped into the president's office with confidence. He shook Trenchard's hand. He sank down in one of the president's comfortable, oversized leather armchairs. He asked how Bill's golf game was going, but for once, the president didn't want to talk about golf. Sam noticed that his friend seemed fidgety. Suddenly, the nervousness he'd felt in the auditorium when Sheraye had stepped up to the microphone gripped him again. The flap of wings—bats this time—forced him to swallow hard.

"I'm sorry to have to ask you this, Sam, but we've had a . . . complaint."

"Complaint?" Sam's voice was as high as a girl's. He wanted to find a sword and thrust it into something. He sat stupidly in the large chair and wondered if his mouth was open. Bill Trenchard began again:

"Someone is alleging that . . . that you're not . . . how shall I put this? That you're not really . . . well . . . black."

"*Ha!*" Sam exclaimed. It was a ridiculous thing to say and it came out of nowhere. It sounded like half of a guilty guffaw and confirmed to them both that he was losing it. He made a desperate effort to recover. "Who . . . who is saying this, Bill? It's absurd! I've always been . . . I mean, my father . . . Ibo."

"That's just it, Sam. Apparently, some reporter from *African American Activism* called your mother. She says your father was

Scottish—from Glasgow. Met him in Ireland. Says he wasn't black at all. Claims she's never heard of an Ibo."

"But my mom's *senile*, for Christ's sake!"

"Precisely. The point I made . . . precisely. You had to commit her to care, I told them that. But they seem to think they're onto something. We need to clear this up somehow. Maybe your siblings?"

"Different dads," Sam said, his voice a monotone. He stifled an urge to throw up.

"Oh, I see. Well, perhaps some other relative can be of assistance?"

"There are no *other relatives*, Bill." Sam spoke so harshly that Bill's eyebrows flicked up in surprise. "Sorry, sorry, Bill. This is upsetting. I mean, I'm *black* for God's sake! You think I'd make that up? I'm not crazy! Look at me. You think you get hair like this from a Scot?"

"Actually, I knew a white fellow from Blackpool who had a head of hair every bit as frizzy as . . . never mind. Sam, this is *very* awkward—very awkward indeed. The Board feels that—"

"The Board of Regents knows about this! *Jesus*, Bill! Why'd you go tattling to them?"

"It wasn't I who told them," Bill said coldly. "Jim McFadden received a call from the reporter last night. Felt he should share it with the rector."

"You know who's behind this, don't you?" Sam sneered.

"Who?"

"That woman, that *bitch* of a woman! Sheraye Underwood! She's responsible for all this, I know it. She *hates* me!"

Bill refused to bite; his expression said that Sheraye Underwood was off limits. Defeat tore at Sam's intestines. He felt his whole body sag into itself as if someone had sucked the old Sam out through his own navel. He felt Sheraye Agness-with-a-double-hiss Underwood jabbing at him with her braids. The razor nick he'd sustained the morning before stung anew. He made one last effort to reestablish his good name:

"Bill, you can't do this to me. I'm biracial. *Black!* Look at me! My work—all of it. You think I could have written those things if I hadn't got some insight into what it's like to straddle two different cultures? My mom's crazy. Most of the time she doesn't even remember my name!"

"What about your father's name, Sam?" Bill suggested. "Maybe we can trace him."

"It was nearly fifty years ago, for Christ's sake! He was a drummer with some band, Mom said. Kojo, she called him. Family owned some cocoa farm. You think we're going to find him now? I don't even know his full name."

"Is it on your birth certificate?"

"No, it's not. Mom's a private person." In light of her sexual history, Sam's assertion seemed ludicrous to both of them.

"Look, Sam, I'm not the one who's raising objections. I think your work is valid even if you're not . . . well, I think it's valid no matter what. But others feel you may have . . . misrepresented yourself. The African-American Student Caucus has asked us to investigate. Look, you're understandably upset. Why don't we leave things as they are for now and talk later. I'm in your corner, Bill. I'm your pal—you know that."

Bill held out his hand. Sam realized he was being dismissed. He tried to remember what it was he was meant to do with the pink and fleshy hand that was being offered to him; he was at a loss. The president patted him on the shoulder: "I'm on your side, pal," Bill repeated. Sam stared at the president for a moment, blinked hard, then stumbled out of the office.

I don't remember," the old woman said. She was irritated and tired. When Sam had first walked into her room in the nursing home in New Jersey, she hadn't recognized him.

"You told him I was white, Mom. The reporter. You've got to tell him the truth. Tell him who my father was."

His mother looked at him. For a moment, he saw a face he

recognized peeking out from behind her eyes, then they clouded over and his mother disappeared. The flesh around her red-rimmed eyes looked colorless, transparent almost. The eyes that were once vivid green had lost their sparkle.

"Mom, you don't understand. This could *ruin* me! I need to be who I said I was. They think I'm a fraud. They think I made it up, Mom. Only you know the truth. Are there any letters from him—*anything*?"

Marie shrugged.

Sam began to feel overwhelmed. He sank down in his chair.

He'd called his half-brothers and stepsister before he left for New Jersey, but none of them could swear his father was even black, let alone Ibo.

"Marie was always cagey 'bout you boys," his stepsister, Sissy, had told him. "Dad—my dad I mean—was the only one she married. The *only* one. Glad she ain't my mama, tell you that right now. Don't know how you boys stand it being mixed. I couldn't be mixed in this day and age. Mariah Carey's 'bout the only one who can pull it off, in my opinion. That girl has class. My mama was a lady. Marie, she was ashamed of the others—the other men she had. All you boys had different daddies. She had a thing for blacks, though, so it stands to reason your daddy was black. Shit!—you *are* pretty light skinned, now I think about it." She laughed. Sam wanted to tell her how vulgar she seemed to him, but he said nothing. "We used to call you Skinnywhiteass—remember?" She laughed. "Funny if you turned out to be white after all. I mean, it would change every damn thing for you, I guess—your books and shit. Almost worser 'n being mixed in a way. Hey, you got any cash you can spare, Sam? My kids is milkin' me dry and their kids is playin' the same damn tune. I'm tellin' you, ain't no picnic bein' a mother in this day an' age."

Sam studied his mother's face looking for a way in.

"Remember the stories you told me? A man as dark as your hair, you used to say. Ibo, from Nigeria—a drummer. Said you couldn't understand why I was so light given the fact that he was the darkest one of all. Melvin, Charles, Wyatt—all of us. All your children are black, for Christ's sake! You love black men. The only man you married was black, right? Stands to reason I'm black too, right?"

"Yes," the old woman replied.

"*Yes!*" Sam could hardly contain his joy. "Say it again, Mom, into the recorder! Tell them my dad was black!"

Sam was so excited he could barely press the record button.

"*Say it!* He was Nigerian, right?"

The old woman passed a mottled hand over her mouth like someone who is very thirsty. In a moment of supreme lucidity, her eyes bored into his, scorching them. His mother saw him at last.

"*You* put me here, you *bastard*," she told him. "You put me in this shit-hole and left me to die."

"Oh my God! Is this some kind of sick revenge? Is that what this is about?"

"You were never kind to anyone," his mother told him. "You treat women like dirt. Carly loved you. You spat on her; you spat on me. So many betrayals . . . all those women, all those young college girls. I love black men, but I don't love you, Sam. Not one bit. Your father would be ashamed. . . ."

He was standing over her now, shouting at the top of his lungs.

"Tell them about my father, you *stupid bitch!*"

He shoved the microphone under the folds of flesh that hung from her chin. But it was too late. Marie had retreated again. A nurse came in and asked him to leave. He snatched up his recorder and ran out of the room.

On the drive home, Sam felt the kind of gut-wrenching panic he'd only experienced once before. It was an evening in June; his skin in Brooklyn summers was dark. He was walking back from the library carrying his boom box. He was late, stayed too long. His mom would be mad when he got home. His pick was lodged in his back pocket in case he needed to prettify his hair. Suddenly, four white men stood in front of him blocking his path. All of them were drunk and mean as snakes. He was fourteen. "Come here, Nigger," one of them said. "An' give us that nice big music machine. A donation of sorts." "How 'bout we run our hands through that gorgeous, girly hair you got?" another said. "Tie it up in some pretty bows, make you feel like a natural woman."

They'd tackled him, all four together. But somehow, maybe because they were so drunk they could barely stand, he'd fought them off. He'd lost his boom box and all his change had fallen out of his pocket. One of the white men had unzipped Sam's jeans and touched him there before Sam had been able to kick him in the crotch. One of the others had shoved him against a wall and rubbed up against him as if he were some whore. He'd stabbed one of them in the leg with his pick. The white man had howled in pain when he'd done it, and the boy who had avoided violence up until then understood for the first time what it meant to draw blood, how thrilling and terrible it felt when it wasn't your own. He'd left his pick there, deep inside the white man's fleshy thigh, and ran.

He had run all the way home—eight miles. Too afraid to wait at a bus stop or enter the subway, too afraid to stop.

He'd never told his mother how he'd got a black eye or where he'd lost his boom box. It wasn't her business. She was white; she wouldn't get it. In those days, it wasn't the kind of thing a boy talked about. He'd sealed it up inside himself. And that was when he'd been born into something different, something set apart. And until now, he'd clung to that, drawn upon it as a rite of passage. But what value did it have if he weren't black? What did all that mean if he'd been duped from the start? If it was a farce, all of it.

He banged his fist on the steering wheel and cried out in rage and humiliation. His eyes were dry and red and swollen.

As soon as he got home, he hurried to the bathroom and grabbed a pair of scissors. A few minutes later, his beautiful hair lay in long swirls on the bathroom floor. He stared at them. The strands seemed to writhe under his gaze, then they became still.

Exhausted, he fell to his knees. He picked up handfuls of his bushy hair and rubbed them against his swollen face, letting the tears come at last. "Oh mother, mother!" he cried, not knowing if what he felt was pain for himself or pain for her, because they were both trapped now, and the long shadows that followed them could never be untangled.

And soon, as he swept up the strands of hair that littered the bathroom floor, the pity he felt was replaced by a thirst for vengeance. He thought of an old woman with white hair and pale skin; he thought of her opposite. He stabbed at them both as he poured his gorgeous hair into the garbage can and slammed the lid shut.

Late that night he made a phone call.

"Carly?" He wanted to wound her.

"Sam? Is that you?" But her voice was gentle, kind. He thought of the twins she bore. He thought of the way she used to grab his hair in both hands when they made love and cling to him as if he had the power to take her somewhere that mattered.

"Carly, they tried to kill me. I ran, but they caught up. Been running all my life."

"Sam—you OK? You been attacked? You need me to call the police?"

"All these years they've been running after me. I never looked back. Not once. Turn to salt if you look back—too many tears. I loved you, Carly, more than I loved myself. Was I loved, Carly? Did you love me once? Or was I always a pompous ass?"

"You were always a pompous ass," she told him. "But I loved you anyway," she said.

"Thank you," he replied, his voice barely above a whisper.

He said good-bye while she was still speaking to him.

He ran his hand over his shorn head, and felt the shock of what had been taken away.

"Effigies" began with a man who hovered in my imagination, much like the flock of angry birds that reappear in the story. Wild haired and physically imposing, Sam was in my peripheral vision; the more he took center stage, the more I realized this would be his story. It was his hair that defined him at first, but soon he evolved into a man trying to escape from his own history, oddly complacent in the world he'd managed to mold for himself. I was drawn to a narrative in which someone is robbed of his identity because it obliged me to ask hard questions. Having worked as a university professor and as a high school teacher for many years on three different continents, I am fascinated (and sometimes appalled) by the culture of academe and by the protocols that have evolved around it. In a culture in which dialogue is essential, remarkably few people learn to speak across difference. When race and ethnicity enter the picture, the culture adjusts itself—all too often in a confrontational way. Racial and gender conflicts often involve the creation of effigies: alien figures we feel comfortable thrusting pins into, creatures we believe will never be "us."

The episode toward the end of the story when Sam recalls the attack by white racists is based upon a series of personal experiences. The attack profoundly alters who Sam is and becomes the catalyst for the role he decrees for himself. I hope that "Effigies" is a story seething with questions; a story of terrible loss and intensely private revelation.

Peter Ho Davies

Born in Britain to Welsh and Chinese parents, Peter Ho Davies is the author of the story collections *The Ugliest House in the World* and *Equal Love*. His work has appeared in *Harper's*, *The Atlantic Monthly*, *Granta*, and *The Paris Review*, among others, and his short fiction has been anthologized in *O. Henry Prize Stories* and *Best American Short Stories*.

Minotaur

Half man, half bull, that's me. Half myth; half monster. And you thought you had it bad. *My* mother fell for a white *bull*. Not that he ever loved her back. She had to have a false cow constructed, climb inside, and have it rolled into his field before he'd give her a second look. Try explaining that next time someone asks "And how did your parents meet?" Even the most liberal have difficulty understanding a woman degrading herself like that. Half pathetic; half contemptible. I just tell them: "Don't have a cow!"

Not that I get out much, not since I entered my teens. My stepfather's ashamed of me, won't be seen dead with me. Oh, it was cute enough when I was a kid—people liked to pet my muzzle, watch me flare my silky nostrils—and I was always a hit at Halloween. But now I'm an adolescent—half child, half adult—now it's clear I'm not growing out of it, that it isn't just "a phase," he's lost patience.

"What?" he asked my mother. "I suppose you'd like to take him to a china shop?" It was his idea to confine me to this basement labyrinth. "Not confined," I can hear him telling her, overhead. "He can come out anytime he wants. I'm a man, not a beast. Maybe you've forgotten the difference?" Which always shuts her up. I feel sorry for her, in truth. Anyone can make a mistake. The heart is the heart. And now she's gone from bull to bully. She visits me every day—I'm homeschooled—and even slips down in the night sometimes to cradle my head in her lap, strokes my velvety head. I lie very still so as not to gore her. *Your father,* she whispers, *was a god; Zeus in disguise.* She means it as a consolation, but I fear I inherited only the disguise, none of the godliness.

My demigod, she calls me. "Demi" being the polite word for a half of something worth having, the cup half full, the *demitasse.*

Technically, of course, he's correct, my stepfather: I'm not confined. There are no locks, no gates, no chains, no bars. I'm just here at the center of the labyrinth. The room's pretty comfortable—cable, microwave, internet, even a cramped little bathroom (it's hard to maneuver in a shower stall with horns). All the usual amenities you'd expect in a finished basement. Bow-flex, knotty pine, futon. And I can call out, order in—half pepperoni, half field-greens (the pizza guy used to bring his own thread, but now he's got the route down). But it's *hard* to leave, you know. Agoraphobia, is what I tell people if they ask (they often do in chatrooms). Sometimes, I say, I don't have the use of my legs.

But really, it's this—at the door of my room, there are two choices: left or right. I stand there for hours at a time, looking down one passage, then the other, staring into the darkness. What would it be like to charge down there? Or there? But I can't choose. If I think of going right, start to imagine it, pretty soon I start to feel halfhearted, regret not turning left. Then again, if I'm of half a mind to go left, I soon feel the same thing about the right. And the worst of it is, as I understand from the pizza guy, these choices just keep recurring, every few steps—left or right? Right or left? Of course, even if they didn't, even if the labyrinth is a lie, an invention of my stepfather's—he pays for the pizza, after all, probably tips the guy well—it wouldn't matter. Why ten choices, or a hundred, when two are enough to stop me in my tracks, snorting and pawing a bald spot in the shag?

The horns of a dilemma? My horns *are* my dilemma.

Sometimes I hear my stepfather up there—he drinks, no surprise—when my mother is out. He likes to stamp around, sometimes it sounds like he's doing a jig, sometimes a rain dance. And when he has my attention, he calls down, in a mocking singsong: *Pick me! No, pick me!*

I toss my head and snort hotly.

"Half-breed? Half-wit!" he taunts. "Half man? Half bullshit!"

"Half *father*?" I bellow back. "Half cuckold! These are *your* horns, old man! I got them from *you*!"

"Want to give them back? Come on then!" He pounds the floor. "What are you waiting for? A red rag?"

He wants to make me angry enough to choose, but I can't. *I can't!* For a long time, I thought it was fear, indecisiveness. Half coward; half Hamlet. But why does it have to be left or right? Why settle for half measures? Given those choices, I refuse to choose. And why just those two? Why not up, or down, or straight ahead. Why not a third choice? So I've been trying to make a new way for myself, charging and running my head against the wall, ripping through the pine and particle board with my horns. Beyond them, as I guessed, are dirt walls, hard packed but dry and crumbling. It's hard work—I have awful migraines that flash like sparks from horn tip to horn tip—but the sight of my own blood on the earth only urges me on. What's a bull's head good for, after all, if not butting and battering, gouging and goring.

And all the while, over the ringing in my ears, I tell myself, *This is my choice*, and lower my head once more.

I've been teaching a class in the history of the short story for a few years now, arguing that the form can, very roughly, be divided into two broad traditions—two lines of descent, if you like—the realistic (Chekhov and Carver, say) and, for want of a better word, the fantastical, (Kafka, Borges, and, oh, Donald Barthelme). My own stories have nearly all been in the former mode, and by way of an experiment I've recently been trying to do more work in the latter, an approach that has led to several new pieces, including "Minotaur." The fantastical treatment appealed in that case as a means of getting away from my early earnestly autobiographical attempts at the subject. More broadly, though, the notion behind this stylistic crossover is that while there may be realistic or fantastical stories, that doesn't mean that writers have to be either conventional or experimental (to put the distinction in contemporary terms). And, of course, that interest in dodging dualities, resisting the either/or, in writing and in life, is in a sense what the story is about.

I should add, finally, that my wife and I have just had our own "mixed" child, who heavily influenced the story, in the fundamental sense that it's not easy to write anything longer than a few hundred words during his naps.

CHASTITY WHITAKER

Emily Raboteau

Emily Raboteau is an assistant professor of creative writing in the English Department at the City College of New York. She has a recent M.F.A. in Fiction from New York University, where she was a *New York Times* Fellow, and a B.A. in English from Yale University. Her short stories have appeared in *Transition, Callaloo, African Voices, The Missouri Review, Tin House, Best American Short Stories 2003,* and elsewhere. She is the recipient of the *Chicago Tribune*'s Nelson Algren Award for Short Fiction, a Jacob Javits Fellowship, a Pushcart Prize, and a New York Foundation for the Arts Fellowship. Her first novel is *The Professor's Daughter*.

Mrs. Turner's Lawn Jockeys

'm mowing Mrs. Turner's front yard after school when one of her lawn jockeys tells me to help him. Mrs. Turner has two lawn jockeys that look exactly the same. They have the same white pants and black boots and red jacket and the same lantern in their hand and the same black face with the same dumb little cap on top. It's the one on the left side of her front steps that opens his mouth first. I think I hear someone call my name but the motor is running real loud on the mower and I'm not sure. Then I hear it again.

"Bernie!"

I look around and don't see anybody but those lawn jockeys. I cut the motor anyway and wipe my face with my towel. The one on the left is staring at me with his bubble eyes.

"Hello, Bernie," he says.

I wonder how he knows my name. I started mowing Mrs. Turner's lawn when I was ten. That was two years ago and neither one of them ever talked to me until now. He tells me to come over, so I go over and sit next to him on the steps. He's about three feet tall. The water at the shallow end of a swimming pool would cover his head.

"What do you want?" I ask him. I'm not sure yet if I should trust these guys, 'cause my dad hates them. "I hate those damn lawn jockeys," he always says. He says when Mrs. Turner got us as her neighbors she should have stuck them in the garage or something.

"We need your help," the lawn jockey tells me. The other one is looking at me through the side of his eyes and I feel nervous right away, like they're gonna ask me to do something bad. I just pick at the scab on my knee.

Then the first one starts talking about how awful things are for them and I start to feel kind of bad about what he's saying. The main point is how they're stuck there, "in bondage," he says, and how nothing ever changes. I look out over Mrs. Turner's yard and I think I know what he means. All you can see past the yard is a piece of the street and then our brick house across it. He says they've been there a long time, in the same place, since way before I was born. By the time the lawn jockey gets done talking I really like him. He's very polite and has a way with words.

"What can I do for you?" I ask.

"Come closer," he says, so I lean my ear down to his mouth and he whispers what he wants me to do.

"That doesn't make any sense!" I say. "Wouldn't you rather

just have me take you somewhere with a better view?" I'm thinking I could strap them to my skateboard with dad's whipping belt and pull them down to Carnegie Lake. If I put them there by the water they could watch the Canada geese and the Princeton crew races and the ice skaters when the lake freezes over in the wintertime.

He says I'm missing the point, which is that even if they were in a different place, people would still look at them in the same way and that would spoil it. He has thought about it a lot and this is what he really wants.

"Him too?" I ask about the other one who hasn't said anything.

"Him too."

"I'm not sure," I tell them. I'm thinking about how I just got done getting grounded for my report card. "It seems kinda risky."

The quiet one on the right sighs. "We didn't want to have to resort to this, but . . ."

"But we've got a lot of dirt on you, buddy," the one on the left cuts in. He stomps his little black boot. He's got a real nasty look on his face all of a sudden.

"What do you mean?"

"That pack of Kools you smoked? We saw you do it."

The quiet one is shaking his head, like he is disappointed.

"So?"

"That time you tried on your mother's lipstick and jerked off on your parents' bed? We saw that too. *Disgusting*."

"Please don't think we enjoy spying," the quiet one explains.

But I'm getting a creepy feeling, the same one I get about Dr. Martin Luther King, Jr. My dad always tells me to pretend like Martin Luther King is standing behind me, watching whatever I'm doing. I'm supposed to try to honor his legacy. That way I won't do anything bad.

"We know you like to wipe your boogers on the bathroom wall."

"It's just that there's nothing else for us to watch."

I turn around and see how all the front windows of our house are like little TV screens.

"We also saw you—"

"All right, Lawn Jockey," I say to the loudmouth, "I'll do it."

I excuse myself because I have to finish up Mrs. Turner's front yard. Once I get done cutting the grass I push the lawn mower into her garage and go back dragging the hose to water the rosebushes. She has five different color roses growing in front: white, pink, peach, yellow, and red. Once she got a prize for how pretty they looked. I can tell the roses are thirsty so I give them a lot of water. Then I dig out the dandelions. I put them in my pocket to make my mom a dandelion crown. The lawn jockeys are watching me and I'm wondering how I'm going to do what they asked me without getting in trouble.

I look over Mrs. Turner's yard and I think it looks pretty good. Not like the backyard. Mrs. Turner won't let me mow the backyard. Mr. Turner used to keep bees back there before he died. He used to wear a white space suit so the bees couldn't sting him, and they used to buzz all around and sit on his arms and head. After he died all the bees flew off to find him. Pretty soon the weeds back there grew as tall as my knees and the neighborhood cats started going back there to crap in the broken beehives. The fact is, Mrs. Turner's front yard and backyard don't seem like they go with the same house.

Once, after Mr. Turner died, Mrs. Turner slipped in the bathtub and broke her hip and I asked her what does it feel like to be almost dead. She told me to button my lip. That wasn't fair. I never told her to button her lip when she asked me what it feels like to be half black. "It feels like I'm half white," I told her. But she wouldn't talk about being almost dead. Some things you're just not supposed to talk about even though they're not exactly a secret. Like her backyard; I'm just supposed to pretend it's not there and focus on making the front yard pretty. That just shows how there's two worlds—the one we talk about and the one we don't.

I coil up the garden hose on the side of the house and start back up to Mrs. Turner's front door so I can get my five dollars. The one on the right is crying. He looks a little different from the loudmouth because one of his ears is cracked off and there's bird shit on his cap.

"What's the matter?" I ask him.

"He's fine," snaps the one on the left, even though I wasn't talking to him.

"Don't you ever talk?" I ask the quiet one.

"If you must know, I'm crying because I'm happy," he says.

I go in and find Mrs. Turner in the dining room reading a big mystery book with a magnifying glass and I tell her I'm done with her yard. She says marvelous and will I take some refreshments. I can't say no 'cause she already has a place mat set up across the table from her with a glass of milk and a plate of potato chips. So I sit down and put a chip in my mouth. It's soggy. I make a point to tell her that her hair looks pretty. The fact is her hair is blue and it looks like a helmet, but it's OK to lie if it makes somebody happy. Mrs. Turner blushes and touches her hair. Then she stands up with her walker and hobbles over to the sideboard. That's where she keeps her checkbook.

I drink the milk and look up at her chandelier. I like Mrs. Turner's chandelier 'cause it makes little rainbows all over the wallpaper. I'm pretty sure the rainbows are alive. They're tiny like the size of bees. Once she paid me five dollars extra to climb up on the table in my socks and take down all the pieces of crystal on that chandelier and dip them in a bucket of soapy water. I sneaked one of them in my sweatpants and gave it to my sister for her birthday. I felt kind of bad thinking Dr. Martin Luther King, Jr. knew I stole Mrs. Turner's crystal, but the fact is she couldn't tell it was missing anyway. She's almost blind.

I wipe off my milk mustache and start wondering about Mr. Turner and the bees. If he knew how to talk to them.

"Remind me how to spell your last name, won't you?" Mrs. Turner says. She forgets a lot of stuff. I say the letters in my last name and she says, "That doesn't sound accurate," and she's right 'cause when I try to spell out loud I remember all the letters but I forget which one comes first. I tell her I'll write it myself.

My first name looks just like a little bird hopped around on the check how she wrote it 'cause her handwriting's so shaky. I write my last name next to it: B-O-U-D-R-E-A-U-X. I don't know if the B is pointing the right way or not, and the middle letters are falling down under the line. I know the X is in the right place at the end of our name, just like how at the end of a treasure hunt X marks the spot.

She fills out the rest of the check and says, "There you are, young man." Mrs. Turner gives out teeny tubes of toothpaste at Halloween and says the same thing: "There you are, young man. There you are, young lady. Don't forget to brush." Toothpaste as a treat is even worse than raisins and that's how come she gets eggs in her mailbox.

On my way down her front steps I look at the lawn jockeys again. The one on the left who is now on the right winks at me and says, "Remember your promise," and the other one with the missing ear says, "We're ready when you are, Bernie."

"I'll be ready tonight," I say. My dad always says there's no time like the present. "There's no time like the present," I say. The lawn jockeys smile like they're proud of me.

M y mom is helping me with my homework later in the living room and I keep looking out the window across the street. The lawn jockeys are watching so I wave and they both wave back with the same hand, the one they usually keep on their hips.

"Earth to Bernie," my mom says. She wants to know what I'm looking at.

"Mrs. Turner's lawn jockeys," I tell her. She pulls the string to close the drapes and tells me to concentrate on my book, but the whole time I'm planning out how I'm going to help them.

"Earth to Bernie. Earth to Bernie," my mom keeps saying,

like I'm on another planet. I put the dandelion crown on her head. The yellow flowers look pretty in her brown hair. I'm not lying this time, they really do. I tell her that and she smiles a little and shakes her head. She points at the book, but the letters are smashing into each other like bumper cars.

The same thing happens at dinner. I'm looking at the lawn jockeys through the dining room window and my dad puts down his fork and says, "Pay attention to your plate, son. You're setting a bad example for your sister." Emma isn't really eating her salmon loaf either, but that's 'cause she's so picky she has to pick out all the little bones, not 'cause I'm setting a bad example. She eats like a bird.

I see the lawn jockey on the right put his lantern on the ground and rub his shoulder. I'm thinking how those two lawn jockeys can see right into all the front windows of our house like five TV shows and how they probably know a whole lot about us.

"Why can't you focus?" my dad says. "What's the matter with you?" He always says that. I shrug my shoulders.

"Dad?" says Emma, but he's not listening to her. He wants to know if I did my homework.

"He finished it before dinner," my mom tells him. "Does anyone want another baked potato?"

"Let's see it," he says, "right now." He's mad at me; I can tell from his voice.

"I learned a new word in Spanish today," Emma says.

"Let him finish eating first, Bernard," my mom tells him.

"No. *Now*."

I bring him my geography workbook and show him the page where I copied down the state capitals how my mom showed me.

"What does this say?" he asks. He's pointing at one of the square states in the middle of the country. There's four of them. My teacher told us if you stand in the middle where they touch corners, then you can be in all four states at once. But I can't remember which one it is my dad has his finger on, and I can't remember the name of the capital.

"Does anyone want to hear my new word?" Emma asks. "It's a noun." She's chewing on the end of her braid.

"Read it," my dad tells me.

Everybody's waiting. Even the lawn jockeys. The dining room is too hot. The grandfather clock in the hallway gets louder and that's the only noise. Tick tock. Tick tock. I scratch the scab on my knee. The fact is, I can't read what I wrote. I look away from my book to my seat. I'm hoping Dr. Martin Luther King, Jr. will be sitting there in his robes, and he'll tell me the answer. But he's not. My chair is empty.

"Traje de baño," says Emma, "Guess what it means?" but nobody guesses. Instead, my dad tells me to go upstairs and get the belt.

Later, when they're getting ready to go to bed, I can hear him fighting with my mom. He's saying he moved us here for the school system so we could have a good education. He's not saying he hates it here, but I know that's what he means. The fact is, sometimes I hate it here too. Everybody looks at us like we did something wrong.

He's telling my mom I'm not pulling my weight. He wants me to be like the other boys. "I just want him to fit in," he says.

"Why? Why in the world would you want that?" my mom says.

"Trust me. It's better that way."

"Can't you see how special he is, Bernard?"

"*Trust me*," says my dad.

"I don't understand."

"No. You wouldn't." I hear something slam. Maybe the drawer he keeps his handkerchiefs in with the BB in the corner.

In the middle of the night when I'm getting ready, my sister comes down to the kitchen in her nightgown and her retainer. She asks me what I'm putting on my face.

"What are you doing up, Pocahontas?" I say. I call her that

sometimes when she's wearing braids 'cause she looks like a lit-tle Indian girl. "You should be in bed."

"Yeah, but what are you putting on your face?" she wants to know.

"Shoe polish," I say. A ski mask would be better, but I don't have one of those.

Emma also wants to know where I'm going, and when I won't tell her she says she's coming with me. I think about it and decide it might be good to have a lookout so I say fine with me on one condition: she has to get dressed all in black like I am and keep her mouth closed about the whole thing.

"That's two conditions," she says, and she goes upstairs to change. When she comes down again she's wearing her black tights and her black ballet slippers and my blue Mets jersey. She says she doesn't have anything black to go on top. I tell her that's no good; the point is that we have to be invisible and she better go put on dad's overcoat. She does that and I black up her face with the shoe polish and then we take the flashlight out to the garage to get the things I'm gonna need.

Everything looks different since this is the middle of the night. I notice some things, like how all the houses up and down the street are sleeping but how most of the trees are awake. Also, the air is softer than in the day. Like velvet almost. We cross the street and a raccoon mama crosses the other way with her rac-coon baby in her mouth. She slinks real slow without looking at us. Then I can see the grass in Mrs. Turner's front yard growing back already, but slow, like the raccoon.

"Who's she?" says the lawn jockey on the left.

"That's the sister," says the one on the right.

"She's keeping a lookout," I tell them. Emma is standing by the sidewalk and she's supposed to whistle if she sees a person coming or a car.

I get the lid off the paint can with the screwdriver I brought and ask which one of them wants to go first.

"Me," they both say at the same time, so I flip my lucky

penny and the one on the right calls heads and wins 'cause there's Abraham Lincoln, looking at the rosebushes. I dip the paintbrush and I'm about to get started when Emma tugs on the back of my sweatshirt and scares the shit out of me. She's so quiet I didn't even know she snuck up behind me. Dad's overcoat is hanging down off her hands and dragging in the grass.

"Who are you talking to, Bernie?" she asks.

"The lawn jockeys."

"Oh. You're going to paint them white?"

I nod my head.

"Why?"

"'Cause they're stuck inside their bodies. See?" I point at them with the paintbrush. The one on the right and the one on the left. She looks at them and blinks. Her eyes look real bright and pretty with her face all black like that.

"I don't get it," she says.

"They're stuck inside the way everybody looks at them, and they want me to change it. Now go back over there and do your job." She goes back over to the edge of the sidewalk and I get started. The smell of the paint goes over the smell of the roses. I start under the lawn jockey's cap and brush going down from his forehead, over his cheeks and under his chin to his neck, and I stop at his collar. I'm careful not to drip on his red jacket. I paint his little fists white too. The paint job looks pretty good, but then I think about Dr. Martin Luther King, Jr. watching and decide to do another coat so it's perfect.

"How do I look?" the quiet one whispers when I'm finished.

"Different," I say.

"It's remarkable," says the one on the left. I paint him too. I'm putting the lid back on the can when Emma starts to whistle so I run over.

"What'd you see?" I ask 'cause I don't see anybody coming.

"Look," she whispers and she points up at our attic window. "It's Dad." The light is on and we can see him sitting in the broken highchair eating out of the ice-cream carton. After a while he stops that and puts his head in his hands.

"What's he doing now?" Emma wants to know.

"He's thinking," I tell her. "He had a bad dream." Our dad is in four places at once, and it's giving him a headache, but I don't tell Emma that. She's too little to understand.

He's thinking about who he used to be, who he is, who people think he is, and who he wants me to become.

"Can he see us?"

"No," I say. "We're invisible."

We wait a long time for him to get up and turn out the light, and then we wait some more before we cross the street to go back home. I ask Emma about her new word. "It means bathing suit," she tells me. I tug on one of her braids and tell her I'll teach her the butterfly stroke when the swimming pool opens up for summer. We wipe off the shoe polish in the garage with socks dipped in turpentine, which it turns out later is a bad idea 'cause we both wake up with an itchy rash.

In the night I dream about the bees. I'm following my dad down some train tracks going over the map of America. A dizzy bee comes and stings him on the neck, but he doesn't notice. Then another one comes and another and soon it's a whole swarm of bees stinging him. He doesn't stop walking. He's walking fast in a shell of bees. I can't catch him. I'm pulling a boxcar full of rocks behind me and I can hardly move. He goes away from me fast as a train, down into Mississippi, where he was born.

I wake myself up early in the morning so I can watch him. I scratch my face. I think there's something crawling under there, trying to dig out of my skin.

I look out my window to check on the white lawn jockeys. I wave but they don't wave back. I can tell they're free at last and aren't alive anymore, just plaster.

Then I hear our screen door slam and I watch him go down the path in his pajamas. I hold my breath. He bends down to pick up the newspaper with his hand on his back like maybe it's hurting him. When he stands up he sees them. He drops the newspaper. The lawn jockeys are holding out their lanterns to him like they're giving him a New Year's toast. I can tell by the way my dad's shoulders go up and down, up and down, that he's laughing.

I wrote this story during a residency at the Virginia Center for the Creative Arts where I'd gone to finish working on a collection of linked short stories. They gave me a studio in a converted dairy barn overlooking a cow pasture. I had a routine there: wake up at six, eat breakfast with the other artists, write for three hours, take a nap, eat lunch in the grass, go for a walk along the railroad tracks, write for three hours, eat dinner with the other artists, write for three hours, bed by ten. I've never been as disciplined or as productive with my writing as I was during that time.

Part of the magic of that place (and others like it) is the buzzing consortium of creative minds. I made friends with a prodigious Russian composer, a woodworker who was carving a headless woman out of the trunk of a walnut tree, and an artist who made delightfully mean little sculptures out of porcupine quills. I loved that the individual artistic challenges each of us faced were somehow comparable in spite of the fact that we were working in entirely different disciplines. I remember the woodworker gnashing her teeth over the walnut woman's crotch at the same time I was gnashing mine over some impasse I'd come to in my writing.

Anyway, one day the Russian composer accompanied me on one of my walks along the railroad tracks after lunch. I pointed to a pair of lawn jockeys standing sentinel outside a mobile home on cinder blocks and suggested we sneak back later that night to slap some white paint on them. She didn't understand what I was talking about or why they were offensive, and it occurred to me then that those lawn jockeys are a peculiarly American phe-

nomenon in need of explanation. I returned to my studio and wrote the first draft of "Mrs. Turner's Lawn Jockeys" before dinner. I don't normally write that quickly, but this just flowed. Bernie, who narrates the story, was a secondary character in several other stories I'd written, and his voice came naturally to me because I knew him so well. Bernie decides to paint his neighbor's lawn jockeys white because he sees how much they upset his black father. It's an act of defiance, but more than that, it's an act of love.

After I'd sold the manuscript I finished at VCCA, my editor convinced me that it was not a collection of short stories but a novel, and that "Mrs. Turner's Lawn Jockeys," which was a very good story on its own, did not fit neatly into the larger narrative of the book. I agreed with her, although it stung a bit to expunge it. I didn't throw the story out because I hoped it would find a home somewhere, and now it has.

JON COOPER

Carmit Delman

Carmit Delman is the author of *Burnt Bread and Chutney: Growing Up Between Cultures, A Memoir of an Indian Jewish Girl*. She has a B.A. in Literature and Anthropology from Brandeis University and an M.F.A. in Creative Writing from Emerson College. Currently, she is a professor of Creative Writing at Chester College of New England.

Footnote

The answering machine blinked hopefully at Angie as she entered her apartment. It was Travis, she knew—one message, at least, if not two or three again like yesterday. Last week he left a message that went on for six minutes and twenty-three seconds. In disbelief, she'd actually counted it out. Two weeks ago he left another message, playing a scratchy country song through the phone. Probably, he'd been sitting on his bed while strumming his guitar, and propped the receiver up on a pillow nearby. It slipped down partway through, so the entire second half of Johnny Cash's "I Walk the Line" was muffled through the sheets. But she understood what he was saying all the same, conjuring up Johnny Cash and the love of his life, June Cash. "You've got to stop calling like that," she'd told him later. "It's not going to be that way between us."

Today Angie ignored the answering machine altogether. Dropping her coat on the couch, she headed straight for the refrigerator instead. She opened its door and surveyed the piles of restaurant Styrofoam inside, each filled with a different kind of Indian food. There was almost nothing there but these leftovers. The saag paneer from Jewel of India was the freshest, but she'd just had that last night. She set that carton aside and dug further, moving through Wednesday's takeout, then Monday's doggie bag, then the $12.99 dinner special from across the street, naan and chutneys included. Finally she settled on a samosa from Curry in a Hurry, still cold from the fridge, and at the end of its life soon anyway. Its fried husk was hard; the green peas and yellow potatoes inside had congealed into a block. But it was still good, and she settled with it onto the couch, clicking on the television and purposefully turning her back to the blinking answering machine.

Travis was a remnant of high school back in Braxton County, West Virginia—an old friend she hadn't seen in years. Angie had moved away to Boston for college, and stayed on there after graduating, to work at a small advertising firm downtown. For a couple of years, she made that job everything, loved the creativity, the challenge of finding the one angle and perfect pitch that would resonate for consumers in a real and important way. She spent long hours in the office, spent nights and weekends slaving and networking. That was all she seemed to have in common with people any more. Most of her friends were in advertising too. When she wasn't at work and she was out with them, all they did was talk about this campaign or that. Now and then she dated—men who were in the industry as well, usually. More than once she found herself in bed with a man from a competing agency, half hoping that in the confidance of flannel sheets she might be able to get some good ideas from him.

It began to feel like too much, and a burden sometimes, to know that everything could be bought and sold if only properly marketed. That summer, burned out, she took two weeks vacation in one shot and did nothing but wander the heated streets of Boston, watching people. Mothers wheeling babies, college students in baseball caps, couples. She didn't watch to watch as many people did, for distraction, with glazed eyes at the park. When Angie watched people, she made almost a game of it, searching those who passed by for something they had in common with her. There, that little girl was wearing a shirt that looked like a shirt she herself had gotten for her tenth birthday. There, that man was talking about a computer problem, which reminded her of the computer problem that made her hard drive crash last year. There, she liked that woman's haircut. There, she wanted to buy those shoes too. There, he looked friendly, and maybe they had shared a smile. This cleared Angie's mind, if only a little, so she was rejuvenated when she went back to work. But every now and then when she felt that heaviness again, she took to wandering the streets, watching people, to find something, to shake herself of something else.

In the meantime, back home, Travis had gotten married, had a kid, been divorced, and then lately was transplanted several times with the painting company he worked for. That was how he ended up in Boston. In the last few years while he was on the road, they hadn't seen each other, just exchanged some E-mails. But before he started traveling, they met up a handful of times when she went back to visit her parents. He still kept her updated about what was happening in town, what the old crowd was doing.

Angie's parents—both doctors, and still in West Virginia—knew everyone too, since they all passed through their offices at one point or another. But they couldn't tell her the first thing about what was going on. They had no interest in small-town life themselves, never had. The only reason they ever landed in such a small West Virginia corner in the first place was that they both believed strongly, philosophically, in bringing their skills to places where they were most needed. And by the time Angie was born, they had become close friends with a carefully insulated group including other local doctors, lawyers, an entrepreneur who had bases around the world but kept a country house nearby, and one retired couple who left New York for some clean living. They were all tight-knit, religiously subscribing to the *New York Times*, traveling to Charleston for decent bookstores, and traveling up north several times a year for the symphony. They tried to nurture small bits of culture; once they even brought a traveling theater company doing *South Pacific* to town to raise money for the nearby library. Even their very presence gave a cosmopolitan feel to the community. The Greenbergs were Jewish. Dr. Jameson's wife was Chinese. And of course Angie's mother was half Indian.

Though Angie had rum hair and skin, and wide rum eyes—was darker than her mother even—she herself never felt Indian, at least not until after college. Why would she? Angie had never met a single person from the Indian side of her family, and only a few Indians throughout her childhood at all. Her own mother had been born in Brooklyn—her grandfather Amrit died when she was a baby. It was not pressed upon her by previous genera-tions like a cloying perfume. It was not even a footnote. So that by the time Angie was in high school growing small breasts, finding mutiny, trying on *sullen*, then *angry*, then *deep*, what she pushed against was the circle of her parents. "You're disconnected from everything, think you're better than everyone else," she once told her mother, not long before she left for college, as she was setting the table for a dinner party. "Look," she gestured around. "You've got Beethoven playing. And you asked everyone to bring two canned goods to donate to charity. And you're making lavish stuffed Cornish hens for us to eat. It's all shit."

After dinner that night she met up with Travis and some of their friends from school. They went to the train tracks and built a fire and listened to music. Jamie was there—Travis's long-time girlfriend, the one he eventually married—and Toby and Sean and many of the others. They all accepted Angie no problem, if only because of Travis whom she'd attached herself to from the first day in second grade—instead, to her parents' disappointment, of Dr. Greenberg's twins, who were in her class too.

When they were very young, some of the group had prodded Angie's skin, curious but also looking for differences, telling her, you're so brown. "That's why she's so smart," Travis came to her defense, and that closed it.

"Man," Travis said, leaning into Angie, drunk and nodding his head to the music, "Isn't Johnny Cash something?"

"Yeah." She lay back into the grass and listened to the simple melody and the guitar and the raw voice and the sweet grown-up lyrics, not just like in pop songs about falling in love, but gritty and blushing all at once, about falling in love and changing diapers and growing old and life's hardships. "Yeah. He's something."

Though in the years since then they'd grown apart some, with their history, it was not surprising that Travis should call her up then, when he was working in Boston, would be there for six months probably, could they get a drink? It was only disorienting really to have those two worlds joined together suddenly.

Travis almost didn't recognize her when they first saw each other after all that time. "Christ, you look different," he said into their hug, his words muffled by her hair. "What happened to Dolly?" Angie blushed for a moment, recalling how she used to adore Dolly Parton. For a while in high school, she plastered posters of the country singer wall to wall across her bedroom with her fat blonde hair and sexy lips and big breasts. And after her mother scolded her one time, shaking her head at the poster, saying she's such a cartoon, Angie took up hairspray and lipstick and big padded bras herself.

"Please," she straightened up. "That's long gone."

"No really," Travis said. "You look so fancy and foreign now. You look so Indian." She nodded, agreeing. He held her at a distance, his head cocked to one side to take it all in. Angie's hair was pulled into a long braid down her back. She wore yellow gold earrings, and a yellow gold nose ring, with orange and red and green bangles up and down both wrists. Her shirt was of a thin cotton material, gilded purple, and it had an extra loose length thrown over her shoulders that resembled the style of a sari.

Later at the bar over drinks, she explained it to him. "This is the real me," she told him. "Only I never knew it. I was Dolly Parton and the Judds. And played Garth Brooks all the time. And loved Johnny Cash—well, maybe I always will love Johnny a little bit. But in all that I never knew it."

"Never knew what?" he asked earnestly. "That you were Indian?"

She waved him aside. "I didn't know what it meant to *be* Indian."

"Aren't you only half Indian?"

"Well, a quarter. But that's not the point." She ran a finger around the squat drink glass in front of her, playing with the straw. "One day, must have been in the last couple months, I went into an Indian grocery store and suddenly realized it."

She looked at him expectantly. But all he said was "Ah."

"I can tell you don't understand." She had been wandering the streets of Cambridge that day, to get away from work, watching people in her usual way, searching, searching—there, he had hot chocolate, and she was cold and could use a cup of hot chocolate too. She tried to sniff out a coffee shop. On the way, an old couple walked nearby and the woman stopped short to adjust her shoe. They were Indian, graying, the man in thick old-fashioned glasses, the woman in a sari. They did not walk hand in hand or whisper together, but they were clearly husband and wife, in step with a common history, and with common purpose. After seeing them, Angie forgot about the hot chocolate and followed them instead for several blocks, to watch them some more. They turned into the Indian grocery store and she went in after them, just to keep them in her sight. And as soon as she stepped inside, the heavy scent of spices sank into her hair and skin and mouth all at once. She wanted more of it, didn't know why she was suddenly parched and anxious and empty. The old couple bought their groceries and left. But Angie stayed behind. She bought a couple of CDs, one of the music playing throughout the store. She rented a Bollywood movie. She walked home with a paper bag full of basmati rice and chili powder and fresh foods prepared by the store, plucked out from behind the glass counter and wrapped in plastic for her.

"I'll bet Indian food is good," Travis offered.

She shrugged to end the conversation. And they talked instead about people back home, who was pregnant, who had left, who would never be able to leave. He told her about work, about the Tennessee vacation he was planning, about the music video that Johnny Cash put out for June after she died. She asked about Travis's ex-wife and when he got to see his daughter. And for a while it was like it used to be between them, with Angie easy and calmed near him as she had been that first day in the second grade when her thin brown fingers took hold of him, naturally and clinging. They parted ways, and at his insistence met up a week later for, he himself decided, Indian food. Though he enjoyed the meal while they sat there, each dish a curiousity, later, after midnight, he called her up, miserable with indigestion. By then anyway, Angie felt they had caught up on old times enough, was content to be done.

But Travis had other ideas. "I think you're the most beautiful thing. And I think we can be good together. Really."

"You don't understand me. I'm different from what I once was. And I'm different from you."

"So you like spicy food. Big deal."

Several nights later, the last time she saw Travis, when he was still persisting, he tried to kiss her and she turned her pursed lips away. She sent him home with two CDs of Indian music and three Bollywood movie videos, as if they might speak on her behalf. What could he possibly say to that droning music, to those flashes of color and dancing and exotic landscape, to those many many brown faces and voices?

C hewing her samosa, Angie fast-forwarded through what she'd programed to record while she was at work, watching the pictures race by in static across the television. There was *India Today*, a thirty-minute local cable show which turned out to be a rerun from last week, and also an exposé of child labor in one Indian village on National Geographic which might have been interesting if it weren't so slow. She tossed the remote control across the couch and, licking her fingers of samosa, reached over to the answering machine and played Travis's message. It was simple and pointed. "I left three messages yesterday. I'm leaving another one right now. Call me back."

She called.

"What are those CDs and videos supposed to mean? I was halfway through the lot of them when I started to get mad. This is your answer to me? They say nothing."

"See, that's just it. They're a part of me that I'm just starting to understand myself. You couldn't possibly get them, or me. That's why it would never work between us."

"That's shit. Really. Are you even listening to yourself? You're telling me these songs and stories in a language you don't even understand mean more to you than a flesh-and-blood man who wants to take you out for dinner?" His voice was angry, but controlled in the disbelief.

"Yes. I'm sorry," she said to him, distantly.

"Tell me you only go out with college graduates. Tell me you don't want to get involved with a guy who has a kid. Anything but this."

"I guess there's nothing more to say."

But he would not stop there. "It's not real. Do you know that? You were always the one so concerned with things being real. Do you do anything but eat curry by yourself at home in front of videos? Do you even have Indian friends?"

"I know Sutra at the grocery store. And the guy who has the restaurant across the street."

"That's not real. I still have a photo of you dressed up as Dolly Parton for Halloween one year—you and Jamie are sitting on my lap, drunker than anything and laughing—remember? I was dressed up like Johnny Cash, his photo on the album you borrowed and never returned. And there we are in those photos, I have proof of it, *real* proof." He stopped a bit. "And you're telling me this other crap is what's real?"

"I guess there's nothing more to say," she told him again.

There was silence, further disbelief for a very long minute. "I guess not."

A fter they hung up, Travis's last words remained with Angie. She stepped out of her work shoes and undid her braid slowly in front of the mirror. It was lonely. Friends from work, how could they understand? This had nothing to do with the industry. It was purely intimate. No one could know what a momentous thing she had realized recently. In clinging to her new understanding, she left the office at 5 P.M. sharp, spent more time alone. She had to wrap her arms around herself tightly, closing everything else out.

She went back to the fridge, looking for more to eat. Cauliflower from a few weeks ago seemed OK, so she took a bite or two of that, cold, before dropping the whole container in the garbage. The lentil soup she actually heated up in the microwave for thirty seconds, then tried a spoonful, then poured it down the sink. Finally she took out the packet of delivery menus from the drawer by the stove and returned with them to the couch. Spreading these out before her, she surveyed the choices, the pink and green script of each menu curling together, across glossy photos of heaping plates, and lists of appetizers, then lunch dishes, then dinner entrées.

Angie ordered from a new restaurant, one she'd never tried before, Bombay Bistro. The menu itself had been stuffed into every mailbox in the building. Take-out or delivery, it read. She called up and ordered delivery, since that was easier, chicken tandoori and garlic naan. She stayed on the phone just a little bit longer with the woman who took down her order to explain the directions, but feeling comforted by the company too. "You know that big pizza shop on the corner of Brighton? Well, it's one, two, three apartments down. Take down my phone number and whoever is making the delivery can call me once they're on the street, and I'll walk them through it."

"Got it. Got it," the woman spoke quickly in an Indian accent.

"Are you sure? Remember, it's the third apartment. Sometimes people miss it, because the awning isn't very prominent. Tell them to call me."

The delivery man found the apartment on his own, and buzzed up to Angie, pacing, thirty-three minutes later. She answered the door, still barefoot, with her hair streaming down her back. In the living room, the television played the rerun of *India Today*. In the amount of time it had taken him to come, she'd decided it was worth watching again after all.

The delivery man was Indian himself, very dark, and a bit too thin, his elbows and Adam's apple making sharp, awkward angles. Still, he had a kind face as he handed Angie the paper sack and waited patiently for the money.

"Come in," she told him, looking at the receipt stapled to the front of the bag. "I need more cash." She closed the door behind him. "Will you take a seat? Would you like some water?"

"Thank you." Smiling, he accepted the kitchen chair and the dripping glass. He sipped happily, seeming to look around her apartment.

Angie returned from the other room, cash in hand, but with Travis's words still ringing in her ears, instead of giving it to the delivery man straight off, she pulled another chair close to him and sat down, ready to chat. "Where are you from?"

"Delhi," he swallowed. "My uncle owns this restaurant—I came here to work for him." He spoke in stiff English, with an Indian inflection. "I have been here almost six months now. Maybe I will go to school soon."

Angie nodded and leaned in nearer, smelling the spices that came from his pores, smelling the stink of sweat at his armpits. "What's Dehli like?"

"It is unlike anything here." He smiled cautiously, teeth a bit crooked, disbelieving, she thought to herself, of what seemed to be happening here in this clean apartment, with this fragrant girl pressing close.

He talked about Delhi, and with a bit of encouragement, he came over into the living room, and talked about his family and his friends and life back home. She listened to everything, enchanted, waiting for each new word with excitement, as though at any moment a single detail could have it all make perfect sense. Once, suddenly awkward, he ran out of things to say, and mentioned the new Nikes he had saved up for, pointing them out to her proudly, though they were shiny red and too white and she thought they looked very large at the end of his thin legs, so she told him shush and to take them off and be comfortable. Another time, too, he wandered off into his hopes to someday be a student at Berkeley. But then she pulled him back, saying shush, and asked about what his friends now did at home in Delhi and he was off again, in tales of the dusty over-crowded streets where all of humanity was packed together, sickly, beggarly, gorgeous, dead, or just very very busy, and still you could go to a vendor on the corner and he'd cut open a young green coconut for you so you could drink the sweet water right out of the top, and that was something. When his pager started beeping from the restaurant trying to reach him, he shut it off, recognizing instinctually what might come from this moment. And they opened up the chicken tandoori and garlic naan and ate it with their hands in front of the TV, which by then had run through both recorded shows and had only white static on the screen.

Angie reached for him first, kissing the crooked mouth, still smeared with garlic. She moved straight to pulling him onto the couch on top of her, so that his whole body formed a blanket for her. Piece by piece, they removed their clothes, so that soon they were naked against each other, throats still tight and dry from the spicy food and now from anticipation.

After they were done, she wedged herself sideways into the couch, holding his wet inside her for as long as it would stay. He lay over her still for a long time, both their bodies quiet now. As she leaned back into the pillows, her body pressed up against the remote control buried there by chance which clicked off the video finally, and the static formed into action and color again, too loud with channel three programing. She pulled the remote out to lower the volume, then went to toss it aside. But since they were leaning together like old lovers anyway, he took it from her, and began to flip through the channels. It surprised her, that he knew this cradling posture, like he had had many Sundays of brunch and spooning, sex-lazy and browsing channels. He passed through sitcoms and a movie on cable. He passed right by Book TV, where an Indian man with spectacles was reading. He passed by it quickly and she could not even read the book title captioned at the bottom of the screen, so she didn't mind much, though it surprised her that he would not at least pause there. He stopped for a few moments on the news. At commercial break, he started flipping again, and then he landed on live sports, and as he craned forward eagerly, with the roar of loud Boston fans in the stadium, she could not believe that he was truly interested in the score.

At commercial break again, he started moving through the

channels, landing on MTV. "Look. It's the Johnny Cash video," he told her. "They're playing it all the time now. He died the other day, you know." No, she didn't know. At hearing this, something in her crumbled, like a pastry falling into dust—it was Johnny Cash, her Johnny Cash after all. And he was gone. And she hadn't even known. She tried to harden herself to it, nudged him to change the channel at once, slipping the remote away from him and between her fingers.

"Wait," he stopped her. "It's the song about his wife who died. June," he told her, still absorbed in the screen. Angie would have shushed him, but she could not, because Johnny was dead, but it seemed he was alive again, missing his lost June, and hurting. And even this delivery man from across the ocean knew it.

Angie lay still on her side, all of him leaking out of her now, watching the delivery man watch Johnny Cash. Then he stood up and put on his big shoes again, and smoothed down her hair, and she smiled at him, thinking if she put on a hopeful front then perhaps he would still be the same exotic delivery man who had come to the door two hours ago. She told him, don't forget the money for the food, it's on the table, and maybe if I visit Dehli next year I'll look you up. And because he was suddenly awkward again, fumbling with his laces, he didn't tell her once more that hopefully by next year he would already be a student in town, at Emerson. On his way out, he hesitated a couple of moments over the cash, the ten and the five singles on the kitchen table, wondering if he should take them or leave them or, since he had eaten from the food himself also, to even split the cost. At the end, he left every cent of it there.

A few summers ago, I bought a Greyhound bus ticket and made a pilgrimage of sorts down through the southern states. In my head were the romantic sto-

ries and haunting music that I connected to that part of the country, a world of which I knew little else. But as I traveled I found myself yearning to understand this culture with more authenticity, with the depth of an insider. Of course, in merely passing through, I could never achieve such a thing, could never be more than an observer. Still, I was moved by the power of such yearning. "Footnote" was inspired by that trip.

SCOTT EASON

Diana Abu-Jaber

Diana Abu-Jaber's newest book is a food memoir entitled *The Language of Baklava*, a Booksense Notable Book for April 2005. Her latest novel, *Crescent*, won the PEN Center Award for Literary Fiction and the Before Columbus Foundation American Book Award. It was also named a Notable Book of the Year by the *Christian Science Monitor*. Her first novel, *Arabian Jazz*, won the 1994 Oregon Book Award. Abu-Jaber is currently Writer-in-Residence at Portland State University.

My Elizabeth

I tipped my forehead to the window and watched as we passed another Indian, black-bronze in the sun, thumb in the air. I was twelve and Uncle Orson was six years older. We'd started our trip in New York City. I hadn't paid much attention until about two or three days had passed, when we began passing long wings of pivot irrigation and the sky started to look like it had been scoured with salt water.

We passed power lines that stood like square-shouldered figures at attention, past grain and silo storage bins, glowing aluminum with pointed tops. At the time I didn't know the names for any of those things; I hadn't known that America unraveled as you moved west, until it ran straight as a pulled strand and the trees shrank into acres of sorghum, beans, corn, and wheat. I stared through the truck window at things mysterious to me as letters in a foreign language.

My uncle's name had been Omar Bin Nader, but when he first pulled up to my father's apartment on Central Park, he introduced himself to me as Orson. For the rest of the ride out to Wyoming, he cursed his luck, having to transport this newly orphaned niece and all of her father's worldly goods. Then he would stop himself and apologize, saying, nothing personal, and hold my head against his chest.

I slept curled up on the wide front seat of the cab. The sound of the engine went on and on. It reminded me of my toy train, an electric engine that had run a two-tiered figure eight around the hall outside our bathroom. It chugged and was painted red with "X & Y Railroad" in white on both sides. I used to watch it with Baba when I'd come home from school and he'd be waiting for me in his bathrobe and slippers and smelling of something strong. My mother was "an American," he'd told me. With pale, pale bluish white skin, Irish-Catholic skin. She'd died so young that all I could remember was that pale skin—its bright contrast to mine. Baba said to me, "Someday we will climb on to this train and I'll drive us home."

We passed square hay bales, plumes of irrigation water, torn tires, more trucks: Peterbilt, Kenworth, Mack, Fruehauf, Great Dane. Orson pointed out shacks with tires on the roof, sunflowers pointed toward dusk, the road ringing like an anvil.

Near dawn a train horn woke me, mournful and steady. My father had gone away to work on the train; he'd told me so just before he left. That was why Orson had to come to get me. Baba would be spending his days on the tracks, cross-stitching the same country that Orson and I covered. We were in Wyoming now. "Now you're home," Orson said.

Umptie Nabila came out of her trailer to greet us. New York was not a place for children, she said. Umptie Nabila had become "Great Aunt Winifred" since five Easters ago when we'd last met. What's more, she'd thought it over, and it seemed my name was now Estelle.

"Estelle," I said, turning the name before me. In the following days I often could not remember to answer to it. I put the name on in the morning like a wig. Before long, though, I became accustomed to it. My former name grew faint, then fell from memory.

The land around us was spiced with yellow wildflowers. There were men crawling the construction troughs along the highway, veils of dust and diesel smoke, and grasslands bearing distant ships of mountains. A sign said, "Welcome to Maybell, pop. 437."

My aunt and cousin lived beside a freight yard; all evening long it rang metal on metal. There were yellow-sided Union Pacific cars, railroad ties, pallets, and stacks of lumber. Past the yard was a field of horses where the colts slept on the ground under their mothers' gazes.

By day, I could look out my window and see the train on the horizon, vanishing into the earth and spilling out the other side. Sometimes the mountains were gray, red lightning scratched the sky. I walked past sandstone hills dusted with sage, rows of snow fences, bikers, vans with MIA/POW bumper stickers. The grass gave way to quills of prairie brush, desert green, and downy cows. It was the top of the world, mountains curling at the edges of basin plains like the ocean.

Aunt Nabila/Winifred, her two-year-old son Omar/Orson, and her grown-up nephew—my father—came to America in 1954. My father stayed in New York while she kept traveling, she said, until she felt "at home." She and Orson settled in the Wallabee Acres Trailer Court in a double-wide trailer, three bedrooms and two and a half baths, 1400 square feet.

Now Orson was going to work as a wrangler on a dude ranch thirty miles north of Maybell. Aunt Winifred worked for the oil company, which took her out of the house all day. She fretted over leaving me alone and gave me a lot of advice on how to attract friends, changes involving dress, hair, and speech.

"Never, *ever*, speak Arabic," she told me. "Wipe it out of your brain. It's clutter, you won't need it anymore. And if anyone asks—" she said, then paused a moment, sighing over my brown skin, "—you say you're Mexican—no, no—*Italian*, or Greek—but don't say Palestinian."

Wyoming was a good place for forgetting. The mountains and snow fences repeated like a four-note melody and chased thoughts from my head.

T he week before Orson left he took me driving around in his pickup. My favorite road signs were for the Rifleman Hotel, Bad Boys B.B.Q., Indian Clem's Trading Post, and the Buckaroo Lodge. At a gas station a trucker in a white tee hung his arm out the window and asked, "What kinda mileage you get?" From far away the highway glistened like a snail's trail. At Gay Pearson's Stop, a driver said, "Indians told the white man not to build their highway through here, said there were evil spirits laying all over Elk Mountains. But the white man goes on anyway, and sure enough every winter twenty, thirty drivers get dumped in some blizzard."

Outside the Pies & Eats, a black man pulled up with a little boy beside him in the front seat. The man opened his door and swung his legs out to face us, but didn't get out. "Hey bud," he yelled to Orson. "Hey buddy." He was wearing a striped train-conductor cap. Orson walked over to him. "Hey buddy, could you help a guy? I'm out of gas, I got to get to Colorado Springs. Could you help me fill'er up, buddy?"

Orson pulled a dollar and some change from his pocket.

"Aw, buddy, thank you man," the man said as he took it. "But I don't think that'll fill her. I mean, I don't think that'll do the job."

"That's all I got."

"Well, how many miles *is* it to Colorado Springs?"

"Two-seventy-five," Orson said, his hand on the door handle to the pickup.

"Well, OK then," the man said, got in his car and drove away.

Wallabee Acres Trailer Court and most of the town of Maybell were inside the Sequoya Reservation. On my fifth day there I met Elizabeth Medicine Bow; she was pushing an empty cargo dolly in the freight yard and singing, "Oh the coffee in the army."

Orson and I had seen Indians on the highways and truck-stops, their cars pulled over, white rags tied to the antennas. There was something about their eyes which reminded me of the full-hearted Arabs. Elizabeth and I saw each other and started off, "What are you doing?"

"I don't know. What do you want to do?"

T rains pulled away from my window toward the south, sometimes coal trains, black as their cargo. Beyond the tracks were green-blanketed pyramids, stone mountains hooked with gaps like piles of skulls, mountains like thunderheads at evening, mountains soft as mirages in morning, sandy-backed, oceans of silty land, cinder fields.

The longer Elizabeth and I knew each other the more certain we felt that we were twins separated at birth. There were many similarities between us: we both had secret names—mine already fading and Elizabeth's used only by her grandmother and great-granny; we both had doubled languages, a public one we spoke in common and a private language that haunted us. When Elizabeth's mother was angry, she called Elizabeth inside using the other language. Elizabeth always marched in saying, "Speak *American*."

Also, neither of us knew where our fathers were. We were descended from nations that no map had names or boundaries for.

Elizabeth's mother was twenty-five years old; she was named

Shoshona and she looked like a movie star. She worked for the oil company, but unlike my aunt who was higher up, Shoshona said she was always "getting laid off and laid on—like all the fool Indians there."

She would send us out to Bill Dee's—a mile and a half walk into town—for a new tube of lipstick or bottle of nail polish, and always a flask of something called Yippie Tonic that Bill Dee kept behind the counter. On the laid-off days Shoshona and her girl-friends—the girls, Elizabeth called them—sat around the TV, drinking Yippie Tonic out of sewing thimbles.

Elizabeth's grandmother and great-granny preferred the TV reception in the bars downtown, at the Buckaroo. "The girls getting fancy again?" Grandmother said, sticking out her fingers to show how you drink from a thimble. Great-granny was sleeping, stretched out in a booth.

F rom Elizabeth's window we could see wheat like pink velvet, white floors of grain, and telephone poles going on and on like crucifixes.

"Just wait," she said as we knelt on her bed, elbows propped on her sill. "When we get out of here we'll go where *people* live."

I'd gotten used to the speckled hills and basin. When Elizabeth ran ahead of me through the fields, the sun darkened her skin to eggplant, her hair a whip against the air. In town we played That's-my-father. We would try to be hidden, and pick from the men we saw the gentlest, the sweetest, the tallest, the strongest: a man who inspired us.

The game sometimes made Elizabeth, who'd never seen her own father, very sad. I knew what mine looked like; I knew he was thrumming along the plains, rails singing under the sky, watching from the tracks that would take us back.

Sometimes Elizabeth stayed overnight and shared my bed. Aunt Winifred would tuck us in and give us a cup of tea.

"When I get big I'm gonna go find him," Elizabeth said. "I

got a lot of stuff to ask him about. I plan to have money; you'll get equal half. I also plan to get muscles, so nobody will mess with us. After I get my father, we'll go get yours."

"Oh, mine's coming back, though," I said and closed my eyes. The lights were out and we could hear the freight yard; the bed trembled as a boxcar got hitched and rolled out. "Pretty soon. No question about that, dearie," I said.

Elizabeth threw one leg over mine. We were both tall and bony and traded our clothes. She left her toothbrush in our bathroom, and we woke at the same time in the morning.

T hat year when school started and Elizabeth and I turned thirteen, we began playing That's-your-boyfriend. We chose the most ridiculous boys in the school, poked each other, and said, "That's yours."

We watched the boys in senior high practice football on the field that connected our schools; we thought they looked like soldiers and each claimed one.

The schools were owned by the Sequoya Reservation, seventh to ninth grade and tenth to twelfth, about fifty kids each. The buildings were corrugated aluminum, the words "Halleluja! Church of Christ" still fading off the junior high. Elementary school shared with the Grange. Sometimes we heard singing from Grange meetings float beyond the building.

That winter Frank Atchison, a white history teacher at the junior high, took Elizabeth aside and said she had great potential, and he would work on "cultivating" her. She would have to stay after school for lessons. After the first lesson, Elizabeth came rushing home: Mr. Atchison had proclaimed a "great love" for her, and she had decided she was interested. They would see each other as long as his wife didn't find out.

Why, I brooded, had Elizabeth been selected and not me? Mr. Atchison might have preferred Sequoyans, but my skin was so dark that no one seemed to notice my difference. I was jealous that while once we had shared everything, Elizabeth hadn't offered Mr. Atchison. More than anything else, though, I was jealous of Mr. Atchison taking Elizabeth away. As it turned out, Elizabeth didn't go anywhere, and her sharing stopped just short of bringing him to sleep over.

We went to school, cut out after attendance, and walked back to the flat rocks over at the freight yard. Elizabeth told me everything in detail so small and perfect, we could sink into it, the white sun careening past us, the rails flashing like a trail of coins. Listening was like being hypnotized:

"And then he left me this note—

"And then we went for a ride—

"And then he pulled up my shirt—"

It was February and a snowy wind filled the basin, flicking off the sides of the mountains, whirling like the Milky Way. When it got too bad out we went to my trailer and huddled in bed. Elizabeth said she spent most of the time she was with him figuring out how to describe it to me later. I knew about the chip in his incisor, the mole behind his ear, the pressure of his body as he flattened against her. We drifted on stories, Elizabeth floating free while I stayed moored by ordinary life.

After two months of it Elizabeth decided to stop seeing him. Everything ceased as abruptly as it had started. The only reminder was Mr. Atchison staring at Elizabeth in the hall, all the kids grinning. Everybody knew what had happened. "It's time to get on with my life," she said. "I don't have time for these men. The grandmothers need me to come for them after school."

Winter churned into something like spring. Clouds became mountains, steam, and rain. In the freight yard there were boxes of bawling calves again, hissing cargo brakes, and metal wheels heated like branding irons.

In spring assembly we watched *West Side Story* and Elizabeth and I saw that Shoshona looked like Natalie Wood. She was what Natalie Wood might look like if you took a cloth to her and polished her bronze, so her cheekbones and the wings of her nose gleamed like a statue's.

Shoshona taught us about life. She said Elizabeth wouldn't ever have any brothers or sisters as long as it was a so-called free country. The doctor at the clinic where she had Elizabeth gave her what she called her favorite toys:

"I tell the boys, 'you gotta put on your raincoat in heavy weather.' I say to them, 'No glove, no love.'"

Shoshona usually brought one of her men home when the tonic was gone and she was laid off. Elizabeth would come over to spend the night with me. One morning after we decided Shoshona looked like Natalie Wood, Elizabeth and I walked back to her trailer and found Shoshona sitting at the table with her eyes ringed purple, blue, and black, a crust of blood along one nostril.

"Never let a drunk man hit you," she told us as we walked in. "He hits you, you crack him back in the jaw hard as you can." She showed us how to make a fist, with the thumb on the outside of our fingers. She displayed a broken tooth in a baby jar that she'd extracted the evening before, and clenching her hand, showed us how.

"That was Fred Go Slow's. So's this." She showed us a wallet with what looked like a lot of money in it. "The sad thing is when he finally comes to, he won't even remember who did it to him."

About three weeks later, Shoshona walked through Aunt Winifred's door, sat down on the sofa, and started crying. Elizabeth and I peeked in from the kitchen door.

"I can't *believe* it. Is this my life? Is this really my life?" she kept saying, while Aunt Winifred tried to get her to drink tea. "*Not* another one! A smelling, screaming . . . oh God the screaming. I don't even care about the black eyes, but *this*—those goddamn rubber things *break*."

That was how we found out Elizabeth was going to get a baby to play with after all.

The school yard was quiet and cows wandered across the playground. We stood behind the school, saw a ripple of antelope, the remains of brushfire, puffs of tumbleweed, a skinned possum, its tongue poking out.

Elizabeth didn't want to go to her trailer much anymore. When Shoshona got through with vomiting in the morning she started taking long pulls on the tonic bottle. The girls, some of whom were also pregnant, kept right up with Shoshona, drinking.

Fred Go Slow, who now had a big hole in his teeth, came around the house looking guilty and nervous until Shoshona's friends chased him away. He tried to give Elizabeth and me little toys and candies, but Elizabeth threw them to the ground, saying, "I'm a woman now, I don't play with baby things."

Summer flared like a match; the freight tracks groaned. Linemen stood against the dusk in overalls, swinging lanterns, coal trains sliding in behind them.

Orson came home from the dude ranch and convinced Aunt Winifred to sell my father's possessions. For a year, furniture, books, and clothing had filled her extra bedroom. Bit by bit, Winifred cleared the room, weeping over every piece she sold, getting remarkable prices in the process. She held back a few things: portraits my father had painted, a sandalwood carving, a brass-topped table, and a small prayer rug. She stored a trunk in my room with a few of my baby toys and some odds and ends.

Elizabeth wanted to investigate the trunk, but it proved disappointing: rigid Barbie dolls, Matchbox racecars, books smelly with dust, and a shotglass with the words "Monticello Raceway." At the bottom, Elizabeth found a big white cotton square checked with black.

"Oh. Oh yeah," I said. Words and faces I hadn't thought about for a year rushed back. My hands remembered things my mind didn't know about. Elizabeth sat before my bureau mirror and I began arranging the *hutta* around her head and neck. She looked like Elizabeth Taylor in *Cleopatra*.

Aunt Winifred was just back from work. She glanced in the

doorway, stopped and said, "Oh, children!" Her eyes were bright and her fist knotted against the base of her throat. Elizabeth looked like royalty.

"Keep it," I said. "It's yours, it was made for you."

"Wait," she said and stood up. First I thought she was going out to show her mother, but minutes later she came running back with something in her hand. A long, tufted feather, deeply colored as the earth, strung on a loop of leather.

"A man who said he was my father gave this to me when I was a kid," she said, the feather covering the palms of both hands. "I knew he wasn't any more my father than the rest, but I like to think it came from my real father anyway. He told me it was golden eagle, a warrior's feather. It's for you, my sister Estelle." She slid the leather piece down on my head. It was too big for me and rested on my ears, but the feather glowed like a flame against the black of my hair, brushing my shoulder, lighting my face.

"I love it," I whispered, afraid to move inches to see it. "It's the most beautiful thing."

Elizabeth put her face next to mine. "Remember the Indian girl we saw last week on the late night movie?"

"Pocahontas," Aunt Winifred said.

Not long after Elizabeth and I had traded headdresses, a woman came to Aunt Winifred's door. She was known around town as the Social Welfare Lady. She had dark eyebrows and a powdered face. Elizabeth and I spied from the doorway as she talked to Aunt Winifred and rubbed her matchstick legs together. Aunt Winifred talked to the woman in a pleading voice, but the woman kept talking straight ahead, with her gray gaze and her rubbing legs. Finally Aunt Winifred turned around to where she knew we were watching, and we saw the lady's eyes lift up, following.

Shoshona had gone drinking the night before. We had heard her outside making the mewing sounds when she wasn't feeling right and the earth was moving beneath her, and she couldn't find the front door key. She'd shown up for work the next morning around the time the lunch whistle was blowing and her boss, Sammy Hudson, who was a cousin of Fred Go Slow, up and reported her to the Bureau. The Bureau had started a new program on the Sequoya Reservation: cash reward for anyone reporting willful endangerment of the unborn through alcohol abuse. All willful endangerers would be imprisoned, length of sentence determined by their due date. They had decided to make an example of Shoshona.

The Welfare Lady said that Elizabeth had to stay with her Aunt Shyela on the other side of the reservation, ten miles away. She led Elizabeth to a big green station wagon and they drove off. That night Elizabeth came back to our trailer on her aunt's bicycle. Her hair was blowing around her face and she looked like a beautiful witch who had climbed out of the sky.

"I promise you, I'm gonna help her escape," Elizabeth whispered as we were falling asleep. "There's no way they're gonna keep my mother in their trap."

"No. I know it," I said.

The train crossed my dreams; I saw my father's eyes, clear as the moon. Voices floated through the dawn, filling me, speaking my other language, words I recognized, forget, don't forget, forget.

Orson drove us to town that day, the air humming with insects. We passed pickups in dust clouds, drivers' fingers off the steering wheels, howdy, rifles shaking in the gun racks. We watched land rising away from us, turning transparent in the light, brown and yellow as the desert.

The day before, Shoshona's pregnancy had looked like nothing more than a held breath, but it seemed to have grown overnight. She was held in a building with the words *Maybell Prison* painted on a water tower on the roof, a small reservation jail. Shoshona sat on a narrow bed in a windowless room, facing away from us. I had never been inside the building before, although we'd passed it plenty of times while searching for grandmothers. Iron bars were a shock. I had imagined a kind of special prison for pregnant women.

"Mom?" Elizabeth said. I had never heard her call her anything but Shoshona. Her voice got inside me, gathering tears behind my eyes, and all I wanted to do was get on my knees and beg Shoshona, come out, come out. Elizabeth and I started crying and Shoshona wouldn't face us. A guard came back and said, "What are you girls doing here? You're not supposed to be back here."

Shoshona stood. "Leave them alone, I'm allowed to have visitors!" Her face was puffy and she was shaking. "Now, kids, be good and go get me some of my medicine tonic," she said in a wobbling voice.

"Sorry, little mama," the man said. "These girls ain't bringing you nothing."

As soon as we got out of the prison we ran to Bill Dee's. Some of the girls were inside sitting at the counter, and they quieted fast. Their eyes slid toward us; I heard a whispered mix of languages. Elizabeth refused to look at anyone as we went to the cash register, then we realized neither of us had any money. We stood there, staring at the gun case, as if that was what we'd come in for. Then two of the girls were standing behind us and one of them said, "Bill Dee, we need some Yippie Tonic and we need it on credit and you know what for."

We walked back to the jail, past the Last Chance, "Girls Girls Girls," past scrub, weeds, and alleyways. The guard who'd sent us away was at the front desk. I had a bottle of tonic tucked inside a jacket that was zipped to the neck, though it was already ninety outside. The man fanned himself with a handful of mimeographed sheets and stared at us. We all stood looking at each other, then he sighed and said, "Girls, you know I can't let you back there."

"Please, officer," Elizabeth said, stepping toward him. "I've got to get back there. Maybe—if there's something you want—anything you want—"

He was shaking his head, eyes closed. Elizabeth started to cry, speaking in her other language, blood sounds that made him open his eyes. But he wouldn't stop shaking his head, and then Elizabeth started to scream, and he got up from the desk to grab her. He'd forgotten me—all I had to do was turn down the corridor and find the right bars.

When I got to her, Shoshona was standing, holding the bars. I pulled the bottle out of my jacket and passed it to her. She was shaking so hard she almost dropped it, so I set it on the ground.

"Estelle," she said, her eyes on the bottle, "what's happening to Elizabeth?"

"They won't let her in," I said. "She tried to come in."

Shoshona nodded. "Tell her to keep trying." Then she looked at me and said, "I can kill this baby any time any way I want to. I can hold my breath and starve off its air. I can think evil down into it so it rots before its fifth month. It's my own heart, this baby. They think they can hold onto my own heart for me?"

I had to leave before they found me. Shoshona's hot voice echoed up the corridor, "What did I do? Just tell me, who says I did wrong?"

I walked back alone, past bottles of rubbing alcohol, Lysol, cooking spray, past huddles of black-haired men and women outside the plasma donor center, cigarette butts smashed on the sidewalk.

Elizabeth didn't come over that night or the next. Voices began to fill my sleep. I dreamed of the toy train running its figure eight, a man's hands, white as marble, going to it, and I woke gasping.

I didn't look for Elizabeth; I knew if I found her, I would come to the end of our world, that it would be an outdated, useless place. Weeks went by. Aunt Winifred looked at me, but didn't ask about Elizabeth. Orson returned to the dude ranch. A few days later he called us to say there was an opening for a chef's assistant—mine, if I wanted it. There was a tutor at the ranch, so I wouldn't need to return to the reservation school.

One week before I was supposed to join Orson, Aunt Winifred came home carrying two bags of groceries and said she had something to tell me. She put down the bags and said, "Your friend Elizabeth has been seen in town. On the arm of a prison officer."

I moved my hands to the edge of the table. "What? Where in town? What officer?"

Aunt Winifred moved some of the cans of food around on the counter. "She's trying to help her mother, I guess," she said. "Poor baby."

I went to the door and Aunt Winifred said, "Estelle, you be careful. You are not to stay out late."

It was mid-August; at 5:30 P.M. the reservation was bright and hot as midday. The shadows had barely begun sliding toward evening, things looked blurred, windows and doors shut to the sun. I walked into town, down Main Street, with its line of bars, neon lassos, and dancing girls. Elizabeth and I had gone into all of these places looking for her grandmothers.

I walked to the door of the Tally Ho and tried to will Elizabeth out to me. I slid my hands in my pockets and prayed, oh please come out, Elizabeth, please, please come out.

The door opened, but there was just an old woman with a mouthful of gold teeth and long, red-black hair. I backed up, walking away as quickly as I could. I saw people coming out of the Three Cheers down the block and I walked toward them looking for Elizabeth. It was two men and a woman. They saw me and moved closer.

"Hey, what's this?" one of the men said. "Want to party, youngster?"

"Ain't you Shoshona Medicine Bow's girl?" the woman asked. She stood with her back to the sun, her face in shadows.

"That's my sister. I mean, Elizabeth is," I said, trying to steady my voice. "Have you seen her?"

"No. You want us to help you look?" the other man said in a way that wasn't offering help. I tried to back away, but they moved toward me, so I stood still, arms clasped around my sides.

"She ain't no Indian," one of the men said, reaching out and tipping my face to the sun. "Not much. Look at her, that ain't no kind of Sequoyan *I* know about. What type mixed breed *are* you?"

I remembered Aunt Winifred's warning: never, never tell. I tried to think of the other nationalities she'd offered me, but they vanished from my mind. The only countries I could remember were from the unit on Northern Europe we'd done that year: Belgian chocolate and Swiss clocks.

"Swiss," I said. "I'm Swiss."

They started laughing.

"You're Swiss and I'm the Pope's grandfather," the other man said. But they were already losing interest, walking away. I shivered in the heat, wanting to run after them and ask what they knew about Elizabeth.

I heard Shoshona's voice in my dream that night, mixed with other voices, her cry, banging like a hammer, "What did I do, who says I did wrong. . . ." I dreamed cargo doors, Cottonbelt, Union Pacific, Hydro-lite, satellite dishes, tilting trees, the white face of a church minding the plain.

I went into town every evening for a week, becoming bolder, entering bars, asking everyone if they had seen Elizabeth Medicine Bow. I went to the building with the water tower on top; Elizabeth wasn't there. I tried the school, I tried Bill Dee's, I tried at the houses of Elizabeth's family and friends.

I'd worked down the street of bars and by Friday I was back at the Tally Ho again. It was late in the evening, getting dark, and the edge had come off the heat. Maybell hummed with the neon, insects swarming to the lights. I stopped on the sidewalk outside the bar, saying my prayer, please come out, Elizabeth, oh please, please come.

The bar door opened then and a Sequoyan man walked out. He had big rounded shoulders and hair that fell down over his back. I glanced at him and looked away. Then he was beside me suddenly, whispering, "Little one, what are you doing here?"

Then he said, "Elizabeth Medicine Bow lives with her new lover. Why don't you come with me instead?" It was too dark to see him clearly; that might have been why his words were so persuasive. I followed him away from the strip. It was dream-walking, following this bear-quiet figure.

We went through the sleeping neighborhoods, to where the land got steep and sharp. We walked up. At times he took my hand to help me, the rest of the time I followed, listening to the flow of his breath, his foot on the stones. The earth became soft, as if we were walking in powder. Then we stopped and the man was bent over, looking around in the dirt. "I always lose my house key," he said. "So I keep it hidden outside. Then I have to find it again."

He pulled and opened a rectangle of yellow out of the night. It was a small cottage, filled with skins and bones, an old sofa, kitchen table, chamber pot, and freezer. He led me, identifying the skeletons and skulls that he had collected. He'd found some bones already sun-washed, others came from carcasses he'd found, and skinned, and sometimes eaten: deer, antelope, tiny bones of raccoon hands, cow and coyote skulls, chicken, cat, dog, and the perfect knobs of snake spines. There were various feathers, some small, stitched together, some curling and striped. One, glowing like brown mineral, rested on a pile of books; I touched it. "Golden eagle," I said.

"That's right," he said. "Apparently you know a few things." That was the first time I looked at him directly. He was heavy and strong, and his hair fell all the way down his back, a bed of black, like his eyes.

"See here." He stood at a small nightstand by the bed. "I made these." He showed me a polished comb and brush. "From bear bones and pig bristles. Very valuable, like elk and mountain lions and rattlers."

This was the way he lived, he told me: scavenging, keeping an ear to the ground, sometimes teaching a class in nature appreciation, or sculpture, or taxidermy. Night moved on a slow tide, the house sailing on his voice. We sat on his couch. I picked up his bone brush and began running it down the length of his black hair, over and over, enchanting myself with the repetition, the way it polished. He sat still until I had fallen asleep.

I woke later, drooling a little on his shoulder. His arms were soft around me, his breath deep and regular. I lay still for a few minutes. It was still dark outside, but I could tell morning was coming from the blue sheen in his window and the way my breath made a mist. It must have dropped forty degrees overnight.

He sat up and pulled a knitted shawl off a chair, then lay back and draped it over us. "What did you dream last night?"

"How do you know that I dreamed?"

He propped up on one arm. "You were talking in your sleep, your dreams speaking—"

It came in flashes: Elizabeth running, the blue of her hair melting into black sky. She was telling me, "I've found my father, he's right over there," and I looked, but it was too dark. The little train was running through its circuit on the floor of the trailer house, speeding up and slowing down; the tiny boxcars were trembling; I thought it was an earthquake. Then there were drops of water on me, red drops. I went to turn off the bathtub; it was overflowing, red as velvet, red wine. Then I saw the white shank of my father's leg and his forearm; I tried to ask why he was bathing in wine, but the words wouldn't come.

I realized I wasn't dreaming anymore, but remembering, and my tongue got thick as if the dream-story was choking me. I stopped speaking and sat opening and closing my eyes slowly. Beyond the window I could see the prairie beneath the hill, divided by tracks, a scroll of light.

"Your dream has more than one meaning," he said.

I was shivering, arms wrapped around myself, trying to press fear back into my ribs. I remembered my father, swallowed by pain, like a drop of bitter wine, his red wrists against the white enamel. Outside the train was passing. I thought, I was weak; I wasn't enough to save him. I put down my head and my tears were light as air.

My friend went into the other room then returned, giving me

the eagle feather. He said, "You won't believe me now, but the feelings you have will dry up after awhile. Like everything else, like tears. Your father went where he needed to; some people can't live on this earth. You should prize this pain of yours. This is what will make you human all the way through. Nothing less will do that."

The feather, he told me, was a warrior's prize. At the time, I only cared about my dream, but later I remembered its glow in my hands, softness where he touched me with it on the face.

I walked down to our trailer later that morning, the path clear in the light. Aunt Winifred was quiet when she saw my changed face. I had decided to join Orson at the dude ranch.

Four years later the owner of the ranch sent me through college, a private school back East. I came back to the reservation for just one Christmas break in all those years. Shoshona and Elizabeth had gone away; their trailer stood empty. I walked through the hills, but couldn't find my friend's cottage.

Not until I'd graduated and was working in New York did my memories become insistent, nudging me in the street or the office, making me wonder what had become of Shoshona and her baby. And of Elizabeth. When I called, Aunt Winifred never talked about the reservation. She said to me, "Your life is *there* now, in New York, out in the world. Forget about what's past."

I took an apartment not far from the one I'd lived in with my father. I imagined my father's ghost waiting there, watching over memories. My walk to work led past the old place, and its brownstone windows moved with shadows.

I began to see Elizabeth too, in stores and restaurants, her blue-black hair in crowds of brown and blond. I would get closer and see it wasn't her. Sometimes I would talk to these women anyway, my wish for her was so strong. Often, they were from other tribes, Iroquois, Tillamuck, Cherokee. Once I stopped someone from the Sioux Pine Ridge Reservation who said she knew Elizabeth Medicine Bow. She told me Elizabeth was now Mrs. Jeffrey Harrison, that she had two sons, and lived in South

Dakota. Twice I stopped black-haired women from Korea, once a woman from Bombay, and once a Palestinian.

Orson settled in Denver; Aunt Winifred retired and moved to Florida. Nothing could summon Elizabeth back but imagination.

I'd been living in New York for several years when I found a book in the library that described how the last of the American Indian population was being killed off through alcohol abuse. When I finished reading I walked to the fire escape outside my apartment and stared at the buildings. I didn't believe the story about her and the South Dakota rancher. My Elizabeth would still be wandering, I thought, pushing open church doors and saloon gates, finding her father.

I stood on the fire escape and noticed how the city hooked itself into crags and canyons, rooftops high enough to snag a singing bird.

I saw the way native people wandered in New York, displaced persons. I thought about the way homes, cities, and whole countries disappeared; the faces of your neighbors and the people you loved, the grass of your home, and the name of the place you lived and played were all gone, incredibly, gone.

My artifacts: a feather or two, a name, the image of a toy train that ran in circles. Sometimes in the mornings before I open my eyes, a moment and space come to me, an opening in the past that Elizabeth and I had shared: we are standing together, holding hands, and everywhere we look we see crops of dirt, spouts of smoke and grain, dust devils, plumes of topsoil, burning crops, and the farmers' hay bales stacked like dominoes. And the land goes on across the wide earth, across our separate lives, our futures silent as buffalo. We are left with the precious, mysterious past.

"My Elizabeth" was partially written in tribute to Willa Cather's magnificent novel My Antonia. Cather was my first guide to the Great Plains in the late 1980s, when I moved to Lincoln, to teach at the University of Nebraska for two years. I started jotting notes for the story on one of the cross-country drives I made from New York to Nebraska, as I moved through the solemnity and austere beauty of the plains. I wrote *"My Elizabeth"* shortly after I finished my first novel, Arabian Jazz, and I had just started the exploration of identity and memory that seems to haunt my subsequent work. Cather's story of an immigrant child creating herself in the new world offered a kind of tender hope and wistfulness that struck a powerful chord with me. I felt that there were important parallels between the dispossession of the American Indians with that of the Palestinians—my father's culture—and Cather's plains story gave me an elegant platform from which to explore that connection.

EMILY SHUR

Mat Johnson

Mat Johnson is the author of the novels *Drop* and *Hunting in Harlem*, winner of the 2004 Hurston/Wright Legacy Award. A graduate of Earlham College and a former Thomas J. Watson Fellow, he received his M.F.A. from Columbia University. Johnson's writing has appeared in *Time Out–New York*, *The Washington Post*, and *Callaloo*. He has taught at Columbia and Rutgers Universities and is currently a professor of literature and writing at Bard College, in Annandale-on-Hudson, New York. He is currently working on a historical novella, *The Great Negro Plot*.

Gift Giving

My wife was a pretty yellow woman who wanted a pretty white man but got me. She had all these books on the shelf in our apartment about dealing with interracial love and raising biracial children, and you'd think she would have thrown them out because we'd been married for near a year, had dated for almost two, but there they were. These things seem clear now, to me.

I told her my trauma story, about my grandmother saying I

had "fair" skin and "good" hair and if someone didn't know I was black, don't tell them, and Sam's response was, "She must have really loved you." That was it. Sam was pretty and I was not very pretty, but I was very pale, and she was very color struck and it seemed to be a match well made.

I really loved Sam. I loved that she had the name of a boy. I loved that she was far more attractive than I was. I liked that when she laughed it was like there was this great and glorious club of beautiful people and through her I'd been inducted. I loved that even though she grew up in Flatbush, a fluke of birthplace had left her with a British passport, and now we could both live a comfortable life in South London as exotics. I loved that sometimes, when she went out, her cell phone would bump in her pocketbook and call home and I could sit for an hour listening to the sound of her going about her day before it would turn off again.

There are a bunch of stories I have now that show that Sam clearly didn't love me as much as I loved her, most of which I didn't form into stories until later. At the time I *loved* loving her. I loved that she was mixed and she would still be with mixed me. I didn't know any mixed couples; I still don't. Every biracial woman I've known has wanted to join a "full blood" of whatever ethnic group she wished she was a full part of. The ones I knew who socialized white always had some mythic white ex-boyfriend to whom no Negro could compare. The ones who socialized black wanted a man who could offer a complete black family as well. Of the women I'm thinking of, both types would claim they weren't these types at all, particularly the former category. But they were. Nobody looks specifically for a mixed man. But there was Sam and she was fly and there was I.

Or maybe I just loved that Sam was a beautiful woman, and everything in my experience had taught me I was an ugly man, and she was willing to attach herself to me, let me stare at her. It really could have been nothing more. Years of other excuses, but really nothing more.

We never had a lot of sex, really. But then suddenly we had less. Do I mention that we stopped having sex, altogether, those last months? This is the formal construction of story taking precedence here, because at the time, I chose not to acknowledge that Sam cringed at my nocturnal advances (or rather rolled away from them and pretended to be asleep). At the time I didn't interpret this trend of a few weeks, choosing instead to simply masturbate, which I found less confrontational and a quick solution.

Over a month and no sex, and then Sam had the flu for a bit, then I had to do a bunch of late nights when we were closing the October/November issue of the magazine I worked at, then boom Sam left for her visit to America, to Florida, to visit her family for a month. She would stop up through Philly and visit my family as well. She would stay with my mother who would give her boxes of Tastykakes to bring to me, mostly Krimpets, jelly and butterscotch. Sam left on a Friday and that night my friend Ric (Chilean Ric from Brick Lane) took me out. We went to a pub in Ladbroke Grove, the one covered in the melted wax of white candles and the hair of that overweight orange cat that paced around us named Big Pussy. The one Sam's boss, Ginger, was always on about, always drunk at. That's where the boys and I chose to go.

After my divorce I was overcome with this feeling of being blindsided, but realistically, I must have had some hostility toward Sam at the time, some relief at her leaving for that trip because (a) she hated Ric, who I had revealed often got drunk and went to prostitutes in Surrey, and (b) this pub was Ginger MacDonald's local, Ginger that wrinkled, chain-smoking homunculus of a fucking boss who Sam detested for reasons that she laid out daily as soon as she got home. The bitch who owned the gallery where Sam worked, as Sam would and did often put it. So I must have felt something was going on before I found out about Sam's indiscretion, something I lost as the context of the event changed in my mind in the years that followed that evening. Because I look back, and I think of myself as an innocent at the time. In my memory, I'm like 4 A.M. snow, lying frozen on the road unaware of sun or summer.

After a few rounds my mate Ricardo—who'd brought these coke head French guys who own a café in Clapham Park—told me they'd bought me a gift to help me through while my wife was out of town. The Frenchies were just laughing it up as the package came out. It was a large box in brown shipping paper that Ric lifted onto the table and sat between the pints. My friends and the rest of the pub watched as I took the paper off. "Don't be so fuckin' prissy. Rip it off!" and there were cheers as I did that. The box revealed was covered in pink flowers and yellow lettering that said "Sindy—Action Figure of Love." Pressed against the plastic screen was a life-size blonde ponytailed head that stared back at me with pink skin and painted blue eyes and a round open red mouth that seemed to cling to the plastic window like a sucker-fish to an aquarium's side.

Everyone laughed and there were cheers and I bowed to my friends and those strangers among us. Ricardo said, "This is gonna get you through, mate, those hard times of the month ahead." I think it was then that I saw Ginger, Sam's boss, the fucking hag, sitting at the bar. That's overly dramatic; I'm sure I noticed her before that moment. She was always sitting on one of the stools off in the corner, but let's just say that it was then that I first truly took note of her.

Special consideration should be made here to portray the character and person of Ginger MacDonald, owner of the Post Primitive Gallery of Angel Court, not just because she's relative to the story that I'm sculpting out of these events, but also because a creature like Ginger MacDonald is so rare, her existence should be recorded. My favorite story about Ginger is the one where the police were called to her house after receiving a call from a frantic maid. When the cops arrived, the maid lay battered and bruised, crying on the front steps. When questioned, Ginger said, "Look, it's not my fault, is it? That cunt needs to learn dusting proper." Charges were never pressed because to the poor money can be more valuable than justice. That's how Ginger had managed to keep Sam from quitting each day of the eighteen months of her employment as Ginger hovered behind her, smoking constantly and blowing it toward her because she knew Sam was allergic, dropping little racist slurs where she could. Abusing the lesser, more expendable help as she became progressively drunk during the course of the workday. At that point, having been given a raise every time she had tried to quit, Sam simply couldn't afford to leave her job. In fact, as of the last I heard, Sam's still working for Ginger.

Ginger's physicality was poetic. To my mind, Ginger seemed a five-foot tumor pickled in whiskey, its flesh leather by a constant Silk Cut fog, sculpted into hard wrinkles by seasonal baking in the Ibizan sun. Ginger was a monstrous honky: her oft-present tan simply added to this impression, reddening her skin to the same shade as cafeteria pork. Second Ginger story: the first time I met her she was grinding those hideous vocal cords in my direction and she paused to burp and a cloud of smoke came out of her like a fucking choo-choo train.

So at the bar this chant goes up: "Blow it up! Blow it up!" And I tried, but after a few attempts I stuck Sindy back in her box. I was pretty drunk by then, and out of shape in general, and it just wasn't going to happen. I was still wheezing, reaching for a beer to stop the pain, and I looked up vacantly and there was Ginger, the beast herself, looking dead at me. She was blowing into her fist as she stared, imitating my huffing and puffing of moments before. Crazy thing is, when Ginger sees that she has my eye, she starts pumping her fist in front of her mouth as she laughs at me. I must say, maybe it was just all the propaganda I'd heard from Sam before that point, but it took me a minute to even realize that this gesture was supposed to be sexual, that this pale wretch was mocking the act of fellatio. I looked at Ginger shocked, then embarrassed I shot my eyes back down to my lap where my new pink plastic friend lay waiting. The thoughts I was struck with: How can anyone find white people attractive? How can any black person not find them grotesque? Although I might be rewriting history, I think I was also wondering, behind that, how can Sam love white people so completely, and how long before off-white is no longer enough for her?

My father was white. I consider myself black; I do not consider myself white, or half white. Similar logic: my mother was a woman, but I do not consider myself a woman or a half woman either (I have a penis, fully functional). I consider myself half Irish, but that's different.

I have been confused for white. I am usually confused for white (or rather [insert racial ambigious swarthy ethnic group here]). But I am not. I am black. And if you kick me out of that group, I'm taking Romare Bearden and the Adam Clayton Powells, Jean Toomer, and all the other ambiguous Negroes with me.

At the end of the night I was loaded into a cab with the box. It was a long trip across the river to Brixton, and I tried to read the writing on the packaging but couldn't because I was too drunk. I leaned the box back against the far door and looked at the head staring up at me, its open eyes, its shocked pleading mouth. And then I turned it face down because whatever was wrong with it, I couldn't help.

The phone was ringing when I got to my front door. It rang for a while too, before I realized it was coming from my flat, before I could drunkenly get my keys to work for me. Right then I should have known it was her (I didn't; I didn't figure it out till later), that she wasn't even in the States, because her cell phone didn't work in the States. Later I found out my Sam wasn't in NYC at the time. My Sam was in Croydon, in the flat of a thirty-three-year-old substitute teacher and sometimes game show contestant. That's just wrong.

The phone rings and I pick it up and I hear that familiar sound of the cell phone rustling in her pocketbook and then I hear something—I swear to God—about a "condom" and "can you find one?" as she digs through the bag from which the cell phone is calling. Soon, there is the distinctive audio of my wife getting the shit fucked out of her. Names being screamed and everything.

At first I thought it was a joke, it was so unreal; she's playing a joke and so for a good five minutes I'm on the phone just trying to keep my smile. It wasn't a joke. It was just fucked up. "Who the fuck is *Neal*?" was about the only rational thought I had. Then I remembered he was the shit bag from Croydon who Sam had gone to graduate school with. Even now, I can barely deal with it, the sound of that bastard's neighing name. If I could, I would have been a better storyteller and dropped the hint about this ex-boyfriend bastard, how he'd gotten her pregnant two years before I met her, and how she'd terminated it and they'd broken up, but they still talked on the phone sometimes. If I'd done that, I could have given the foreshadowing, and this wouldn't seem to come out of nowhere, but I don't give a shit because why should you be given more forewarning than I had? It was just some white guy name Neal. Some pink-dicked punk whose hobbies included fucking my wife and laughing at me.

The next morning it was like I didn't even think about it. My body just moved on its own, and what it did was blow up that sex toy.

When Sindy fully inflated, the first thing I noticed was she was too light—she weighed next to nothing. Every time I touched her, her whole body jumped like a beach ball. Sindy's latex flesh, lazily made to look like she was a descendent of the Caucus mountain clan, felt lifeless in my hands, so that morning I took a canister of tire foam out from the trunk of my Fiat. Inside, I dragged Sindy from the living room up the stairs to the bedroom by her inflated foot and she bounced loosely with every step, bounced off the walls. Once I figured out how to aim the nozzle correctly, the tire foam filled her body easily, naturally, and she gained a few pounds. Her legs were firmer, her ass was tight. I put Sindy in Sam's clothes to give her more life. I knew it was sick to do this, but I desired sickness as well. It was Sam's sweatshirt from our days in college, and the blue jeans she used to wear when we were falling in love, the ones she insisted were out of style now. They fit Sindy to perfection and I laid my white puppet's face down on the floor. The slow bass of "Sunshine" carried me as I slipped back her pants and revealed the roundness of her plasticine ass. The tresses of her golden hair bounced with grace as I rhythmically applied my weight to her and then pulled it back again. "Neal!" I said aloud, which kind of woke me up, made me lose my erection and roll to the floor again.

The above scene I've actually talked about in therapy, and in rehashing it the first thing I noticed was the obvious melodrama. It's perverse too, of course, but self-consciously so and as symbolically pathetic (as well as mildly homoerotic) as one could come by. I could tell you that afterward I laid on the floor, crying and wallowing in my shame, but now I feel that was playing into the whole performance of self-pity I was creating.

If there was a rational reason behind my actions, it would be that they were a conscious artificial attempt on my part to hit rock bottom, so that I could speed up the process of rising again.

I would break up with Sam, I told myself. I didn't want to, but I knew, rationally, that I must, and that was an important realization. I would just cut off the whole thing, this marriage, at next contact. Perform the cutting so that the healing could begin.

Sam called the next night, this time on purpose. From Brooklyn, where she said she was visiting sorority sisters from SUNY/New Paltz (note: I also loved that she was AKA, which had only added to her inaccessibility). On this call Sam was talking to them as much as to me; she said they asked how I was doing and she'd thought she'd give me a buzz. She called me her baby again, said she missed me and she didn't want me to burn the house down and she would take care of me when she got home. At first I thought this was all a lie, but then I heard her friends giggling in the background and they yelled an American "Hi!" over her shoulder before she hung up, so it seems Sam was actually in the States by then.

Later, after I was well asleep, the phone rang again and it was Sam, this time alone.

"Tell me what's wrong. You're acting weird. Honey, talk to me. Are you OK? What's going on?"

The funny thing is, the way Sam said all this I could tell she knew that I knew something was up. She was framing it in a way that implied that it was my problem, but you could tell Sam knew it was her shit that was stinking up the room. The reason for the call, I'm sure, was to figure out what I knew, how I knew it, and what I planned on doing about it. She kept pausing, waiting for me to jump in, offer something. I offered: "Everything's fine. No really, I'm just tired." And variations thereof until Sam gave up and hung up once more.

After I hung up I just lay there, in our bed, alone in the dark, unable to go back to sleep, and I came up with an important revelation. It turned out, to my surprise, that I didn't want reconciliation. Rather, I did, but this thing—this image of Sam fucking her dream white man, his ponytail flapping in rhythm with his balls—and then the lies, the lies around it that were like little multiplication Xs; they were too much for me. So foremost, what I required was something more. I required revenge. It was very simple, very pure, very obvious really.

A week later, when Sam came back to London, she looked good, real good. I picked her up from Gatwick myself, and just the sight of her, it was enough to move me. Have I mentioned her fitness, that I loved that too? Sam insisted on spandex pants as a uniform; they were barely pants, really, just thick stockings, and while they bordered on tacky she didn't care because she knew her body looked that good in them. I was not her physical equal; she once said, "I always thought the man I would marry would have this great, athletic body, but there you are." At the time I decided to take the statement as a positive, further proof that I had married above my station.

In the minicab I told her I had a surprise for her, tried to keep the conversation light, ask a lot of questions and not let on to anything. Sam loved surprises, always hinted at wanting more of them, and when she got home she put her bags right down in the doorway and went off in search of this surprise, expecting great things.

It was sitting on the dining room table as I told her, wrapped beautifully (I've learned to pay others as I lack the precision).

"Oh (extended exclamation)! You are—this is just sweet. Can I guess what it is? Let me guess."

I let her guess. It was easy: a medium-sized box, very light, rectangular. As she shook it gleefully, I didn't smile. I didn't revel in the moment as Sam did, but she didn't notice. Whatever apprehension she'd experienced on the phone before was gone; Sam was completely relaxed, which made me relish my revenge more, added to my rationalization about the price I'd paid for it.

"Baby, did you get me something frilly, something silky to welcome me home?"

That I did. Sam looked so happy that I could almost pretend that she hadn't been fucking somebody for at least four months by then, but I knew different. By then, I'd combed her Master-Card receipts, searched through her E-mails. Still, the red that came into Sam's tan cheeks, it almost convinced me she was still in love with me.

It was silk, it was frilly, and Sam's smile didn't dissipate until she held it up before her. The panties were too small; there was no way Sam could fit Africa's blessing into those little things. And they were soiled; this Sam might have deciphered as well, although we never discussed that later.

For Sam, all humor was suddenly gone. The best way to describe it is like she suddenly remembered herself. Suddenly woke up, realized that she was participating in a dream that was no longer relevant anymore.

"What?" she asked me, almost whispered. In her two hands the stained drawers slowly wilted down. That moment, even before I said it. When anyone asks me what it is like to get a divorce, it's that moment, that look on Sam's face that comes to mind immediately. Not the part where I had to come back to Philly, where it took me six months to find another job, or even when I was packing my shit into boxes a day later. That moment even before I said it, when she knew, she knew where this was going. Of course, I said it anyway:

"Those are panties, honey. They're Ginger's panties, honey. She gave them to me after I fucked her. See, I fucked your cracker-ass boss behind your back, just like you've been fucking your ponytailed honky behind my back for months. I fucked Ginger MacDonald, and I told her it was our secret. She said it's our secret, and she gave me those as a trophy."

Sad thing is, I really said all that. Pretty much to the word. And I know that makes me an asshole, but I did it. And I know that makes me a loser, because why should Sam care? Women are not, on the whole, territorial about their mate's physical landscape, and Sam was playing with leaving me anyway. The crazy thing is at the time in my head this was a move to keep Sam in my life. That I still don't understand.

Sam dropped Ginger's shit-stained drawers from her hands, turned from me to the kitchen sink, and started silently washing her hands. Sam took a long time too, the water so hot you could see steam rising up past her shoulders. What I said: "Trying to wash the black right off you? Is that what you wish I could do too?" But Sam was, that quickly, beyond the point of fighting. This woman, my wife, the woman I still wake up to sometimes and remember I'm still in love with, she wasn't there. She was a ghost in the room. I stood there waiting for Sam to finish at the sink and turn to me, to hit me, even hate me, so we could move past that and get on to the next part. But when she was done, my Sam just walked by me without expression, walked by me, got her bags, and went out the door once more. Even locked the door like there was no one home to take care of the chore.

This was not really the ending. This was a divorce, there were lawyers, there were meetings. One time, in the elevator going up to the last arbitration, I asked how life was like with white boy, of course using those words. She looked so beautiful, it hurt my teeth just to stand next to her. Sam's response, "Our problem was that the thing I loved about you, you yourself hated." She had pity in her voice too. If I still have hate for her, it was that in those final interactions, it was still all my fault. She cheated in less than a year, but it was all my fault we were failing.

My response to this, which sadly came to me a few days later, after the divorce was filed, was this: "Not 'hated,' dear, just not isolated and cherished. Our problem was that you see yourself as a half needing to be made whole. I know that I am not the ingredients, but the greater sum. I am the unique creation, who needs someone whole." That I liked, that I repeated to myself, hoping I could run into her somewhere so I could lay it on her.

Looking back now, though, that's a bit romantic and self-important also. I hate mixed people who think they're fucking special because of that boring fact. Still, for a few weeks that imagined response did much to comfort me.

After Sam's late night call from the States, I'd spent that day out shopping for a new battery for my laptop in Kensington, then I walked up to Notting Hill where I met up with Ric again to put a few pints down. Basically I spent that night just saying again and again that I loved Sam without telling Ric what was up, what she'd done to me. Somehow I ended up down the street at that Ladbroke Grove pub again, alone, despondent, and there was the beast. She was at the bar, smiling those brown rocks at me. It was odd because at my table, somehow we got on the topic of race, and this wretch said to me, "Well look at you. You're barely even quarter caste, you're damn near as white as me." Later, when we stumbled around the corner and she stood before me like a bleached prune, Ginger belched, "Well look at the body on you. You're a fine one, blackie."

It was no great victory.

I got dumped by this fiancée, felt betrayed, and wanted revenge. So I got the idea for this story. I wrote the first draft almost a decade ago, and shelved it because it was just insane, a rage-filled, self-indulgent rant. It's not much different now, but luckily in the time since, I've learned more about how to turn my rage-filled self-indulgence into something with entertainment value. So this goes out to that lovely lady of yesteryear, and all the mulat-tresses who wouldn't go out with me because I wasn't white or black enough. Beige power.

Stewart David Ikeda

Stewart David Ikeda is author of *What the Scarecrow Said*, a finalist in Barnes & Noble's Discover Great New Writers Series, and vice president of the publishing company IMDiversity, Inc. He was born in suburban Philadelphia in 1966 to families who, somewhere down the line, started out elsewhere—throughout Europe and in Japan. His short fiction has appeared in *Ploughshares*, *Story*, *Glimmer Train*, and *Pacific Citizen*, as well as the anthologies *Voices of the Xiled* and *Yellow Light*.

Shadey

A seven-year old boy named Bart climbs out the sixth-floor window of the towering city apartment, trying to retrieve his cat, which has slipped out and sits cocked on the sill, gauging the leap to the fire escape. Bart's mother has been yelling at Shadey because there is a mouse in the apartment; clenching the cat by the scruff of the neck, she had thrust it down upon the mouse, but Shadey isn't a mousing cat.

"Shitty cat!" Bart's mother yells too loudly. An accomplished actress in films and musical theater, she wields a voice that carries; it has frightened Shadey into jumping out onto the ledge. She pays for the apartment (pays *a lot*), even though she rarely stays here, and is furious that it has pests. She quakes with irritation; she is an anxious woman. She is not a squeamish woman, however, and chases the mouse around the apartment with a deep saucepan. Fearing that she plans to squash the rodent, Bart starts to wheeze.

When she finally captures the mouse and carries it to the window, she commands, "Get out of the way!" Both boy and cat look at her; only Bart obeys, lowering himself back into the room and onto the rug. She thrusts the pan out the window and slowly rotates her arm until the mouse can barely cling to the nonstick lining and begins to fall.

"Watch out for Shadey, Mama!" Bart cries, climbing beneath her arm, back out the window. Shadey automatically reaches out to skewer the mouse with its claws, and the windowsill has become very cramped with all of them. At the precise moment that Bart catches hold of the shrieking Shadey's tail—losing his footing—his mother catches his belt through the window. The momentum of boy and cat falling drags her face-first into the closed upper pane. Bart, at the end of his toppling arc, rebounds, upside down, off the brick wall below. He does the smart thing—seeing the brown brick onrushing, he parries with the hand *not* holding his cat, but Shadey scratches free and hurtles with the mouse into a protruding air conditioner on the way to the second-floor rooftop. Oddly, it seems to take both animals the same amount of time to land. Hanging upside down, Bart is dazzled by a glint of the chrome pot somersaulting. He sees a small brown spot pause for a moment and then scamper off into the air vent. Neighbors lean out of windows below, looking up at Bart and his mother, shading their eyes with flat hands as if saluting.

"My arm, my arm . . ." says Bart's mother, with the terrible voice, hauling him up.

"My cat, my cat, my cat . . ." cries Bart.

B art awakens to a thundering headache, the slap of ammonia salts, and a stranger's smiling face. Thick fingers tug his eyes open, blind them with a penlight, then close them. His mother's smell floats nearby, mingles with hospital odors. He believes that Shadey saved his life. He knows how cats are always supposed to land on their feet; he knows from Science class that when a cat falls from high up, a loose skin on the underside swells like a parachute. Or was it *squirrels*? Why can't he remember?

L ike many only children, Bart has an imaginary best friend whom he sometimes talks to about things he shouldn't say out loud. His friend is the ghost of the boy King David. Bart is not afraid of ghosts. He has never been in church, nor has he read the Bible, but his father's mother (who is very afraid of ghosts and always seems to be in church, or *talking* about church, or *selling* something for the church) sent him a comic book version of *The Slaying of Goliath* and one night the shepherd/king just moved in beneath Bart's bed.

Bart often wishes that he had been named David.

B art is scared by the sights and sounds and smells of the hospital, and wants his father, who is probably out on some business for his mother. Bart's father is his mother's agent, and Bart thinks that's a very important thing to be. His father works at home during the day most days, and even though he talks on the telephone almost constantly, he often asks Bart to help him. "We have to find jobs for Mama, don't we Bart?" his father says. "And that's a big task. That's a task for *two* men, isn't it Bart?" When Bart returns from school, he joins his father in the office, checks for faxes from his mother, and reports on his day. Then, he helps his father by filing papers and looking for telephone numbers in the Yellow Pages.

"That's 'Theatrical Agencies' . . . Bart, what does that sound like to you?"

"TThhh . . . Thh . . . T . . ."

"Good. And what letter does T need to make a *thhh* sound, Bart?"

"It needs an H," answers Bart with confidence. "T, H, E . . ."

"That's right. Good boy. But what if you were in France? Remember what I said?"

"Except in French," Bart adds knowingly, "the T doesn't need the H. Or it doesn't matter if it has one or not."

"That's true, Bart. You really know your stuff."

W hy "Bart"? His mother named him after her father—he knows that much. *He* was a very famous actor too, as was *his* father. Both were named Bartholomew. Never very good with names (or spelling), it is Bart's mother who dubbed the kitten Shadey (not Shady) for its early ashen color (which had faded to a dirty brown by the time it was a grown cat).

"It's an *English* spelling," she had insisted.

She had not taken her husband's last name, obviously, but Bart had, though the compromise had pained her. She had dearly wanted the boy to retain, to benefit from, carrying a "great name." Hers was after all a great English family, she said—a *famed* family, she said—and a name that opened doors. Ultimately, she would endure the convention of her son's surname "as long as it's fifty-fifty," she had said.

"Really, it's sixty-six-point-six to thirty-three-point-three and change," her husband had corrected, for she insisted on shoehorning her famous family name in between "Bartholomew" and the caboose of his own last name which, she complained, was unpronounceable.

(Bart's father's family did not use middle names, and he had never suffered for lacking one himself.)

Truly, all together, Bart's full name is a real tongue twister. It has nine syllables, not even counting his middle name.

"It's a whole lotta name," his mother would say.

"For a whole lotta boy," his father would say.

Bart's father, however, refuses to call him Bartholomew. Even when identifying his son in writing on an official document, he will not use the longer form. No matter what they are discussing, his father liberally peppers his sentences with the shorter nickname, as if there were other people in the room who might think the comment was directed at them.

Bart wonders why his parents couldn't have found some other name they agreed on. "They can do so many things, my parents," Bart tells David, "but some of the simplest things they just don't get."

But David, a worldly boy-king, so much more familiar with big people and wary of their ways, is not surprised at all.

B art's mother had rushed him to the hospital in a panic, but the emergency room doctor assured her "the bleeding looks worse than it really is," so she immediately set out through the hospital to locate a phone to call her husband.

When he arrives, his eyes are red, his wide face ashen. He takes her face between his palms, scrutinizes her scratches until certain that she is not badly hurt, administers a light caress to each one. As she begins telling the story, he turns on his heels and drags her down the corridor, peering frantically into each cubicle, looking for Bart. She says she never suffered such a fright as when she heard her boy slap against the wall outside and felt that single belt loop snap . . . no, *tear* from the boy's jeans as she hauled him up. "I would have thrown myself out to save him, you know," she says. "I would have . . ."

"Enough drama!" he tells her. "It's self-indulgent. Where is my son?"

She knows she's talking too much—it's nerves. She has never seen her husband so distraught—and certainly never tearing up so (although Bart has), and it badly shakes her. She had bloodied her nose, she blurts, and the boy had seven stitches sewed across his lip and right cheek . . .

Suddenly pivoting about-face, he covers her mouth with his hand. They have reached the door to the cubicle where the boy waits, legs dangling from the cold steel gurney, dabbing his cheek with a gauze pad saturated brown with iodine or blood.

"Go home," Bart's father growls to her, as if—as if everything were *her* fault. "Go home and get it cleaned up before he comes home to see it."

"Clean what?" she asks pointlessly. And he doesn't *say* it, no, but she imagines that he *looks* at her like *she'd* killed the dumb animal. "Clean *it*?"

"Shadey," he says, and he turns from her.

Letting him slide her into her overcoat, she mumbles, "Go on, make everything better. Go in and clean up my mess," but she is humble, following him into the cubicle to say good-bye. She cries when she signs the cast running down Bart's arm, but Bart's father makes them all laugh, pilfering rolls of surgical tape and gauze from the cabinet and swaddling everyone's hands into fist-balls, saying, "Look, Bart. Now *we* have monkey paws too."

It's like your mother is always angry, David says, and Bart does not correct him. David is Bart's best friend—they like all the same things: cats, ecology, books, inarizushi—and David even accompanies Bart to school on occasion, dematerializing into a back pocket or textbook or pencil eraser. Together, they make the smartest pair of boys in class; only David can keep up with Bart in science, for example.

Although adored by teachers and envied by classmates for his intelligence (and diligence), Bart suffered sporadic but distressing asthma that prevented him from playing sports with the others. Asthma aside, Bart enjoys general good health, but he is small and delicate looking compared to other boys his age; in the slightest direct light, his pale, transparent skin seems to luminesce like a paper lantern at the end of its wick. In the manner that an older schoolboy might win borrowed self-confidence by befriending the captain of the football team, Bart finds comfort in the company of the resourceful giant-killer.

It's like your mother has angry bones, says David firmly, now that they are talking of bones. Bart is fascinated to have broken small ones in his right wrist and middle finger. His hand is wrapped in a complicated cast and steel-reinforced splint—a robot arm—locking his wrist up in a constant patty-cake position; two padded digit-splints like ninja claws curve over his fingers in an impressive fashion.

Waiting for his father to return from the hospital cafeteria with the dinner tray, Bart and David hunch over a book of anatomical sketches the doctor has left for them, absentmindedly raising and lowering the mechanical bed with a control pad taped to the railing. Squinting at the X rays, then the book, then the bandaged real thing, Bart locates the exact point of breakage in one of the fingers and names it; he reads, "Prox-i-mal phal-an-x," and pronounces, "It's just a small bone."

A small, painful *bone*, says David, shivering.

"Proximal phalanx," Bart repeats slowly.

A broken phalanx, says David.

At home, when his parents are occupied, Bart sometimes sits alone in his room, or on the bathroom tile, or in the back of his mother's closet, scanning the phone book. He likes to get a head start so that he will be prepared when his father next calls on him for assistance. He and David scan it for the funniest, foreign-sounding names sometimes, but mostly Bart takes his responsibilities very seriously.

D avid fears and sometimes hates Bart's mother, especially when she hits Bart's father (who is a sturdy, gentle man who always laughs and never seems to be hurt, but that is not the point). She doesn't have much time to spend at home, but when she's between jobs she takes Bart with her everywhere.

"There's spending time together, a lot of time even, but then there's *quality* time," she tells him often. "Of course you and Daddy see each other all the time, but I miss you very, very, very much when I'm away. I want you with me *all* the time when I'm home because I miss you so much."

"*How* much do you miss me?" Bart always asks, making her say it again, multiplying by another "very" each time.

W hen Bart's mother finds Shadey on the second floor rooftop, she is both dismayed and a little impressed that it is still alive, barely. Mostly, she is grateful, thinking she might be able to carry it back upstairs and call a vet to have it fixed before the boy comes home. She knows she'll have time to clean up the blood because her husband has phoned from the hospital to say they have admitted Bart for the night in case of concussion.

The beast purrs, at first. It lets her stroke its head and soothe it. She wonders at this because it should be obvious to them both that she doesn't like cats, but she pets it anyway and soon finds herself *talking* to it too. "I should try it soon," she says, eyeing the treacherous climb up the fire escape, "or it will be too late for you, cat."

Hauling the cat up like a sack under her arm, she begins to climb the straight-upward ladder-stairs, but it releases such a moan that she almost drops it again. When she finally slips back inside the apartment and looks down, she notices several of the cat's ribs protruding through its side. It swipes at her arm and jumps heavily to the floor, alighting with a liquid sound like a water balloon; she feels she will vomit. Dragging its broken body under the bed, it forces itself to die before she can move the furniture out of the way to fetch it. Disposal is easy: she scoops Shadey up in a thick black garbage bag and dumps it down the incinerator chute. She will remember this; she has a remarkable capacity for sense memory.

It is difficult to breathe now that the blood in her nose has congealed. Wheezing, she lugs a three-gallon lobster pot full of hot water to the windowsill and mixes a solution of several household cleansers, dish detergent, and Softsoap, blinking from the fumes. Tipping the brew is a strain; she has not played Lady Macbeth before, but with an actress's kitsch and some pain, the moment reminds her that she is nearly old enough, now. With the slow heaviness of a dinosaur's tongue, the green liquid unfurls past the amazed nosy-bodies below—again perched at their windows—and obliterates the stain (and a good portion of the roof tar) where the mouse had finally foiled Shadey.

When she is done, she kindles a long, gold-tipped Sobranie Black Russian, selects an *Interview* from the magazine basket, and settles into a scented bath.

S itting between his parents during the cab ride home from the hospital, Bart watches the dashboard meter count the fare. He feels bad and wants to talk to David, but he cannot do this in front of his parents. On the meter is a picture of the cabdriver, who has one of those funny, foreign names.

His father sounds tired as he explains that Shadey "has gone to play in the Place where the cats all answer only to their real secret names." Although Bart knows the book by heart—and knows it's a pretty good Place to go—still, he hopes. He suspects that perhaps his mother has done something with Shadey . . .

perhaps *hidden* him somewhere, given him away, or taken him to a pound. But he says, "Maybe, Mama . . . just maybe . . . did you see . . . ?"

"No," says his mother, looking out the window, a scarf of blue cigarette smoke wafting around her. "It's gone."

Bart feels his parents both stiffen on either side of him.

O n the occasions when Bart's mother returns home from an extended film shoot or play run, Bart is eager to tell her about the jobs he and Daddy have found for her. She always thanks Bart enthusiastically with hugs and kisses, but she doesn't seem to think that being an agent is such a good job for his father. They can have terrible fights sometimes. Once not long ago Bart overheard his mother shouting about a part. She not only had to wear the *pants* in the house, but the *jockstraps*, too, she said. Bart didn't know what that meant, but from the tone of her voice he felt fortunate that *he* didn't have to wear them.

Bart rarely sees his father get angry. He was once a kind of actor too, but then stopped. The one time Bart asked him why, his father thought for a long time, then said that there were only so many good acting jobs to go around. "Having one good actor in the family is plenty," he had said. "Every family needs a good agent too."

H aving slept badly his first night home from the hospital, Bart wakes very late to his mother's voice coming from the den. Still sleepy, he rises and crosses to peek out through his bedroom door, which his father is used to leaving cracked open at night, just wide enough that Shadey could slip in and out. His mother is seated on the divan. She has a lot of makeup on, he notices, and appears very shiny.

He can't see who she is talking to, but knows it must be the friend from the *Daily News* who was to come by for "a little chat," because Bart had been allowed to mark this appointment in her calendar. She (the friend) is a *newspaperman*, which is one of the things Bart thinks he might be if he doesn't have to be an actor, so he listens attentively from behind his bedroom door while dressing himself.

"Just between you and me," he hears his mother tell the woman, "I'm not getting the kind of roles I *really* want to be doing. Strictly off the record, my agent isn't exactly working out the way I'd like." She doesn't say, "my *husband* isn't working out the way I'd like," Bart notices.

Bart's mother dresses very well; she prefers to look "classic," as she says. To Bart, she always looks busy, clean, and . . . big. Big hair, big eyes, big coats; clanking belts with mighty buckles and shoes that make her taller than his father. She has painted tins on her vanity overflowing with pins and feathers and bangles like tackle boxes. On each wall of her closet—as spacious as Bart's bedroom—hangs a poster of a regally dressed woman. Four in all, each representing a season of the year; their various wafting scarves and gowns snake through a block of script lettering below: *le Printemps, l'Été, l'Automne, l'Hiver.*

When she is away, Bart shuts himself in her closet and presses his face against her boas and scarves and gowns hanging from hooks scented with potpourri, or clacks her faux-pearls between his teeth. And garters: his mother owns the world's largest collection, matching pairs, all of them. In cowboy movies, it is always the fat mustached saloon keepers who wear garters . . . on their sleeves. Bart's mother, however, wears hers beneath her dress, and they always smell of her custom-mixed perfume. Bart wonders if those accessories are the dreaded *jockstraps* wrapping her thighs instead of his father's arms, but senses it is a sore subject and doesn't ask. Besides, she has several times forbidden him to play in her closet.

It is Bart's father who arranges his wardrobe. "A man knows a boy needs sensible clothes," his father says. Tough pants with rubber patches glued inside over the knees. Winter coats with clips in the sleeves for mittens. Two-toned shoes with thick soles and hard caps in the front, because he tends to drag his toes when he walks. His mother, however, doesn't approve of his appearance.

"Jesus Christ, *look* at him!" she had said to his father once when they returned from back-to-school clothes shopping and getting a bowl cut at the barbershop. "He looks like a queer Bowery Boy, for God's sake!"

"You like your clothes, don't you Bart?" his father had asked quietly.

"My kid cannot go to school looking like that, goddamn it!"

"What do you think, Bart?" his father had asked again.

"He thinks he looks goddamn foolish," his mother had said, advancing angrily toward them. "What the hell does a seven-year-old think? He thinks what his goddamn mother thinks!"

"And his father?"

Bart had turned away because he was crying. His mother had turned away and stormed out of the apartment. His father had turned to him and patted him on the head.

His mother doesn't seem to think that a father is such a good thing to be either.

When Bart sneaks out of his room, the woman from the *Daily News* is scribbling crazily on a spiral notebook as his mother talks about his grandfather.

"And speaking of Bart!" his mother says. She holds both arms open until he crosses to the divan, then hugs him to her, bigger and longer than usual, and kisses him four times on the top of his hair, and once on the cheek, which leaves a circle of bright red lipstick but that's OK by him. Noticing his splinted hand, the reporter *tsks* and shivers with sympathy. For a while the women give him all their attention, but it is the good kind, and he is happy and decides to stay here as long as he can instead of continuing on into the kitchen. Putting down her notebook, the *Daily News* woman extends her arms toward him too, saying, "Oh!" and "Oh, don't you two make the most delightful picture!" and to him alone, "Let me look at you!" and it is like he is in a fashion show.

His mother lightly pushes him forward, and the reporter's fingers close around his shoulders, pulling him close. He must stand on tiptoes—like he sometimes held Shadey when they had a serious conversation—while she draws him nearer to her face, which is stretched and pink. "Oh!" she says, studying him. "You look just like a little doll! Now where *ever* did they *find* you?" And although she's smiling, she says it like he's done something a little naughty. Bart doesn't know what to say to that.

"Oh," his mother says with a little laugh, although she sounds annoyed. "We found him down by the river one day, floating along inside a giant peach. Right, Bart?"

She means like Momotaro the Peach-Pit Boy—another ogre-slaying boy-hero, like David, in another favorite storybook from his father's mother, but the *Daily News* lady doesn't seem to understand.

"Well," she says, "he certainly *looks* it! His cheeks are round and soft as a peach! And as sweet, I'll bet . . . ," she says. She looks curiously from Bart to his mother, commenting on *her* cheekbones—saying that his mother has inherited her "father's *famous* cheekbones," and, "Did you know your Grandpa Bart, Bart?" she asks, and chuckles.

Bart has never met his grandfather, who ran off when his mother was very young.

"He was *long* gone," his mother says testily. "Dead, actually," she says, to Bart, although he knows this already.

In the kitchen, among a great collection of old photos, is a still from her first film (and only film with her father). She is Bart's age, dressed in rags like a character from *Oliver Twist*, but her face is shining. Bart's grandfather, looking like a tycoon with his slick hair, expensive suit, and big cigar, cups her beaming face in his palm. Bart has never seen the movie and it isn't on video so he's not likely to.

He is grateful when finally the reporter releases her grip on him, and he quickly moves to sit at his mother's feet as the women continue talking. The reporter is asking, "What do you say to people who claim you're only successful because you're the famous Bartholomew's daughter?"

"What do I say?" Looking down to the floor, she reaches over and picks up a red plastic ball with a bell from beneath the coffee table. Bart recognizes it as one of Shadey's toys. Rolling it in her palm, smoking hard on her cigarette, she finally says, "Having your old man leave you when you're seven, write an autobiography about the misery your mother caused him and all her friends he screwed, and then die two years later leaving only a pile of bills isn't exactly a guaranteed ticket to success." Like cracking open a walnut, she squeezes until the ball crumbles and only the tinkling tin bell remains. "The only link between us is we both were *real* actors. And if that makes some people jealous, well let them eat their fucking cake, is what I say."

Bart believes her: he knows how hard things can be for her. He knows he and his father have really helped her the most.

B art is a light sleeper and already a veteran midnight-snacker. His mother maintains a never-empty hoard of well-sugared junk food in the pantry, with staples of cream-filled powdered donuts and vats of ice cream. His father (who cannot eat such things) usually can sleep soundly, so Bart often sits alone at night watching his white-mustached reflection on the surface of the polished granite table.

As Bart sits scanning the kitchen walls, so cluttered with photos—mostly black and white, chronicling his mother's career—massaging his wrapped arm, David whispers into his ear that his splint and scary claws might be good for some mischievous fun. *We could play a trick*, says David. *We could play a trick on your mother*.

But Bart is generally a well-behaved boy and doesn't like to think about such things. "I'm not listening to you," he says, and directs his attention to the photos—the film still with old Bartholomew, several shots of his mother in scintillating poses, and a particularly funny one where she's dressed like a Viking.

There is also a picture of Bart's parents by the stage of a summerstock theater in the Poconos. They look like different people, but also, in Bart's opinion, very beautiful. They look happier. His mother, stunning in her silky red gown, a tiara sparkling in her gold hair, hangs around her fiancé's neck. Shirtless, his jet hair pulled into a tight ponytail, his jeans splotched with paint but new, Bart's father looks handsome and rugged, but wears a grin that is a little goofy. One strong arm holds her aloft while the other raises above his head a barbell boasting 5,000 LBS on each end. Scrawled across the photo, in a pretty but misspelled script, a dedication reads,

> *To the Daydream Beleaver from the Homcoming Queen:*
> *I loveyouloveyouloveyouloveyouloveYOU!*

But it is another photo that gives him the idea to do a play, a shot that sometimes unsettles him. It shows his grandfather and child-mother posing before a stone cottage with a slightly spooky man, thin lipped and stern looking even though he is smiling. Leaning over to pat the little girl's head, he appears more like he's leaning *on* her, like a walking stick. Bart's mother told him this same cadaverous man, who signed the photo "Ever and affectionately your Old Possum," had also written their favorite "cat book." She said she had met the aging poet twice in England and once in Boston, and remembered that although he and old Bartholomew were mutually respectful, they did not seem particularly fond of each other. "Eliot may be a tight-ass in person . . ." she remembered her father saying, "and you might never guess it just to look at him, but he's an *actor's* poet, that's for sure. When he isn't *fretting* and gets down to *writing*, he's the best actor's poet since Bill Shakespeare and I'll fight anyone who contradicts me!" Still, the man had come to visit her mother after the divorce and had been kind to them.

Examining his grandfather's famous cheekbones in the photo, Bart decides he doesn't like that *Daily News* woman. He decides he won't be a reporter.

You'll have to be an actor anyway, David says. *She'll make you be one.*

Bart brushes the powder from his face with his cast, wipes the tabletop, turns off the light; he knows he will fall asleep in the kitchen again if he doesn't go to bed right now. Out of habit, he peeks into the moonlit office to the fax machine, now quiet and empty, then continues down the corridor. Tracing the wall with his good hand, he brushes the knob of the door to his parents' bedroom; there are sounds faintly feline. He decides he will give his parents a play. Following the long black road toward the distant nightlight, he is already dreaming on his feet. Dreaming of cats.

I n the morning, before his performance, Bart sits at his usual window seat in the study, flipping awkwardly through the phone book with his splinted hand and chewing a fingernail on the other. "*Ohayo*," his mother says, entering the room, still sleepy in her pink robe. "Hey, I thought we said no more biting nails." She lifts the pyramid of mail he so neatly erected on the desktop—a parcel, a women's magazine, then bills, then airline tickets.

"When you stop smoking cigarettes," he replies, but doesn't look up.

"Christ, you sound like your father," she says. She pauses, then crosses to him and rumples his hair. "What are you doing?"

"Finding you a job," he says.

"Oh, if *that's* all," she says, hugging him, "then you can take a break. I'm going out shopping and I want you to come with me. We'll go to the river for lunch, OK?"

"But I have to find something for you to do," he says, more insistently.

"Hmm. I'd almost think you were trying to get rid of me, Honey."

Huffing, Bart closes the book and rises.

That boy has the theater in his blood!" Bart's mother cries delightedly.

"Born to walk the boards, old Bart!" shouts his father.

"I hear tell from folks who know his Hamlet is reminiscent of the young Booth!"

Bart is almost ready. His parents sit attentively but apart on the wide leather sofa. Bart requires them to skootch close together, making room for David who conceived and directed his "staged recitation" of a poem from his favorite bedtime book. Magenta and emerald lighting gels are taped over lamps; except for those dim spotlights and his mother's cigarette ash and the "recording" indicator on the camcorder, the living room is all expectant darkness.

Waiting for the scene to be set, the stage lights to rise, Bart's parents indulge themselves in the first relieved gaiety this living room has heard in many days. Outwardly trading encouraging theatrical clichés, they inwardly sink into that private and peaceful place where parents go to recoup when the storms of perilous might-have-beens abate, exhausted from the anxious three-day vigil. As Bart clatters properties around in the curtained-off hallway, it is the first moment they've been alone and able to talk, but they don't. Each thinks, "He's such a smart boy, he's a good boy. The boy's all right."

Bart's mother feels unusually secure. Usually, when she's working, she fears that Bart will somehow forget her during her long absences. If she would confide this to her husband, he'd tell her that, on the contrary, Bart remembers everything. In fact, *she* is more likely to put *him* out of mind when work demands her solid concentration, which has become increasingly difficult to muster.

Not that she *forgets* him. How many makeup artists, hairdressers, gaffers, grips, and other grunts could tell you: Bart's grade average; the age Bart grew his first tooth; how tall (in crayon notches, etched into the refrigerator door) Bart had grown; or the joyful circumstances when Bart first poo-pooed-in-potty by his own volition? *Hollywood, Burbank, and the Great White Way could attest to her devotion!* And doesn't she send gifts from every new location? Across the country and across the world?

And not that she doesn't *love* Bart. Oh, God! Watching him, she knows she loves him, but . . .

It was as though they had begun rejecting each other even before his emergence. The obstetrician had explained carefully, but it sounded like Greek to her: "There is an incompatibility between the Rh factors in your bloods."

"Which means . . . ?"

"Your Rh negative blood contains antibodies which attack certain proteins in your fetus's Rh *positive* blood. You with me?" But what did she know about such things? Was he saying that something was *wrong* with her?

"Which means . . . ?"

Her first pregnancy, ending in a wholly unlooked-for miscarriage, "had caused a hemolytic reaction in her blood. Antibodies developed to reject and kill foreign proteins." *Hadn't she had any medical care?* the obstetrician demanded, frowning. "Hard luck," he said, "and avoidable too. It's virtually impossible in the world of modern medicine to have Rh incompatibility threaten a pregnancy." But then, she hadn't been in the modern world that first time.

She had been shooting on the coast of Kenya for the three months of her pregnancy: the story of the daredevil American anthropologist Madeleine Jean Porter—Mama Maddy-Jean, the Kenyans used to call her. Two weeks into the shoot, it was too hot to work from 11 to 2, so she daily rented a donkey to carry her to the spot where she would stretch unclothed without a towel exactly halfway within the frothy skirt of the Indian Ocean, listening to the tidal tongue lapping her and the other tides within her. Sometimes local boys were brave enough to approach her under the pretense of selling coconut or warm Coke or fresh tigerfish; but most often, they watched from afar as warily as if she were a lioness—as if she were the *real* Maddy-Jean, rather than a lonely, nervous, increasingly queasy woman. It did not show—scrutinizing every centimeter of her smooth flat hide, they could not have guessed that Bart's minus-seven-months-old sibling waited inside her. A *good* doctor would have known, of course. On that island, however, where mute, clitoridectomized women also hid their nearly constant pregnancies beneath top-to-toe black bui-bui wraps, modern pre- and postnatal care was not readily available. Still, the producers had assured her that a doctor would be available to her throughout the shoot; a "respected English doctor," they had said. They had not said that that gentleman, scion of well-landed colonialists, spent more time in the bush treating rich expats' hangovers and clap, or acquiring these himself, than keeping abreast on medical procedure.

It happened quickly. Having dreamt of the delivery, she awoke one morning racked by cramps; enclosed in the four-posted bed canopied with mosquito netting, she had the sensation also of being an infant in an incubator. The sheets were soiled with blood and other discharge. She knew, of course, that her pregnancy had miscarried, though it appeared to her as little more than a heavy period. A helicopter flew her to a Mombasa hospital, where she waited for her husband to arrive twenty-four hours later. The staff had barred him at first, not believing he was her husband, and his appearance was wild when he found her. The first thing she'd said to him was, "I blew it." Scared and enraged, asserting the crew could shoot around her scenes for a week, he insisted that she return home immediately, but the doctors kept saying, "*Rest*, Bwana, rest is what she needs. Be patient." That's what the Kenyans were always saying: "Patience. Be patient."

But a year later, to the other doctor, the man who would deliver Bart to her, she had begged, "In plain English, please," not actually wanting to hear—not yet—wanting time, wanting that convenient compression of *thinking* time afforded when one knows the script.

"That means," the doctor said, "your blood destroys the fetus's red blood cells, and its waste flows into the amniotic sac. We can do a transfusion of new blood into the fetus in utero. Or, we may have to force delivery by C-section, which would entail . . ."

"Even *I* know what that means."

"The child will be premature. We will probably perform two or three more transfusions, and we'll monitor it for a time for infection. Do you understand? We have to make sure that the exchange is complete, that the fetus accepts the new blood."

But what she had wanted to know was, "My blood? I want my baby to have *my* blood. Or my husband's?" It seemed, for some unclear reason, important to know.

"No, no, no," the doctor explained, "a *donor's* blood. It cannot be your blood; your blood is what is killing it. Do you understand? Your blood is what we must take *out*. If any of it were to stay in the child's system after delivery, it would continue to eat it from inside." The swollen scarlet blobs in the photographs he showed her were creatures of horror films . . . not babies. She was determined to do better than that. Try, try again.

How could she but love the child?

Still, Bart's mother, the aging starlet, frequently lies insomniac in hotels and location trailers, reading advice columns in parenting magazines by women she would never talk to in real life, thinking, "I don't know my boy very well"; thinking, "I complicate things, I know it"; thinking, "I miss him very, very, very much."

And now, she watches the boy strut across the living room.

Swathed in her scarves and her chain belts, Bart knows how to make an entrance. She tells herself, *He does, he does have my blood!* And she thinks, *I almost killed my son. Again.*

M acavity's a Mystery Cat: he's called the Hidden *Paw*—" whispers Bart, the little actor, brandishing the claws of his own. A smart boy. He thinks he's caught the sense of his character: his "brow deeply lined with thought," swaying "with movements like a snake," and licking his thumbs. Red-green spotlights melt to brown, saturate the airy scarves from his mother's closet: his neglected, dusty coat.

He wants to please his parents; he wants his performance to be good.

Bart hops from piano stool to divan, slinking through gloomy streets of inner London. Rising above and before his parents, perched on the coffee table and clawing at the air, he makes a good semblance of the respectable monster of depravity. His character posture is impeccable; his projection too, for his mother has taught him to "cheat out" to the audience. And although he doesn't know much of the poem's meaning, he captures its music, the same mellifluous reading voice learnt from his mother, which she in turn had learnt from Bartholomew the Elder.

But the better his performance goes, pacing the room, mewing, the more displeased his mother seems. He begins to swing her scarf above his head—just like he'd seen his mother do in a movie, as the nightclub singer who sang to men and lassoed them for a kiss—but a nervous laughter replaces his parents' applause. The more convincingly he rages and roars, as he has seen his mother do onstage so many times, the tighter his parents' hands press.

"You may seek him in the basement," Bart sings, confused by the wetness below his mother's eyes. "You may look up in the air . . ."

He lets the scarf fly, and as it hangs there, Bart, his mother, his father, everyone thinks of Shadey.

"But I tell you once and once again, *Macavity's not there!*"

The scarf arcs up, falls soft, like a swallow—or a kitten—onto her shoulders, and Bart reaches to kiss her. He doesn't want her to cry; it frightens him. He tries to wipe her cheeks, forgetting about his cast, raking her face with it. She flinches, clenches her husband's arm, and screams. This is not the way Bart wanted it to be. And David? He looks to the couch and sees David chuckling. His mother looks to the empty space beside her and sees nothing.

"Go away!" Bart shouts to David. "Please go away!"

"Oh God!" his mother moans, so loudly, so terribly, that Bart can only run away. He runs down the hall to the door of their bedroom. Groping at the doorknob, bending one of the digit splints on his cast, he screams, slams the door. Unable to breathe, he runs wheezing to the window.

"I'm sorry," he hears his mother shout from behind the door. "I'm so sorry."

T he veins lining her husband's hands deflate as she releases him from her tourniquet grip and he lightly traces the scratch on her face. He dabs at a tiny bead of blood from above her sharp left cheekbone, making her wince and grab his hand away again.

"He didn't mean it," says her husband, her agent, the go-between even at home—especially at home—but not sounding wholly sure.

"No," she says. "I blew it."

They can hear Bart's muffled sobs from the direction of their bedroom, and she knows her husband is aching to go to the boy, but pulls him back onto the couch.

"I'll go," she says. "I have to."

Standing is dizzying. The blinking light of the camcorder revives her. By instinct, she gathers her thoughts, inhales, brushes her hair back from her face, and then depresses the power button. She turns to her husband, who, without looking at her, extends two fingers to relieve her of the cigarette. Then, her gaze floats above and beyond him to the bedroom door and she slowly starts in after the boy.

S eated on the narrow fire escape off his parents' bedroom, legs dangling, Bart refuses to heed his mother's request to come back inside. "You come out with me," he says, watching her.

Hugging herself, she whispers, "I'm the mother here."

It occurs to Bart that she might be afraid, afraid of the rickety fire escape or afraid of David. Reaching into his pocket, he removes the giant-killer. Holding David flat in his palm, Bart takes a wheezing breath and exhales like blowing a kiss, and watches his protector float away over the street, across the city, into the sky. He doesn't like his mother to be afraid.

"It's OK," he says, watching her. "You can come out now."

And slowly, carefully, she removes her shoes and slips one foot out the window. She swings her body out, squats on her haunches, not looking down. There is a ripping sound as the soles of her stockings tear on the rusty iron platform. Holding her breath, she crawls next to him.

"I think I'm going to stick around," she tells him, looking down over the edge, and Bart lets her take his good hand. "For a little while."

"Shadey" is the perennial bridesmaid among my short stories—serially rejected and most dear to me for it. Popular in workshops and at public readings, it was the pearl of a manuscript that won a Hopwood Award, then went on to protracted courtships by multiple editors, only to be repeatedly left at the altar following several rounds of correspondence and tweakings.

It was an experiment in the unsaid. I wanted to explore the intersection of race, ethnicity, culture, class, belonging, and fame and infamy in a multicultural family without naming these things. Although these had been close to the surface in early drafts, I set to removing explicit references to the concepts, which seemed unsuited to the perspective and emotional logic of a child who had not yet been socialized to them—or, at least, had not yet been equipped with a vocabulary for expressing what he knew of them. For, in my experience, the facts of being a biracial child were wholly different from how I later learned to define them verbally. Parsing by race, cultural tradition, and blood quantum is an adult preoccupation. What child innately conceives of himself as half this or that until taught to do so? For some editors, this approach and the ending presented difficulties. After holding onto the story through months of close revision work, one wrote, "[I am] so drawn to 'Shadey' emotionally . . . but am left with more unanswered questions than I can comfortably handle."

Finally, after a decade's hibernation, this version restores a few of the more explicitly stated explorations of blood and inheritance and cultural distances, and it is clearer for it.

Brian Ascalon Roley

Brian Ascalon Roley, who is half Caucasian and half Filipino, was born in 1966 and grew up in Los Angeles. His novel, *American Son*, was published in 2001 and was a *New York Times* Notable Book, a *Los Angeles Times* Best Book, a Kiriyami Prize Finalist, and winner of the AAAS Prose Book Award (given by the Association of Asian American Studies). His work has been translated, anthologized, and chosen for the California Council of the Humanities' statewide reading series, California Uncovered. He teaches at Miami University of Ohio.

Unacknowledged

I

During the year I entered junior high school, my mother convinced my father to import a maid from the Philippines. She arranged for her brother, Betino, who still lived in Manila, to send one over to us; Father mailed him a check for ten thousand dollars to bribe the customs officials on the Asian side and to purchase a false visa for the agents here in Los Angeles. To get ready for the maid, we cleared out our garage.

Father and my older brother, Matt, and I put up drywall and laid in plywood floors and carpeting, and we bought a futon for the maid to sleep on. The cars had to be parked on the street. We painted the walls a cream color, which Father thought would be more cheerful than stark white, but he stared at the bare walls and frowned. Then he asked Mother to help him decorate the room. She laughed and told him the room was fine, that it was far nicer than the shanties most urban Filipinos lived in, or the *nipa* huts you found out in the countryside. Our father was from the Midwest and had only lived in nice areas of Palawan, a beachy outpost popular with European scuba divers and tourists, where he'd worked as an attorney for an American corporation, met our mother, and where Matt and Kara and I had been born.

Kara and I cleared out our car trunks to make room for the maid's luggage, and we drove to the airport in a caravan of two cars—Father and Matt behind the steering wheels. We had never had a live-in maid before, at least not since we left Manila when I was three. Over the years, our mother had hired some Hispanic women to help her take care of us in the afternoons, after school when she was at work, but they never lasted long. She either complained that they were lazy, did not know English, or—if she liked them—that they ended up leaving us for better jobs.

"What's this maid like?" Kara asked her.

Startled out of her thoughts, Mother turned to my sister: "Your Tito Betino says she's very hardworking and responsible. A good person."

"Is she one of his maids?"

"No," Mother frowned. She had wanted one of her brother's own maids—strictly trained by his wife, Millie—but Tito Betino had insisted none were available. "He says this one is very professional."

Father was quiet this whole time. He did not believe people needed maids (he was from a family of farmers), and he would frown at her use of that word (preferring "housekeeper"), but Mother would make fun of him and tell him to make his own burgers at McDonald's and to bus his own tables at restaurants if he did not like the division of labor. And anyway, he was not the one who did most of the housework.

According to our mother, even lower middle-class people had maids in the Philippines. Each time we went to visit Tito Betino, we stayed at his house and were looked after by four maids, a houseboy, and three chauffeurs, who drove our uncle, aunt, and three cousins—Malaya, Juliet, and Anna. The drivers took us to the shopping centers, where they would drop us off at the entrance; then they would wait at the curb nearby, parked illegally in a car which baked in the wrenchingly hot sun, keeping an eye on the mall entrance so that as soon as we stepped outside they could hurry over and pick us up. One time our aunt came too. The driver did not immediately see us, causing Tita Millie to frown. She gave the man a huge scolding in front of us kids.

At family meals the maids would hover behind us, filling our glasses, serving us from dishes we could easily have reached ourselves, fanning flies away with huge banana fronds as if we were Egyptian royalty in the old MGM movies our father liked to watch.

Our mother was much more circumspect about the whole situation. Occasionally her sister-in-law would scold a maid in front of us, driving the poor girl to look at the ground as Millie told her how incompetent she was, stupid and inconsiderate, and later, privately, Mother would criticize that behavior. "There's no excuse for Millie to be scolding her maids so harshly," she said. "That kind of humiliation is hardly Catholic. Not all rich Filipinos treat their employees that way just because they're poor and can't afford to quit. I hope you kids don't learn bad habits from seeing her do this."

"Of course we won't, Mom," Kara said, offended.

Mother ignored her and continued, "Rich people here walk all over their help, because the poor people are so desperate for work. If we treated them even twice as kindly as Millie does, they would be grateful. Not like the spoiled housekeepers you find in America. No matter how much you pay them, they feel they deserve more." She shook her head. "Americans are so spoiled," she added and glanced pointedly at Kara, who frowned.

After we returned to Los Angeles our mother began her campaign to convince her brother to send over one of his well-trained maids—a girl so yelled at and overworked she would be thankful to be in our house. As the woman's arrival date neared, our house grew thick with excitement. My sister told her friends at school we would be getting one of our rich Filipino uncle's maids. For her, this was an opportunity to distinguish us from the masses of poor Filipinos you saw in California, if you noticed Filipinos at all. Kara had always been sensitive to what most people thought of Filipinos, and hated being lumped together with mail-order brides and prostitutes and farm laborers and domestic help, who were thought of as so lowly that they were routinely beaten by their Saudi Arabian and Singaporean masters, or so we heard on television. Her friends related the condescending sneer a new Hong Kong girl made at school when she found out Kara was a Filipina ("Oh, yes, we get a lot of cheap Filipino laborers in Hong Kong because local workers are so expensive," she scoffed), and Kara always avoided the half-Filipino girl whose father had been a soldier based in Subic Bay and reputedly married her bargirl mother. Kara told our classmates that it was wrong for anyone to lump all Filipinos together. She always pointed to the fact that our great great granduncle was a famous poet and martyr, who had also been a surgeon in Europe, and that her round eyes came from Spanish blood. At other times she lied and told people we were actually of Chinese ancestry, descended from Sino traders of high intelligence and an ancient written culture who settled in the Visayan Islands south of Luzon.

· · ·

We drove to the airport together and stood behind the rope watching the passengers swarm out of customs, as Matt held up a cardboard sign with our mother's family name—"Laurel"—written in red felt-tip letters. We scoured all the women's faces, to see if they were looking for us, for any eyes that found our sign and showed recognition. Time and again people looked it over, but kept going. Finally, a fat, pleasant-faced woman saw the sign and her eyes brightened, still a bit apprehensive, and she smiled as she waddled over toward us.

"That must be her," Matt said.

Our mother eagerly looked for her. Suddenly Mother's expression changed. "Oh, I can't believe it."

"What?" Kara said.

Mother bit her lip, looking aside. "I can't believe my brother did this to us."

"What, Mom—would you please tell us what you're talking about?"

And then we noticed the girl behind the maid. She shyly followed her mother with her eyes focused on the floor. She wore a knee-length dress that hugged her slender figure, showing an outline of her hipbones, and wore cranberry lipstick.

Kara tensed and turned to our mother: "Who's that, Mom?"

Mother did not answer her, but simply shook her head.

What our mother would not tell us, but which we discovered later—through the gossip network of cousins—was that this woman had been the mistress of Mother's deceased uncle—Lolo Bong—and that the girl was their fifteen-year-old illegitimate daughter. On the drive home, our parents looked grim and silent. Our father must have felt betrayed and taken advantage of. Our mother must have sensed this; she was also seething at her brother.

Apparently my uncle had decided on his own that we would have to take care of this mistress and her illegitimate daughter, because of irresponsible Lolo Bong's sins. But Father was an

American, already providing for our widowed maternal grand-mother who lived in our house. This mistress was something of a third wife, complete with a household and children, but she had inherited nothing because Bong's first wife (though long sepa-rated) was the only one recognized by the church.

Sepa kept smiling at us, nervously, glancing at our parents in the front seats. The daughter, Teresa, was frail and pretty and sat squashed against the door, her thin shoulders hunched together, her cheap handbag hugged protectively on her lap. She stared out the window. As much as I was drawn to her enormous black eyes, I could barely look at her—I was so afraid—but my brother could not help regarding her. I had seen that look on Matt before—whenever he saw something he wanted to protect: a wounded animal, a new scrawny kid at school, me.

That night our new maid slept on the garage bed, the daugh-ter on the floor, their twine-wrapped boxes pushed against the wall. I went to the kitchen, pretending to get milk, and listened to their muffled Tagalog whispers through the door. I could no longer understand the language, but their tones were hushed and anxious. I took it the daughter was unhappy and the mother only wanted her to quiet down.

II

At breakfast, as the mother served us eggs, we sat restlessly and quietly—unaccustomed to all this sitting.

The daughter was sitting outside, grim as she poked at her own sorry breakfast of leftover, coagulated eggs; her mother had given her the ones with broken yokes and saved the whole ones for us.

Matt kept going up to the window. He would watch her, shake his head, and return to our table. He would not speak when Mother or Father tried to engage him in conversation. Each time he went to the window, it made all of us nervous, and even the girl's mother paced anxiously about the room whenever he showed concern.

Though he was already nearsighted from reading too much and looked bookish in his wire-rimmed glasses, my brother was also large, a Hapkido black belt and member of the varsity soccer team. When I first entered Westwind High School, a new boy in my class taunted me about my yellow backpack (my mother had bought it for me, and refused to spend the money on a new one in a different color) and took my lunch money. Matt heard about this, enraged, and sought out the bully and came upon him in a nearby alleyway after school, with a couple of friends from the soccer team. They beat the boy to the asphalt, kicked his ribs in, and dislocated the boy's shoulder and then retrieved my lunch money from his pocket.

When Matt came home with a bruised face, suspended from class, our mother was angry with him. He had gotten into a number of fights in elementary school, and had had problems with his grades; he'd seemed to be moving in a bad direction then, but she had been strict, lecturing him and setting up rules and chores and bringing him to a streetwise Paulist priest who tutored him in moral philosophy and made him read the biographies of good men. She hired tutors and got him to calm down and even gain entrance into a private school fashionable with the children of movie industry people, Westwind for the Arts and Sciences. So she'd been disappointed, worried he would turn bad again, though when I told her why Matt had beaten up that boy she looked conflicted and even, if reluctantly, proud. It was easy for her to be proud of my brother, and I knew he was her favorite.

While our mother showed our new maid her duties around the house, the daughter remained outside, reading a book in English; she seemed to be more educated than the mother, who could only speak Tagalog. The girl sat there all afternoon. Kara and I would go outside and sit on chairs across the lawn, reading our own books, but only Matt went up to her. He offered her iced tea and cookies, and though she at first declined, on his third try she accepted one cookie—embarrassed—then bowed her head and took a bite.

He returned to us.

"Why's she just sitting around out there?" Kara said, looking bothered.

"I think she doesn't know what else to do."

"She could help her mother."

"I don't think so."

"Why not?"

"That's not her job," he said, and his eyes steadied on our sister. "We're not paying them two salaries, Kara."

She blushed and glanced down, then looked up at him again. "So am I supposed to entertain her, or what?"

"That would be up to you."

My sister peered sheepishly over at the girl. Teresa was probably older than Kara by a year, but seemed both shyer and yet mysteriously far older. She wore a thin dress that accentuated her figure and pantyhose that only came up to her calves, like socks. Her very manner, even simply the composed way she held herself, seemed more feminine than that of Kara's friends, who all wore jeans and oversized sweaters. "My friends wouldn't have anything in common with her."

Matt noticed that Kara was afraid to meet his glance and warmth returned to his face. "She just dresses differently, Kara. You could make her fashionable. Show her the local ways, since you're so good at that."

Kara's face softened. "She is pretty. Maybe Mom will take us shopping on the Promenade."

He nodded.

We did not intrude on the girl's side of the yard, but Matt assembled some of his novels he thought she might like to read, and finally chose a book by Isaac Bashevis Singer because the man wrote about immigrants and as Teresa was an immigrant he thought she might be able to relate to it. I told Matt I did not see why she would care about Jews in 1950s New York, but he did not listen to me. Lately, ever since transferring to Westwind and finding Jewish friends there, he had discarded his surfboards and bleached hair and now went to synagogue with them and always spoke about moving to New York. As I myself had followed his lead and bleached my hair and spent my savings on a surfboard, I now felt foolish and was not completely happy about this change. When he told Mother that he wanted to convert to Judaism, she accused him of merely wanting a bar mitzvah with a fancy reception and expensive presents. He persisted, and she asked him what was wrong with him. He asked what was wrong with being Jewish. She said nothing but so long as you live in my house and until you are eighteen you are going to mass every week. He said that you could not force someone to be Catholic if they did not believe in it, and she said oh yes you could. He said even the priests at St. Martin's wouldn't have confirmed him if he had told them he did not want it, and he had only lied to them about believing in Jesus to get confirmed and therefore to please Mother, and now he wished he hadn't. In the end she let him go to synagogue on Saturdays with his girlfriend, Brenda, and her family, so long as he also went to Sunday mass with us. The Jewish girlfriend's father, Stan Goldman, would come to the house to pick him up, and he seemed to believe Matt's interest in temple was bizarre. He made jokes about Filipino Jews to my mother, who attempted to laugh. Stan Goldman kept asking if all this was OK with our mother, and she said yes. But Matt still had to go to mass with us and he would sit erectly in a rear pew with a pained look on his face.

He now offered the Jewish book to Teresa after dinner. She looked at him curiously but thanked him.

"You can read it here in the family room with us," he said. "I mean, if you want to."

"OK," she said shyly, lowering her head.

Matt and I stayed in the same room, doing our homework, though I kept on the farthest chair from her. She crossed her legs and smoothed her skirt over her pretty knees, and fingered her long hair over one shoulder, then concentrated on the page. Mother kept coming down to the kitchen and making loud irritated noises with glasses and food in the fridge.

At ten o'clock the girl stood and hesitated, as if unsure whether she should address us, and said she was going to sleep. Matt stood. He said he would be interested in hearing what she thought of the book he had loaned her when she finished, and she agreed. After she left the room my brother paced around a while and went upstairs.

When I later came up to the landing, muffled voices reverberated from my parents' room, and I listened for a long time to their concerned voices before I went to bed.

The next morning we left for school, but of course the girl did not come with us; no one had had time to register her for classes.

Over the next few days her mother turned out to be a better maid than my mother had expected. Sepa woke early, before five, to begin cleaning the house. At first she made breakfast ahead of time and put it in the oven to keep warm while she did other chores, then took the warm plates out for us; we had to peel the damp cellophane off the food. The eggs were dried and oily and the yokes solid and sometimes broken on the crispy rice. I frowned and Kara complained to Mother. But Sepa soon figured out how to prepare the food the way we liked it. She made Father oatmeal with walnuts and brown sugar, rice and *isda* with tamarind for our mother. And we found that Sepa often fetched us Cokes and snacks without our even asking—even us kids—and she did all this with a cheerful smile. She particularly liked to pamper Father, and treated him like the man of the castle, bringing his paper to him on the couch along with a bourbon and ginger ale. It was hard to keep in mind that she'd been a relative's mistress, because she seemed so devoid of resentment, and in fact appeared grateful for her place in our house.

Yet though the daughter did not openly complain, and kept to her corner with her books, she would glance at her mother and disgust came over her face. She never spoke to my mother. On several occasions when my mother criticized Sepa for some mistake, or sighed impatiently while explaining some chore, I noticed Teresa angrily walk away. One time she slammed a door. Sepa followed Teresa and told her to be more polite, but Teresa merely looked at her mother condescendingly, then wordlessly went to her reading spot in our yard.

Her face showed none of this disgust, however, when my brother returned from soccer practice and found her outside; she liked to sit on a lawn chair beneath the sycamore tree, sunlight dappling over her calves and feet. She kept her face in the shade as she read, however, no doubt so her skin would not get darker. She was pale and tall for a Filipina—paler even than my own mother, who had much Spanish blood—and Matt would stand a few feet from her, his hands in his pockets as he tried to make conversation.

Something about his posture bothered me. My brother had always been a giant to me, but before her his face seemed almost vulnerable. That his expression would be this way was odd, because around him she always smiled shyly. Mother sometimes watched them from the back window, her expression dark and mysterious.

From his conversations with Teresa, Matt pieced together her story, that she grew up on the farm in a house her father had built for her mother, and he would visit every month from his main home in San Pablo. Teresa liked living near her mother's relatives and had many friends and cousins to play with, but her father's relatives would not speak to her or Sepa, for fear of angering his Catholic wife, and as Teresa grew older it began to bother her. Her father paid for her to go to private boarding school, against his estranged first wife's wishes, and she was more educated (and harder working) than her legitimate cousins, but still shunned.

Her father told her he would send her to private college in Manila, but after he died all the estate went to his first wife, though they had long ago separated, and the woman refused to pay for Teresa's education. Betino had taken pity on them, and had them sent over to us.

One day Matt arranged for Teresa to visit his Westwind classes with him. Mother was annoyed, but he told her his teacher had suggested it as a chance for the other students to learn something about another country from a "guest." Mother, who had been brought up to worship schoolteachers, allowed it.

Teresa looked frightened that morning as she and Matt drove off, but when they returned she wore a happy expression. Apparently she had been a hit with Matt's friends at Westwind. At first Teresa had been shocked to learn that nobody knew that the Philippines had been a U.S. colony, though they all knew India had once belonged to Britain. She could not believe it. She had assumed that a special, benevolent relationship existed between the Filipinos and their former colonizers ("Our older brothers," her titos had called the Americans they fought with against the Japanese). She felt like an idiot. There was actually this whole huge country over there which the Americans had fashioned after themselves, where everybody assumed Americans still thought about them. However, Matt's history teacher saw that she looked hurt and he showed an interest in what she had to tell the class, and even the headmaster met her and acknowledged it was strange that the countries' common history was not in his American history course material, and he promised to add it. He later took Matt aside and asked him if Teresa was interested in applying to enter, perhaps on a scholarship, and that even midyear something might be able to be arranged.

At night, as we lay in our beds trying to fall asleep, Matt would talk about her, even telling me about his intention of bringing her to synagogue. Lately he had been showing her Los Angeles, driving her to all the same places he used to bring me with his friends, excursions to Venice and Hollywood pool houses and Mar Vista parties that had made me feel older and important. He told me, "Ben, she's a lot smarter than you'd think."

"I wouldn't know," I said. "She's so quiet."

"Her English is damn good."

"How? Her mother sure doesn't speak it right."

He paused, and even in the darkness I could feel his irritation. Our wall vibrated from Father's noisy bedroom television.

"Well, the girl got sent to a convent school," he said briskly. "Her teachers don't let them speak Tagalog there or teach them anything about their own country. She actually knows more about American history than we do."

You should speak for yourself, I thought, but said, "Why would she want to know about that?"

"It has nothing to do with what they want to know, Ben," he said in a newly condescending manner.

I rolled over on my side with my eyes open and did not say anything; his indignant breathing slowed and deepened and he drifted off to sleep.

One evening a few weeks after her arrival, I saw them in the living room kissing on the couch. I had come down from our bedroom for a late-night glass of water, and had heard the low sounds of the television and seen its flickering light coming through the doorless opening to the dining room. I quietly walked into the dark dining room, where I could see them without easily being seen. He had his hands in her hair, and beneath a few pillows that attempted to cover their lower bodies he appeared to be rubbing his crotch against her. The motions appeared rough and ugly. I had never necked with a girl before, nor had I seen my brother doing this, and it surprised me how he rubbed against her like a dog. It bothered me, but I watched for a while before leaving.

The next morning I was working on a model rocket alone at

the outdoor table when she sat down near me with a glass of water, a slice of lemon bobbing amid glistening cubes of ice.

"Do you mind if I sit here, Ben?" she said, although she was already seated.

"No."

"Why don't you look at me? You don't need to be afraid. I don't bite."

I blushed and felt angry with her for embarrassing me. But she was smiling at me, like a nice older sister, which made me confused about how to feel about her. She had never, after all, been mean to me personally.

"I know you don't bite."

"Good." She tossed her hair over her shoulder, then fingered it over an ear. "You know, your brother loves you very much."

I shrugged. This was not the sort of comment I answered to.

She laughed, and then asked, "Ben, what is it like to go to your school?"

"It pretty much sucks."

"Don't worry, soon you will make friends. Just give it time, and give people a chance," she said, thus betraying the fact that my brother had told her I was lonely there, something he should not have done.

"I have friends there," I said.

"Yes, of course you do," she said and disappeared into her thoughts, looking over the canyon at the purple woods on the opposite wall, and said, "I think I would like to go there someday."

Over the next several weeks, Matt made certain he was around for her to talk to him about her native country. They took walks; they went to Westwood to watch films and amble among the teenaged crowds; he showed her the tourist attractions where our mother usually brought visiting relatives: Disneyland, Universal Studios, Knottsberry Farm. At night he informed me of the fantastic things Teresa told him. About dark river-caves you could boat into, filled with blind sparrows that found their way around by chirping, the ceilings lined by red-eyed sleeping bats. About enchanted volcanoes whose springs had procured visions of the Virgin Mary and whose waters cured deformity and disease. About slave ships that had crashed in the nineteenth century and shipwrecked people whose descendants live on some island where they practice a strange mix of voodoo and Catholicism and people take boats there from all over the Philippines to obtain cures for their loved ones and curses for their enemies. About the farm she grew up on, Tagkawayan, a vast coconut and rice plantation that had been in our family for generations, but which Matt, Kara, and I had never seen; Teresa said its beaches had azure water so clear you could see sunny coral reefs out in the bay. Hundreds of poor people lived on the land.

I had my own enchanting memories. I recalled the sweet dry breezes that blew through the sugarcane stalks on our grandfather's Visayan island. I remembered the magical fiestas, so full of life and family laughing, of dancing for adults who threw coins at our feet, of playing with our cousins at Chu Checerida's beach house, walking over coral reefs in search of starfish and octopus, of learning to climb coconut trees with the houseboys. I recollected a three-month return visit to our cousins' school and what a curious, big deal their friends made of us for being Americans. But in recent years, ever since my brother had entered puberty and began trying to fit in at junior high school, we had stopped speaking about returning, and the country seemed to have left our minds.

I had wondered if our mother's disparaging comments about the country ("it's hot, corrupt, and there's a huge difference between the rich and poor") had poisoned my brother's memories. But now I asked myself why if Teresa loved it so much there, she and Sepa wanted to live in the U.S., and I suspected she was telling Matt what he wanted to hear. I found his new interest mysterious and disconcerting.

. . .

At breakfast one morning as Father ate the oatmeal Sepa had made for him, and the rest of us enjoyed poached eggs brushed with hollandaise sauce, Matt turned to Mother, and said, "So I didn't realize that the farm in your family was so huge."

"What farm?"

"The hacienda. Tagkawayan."

She waved her hand dismissively. "It's nothing. It has no electricity or running water."

"But hundreds of people live on it—on your farm."

"Their grandparents worked for my grandfather, but coconut prices dropped during the '60s and communists over-ran it. It's worthless now."

"All those people, though. It sounds like something out of feudal Europe. Like our relatives are some sort of aristocracy over there."

Mother laughed. "We are talking about the Philippines, Matt—that's hardly like owning a piece of Tuscany or southern France."

Matt reddened. "You know, that sounds somewhat like an imperialistic value judgment," he said. "To say that a piece of Europe is more important than a piece of the Philippines. Actually, Teresa says the farm is beautiful, that it has mountains and valleys and beaches as blue and as clear as Hawaii."

"Well, if she wants to live where there's no jobs or electricity or running water, where there's no hospitals so that if you get sick you die—well, then she can go back. Fine."

Mother took a bite of food, conscious of our quieted table.

"I want to visit," he announced.

"Matt, you wouldn't like the insects, and you're too fussy about your food. You'd be afraid of germs, just like your father. Besides, it's dangerous. The communist guerrillas would kidnap you."

"People live there and don't get kidnapped."

"They aren't Americans like you."

"Excuse me, but I'm not American."

"You could have fooled me."

He turned a deep, indignant red. "Try telling that to all the white kids who teased me about being an Asian in elementary school."

"Well, the Marxist guerrillas would certainly think you were American. As long as you look pale enough to have a big bank account." Mother alone laughed. The rest of us quietly regarded our plates.

"I'm going anyway. And you can't stop me, because I'm *right* about this," he said, his jaw trembling, then put down his fork and crossed his arms and looked aside, out the window, at the vines which grew up the backyard fence like snakes and glittered in the late afternoon sunshine.

Mother observed him across the table. He stood up without finishing the *babingka* dessert she had made for him, and he left the room.

A few mornings later, while Matt was at Saturday soccer practice, my mother asked me to help Teresa bring her bags to the car.

"Why?" I said.

Mother avoided my eyes. "She'll be moving to my cousin Cherry's place in Torrance."

"But what for?"

"There's not enough room in our house."

"Is Sepa going too?"

"No."

"I don't get it."

"They'll spend their weekends together."

"Does Matt know about this?"

"Look. This isn't up to your brother," my mother said crisply. "Now can you please help with the bags?"

The girl was in the living room beside the boxes she had packed, and she stood by the bar, her arms crossed, as I hesitated in the doorway. Behind her in my father's bar the rear wall was a smoky mirror in which I could see her reflection. She looked stylish—like an advertisement—and deeper in the mirror there stood my reflection in the doorway, small, brown, and ugly: for all my Americanness, compared to her pale Spanish features I looked like an insignificant little Malay.

"I'm supposed to get your bags," I said.

She turned to me. "What?"

"My mother wants me to help get your bags to the car."

"Then why are you all the way over there in the doorway?"

I tried to hide my blush and crossed the room and picked up a box. It was not too heavy for her to handle herself, but she made no move to help. She continued to watch as I passed her like some houseboy, and then I felt her hand touch my shoulder—only a tap, but enough to stop me and cause my blood to swell in my throat.

"What?" I said in the irritated voice I often used when confronted with pretty females.

"You will miss having me around?" she said, coming closer and touching my bicep in a feminine manner which happened to me so rarely that it roused a confusing heat. I could not tell if she was mocking me. Her mysterious eyes seemed sad, but complicated and full of yearning.

"Yeah, sure," I said uncertainly.

Yet before I could say anything more, we heard my mother jiggling her keys in the other room, and my face must have shown my worry, because Teresa's expression grew cold and irritated with me again. I tried to say something, but she brushed past me and walked into the entryway.

In the rearview mirror, I spied Teresa in the backseat. She watched the green streets of Brentwood disperse, as we drove south toward Torrance, into a bare sprawl of glaring white sidewalks and identical houses. Physically even this was nicer than Manila or San Pablo, but there were no pedestrians, no lively crowds, no colorful *Jeepney* taxis, no vendor markets, no boys wandering through traffic trying to sell Marlboros and newspapers, no *tsismis* laughter, no azure skies, no coconut palms and sandy beaches and cheerful yellow Jolibees, only cars and a few Mexicans and deflated-looking teenagers at the dilapidated bus-stop benches.

I was surprised at how small the apartment was. It had avocado shag carpeting and smelled of kitchen grease from the in-room kitchenette, and I could hear the neighbor's television through the thin walls. Mother avoided Cherry's eyes as her cousin greeted first us, then Teresa, and showed us around. The apartment had only one bedroom and Teresa would be sleeping on the couch. Mother's cousin offered us lunch and we ate pork *adobo* and *lumpia* at a small table in the living room and the apartment windows steamed from her cooking.

Teresa did not look at us when we departed.

On the ride home Mother was quiet. The car felt empty. As we entered Brentwood's familiar lush streets, she pulled over to the curb and sighed. "That was terrible," she said.

III

Matt came home from Saturday soccer practice with an eager smile and a large book in hand. He had checked it out from the school library for Teresa, a bulky tome on postwar Jewish immigrants in the Bronx. He looked out at the yard, but she wasn't there, as she normally was before dinner. He sat and began peeling an orange. I avoided his eyes.

"You want some of my orange, Junior?"

"No thanks," I said.

Later, when Teresa was not eating dinner with her mother in the kitchen, our parents finally told him that she was gone.

"What?" Matt said. He held his fork in the air. "Gone—where?"

"To live with your mother's cousin in Torrance," Father said, in a tone protective of our mother.

"Why'd she go there?"

"There's not enough room in this house for all of us."

"But shouldn't she stay here together with Sepa? Sepa *is* her mother." He stared at our mother, and she softly fingered her plate's azure and gold leaf edges.

"Look," Father said. "We asked Betino for a housekeeper. We didn't know she was a mistress or a concubine or whatever you want to call what she did. We didn't know she had a teenage daughter coming. That wasn't part of the bargain. That wasn't reasonable, and it wasn't asked of us. But Teresa will be going to school here, getting an American education."

"An American education. A lot of good that does most Americans."

Father frowned. "Seriously, it'll be a great advantage to her."

He tried to adopt a stern and patriarchal tone, one which did not suit him, and Matt ignored it and turned to our mother. He seemed to stare down at the top of her head as she fingered the wine glass before her. "Did she want to leave us, Mom?"

She continued looking at her glass. "I will not allow her to get back at me by hurting you."

"Jesus, Mom, are you *kidding* me?"

"I will not have that teenage girl in this house disrupting my family," she said in a cold voice I had not heard from her before. Her tone made my bones contract like a house in winter.

"Jesus, I can't believe you could be so retarded in your thinking," he said.

Our father scolded my brother, but Matt ignored him.

"And I asked you a question, Mom. Did she want to leave us?"

Mother crossed her arms and looked aside, refusing to answer him.

"Excuse me, but can you please answer me, Mom? Hello? If you're going to try to self-righteously dictate rules to me and then behave in a certain way, then I think I deserve an answer."

He left the room then, and we heard him climb the stairs,

slamming shut his bedroom door. He began playing his saxophone, something he knew our parents hated the sound of, and we sat there listening to the grating noise that came muted through the ceiling and vibrated the glass chandelier—and we spoke no more words.

Sepa came in to clear the dishes. My father and I avoided her eyes, but when she asked me if I was finished with my Coke, I could not avoid meeting them. They were huge and wet looking and childlike and I could see how she might have once been pretty and attractive to my mother's uncle. If she was sad she didn't show it. She smiled at me in her usual cheerful manner, and then at my mother with no sign of resentment.

Later, I noticed Sepa bending over plates she was drying, and I thought I saw a glimmer of hurt in her eyes, though of course this could be my faulty memory.

That night, when I came into our room, Matt was on his bed. It was dark and he had the window open—which meant he had been smoking, something I hated him doing because I did not like to lie to our parents about it, or to get into trouble for keeping quiet.

We lay silently. He did not speak, though he often did on those nights. The open window let in the warm night air, dusty with a chaparral scent that emanated from the Santa Monica canyons below us. A warm wind blew and dry branches clattered gently in the treetops only fifteen feet away.

"You didn't need to be so mean to Mom," I said.

His bed squeaked as he turned to me. "What?" he said, and there was surprise in his voice at hearing my anger.

"It wasn't her fault."

"Junior, what are you so upset about?" he said, sounding bewildered and somewhat amused as he came over and tried to place a hand on my shoulder. I shrugged it off. "Don't touch me."

He recoiled, holding his hands up as if he had touched a hot stove, then regarded me for a long moment. "Junior, you don't know anything, do you?" he said.

"You're the mean person. You made Mom feel bad."

He sat back on his bed and sighed in the dark. "So, does this mean you're not going to hang out with me and ask my advice on things anymore?" He sounded more resigned now than angry, and waited for an answer. But I gave none.

"She's the daughter of Mom's uncle's mistress," he finally said.

"So? That doesn't mean Mom should have to take care of them."

"You know, he could very well have forced himself on Sepa. He might have raped her, Ben."

"That's still not Mom's fault."

"Don't you get who that girl is?"

I hesitated.

"It should be obvious, Ben."

Wind gusted. Somewhere down the street an empty rubber trash can fell over and rolled about on the gravelly asphalt.

"She's Mom's first cousin."

He leaned back against his headboard again, and though it was dark, I could see by the moonlight that he was waiting for a response but, getting none, shook his head and looked outside at the moonlit clouds that crept over the eastern horizon.

For some reason those last words failed to make much of an impact on me that night, though I remember them well now. Over the following days Matt refused to speak to our parents, except in critical tones—finding fault with Father's country club and career as an attorney, accusing our mother of vanity in the obsessiveness with which she applied her makeup and the fastidiousness by which she avoided the sunlight so as to keep her skin from getting dark. He called her colonialized, a snob, ignorant. She never berated him back, only defended herself meekly, but when he was out at night, my father still at work, I found her crying in the dark living room, lights off. My brother continued to drive to Torrance to see the daughter. He met her after she got out of classes, because Cherry felt uncomfortable letting them see each other knowing how our mother felt about this. But Mother knew what he was up to, and they argued over it loudly enough for me to hear them through the walls. One time I was in the family room as Sepa was ironing clothes and watching TV with me, when we could hear Matt shouting at Mother about what a terrible person Mother was. Sepa did not meet my eyes.

Nothing my mother said, no matter how angry or heartfelt or humiliated or tearful or pleading, stopped him from going down to Torrance. I decided it was up to me to protect her.

On Monday, a day Matt and I usually rode our bikes to Tae Kwon Do together, I purposely left before he returned home from soccer practice. No doubt he must have waited around for me, because he came into the dojo late, having to bow before the instructor and ask humbly for permission to enter the class. His forehead touched the sweaty blue mat. Then he raised his face. With the instructor watching, he did not dare catch my eye in the workout mirror. Master Lee Cho III grunted at him, then made him do fifty push-ups in front of everyone, causing my brother's face to go red. Our master then let Matt find his humiliating place at the rear of the studio with the white belts who were several ranks below him.

During the sparring sessions, I avoided being paired up with my brother, and would not meet his glance.

Afterward I hurried to my bicycle, but my fingers had trouble unlocking the rusty chain that ran through the wheel spokes. Matt caught up with me.

"Why aren't you looking at me, Junior?" he said, stopping several yards away.

"I'm busy unlocking the chain."

My fingers jittered on the links as I pulled them through the spokes. He glanced aside, at the departing cars and the gregarious students so happy to be in their street clothes again, then turned back to me. "I missed you earlier."

"I'd left already."

"I noticed that."

I did not say anything more, and he added, "Look. I'll buy you a sundae. My treat."

"You know, she was talking about you the other day."

A change came over my brother's face and he seemed suddenly aware of the other students around us, in earshot, walking to their cars.

"Who?"

"Teresa."

"What did she say?"

"She was laughing at you. She said you had a crush on her, but she didn't like the way you walk all awkwardly and nervous, and that she thought you were creepy the way you always looked at her with big puppy-dog eyes. But she put up with you because she felt sorry for you and had nothing better to do. She said she couldn't understand why you kept on giving her books written by Jews, and she could tell your Jewish high school friends laughed at you behind your back for going to synagogue."

I gripped my handlebars, intending to pedal off immediately, but my shoe slipped off the pedal onto the sidewalk, the aluminum teeth cutting into my ankle. Recovering, I could not avoid my brother's eyes: his face was crumpled with hurt. I finally managed to bike away, cutting tire marks in the yellow pollen, the sun warm on my face as it poked through the overhead branches and flickered, stinging my eyes.

Later I would, of course, spar with him again. And we would have conversations in the dark when we should have been sleeping. But they were never the same as they had been—whether this was mostly due to him or me, I do not know—and he soon left for college. Perhaps this is the nature of things between siblings as they get older, and what happened with Sepa and her daughter was only incidental. But after he was gone I could not help thinking about how I had acted and the way he looked at me, and how all this happened so soon before he left for Vassar, without proper time to make amends. We live in separate cities now and though for a time we did not speak much to each other, we now do annual ski trips with our families. It is often a merry occasion, and our children play well together. But we never talk about Sepa and her daughter.

IV

She actually did go to high school in Torrance, where she received an American education. She did not do well in my mother's cousin's home, that small one bedroom apartment in a cheap complex with fake grass in the courtyard. I heard about her "wildness," the drinking, the drugs, the pregnancy, her many boyfriends, and how she dropped out of school. The times she came to pick Sepa up she sat in the running car, honking but refusing to come inside. Her mother would hurry out, signaling for her to be quiet, and the daughter seemed to have disgust on her face as she stared forward and as she drove them away. A year after her pregnancy she moved to San Francisco with some boyfriend, and her mother—whom we had grown to love having around—sadly left us (she cried as she hugged each one of us, and especially Matt), to live closer to her granddaughter.

For several years Mother tried to convince Sepa to return, and Sepa, who had always fondly pampered my father, would think about it but finally say she could not leave the city her daughter and grandchild lived in. We received a few postcards from the area—Daly City, Milapitas, Hercules, Vallejo—then they tapered off. Somehow Sepa and her daughter seemed to have vanished into the vast diaspora of Filipinos who lived up there but whom, for some reason, nobody ever seemed to notice. We heard fragments of biography about them, some contradictory, that Sepa had taken up with a widower boxer she'd nursed while working in a hospital, that Teresa had taken up with another guy—a black man—but none of these were substantiated and I do not know where they live or what became of them.

I began this story, about three biracial siblings and their encounter with their Filipino mother's imported maid (and her illegitimate daughter), approximately ten years ago.

I probably should not admit this, but the rough seed of the idea for this story came from the observation of real-life events in my extended family. I was raised by strict Filipino Catholics, who fortunately did not let their religious pieties interfere with a deep love of gossip, even when that gossip involved the revelation of family scandal. In fact, the women seemed the most excited when they were talking about the beautiful illegitimate daughters of my grandmother's brothers and their sometimes tragic, sometimes glamorous adult lives.

The mother in my story was the original point-of-view character. However, her conflict was essentially one between her sense of shame with her American husband at having a maid who was an uncle's concubine, and her desire to have a Filipino maid. It was a conflict that seemed understandable enough to a middle- or upper-class Filipino, but less than sympathetic to an American reader, and I stuck the story in a drawer for a number of years.

I went to grad school, wrote a novel, had two children, and looked at the story again. I realized right off that the material—with its cross-cultural conflicts and moral complexities—was better told from one of the biracial children's vantage points. It wrote itself rather quickly this time, though I probably spent another year or two polishing it.

Mary Yukari Waters

Mary Yukari Waters' fiction has appeared in various venues: *Best American Short Stories 2002, 2003,* and *2004; The O. Henry Prize Stories; The Pushcart Book of Short Stories: The Best Short Stories from a Quarter-Century of the Pushcart Prize; Zoetrope Anthology 2;* and *NPR's Selected Shorts.* She is the recipient of a grant from the National Endowment for the Arts. Her debut collection, *The Laws of Evening,* was a Barnes & Noble Discover Great New Writers selection, a Booksense 76 selection, and a Kiriyama Prize Notable Book. *The Laws of Evening* was also selected as one of the Best Books of 2003 by *Newsday* and the *San Francisco Chronicle.*

Caste System

I t started innocuously enough, after Sarah Rexford had been in Japan for several days. By this time, she had long since unpacked and eaten her fill of *hiramasa* sushi and roadstand octopus balls, available only in late autumn. Accompanied by her grandmother—the two were inseparable—she had already visited her mother's grave and ridden the bus over to Ikebari Temple to give thanks for her safe flight. Only after the initial flurry had passed, leaving them in the quiet lull of daily life, did her grandmother remember to mention that Aunt Kimiko's choir was performing next week at Kyoto Civic Auditorium.

Grandma's forgetfulness was understandable. In her eyes, her eldest granddaughter took precedence over anyone else in the family. Sarah knew, deep down, that this was by default; her late mother had been Grandma's favorite child. The reasons for this favoritism had been complex, as such reasons always are. It boiled down to a series of lucky coincidences: the right father (her grandmother had married her first husband for love, her second husband for financial security), the level of happiness associated with each child's birth (Sarah's mother had been born in the prosperous days before the war, Uncle Masahiro shortly before the surrender, and Aunt Kimiko during the American occupation). The children's positions were further sealed by the compatibility between their mother's personality and their own—which were mostly inherited, but also surely influenced by the circumstances of their birth. At any rate, when Sarah's mother died seven years ago, the full force of Grandma's passions had shifted to the child she left behind. And after some initial guilt, Sarah had accepted this as her due. What did it matter in the end, whether love was earned or inherited?

"Aunt Kimiko's in a choir?" Sarah said. "You mean the PTA choir?"

"PTA? What are you talking . . . aaa, I see. No, she stopped that years ago, when your cousins finished elementary school." Her grandmother looked amused at Sarah's confused expression. "No wonder we're at cross-purposes all the time. Your information's all outdated."

This was true. Sarah Rexford had grown up here in Kyoto, but America had been home for most of her twenty-six years. She was a mixed child—or as they said in Japan, a "half"—and her features leaned heavily toward the Caucasian: gray eyes, straight nose, and dark hair with brown highlights instead of blue. Every other year, she took two weeks off from her office job and flew out to stay with her grandmother. But she was never fully inside the family loop. By the time she arrived, most of what had happened during the two years of her absence—barring the exceptional—had already drained from everyday conversation. So there were lapses, like now for instance. This was the first year Sarah had visited during concert season.

"Your aunt's in a *real* choir now," Grandma said. She had turned away to rummage through a drawer filled with bills and receipts; now she turned back around, triumphantly holding up an envelope. "Look! Complimentary tickets."

Sarah remembered the source of her "outdated information": a conversation she had once heard as a young girl. Back then, her mother was still alive. She and Sarah used to fly out together during summer vacations.

The three of them—Grandma, Mama, and Sarah—had been sitting out in the garden one muggy afternoon, fanning their moist faces with round paper uchiwas as cicadas droned *meeeee* in the pine branches overhead. Hearing the rapid *k'sha k'sha* of crunching gravel, they turned their heads to see Aunt Kimiko hurrying past along the alley, her slender form flashing in and out of view through slats in the bamboo fence.

"A! Late for the bus again," Grandma said. "Choir day."

"Choir? Really!" The corners of Mama's mouth twitched with a repressed smile. "Well, well—good for *her*!"

"It's with some other PTA mothers," Grandma said. "They've formed some kind of a group." She leaned over and twisted off a dead leaf from a nearby fuchsia bush, placing it carefully in the center of her lap to throw away later. "By the way, I'm thinking about making gyoza for dinner. Or do you think it's too hot for that?"

Sarah, who was eleven at the time, had asked whether Aunt Kimiko was a good singer.

Her grandmother had considered this for a moment, gazing vaguely at a corner of the garden. "I suppose so," she had finally said, "but nothing outstanding, I think. It was always your mother they picked for the solos in school."

Sarah now examined the contents of the envelope. The concert tickets, glossy and professional looking, had an unexpectedly high admission price. The title was printed in raised Chinese characters: "Songs That Got Us Through: A Wartime Retrospective."

"Have I even heard her sing?" she said. But her grandmother had gone to another room.

Sarah couldn't remember if she had always felt guilty about her aunt, or if this was an adult development in the wake of her mother's death. The perspective of time was unreliable—old memories had a sneaky way of shifting shape and focus—but she was inclined to believe the guilt had always been there, like one of those elusive baseline flavors in cooking: fish stock, or MSG. Part of her uncertainty lay in the fact that her aunt had never been the type to make a strong impression on people's minds.

Aunt Kimiko's family lived at the other end of the lane. If Sarah looked out from her grandmother's parlor window, from a slightly stooped position, it was possible to peer under the eaves, over the wooden garden fence and the top of the miniature yuzu tree, and glimpse their second-story windows. Granny Sono was usually out on the balcony in the mornings, pinning up socks and handkerchiefs to dry. Granny Sono was Aunt Kimiko's mother-in-law, and upstairs was her chosen domain.

As a child, Sarah had spent many hours playing in that house with her cousins. Aunt Kimiko inhabited the lower floor which, unlike the sunlit rooms above, was filled with restful, leaf-filtered light. The formal dining room was rarely used, so the children gravitated toward the informal eating area that directly adjoined the kitchen. Under the large low table, stacked in tin boxes, were snacks: rice crackers, wasabi-coated soybeans, curry-flavored puffs.

In the pale green light, Aunt Kimiko glided in and out of the kitchen bearing delicate glass dishes of flan pudding, or crustless sandwich triangles, or frilled drumsticks adorned with parsley sprigs. "Hai, this is to wipe your fingers," she said, handing them dampened towels folded into neat squares. Her conversation was as soft and serene as the light. "Do you like juice?" she would ask gently, as if Sarah were still six years old instead of eleven, or thirteen, or sixteen. Referring to one of her children, she would remark, "Yashiko's favorite spoons have Hello Kitty on them. Don't they, Yashiko?"

Sarah figured her aunt just wasn't used to children from America. This made her anxious, for she was particularly sensitive about not belonging. She still remembered her early childhood here, how it had felt to board a bus or walk down a street: the baleful stares of children, the frank curiosity of vendors or those people from the weaving district—revealing, by their undeveloped graces, the truth behind the normal grown-ups' tactful indifference. Young Sarah, growing up among Japanese faces, had been taken aback each time she glanced in a mirror and saw her own features: a pointy nose covered with freckles, a sharp little chin that was severe, almost foxlike, compared with the softer, more pleasing contours of those around her.

She wondered if Aunt Kimiko switched personas the minute she was alone with her own children, shedding her opaqueness along with her apron and talking in fast, careless sentences like Mama, or Grandma, or Granny Sono. She watched her aunt carefully when she was in the company of other adults. Although Aunt Kimiko did switch to an adult-level vocabulary, her demeanor remained as soft and muted as with the children. She had none of the impulsive, gossipy spark that the other women had in abundance. Once, in a private uncharitable moment, Sarah's mother had sighed sharply and said to Grandma, "I swear! She's like a blancmange pudding."

And then, as always, Mama rectified her blunder ("Because blancmange pudding is pure and white, never sullied by anything ugly") to ensure that there would be no misunderstanding on her daughter's part.

"It's OK, Mama, I know," Sarah said. "She's sort of like a Christian Madonna, isn't she."

"Exactly." Her mother's relieved eyes met hers, and there had been a perfect adult moment of understanding.

There were other occasional slipups. Once a pun came up during a particularly uninhibited teatime conversation in which Grandma and Mama sat doubled over with helpless laughter, like a pair of schoolgirls. The pun was about a local Christian women's college, Notre Dame, run by elderly Catholic nuns from Canada. It was attended by students whose grades weren't high enough for the desirable colleges. Notre Dame was pronounced *Noh tolu dah-meh. Noh* meant brains, *tolu* was to take away, and *dah-meh* meant hopeless. That pun had been—and still was— used by young elitists from Kyoto University, her mother's alma mater. When it occurred to Mama, in midsentence, that her own sister had attended Notre Dame, her face took on a stricken expression. She turned to Sarah, who was laughing hysterically, and made her promise never to repeat that pun, *ever*.

It wasn't that the two sisters disliked each other. It was quite the opposite; Sarah's mother was fiercely protective toward Aunt Kimiko, who in turn looked up to her big sister with humble admiration. But they weren't true friends, the way Mama and Grandma were. Perhaps it was too much to ask. They belonged in different leagues—Mama had so much personal charisma, and Aunt Kimiko had so little. Elderly neighbors recounted numerous childhood anecdotes about Sarah's mother, but seemed to recall very little about her aunt. "Kimi-chan? Aaa, I remember she was a cute little thing," someone once told Sarah. "Always running after your mother on her tiny legs, losing her sandal and calling out, 'Big Sister, wait for me . . .'"

Every so often, when Sarah and her cousins were playing outside in Aunt Kimiko's garden, they would hear a faint peal of laughter coming from Grandma's house (it was midsummer, and the windows were all open). They would pause in their play, picturing the two women wiping away tears of laughter, or playfully slapping at each other's arm.

After a minute or two, one of her cousins would predictably ask, "Can we go play at *your* house now?" Sarah was in no hurry to return home; she liked being the guest in an unfamiliar household, and besides, Aunt Kimiko served lovely snacks. But she yielded to her cousins, whose mute urgency was like that of dogs straining at the leash. She felt she owed it to them, for some reason she could not define.

"Don't stay too long and become a bother," Aunt Kimiko called gently from the gate, waving after her children who had, by now, broken into a run. And Sarah, lingering behind to return her aunt's wave, felt once again that strange compunction.

But of all her childhood memories, the most significant was of a winter afternoon when she was six years old, before her family had moved to America. She was walking to the park with Aunt Kimiko and her cousins. "Hold onto Big Sister's hand, for safety," her aunt told her two girls. As young as she was, Sarah knew her aunt had done this to flatter her, for she was only a few years older than her cousins. The little girls obediently clutched her hands with their mittened ones, looking up at her with chubby, trusting faces framed by knitted hoods with animal ears. Sarah had felt a rush of importance, followed by an overwhelming love for her aunt. The four of them held hands and strolled down the lane. "Ten ten ten—ten koro rin—" Aunt Kimiko chanted softly as they swung their joined hands back and forth.

It had struck Sarah, with a small child's intuitiveness, that no one but her aunt could have been capable of such sensitivity. Looking back now, she wondered if she had sensed a kinship between them, for they both knew how it was to be on the outside.

. . .

That evening, Sarah visited her aunt under the guise of using her shower. It was years since she had showered at Aunt Kimiko's house. She used to do it often, back when her mother was alive; it was quicker than public bathing, and left more time to play or watch television. Her mother and grandmother preferred to spend hours at the public bathhouse, immersed up to their chins in the steaming water, chattering away with the other bathers. They didn't particularly care if Sarah came along or not. As long as they had each other, they were happy.

Since then, Sarah had taken over her mother's role. At the bathhouse, even after seven years, her mother's legacy lived on. Naked dripping women still sighed by way of a conversation opener: "Such a pity, ne—your mother used to light up a room, she was so full of life."

"Thank you, it's so kind of you to remember," Sarah would reply. And her grandmother chimed in, "And this one here's becoming more and more like her mother, every day."

The naked women nodded and beamed at Sarah, and she smiled back modestly.

Her grandmother was correct, to a certain extent. Sarah, unlike her aunt, had benefited from living in her mother's shadow. An observant child, she had gradually adopted many of the social mannerisms that had endeared her mother to the public—some as specific as the proud way she held up her head, or her habit of clapping once when she had a bright idea; others more general, like a sunny demeanor and a propensity for easy chatter. More importantly, she had internalized her mother's carefree attitude of taking others' approval for granted. It hadn't come easily, given her earlier insecurity over being a "half." She had attained it only through close identification with her mother—before and after her death—almost blurring their identities, the way she had once learned to waltz by standing on her father's feet. No one would call *her* a blancmange pudding. Yet there was a difference: Sarah's behavior was learned, whereas her mother's had been instinctive. Sarah knew, and realized her grandmother knew, that she would never have the true spark of the original.

Tonight, Aunt Kimiko was alone in the kitchen, listening to music as she prepared dinner. She had a Hello Kitty radio, long outgrown by one of her daughters. For as long as Sarah could remember, it had been tuned to the same classical station, which played everything from the western melodies of Strauss and Puccini to the elegant notes of stringed koto, punctuated by a shamisen's bitter twangs.

Aunt Kimiko never seemed to change either. She wore the same short bob from her college photos, parted on one side and pinned with a barrette. There was a virginal quality about her, emphasized tonight by a pale pink sweater worn over a white Peter Pan collar. Since babyhood Sarah had registered, like abstract art, those shades and shapes that made up her aunt. Even now, certain combinations—pastel fabric against the whitish cast of Japanese cosmetics, a round bob above a round collar—triggered childhood impressions of her aunt: someone infinitely patient, hovering with a damp cloth for wiping children's dirty fingers; a soft, gentle face unmarred by frowns or grimaces.

"Auntie, I'm really looking forward to your concert," Sarah said. She stood wrapped in a towel, ready to enter the shower. Oddly enough, the showering room was right next to the kitchen: one entered it through the informal dining area. This was a typical phenomenon in older neighborhoods; many families had added on western-style showers to their traditional homes.

Over in the kitchen, her aunt glanced up from washing the rice. She laughed, waving a dripping palm before her face in a no-no motion as if the very idea of her participating in a concert was absurd. "Sarah-chan, you'll catch cold," she said.

Several minutes later, Sarah was in the middle of shampooing her hair when she recognized Pavarotti's soulful tenor on the radio, launching into "Ave Maria." She almost called out—Auntie! This is the song Granny Sono used to tell us about!—but she caught herself in time.

When Sarah and her cousins were little, they had often climbed upstairs to visit Granny Sono, who entertained them with games and stories. One of the funniest—and most intriguing—was the Ave Maria story.

"It happened a couple of times, the first year Kimiko-san came here as a new bride," Granny Sono told them. "Every morning after breakfast, she'd climb upstairs to the balcony and hang the shirts and towels and socks out on the line. I'd be downstairs, washing the dishes quietly, and then, A! I'd hear . . ." The children waited eagerly as she placed her teacup deliberately onto the saucer with an elderly hand that, even back then, trembled. "Ave Maria!" She said it ominously: *ah-beh-mah-lih-ah!* "Foreign songs from that *Christian* college—" Granny Sono threw back her wrinkled face and trilled an affected operatic tune. "Aaah . . . oooh . . . So loud! All over the neighborhood! Maa, what the neighbors must have thought!"

Sarah and her cousins had sprawled on the tatami floor, shrieking with laughter. What a foolish thing for Aunt Kimiko to do! Granny Sono was right about the neighbors. This neighborhood was extremely quiet. Mornings here, except for a brief half hour when clusters of children tramped their raucous paths to school through the narrow lanes, were thick with silence. The wooden houses stood, somber and shrinelike, beneath aged pines from which a crow, every so often, cawed.

Her aunt must have been reckless with bridal bliss!

But tonight, something about the story didn't add up.

It was the music—the music was wrong. Sarah turned off the water and stood very still in the shower room, listening to the stately notes of "Ave Maria." And this time, as an adult, she understood what she was hearing: a plea, heartrending in its humility.

We meant no harm, she thought. And then, perhaps triggered by the sorrowful swell of music, a random remark flashed through her mind: her mother (or grandmother) saying, "Let's not mention to your Aunt Kimiko that we went out for sushi without her—it's just easier this way." She felt a sweep of remorse: partly on behalf of her mother and grandmother, but mostly for the eager, happy way she herself had complied, proud of her place within their golden, laughter-filled circle. But they had meant no harm. And they had caused none, for Aunt Kimiko had never heard them. Surely it was something else that had made her aunt sing out her long-ago lament on the balcony.

It occurred to Sarah, at the height of this sentimental surge, that her regret wasn't merely for Aunt Kimiko. It was also for the part of herself that had been akin to her aunt. Her memory of the winter afternoon, when they had held hands against the world, glowed now with a guileless purity that seemed lost forever. And she was aware that once again, she was shifting Aunt Kimiko to second place.

T ea for Two" was playing when Sarah came out of the shower. Aunt Kimiko hummed the *cha cha cha*s, softly. The kitchen was fragrant with soy sauce and ginger, and a small plate of seasonal chestnut dumplings was waiting on the low table in the informal eating area.

Maybe she had read too much into the Ave Maria.

Aunt Kimiko, taking off her apron, joined Sarah at the low table to keep her company as she ate the dumplings. "Sarah-chan, are you finding this Japanese weather too chilly?" she asked.

"Not at all, Auntie. It's warmer than usual, I thought, for November."

"Yes, you're right!" she said. "It's unseasonably warm."

It was difficult, conversing with Aunt Kimiko. On a purely technical level, she wasn't used to making allowances for Sarah's less advanced Japanese vocabulary. Grandma had the knack—as had Sarah's mother—for putting complex ideas into simple terms: nuclear physics, for instance, became "the rules of science involving—" followed by an exploding sound, with both hands outlining an enormous H-bomb mushroom. "Right, right!" Sarah would say, laughing and nodding. But Aunt Kimiko would use the term "nuclear physics," then falter when Sarah didn't understand. Gradually, she had given up on any but the simplest conversation.

But language aside—for Sarah had watched her aunt around others—direct emotional entry was difficult. Hers was a particularly traditional sensibility, with overtones that Sarah vaguely recognized from historical dramas on television. Sarah often had to remind herself that her mother, who after all had married an American, was the atypical one. Mama had no patience for old-school Japanese obliquity. I have a cosmopolitan soul, she used to say, only half joking.

"Auntie." Sarah was aware of the woeful inadequacy of her words. "I feel so bad, that I never even knew about your choir."

"Ara! Why should you feel bad!" her aunt exclaimed, as dismayed as if Sarah had just announced she was coming down with a cold. She quickly poured some tea. "Drink this," she said.

"It's just that I don't remember you ever talking about your singing."

"Is that so? That's probably so." She eyed Sarah's teacup, which was still untouched. "Oh—do you not drink Japanese tea?"

"Of course I do!" Sarah felt a twinge of her old childhood insecurity. "Auntie, don't you remember?" She took a sip of her tea, and after a suitably appreciative silence asked, "Are you a soprano?"

"No—I sing with a low voice," her aunt replied. Her grandmother would have given Sarah credit for an easy word like "alto," considering it was English to start with.

The room was very quiet. Granny Sono was upstairs, waiting for her dinner; Uncle and the girls hadn't come home yet. It occurred to Sarah that she was holding up dinner preparations. The rice cooker was bubbling in the kitchen. The table was still unset.

"But your mother used to sing with a high voice," Aunt

Kimiko said. "A beautiful high voice. I still remember the day she sang 'Days of Yore' at our school assembly."

"Really? Tell me. . . ." Now they were on familiar ground. Sarah relaxed and listened, feeling quiet pride for her mother. Even in death, Mama was able to fill up a conversational vacuum.

Some time later, sated with tea and dumplings, she got up to leave, maneuvering carefully around the low table so as not to poke a hole in the shoji panels behind her.

Aunt Kimiko walked her out. "Your grandma must be waiting," she said, but with none of the sarcasm or strained pride of a daughter who had been passed over. At that moment Sarah was ashamed: ashamed that she had allowed her aunt to comfort her with details of her big sister's superiority, ashamed that her aunt had never been anything but generous, not once taking it out on Sarah for usurping her territory.

"You must really love singing," Sarah said as she followed her aunt down the unlit hallway, "to have done it for so long."

"Aaa, I know." Aunt Kimiko sighed, as if admitting to a bad habit. "Much too long."

You and I are *family*, Sarah wanted to say. Don't use such good manners.

They came out onto the lane. It was indeed warm for November, reminiscent of summer and childhood. The crickets ticked *reen reen reen*. The night air was cool; Sarah stood still before the slatted gate holding her washbasin and towel, feeling the faint breeze waft against her freshly scrubbed skin. Caught in the knobby branches of a neighbor's pine tree, heavy with white light and almost touchable, was a full moon.

"Look at the moon," Sarah said.

"Aaa, isn't it pretty," Aunt Kimiko answered.

They were silent awhile, looking up.

"I look at the moon a lot," her aunt said, and this time there was something different in her voice. "Like this, with the branches silhouetted on it. In classical art, you know, the moon is never bare. It's always half hidden behind branches or clouds." Sarah knew the art to which she was referring. She, too, had been affected by those old Japanese tableaux, by the sorrowful beauty of a shining thing glimpsed, only partially, through a layer of impediments. And she felt strongly (although later she would second-guess herself), that this was her aunt's response to her own clumsy attempts earlier. For a brief instant, the communion of that long-ago winter afternoon was fully restored.

Halfway down the lane, she looked back. Her aunt was standing by the gate waiting to return her wave, her Aunt Kimiko with such thin shoulders.

The remaining days were quiet, uneventful. Scarlet maple leaves floated down in the garden. Sarah and her grandmother gossiped idly over pots of tea. Their intimacy was secure and comfortable; gone was the fierce emotional urgency of those early years after her mother's death.

Thus, for the first time, their conversations revolved around Aunt Kimiko. Sarah had many questions, which she tried to pose subtly to honor the delicate moment she and her aunt had shared. It was surprising how much she could glean, once she knew what to look for. For instance, her grandmother, who was skilled at identifying footsteps on gravel, once remarked that Uncle came home from work around 11:00 each night. Was there, or wasn't there, a slight emphasis on *work*? Her uncle and aunt had a traditional arranged marriage. As a child, Sarah had seen wedding pictures: Aunt Kimiko's neck, frail under the bulk of her headdress, bent to expose a white-painted nape. That pose, so sensual and alluring on others, made her look like a penitent child. "What do you expect—Canadian nuns," someone had once remarked dryly.

Sarah had seen no evidence of tension in that house, but then, she was so seldom here. From her grandmother's comments, however—and her own mother's, from when she was alive—she could deduce the situation: Uncle, trapped in an arranged marriage under his mother's roof; Granny Sono (who had once been beautiful and rather spoiled), accustomed to wielding power all her life; Aunt Kimiko's daughters as teenagers, rebelling American-style at anyone with authority; and her aunt tiptoeing through a minefield of resentments.

At some point Sarah abandoned subtlety altogether, as she and her grandmother openly pondered the state of affairs in that house.

They also discussed Aunt Kimiko's health. When Grandma worked in the garden, she always looked up to check Aunt Kimiko's balcony. If the drapes were drawn behind the sliding glass doors, it meant she was sleeping off an attack of headache and fatigue. (Sarah was beginning to realize her grandmother was a keen observer—she watched her less-favored daughter more carefully than one would have expected). It had never before occurred to Sarah that her aunt had a condition. "She gets tired," Grandma said. She suspected anemia, although Sarah's mother had apparently argued in favor of migraines, having heard Aunt Kimiko mention "flashing lights."

"And you never learned what it was?" asked Sarah.

Her grandmother shook her head. "Your aunt is a very private person," she said.

After such talk, it was a letdown to run into Aunt Kimiko at the open-air market. She seemed so ordinary, chatting about Fuji-ya's new crop of persimmons or whose turn it was on neighborhood watch. Sarah felt the same double take of confusion she had on the night she stepped out of the shower.

Although their musings about Aunt Kimiko yielded little, the discussions themselves were revealing a new state of affairs of which Sarah had not been aware. There was casual mention of Aunt Kimiko planting violets under Grandma's mailbox last spring—the kind of romantic gesture for which Mama had been known. And her grandmother had begun buying roasted eel fillets for Aunt Kimiko's anemia. "Your aunt can't afford it on her household budget," she told Sarah, "because she'd never buy just one for herself, she'd buy them for everyone in the house. So this way, things are taken care of gracefully—I sneak her over here for a quick bite, and no one's the wiser. If Uncle or Granny Sono knew I was buying it for her, they'd be *so* insulted!"

This was the first Sarah had heard of her grandmother keeping secrets with anyone but her mother and herself. The situation was becoming clear: a tentative coming together of mother and child, as belated and autumnal as the weather around them. Her grandmother discussed it hesitantly at first, as if guilty for betraying her favorite daughter, then with something like relief. Sarah was all encouragement; she was glad for them, of course. But she felt a new, unfamiliar emptiness. Her mother was gone—really, finally gone.

"Doesn't Auntie have hard feelings about before?" she asked. She took a hard pleasure in being so direct.

Her grandmother looked down at her tea. Surprise and shame mingled on her face. "I don't know," she finally said. "She must, deep down. Don't you think? I don't know."

Sarah was instantly sorry. "I'm sure she doesn't, Grandma," she consoled. "Blood ties always win out in the end."

"I wasn't a good mother," Grandma said. "I know that. But if I had it to do over, I don't know if things would be any different. When your grandfather died . . . and then I married Kimiko's father . . . it was so hard . . ."

"Plus the war," Sarah offered. She had a sudden need to comfort this old woman, hunched sadly over her tea.

"And there was the war, yes," her grandmother said. "Your mother was all I had left in the world. At least that's how it felt back then. I was a weak woman."

"No, you weren't. Grandma, you weren't!"

"I was. I focused on your mother, then I just shut my eyes to everything else and clung. I clung for years and years, till the pain went away. I wonder, are you old enough to understand?"

"Yes," Sarah said. Her own recent remorse over Aunt Kimiko flared up to meet her grandmother's, creating a strange, quivering synergy between them. I was weak too, she thought. I needed my mother. "*Yes,*" she repeated, and reaching across the table, she gripped her grandmother's hand.

"I wonder if *she* understands," Grandma said.

A unt Kimiko's concert took place on a chilly, gray evening, after the warm spell had passed. Sarah and her grandmother went alone. Uncle was working, and Sarah's cousins, having already attended their mother's opening performance as well as numerous other concerts over the years, had begged off on this one.

The orchestra was warming up. Flipping through the program to the "Choir Facts" section, Sarah saw that this choir had performed in Paris, Berlin, and New York—Carnegie Hall. Last year, it had received the prestigious national Tanaka Foundation Award. She gazed at the page long after she had finished reading. This is an outstanding choir, she thought with a belated rise of understanding. It must have taken persistence for her aunt to qualify—hours upon hours, years upon years, of practice.

"Did she go to these countries?" she whispered to her grandmother, pointing to the program.

"Oh no. Just the members who can afford to travel," Grandma whispered back. "And money aside . . ." She stopped because the instruments had become silent.

"She takes naps, goes singing. Goes singing, takes naps," Granny Sono had complained to Sarah just this morning. "Oh my, what a nice life!"

The choir filed onstage: unassuming women, middle-aged to elderly, wearing black, knee-length dresses. They flowed into their assigned lines smoothly, like a marching band. Sarah could make out her aunt in the front row, third from left. Black was too severe; it overpowered her. She needed some rouge.

The conductor strode swiftly to the center of the stage, bowed deeply, then turned his back to the audience, baton raised, and waited. The clapping died down. Someone coughed. Row upon row of pale faces rose up in the darkness around them, waiting. On this threshold, Sarah felt a deep, sharp joy for her aunt, and also a foreshadowing of what lay ahead for the three of them: not the shining, laughing summers of her mother's time but a brave new season that would resonate, like those bittersweet Japanese tableaux, with all the complexities of time's passage.

The first soprano was a lone voice, barely audible. Then the others—second soprano, then first alto (Aunt Kimiko's section)—joined in with steadily gathering force, and finally the second alto, its heft overtaking all the others; their voices swelled to a crescendo then paused, the notes spreading out like ink in water.

They sang of little yellow flowers, blooming by the roadside in spring. Sarah's mother had sung this to her as a child. Sarah hadn't learned until later that Buraki, the wartime composer, had written it about a bomb-shelled Hiroshima. Today, through the orchestra and the sheer power of voices, its old familiar words were elevated as she had never heard them; rich, omniscient. *Small flowers are nodding*—they sang out with one voice. *Cheery and bright*—.

Sarah thought of young Aunt Kimiko standing alone amidst flapping laundry, singing out to an empty sky. How tightly she must have clung, for her voice to turn so pure and far-reaching and resonant with wonder.

I'm a mixed child myself, half Japanese and half Irish-American. I was born and raised in Japan; my family moved to the States when I was eleven.

Because I'm mixed, people often ask how race affects my sense of identity, whether I see myself as white or Asian, etc. When I was a little girl, I remember answering, "I don't know—I'm just me." I think the nice thing about being mixed is that it frees you from having to pick sides, from defining yourself in such a limited way. I have both an American side and a Japanese side—the same way one might have a city house and a country house—and I like moving back and forth between them. I think this is why I enjoy writing about Japan for western readers. One of my greatest goals in writing is to present the Japanese sensibility in such a way that English readers feel, if only for a brief time, that they have left their own race and somehow become Japanese without realizing it.

Chandra Prasad

Chandra Prasad is a mix of Italian, English, Swedish, and Indian. Her novel *One of the Boys*, about a girl who poses as a male student at Yale University in the 1930s, will be published in 2007. She's the author of the book *Death of a Circus* and the careers guide *Outwitting the Job Market*, as well as numerous articles on diversity and the workplace, which have been published in the *Wall Street Journal*, *India Abroad*, *India New England*, Vault.com, and IMDiversity.com, among others.

Wayward

The scents bring us back. That's what Mr. Agrawal says. He says the scents of summer are the most potent, the most enduring.

The sun beats hard in Duxton, Massachusetts, in late July. It shrivels soft things: flower petals, the worms that struggle up through the ground after a midday shower. The sun here cares nothing for exteriors. It is interested only in essences, the soft middles. Mr. Agrawal doesn't bother to pick the ripening tomatoes in the garden, infested with rangy weeds and fat iridescent beetles. He says he likes the smell of the flesh once the heat has sizzled the peel.

It's dusk and Mr. Agrawal and I laze on the porch. He's breathing slowly, enjoying wafts of wild mint carried by a breeze. Sunk in a dirty plastic lawn chair, eyes closed, he tells me wild mint is his favorite of all summer scents.

"Breathe it in, Jai. It soothes a weary spirit."

I'm not sure if he means "weary" or "wary," but I don't ask, and in either case, I don't agree with him. The heat of the day has baked the mint sprigs that spangle the edge of the bog nearby. For hours, the aroma has struck me as heady, overwhelming, not so different from the smell at the back of the parking lot behind my school.

Mr. Agrawal opens his eyes. They roll slowly down my torn T-shirt and jeans.

"Your mother would kill me if she saw the way you dress."

"I dress like this at home."

"Like a vagabond?"

"Not like a bitchy beauty queen."

"I told you not to swear," he snaps.

Technically, "bitchy" isn't a swear, but I keep my mouth shut. Although he's lived in America since he was ten, Mr. Agrawal opportunistically champions certain Indian traditions, like how arranged marriages are preferable to love marriages, and how youngsters should hush up when their elders speak.

Mr. Agrawal turns his attention to the newspaper I'm trying to hide behind. When I first arrived here for the summer, he was surprised I read so much. Over the years my mother had no doubt mailed him my report cards.

"Still Whitney Swinn on the cover?" he asks dolefully.

"Yup."

Whitney Swinn is famous in Duxton. Somebody snatched her from her parents' house and there's been no trace of her since. Every day the *Duxton Clipper* flashes the same photograph of her.

She's wearing the kind of clothes Mr. Agrawal would love: anklets, glossy Mary Jane shoes, a white eyelet dress. Doll's clothes.

Seeing Whitney's image so often, she's imprinted on my brain. She's pixie-small with corn silk hair, butterfly barrettes, and braces. Her large eyes are muddy green, like two lily pads on a pond. I see eyes like that and I know she's been floating through life.

"What's it been now, three weeks?" Mr. Agrawal asks.

"Twenty days, sir," I tell him, and I'm certain. Like I said, she's been imprinted.

"You'd think they would have found her."

By his tone I know he means crumpled in a ditch. He isn't trying to be pessimistic or cruel, it's just that the odds are stacked against girls like Whitney. Every year, it seems, another few disappear. Parents plead on TV, well-doers wave signs, newscasters salivate. But the end almost always reads like an old Russian novel.

Stuff like this doesn't happen in Duxton, and the whole town's gone haywire. The hardware store has a waiting list for locks and chains, and then there are the people buying surveillance cameras and handguns. I've been affected too. I worry when I see little kids playing outside. I wonder if they'll edge too close to the street, if they'll pause when a car sidles up, engine softly thrumming.

"You remember where she lived?" Mr. Agrawal asks. He's trying to catch my eye.

"Over on that tract near Grove Street. The one with the huge houses."

"Like mansions."

"Yup."

Mr. Agrawal wouldn't admit it, but it's obvious to me he doesn't care much for little girls. My grandmother told me that when my mother was born, he'd asked a nurse to double-check under the swaddle. My mother was his only child too. There were complications, as they say—something twisted, clotted, and terribly wrong.

"I told your mother I'd find you a job," Mr. Agrawal says suddenly.

"Isn't studying all summer enough?"

"That's nothing," he huffs, and I wait for the inevitable when-I-was-young speech, but instead he murmurs, "Too much time on your hands and your mind will start to stray."

The sun's disappearing now. It dips into the thick creepers that hem Mr. Agrawal's property. The night creatures are starting to make noise.

"I could work at that garage off Howe Street. I met the owner—Eddie. He's cool."

"A girl changing tires all day?"

"Yeah—so?"

He snorts for effect. "No way, José. I promised your mother you'd come back straightened."

"I'm straightened."

"You're about as straight as this," he says, pointing to his nose, which is lopsided and bulbous. He likes to tell the story of how he broke it when he was fifteen. How he'd gone head-to-head with an armed robber when the family used to live in Queens.

"You got another option?" I ask him.

"Yes, hotshot. You're going to fill that old well in the back. I've ordered the clay."

"Why don't you just nail the plywood you've got over it?"

"That's a job half done."

"Mom wants me to get a job to make money," I point out, my shoulders tensing.

"She wants you to show you're not a deadbeat like your father."

Mr. Agrawal knows exactly how to push my buttons. He's the only relative I've got who'll openly badmouth my dad. He's always harbored the suspicion that my father married my mother to stay in this country. But that doesn't make sense; after the divorce my father packed his bags and hightailed it back home, and besides, my mother's not exactly the baseball-and-apple-pie type.

My dad's Russian, but not just any Russian. He's a Russian from Odessa. If you don't know the difference, he'll be happy to tell you. You'll need a comfortable chair, a few bottles of wine, and most of a night. Then you'll know why Odessa is to Ukraine like New York City is to the U.S.

"You start tomorrow," Mr. Agrawal informs me. He stretches his bare feet. They're skinny, with dry, cracked heels and long sallow nails that curve at the ends—a raptor's feet.

"How deep is it?"

"Deep."

"Thirty feet? Forty?"

He waves me off and stares ahead as fireflies blink to life.

"I have to know for logistical purposes."

"I don't know. It's probably not up to code."

"Wait—you never told the town about it?"

"You sound like a bureaucrat, Jaishri. You would do well in India."

I want to remind him that he's lived here longer than he ever lived in Lucknow, but he's distracted by the brief snips of light, and anyway, I know better.

Abruptly, he announces he's going for a drive. He likes the evening hunt: raccoons and possums, mostly. That's part of why he moved here, to so remote a place. I can't understand what he enjoys about killing harmless little animals, about ripping fur off skin that was never meant to be seen. His whole basement is draped with pelts, and still he keeps a rifle in the trunk.

He used to have a dog named Burger King, a shag carpet of a mutt with a dirty-looking muzzle and cute, clownishly large paws. Mr. Agrawal cherished that dog. My mother said he fed it to death, maybe, with all the bacon strips and soup bones he bought for it. I asked Mr. Agrawal once, how could he have loved

Burger King so much but feel nothing for the animals he hunted? They no doubt felt the pain, as much as Burger King must have felt when he died: a growth in his stomach, a tumor—something random and unfair.

"There's a difference," Mr. Agrawal had said.

"No," I'd replied, a flare of anger suddenly ignited.

"There is. You've got to learn who's in your pack—who's in your pack and who's not." Even now I think back on that answer, how, inexplicably, it makes sense.

I watch him hobble away, a thinly muscled silhouette. His skin's so dark it melts into the air. A minute later his battered Buick Le Sabre crunches the winding gravel road.

Loneliness and a bit of fright come as soon as Mr. Agrawal goes. The noises seem to intensify: bullfrogs croaking, crickets chirping, twigs cracking under invisible paws. I realize, not for the first time, that Mr. Agrawal lives along the borderland of the wild. His nearest neighbor is a half mile away. Coyotes and foxes have been known to scurry across his yard, a jungle of unmowed grass, dandelions, ragweed, and goldenrod. Somewhere beyond, in the overgrowth, a well needs filling. Before darkness falls for good, I will myself to take a look.

I have to claw my way through. The creepers are thorny, unforgiving. They give way just before the well, as if in fear of it, or reverence. In that dim clearing I catch my breath and feel the itchy, raised scratches along my arms. The well's marked by a waist-high circle of joined stones. For as long as I can remember, there's been the same sheet of weathered plywood over the hole, and on top of that, a pile of loose bricks. Reluctantly I decide that Mr. Agrawal is right: boarding it up wouldn't be enough. Years from now the wood would rot, give way. A shiver jerks my spine when I consider the possibilities. Wells and silos have always spooked me. As a kid, I used to have nightmares about falling down one of those man-made throats, flailing haplessly in grain or water, scraping the sleek, cylindrical walls until my strength gives and my mouth fills.

I pick off the bricks one by one, and push the plywood aside. Then I bend over the hole and shout, "Mader chod! Bhen chod! Otsoseé!" I wonder if somewhere, way off in the woods, Mr. Agrawal can hear me. I don't curse much now that I'm in the middle of nowhere, but old habits die hard. The words strike bottom, way down deep in Hades, and echo back. I peer into the gloom. Taking a long slow breath, I expect to inhale something rancid, but all I taste is stale water.

F ive years ago my dad left me and my mom. It was a hot summer, like this one. I remember that the heat added to our torment. When Mr. Agrawal found out, he convinced the two of us to pack up our apartment in the city and stay with him in Duxton. Just temporarily, he'd said, until my mother was through with crying and back on her feet.

Back then Mr. Agrawal wasn't determined to find me work, but my mother was—she wanted me out of her hair—and she got her way over at the A&P. A chatty checkout girl remarked that she'd be leaving for college in the fall, and that on Saturday nights she sometimes babysat.

"I just can't do it anymore," she said, stretching pink gum across her pinker tongue. "I need my weekends free, so I can let loose a little. Ya know what I mean?"

I ducked behind my mother's voluminous salwar, watching this girl with permed, fawn-colored hair and tight Jordache jeans sort groceries into bags. At the time, she'd seemed beautiful.

"Yes, I know what you mean," my mother responded.

"What's your name? I've seen you around."

"Anita Obolensk . . . *Agrawal*."

"You're Indian, right?"

The girl, whose nametag read "AMY," nodded approvingly. I recognized her reaction. It was the one most people have upon meeting my mother—if they haven't been disillusioned by Indian cabdrivers or gas station owners. It was the one associated with doctors, scientists in crisp white lab coats, and children who won national spelling bees. It was the one that conjured phrases like "model minority," "brain drain," and "forehead dot," and images like that from a recent *Time* magazine cover article: "Those Asian American Whiz Kids."

Amy glanced at me. "Is that your daughter?" My mother nodded.

"How old is she?"

"She's thirteen."

"So she's old enough to sit. Do you think she could handle a six-year-old?"

My mother looked me over as if I were stuck with pins on a corkboard. "I think so. She's become more mature this year."

"Let me ask the parents, 'kay? Give me your number and I'll let you know."

"I would really appreciate that, Amy. She could use some responsibility." My mother bowed slightly, as was her habit.

That bow, now that I look back, seemed like an apology.

Not long after, I met the little girl's parents at their front door. They showed me around their gleaming three-story house, encouraged me to raid the fridge, and outlined Amy's old routine. They told me which rooms were off-limits. I wondered if they would have imposed such boundaries if I'd looked different. Maybe if I had the mother's frizzled blonde hair or electric blue headband.

But to be fair I'd been assessing them too, though my head was bent, though I observed everything out of the corner of my eye. I watched the way the father doted on Whitney, plucking a plastic bangle bracelet from his sports coat before leaving. He slipped it on her wrist and called her "jellybean," and she beamed at him with big gorgeous eyes. Under Whitney's spell, he followed in the fog of his wife's acrid, woozy perfume. It had taken me a long time to figure out what that smell had reminded me of. Marigolds.

With her parents gone, Whitney dragged out the Barbies. I'd always shunned dolls, Barbies above all others. She came out of her room with a tub of them and dumped the whole blonde sorority onto the living room carpet. Strangely, every doll was damaged. Whitney or one of her friends had scratched out eyes, amputated limbs, and cropped hair into crew cuts and asymmetrical bobs. Whitney gave me the lone black Barbie, and the first thing I thought was not that this doll was the least cherished and most abused—which it was—but that it was entirely out of place in the Swinn household. Some out-of-touch relative must have picked it up as a last-minute birthday present.

I hadn't had many toys growing up, and those that I did have were generally hand-me-downs, cheap stuffed animals and the like. I had no idea how to "play Barbies," as Whitney put it. But I soon learned her method involved taking off their clothes and rubbing their robotic bodies against each other.

"Ooohh . . . Ahhhh," Whitney moaned graphically, and the way she did it, I knew she was trying to get a rise out of me. She was testing me; more than that, she was testing the night's potential.

"Are you Porto Rican?" she wanted to know, moving her doll on top of mine.

"Why do you ask?"

"My mother says Porto Ricans smell."

"I'm not Puerto Rican."

"But you're dirty like one."

"What?"

"You're dirty like one," she repeated. "Is your daddy Porto Rican?"

I moved my doll to the dominant position. "He's Russian."

Whitney looked at me quizzically.

"Russian—from Russia," I clarified. "You know, one of those places that's not America?"

"He lives there?"

"Let's do something else," I said hastily, throwing the Barbies back into the tub, all of them, except for the black one; that one I placed back gently. The whole time I wondered what she'd been getting at—that my skin was darker than hers, that I had a few pimples? I wondered if I'd forgotten to put on deodorant.

"Do you want a snack—something to drink?" I asked her, to distract myself.

"Uh huh. Coca Cola."

"Well, I don't know about that." The kid was already hyper.

She ogled me, all lashes and cloying sweetness. Then she traipsed into the kitchen, where she filled a bowl with a combination of Lucky Charms and Count Chocula. I let her too, until she insisted on pouring the milk herself. Predictably, it sloshed over the bowl, cascading over the counter like a white waterfall.

"Hey, gimme that," I snapped, grabbing for the carton. Whitney screeched gleefully as she stomped the puddle on the floor.

"Stop that!" I cried, on my hands and knees with a roll of paper towels, thinking that my mother would soon put up with some variation of this exact same scenario. She'd decided that once we moved back to the city, she'd become a maid in a hotel or office complex. She'd been one when she was younger, before she'd met my father. She said she was used to stained uniforms and rug-burned knees.

Whitney giggled hysterically and bolted away, leaving creamy footprints in her wake.

After cleaning the mess I was determined to establish control. I resolved to give the little demon a bath. I ordered her to undress, then rinsed off her sneakers and shoved her damp clothes into the hamper. I made sure the water was warm and plunked in all her bath toys to give her something to do.

Surprisingly, she climbed in of her own accord. "How long do I have to stay here?"

"For as long as I tell you to."

At first I monitored her carefully. She sang some tune from Annie. "It's the hard-knock life—for us!" and a bunch of other lyrics that in no way applied to her situation. I looked through the medicine cabinet, noting condoms, K-Y Jelly, hair peroxide, Valium, laxatives, razorblades. I examined the fancy star-shape clasp of the window lock. Sitting atop the toilet cover, I whizzed through a basket of fashion magazines and diet books. For all that time Whitney busily amused herself, and I decided it was safe to leave for a minute. Five minutes tops.

I chose her parents' bedroom, one of the off-limit places. Carefully, with only the tips of my fingers, I opened a dresser drawer and felt the cool, slippery fabric of Mrs. Swinn's panties and slips. In the closet I unearthed a box at the back. It was full of *Playboys*. The women inside all looked like Christie Brinkley, if Christie Brinkley were to have helium in her boobs. I put back the magazines in the same order I'd taken them out, pushed the box into place, and slid the bypassing door to its original position: roughly four inches from the jamb.

I was about to move on to another room when I noticed the bed, how it was different somehow—more swollen and roly-poly than a normal bed. A black satin spread kept it shrouded like something under a magician's cloth. I touched the spread and it reacted, sending shiny ripples down the sleek fabric. I'd never seen a waterbed before and it seemed terribly exotic, too enticing to pass up. I sat on it gingerly at first, but gaining confidence, I lay down and stretched out, twisting, squirming, and bobbing atop the wavy surface. I felt like a manatee I'd seen once at the Mystic Aquarium in Connecticut. The constant undulation reminded me of the time I'd been invited to a pool party, how the chlorine water had braced my back while also absorbing the motion of the other girls.

I was still thinking back to the pool, having the time of my life, when Whitney walked in sopping naked.

She gazed at me reproachfully, and for a second I forgot she was only six. Then I got up, smoothed the bedspread, and made sure I hadn't left any stray hairs. Dragging her back to the bathroom, I cleared the toys she'd strewn over the flooded tile floor. It was only while I was toweling her off that I noticed how the toilet cover was up. The water was bubbling and foaming over the seat. Above the sink, the porcelain soap holder stood empty.

I wanted to slap her, I really did, but I clenched her wrist instead, to keep her from running. She showed no fear, not even a trace, and why should she? By then the truth was painfully clear to both of us: I was neither a worthy accomplice nor a worthy foe.

To retrieve the bar of soap, I'd need time, and to buy time, I'd need to send her to bed early. I was considering this when I spotted it: a large mole poking out from beneath one of Whitney's shoulder blades. It was fat, misshapen, and startlingly distinct on her vanilla skin. It reminded me of a Raisinet when two of the raisins get stuck together under the chocolate.

Whitney couldn't follow my gaze—her neck couldn't crane that far—but she knew what I was looking at.

"I've tried to wash it off," she explained sheepishly.

She sounded so embarrassed, I was momentarily overcome. I thought maybe I'd been misjudging her all this time. She was only a kid, for god's sake, and what the hell do kids know?

"No, honey, you can't. It's a beauty mark. It doesn't come off."

"Why's it called a 'beauty mark' when it's so ugly? It's the color of poop."

"It's not ugly."

"I can hide it."

"You don't have to hide it. Lots of people have them."

"You can't see it under a bathing suit," she insisted, her voice increasingly desperate.

"It's *OK* to see it. It's normal—natural. Nothing to be ashamed of." I was trying to maintain my composure, to sound like I knew a thing or two, but my face was going red under her challenging stare. I was still drying her, and her face was close to mine. Her tiny hairless body smelled like baby oil, springtime, Bounce fabric softener. Her lips reminded me of the buds on the miniature, overpruned rosebushes that glutted this neighborhood. Her hair, even wet, shone golden. And I couldn't help it—I

felt defective beside her, like I was this grimy, greasy, giant foreigner next to an Ivory Snow princess.

"Do you understand what I'm telling you?" I continued,
struggling to keep my voice even. "That there's nothing wrong
with you?"

"Do *you* have a beauty mark?"

"Sure—sure I do," I lied. "Tons of 'em."

Teasingly, maybe provokingly, she cocked her head to one
side. "So that's why your daddy left you."

I babysat Whitney Swinn the second and final time exactly a
week later. Her parents were going to a party that night. The
mother, despite her wrinkled skin, looked smashing in a tight
turquoise tube-dress and shimmery lipstick. She wasn't quite
as friendly as last time, and mentioned something about
mildew in the hamper, how they liked to keep *their* house neat
and sanitary, did I understand? I nodded and smiled, peering
at her high-heeled pumps, listening to them click, clack, click
as the father kissed Whitney twice on the top of the head
before heading out.

In the time since seeing Whitney, I'd thought about her constantly. Not really about her, but about that mole on her back.
That one smirch on her otherwise pristine body. I couldn't get
over how separate it looked from the rest of her, like you could
pluck if off and stick it anywhere, maybe between the eyebrows
like a bindi. I went to bed and dreamed about the mole, imagining Whitney covered with Raisinet spots, how her father would
pull out his hair if he ever saw her like that. I envisioned her covered in so many moles that her skin looked brown from a distance, brown as Mr. Agrawal's. Only up close could you see the
contrast between light and dark.

This time around, I wasn't cautious in the house. I roved the
place like I owned it, opening cabinets as I pleased and fingering

white marble counters, cold steel appliances, a coffee machine with so many buttons, knobs, and lights it looked like a computer. Yoo-hoo and individual-size bags of Doritos and Cheetos lined the pantry. All this junk, I thought, and still the family's skinny.

I descended into the den, which was really the basement—another No Trespassing Zone. But while Mr. Agrawal's basement smelled putrid and crawled with centipedes every spring, the Swinn's boasted a full-size Ms. Pac-Man arcade, gumball machine, pool table, and real-life traffic light hanging from the ceiling. I watched it blink green, red, yellow, then back to green again.

Whitney followed me downstairs. She was talking a mile a minute, asking all sorts of questions. I think she was trying to win me over, just for the sport of it, like luring a dog with meat scraps only to smack it in the nose when it comes near. When she understood that I intended to ignore her, she stomped back upstairs hostilely, and I spent the rest of the night playing Ms. Pac-Man.

At eleven-thirty the Swinns returned, their breath smelling sour-malty like my father's used to. Mrs. Swinn wobbled unsteadily in her high heels.

"So how did it go?" she asked.

"Fine, ma'am."

"Whitney went to bed without a problem?"

I'd ordered her to her room at nine o'clock. "Put on your pajamas" and "get under the sheets" were the only words out of my mouth all night.

"She was an angel."

"Good. Glad to hear it. Wait a minute now."

She and Mr. Swinn disappeared into the kitchen and I could I hear them discussing how much they ought to pay me. They'd forgotten to give me anything last time, and I'd been too sheepish to ask. While Mrs. Swinn complained, Mr. Swinn mentioned how they used to give Amy three times as much.

"But in her country the dollar is worth more," she argued. The debate degenerated until finally she left with a huff, nearly grazing me as she tottered to the bedroom.

I was still waiting for Mr. Swinn and whatever money he was going to give me when she reappeared, glowering and panting. For the first time I noticed that her nostrils were inflamed and a little crusty. She threw her hands into the air and hollered for her husband to come. When he did, bills in hand, she pointed at me, her rawhide face streaky with mascara and tears.

"She's gone through my jewelry box. I found it wide open. One of my diamond earrings is missing."

Although I couldn't see Whitney, I could imagine her well enough: opening her door a crack, her hair a nimbus in the darkness. She'd be covering a smirk with her hand. Maybe she was clutching the earring with the other, or maybe she'd had another adventure with the toilet.

"Ma'am, I didn't take anything. I swear to you."

"Empty your pockets right now." I winced. "I said, 'now!'"

I did better than that. I took off my clothes and shook them out, even my shoes and socks. I stood in my underwear, my potbelly hanging over my flower-dotted underpants, anything to put Whitney in her place.

"She must have given it to someone. Who knows what kind of people she let in? Half of Mexico could have tromped through this house by now."

"Calm down, Misty. Let's think this through." Stony faced, Mr. Swinn turned to me. "I think it's time for you to go home, Jaishri." He surprised me by pronouncing my name correctly.

I wanted to defend myself, to point out the obvious, like if I were going to steal jewelry, why would I take *one* earring? But then, as so often happened when I got nervous, the words clogged in my throat and I felt choked. Before I knew it, Mrs. Swinn was throwing my clothes at me and showing me to the door, her hand like a vice on my shoulder. I didn't even have time to get my shoes on before finding myself on the doorstep. As I tied my laces, I could hear them raging inside.

"What the hell was that about? We're supposed to drop her home," Mr. Swinn said.

"You've got to be kidding. There's no way you're driving that scum. Let her walk."

I did walk, all the way to Mr. Agrawal's house. I didn't have the money or inclination to call my mother and explain the situation; and anyhow, I felt guilty, even if I knew I hadn't done anything wrong—or much wrong. It took me four hours to walk all the way (I got lost in the dark once or twice), and by the time I got there, she was pacing on the porch. She looked like she wasn't sure whether to hit me or hug me, and so she started talking instead. She told me that Mr. Agrawal had called the Swinns. They'd said I'd decided to walk home, and that they wouldn't be needing my services anymore. I listened carefully, waiting for a crescendo, but she didn't mention anything about the earring, only that Mr. Agrawal was out in the Buick, trolling the streets.

After calling me reckless and stupid, she started to fire questions. But then she saw how exhausted I must have looked, and sat me down to feed me warm gulab jamen balls and a glass of milk. Kneeling on the floor, she took off my shoes and looked at the newly sprung blisters on my feet.

When Mr. Agrawal appeared, I was so tired I could barely stay upright in the chair. They sent me to bed. Long into the night I glided in and out of sleep, listening to them prattle on. They discussed how badly the little girl's parents had treated me—what kind of people were they? They tried to agree on a course of action, whether they should contact the police, the Department of Children's Services, or if they should see the Swinns in person. Maybe write a letter of complaint? But in the end, my mother nixed all those options. She decided she didn't want to pursue the matter any further, and she didn't want to hear the Swinns' name, not ever again.

T he Buick's surprisingly quiet for such a bulky old clunker. I remember that when Mr. Agrawal purrs up behind me. I'm gazing at the creepers. He gets out and points to a looming pile of clay in the yard.

"It's hard to miss," I tell him.

"Got more on the way, once you're done with this one."

"Great."

"There are buckets in the shed. You'll have to haul it a little at a time."

"The creepers aren't nice," I say, flashing my scraped arms— a last-ditch effort.

"I'll clear a path for you. The machete's in the shed too."

"The *machete*? What are you—an Amazon?"

He ignores this. "Your mother called while you were gone."

"Yeah? What did she want?"

"How should I know, Sherlock? She wants you to call her back."

He goes to retrieve the machete, which looks as menacing as you'd think. Oil glistens on the blade. Mr. Agrawal has done this before, I can tell, as he starts hacking through the vines. The machete seems to slice effortlessly through the riotous vegetation.

When the path materializes in full, Mr. Agrawal deposits the machete in the shed and comes out with the buckets. He sets them at my feet and says the rest is up to me.

I work for hours that first day, shoveling, hauling, heaving, and pouring. Calluses start to mottle my palms. I work until the sun descends and the stench of wild mint fills my nostrils. I work until Mr. Agrawal comes out with a glass of iced tea, mint sprigs drowning at the bottom, and tells me dinner's ready.

"Borsh," he says, sounding both hopeful and ashamed. "I got your mother's recipe."

"Dad's recipe," I correct him. "I don't want dinner. I'm not hungry—sorry." All I want is to fill that well, to see clay brimming over the top.

He looks glum, but shrugs resignedly. "Suit yourself."

After that, I don't take my meals regularly, but I gorge myself on the overripe tomatoes. I eat them like apples, a dozen a day, biting into the pinched, puckered skin, letting the sun-warmed juices dribble down my chin.

Even without the tomatoes, though, I'm filled. Working on the well I feel the clay sliding coarse down my gullet, grinding away at my tender parts. I'm pressed, packed down, and I don't anticipate any lightening of the weight.

I polish off the first pile in four days. A new one, even higher, arrives soon after. Late afternoon, when I'm hardest at work, Mr. Agrawal sees my concentration. It's marked by my cross expression, by the hardening of my hands. He says he's always known I could buckle down.

Occasionally I'll take a break and go to the library, taking the long way, past the Swinns' property. The deterioration of hope has begun. I see it in the wind-torn corners of Whitney's posters and in the fortress silence of the house. Someone has placed a bouquet at the base of an elm tree, under Whitney's photograph, and the sight reminds me of the mini-shrines people set up at the scenes of car accidents.

There's an air of mourning here, but elsewhere, neglect predominates. Today, Whitney's picture wasn't on the front page or even the second. I've been thinking about how her father must feel.

Another week passes and I'm finished with the second pile. I shine a flashlight down the well, but still I can't see where the filler ends and the emptiness begins. I shout into the darkness— no swearing this time. My echo bounces back quicker than before. From behind, Mr. Agrawal approaches. I can hear his bare feet padding over the stumps and nubs of the creepers, which have already started to recover.

"I reckon you'll need another truckload," he says.

"I reckon you're right."

"Fine, I'll place the order."

With my buckets empty, I decide to return my mother's call, finally.

The trill of her voice irritates me as soon as she answers. "Jaishri," she stresses the first syllable urgently. "Didn't you get my message"

"How are you?" I stammer. We never really have conversations any more, just these awkward volleys.

"I'm OK. I hope you're taking care of Grandfather. Have you been studying your geometry book? And what of chemistry?"

It's true that I failed two classes this past year. English is the only one I consistently pass. I scrape by not because I do the assignments, but because the teacher knows that when I'm not paying attention, it's usually because I have a novel in my lap. She's taken me aside a couple of times. Why don't I do my homework, why don't I participate, why don't I live up to my potential, she wants to know? I tell her the truth. I don't pay attention to her lectures, I don't study, and I don't care. I tell her, flat out, I can't be what she wants me to.

"I want to come home," I mutter, realizing immediately that I've chosen the wrong tactic.

"What's wrong? What's going on?"

But I don't know how to explain, or even where to begin. My silence, as usual, presumes guilt.

"You're not going anywhere, Jai. Not until September. I have to put my foot down this time. I told you that before you left. The counselor did too, remember?"

I'm still thinking of how to reframe my argument when she hangs up. I hold out the receiver, which is old and chunky, then start pounding it on a La-Z-Boy. Ten, twenty, thirty times. I pound it until the hatred ebbs, until my fingers gnarl up pale and rigid.

Mr. Agrawal's there when I stop. I have no idea how long he's been observing me. He walks out the door and onto the porch, and I follow behind. There, we assume our usual positions, him on the plastic chair, me on a busted, moldy sofa. I inhale deeply, tasting lemon balm, sage, basil, and, of course, mint. The lush, unruly leftovers from before my grandmother died. That's when I remember the most lovely scent of all: the fragrance of Whitney Swinn's hair. I'd caught it only once—maybe twice—but what a bit of heaven it was.

I wrote the first draft of this story when I was a teenager. As I reworked it for the anthology, I felt a little worried. Though this is a work of fiction, I wondered if people would think I was trying to justify—or even worse, endorse—violence. What I did intend to do is explore the narrator's specific brand of resentment and alienation, common to some teenagers, but magnified, and potentially monstrous, in this case.

NORMA QUINTATA

Cristina Garcia

Cristina Garcia is the author of *Dreaming in Cuban* (nominated for a National Book Award), *The Aguero Sisters*, *Monkey Hunting*, and the forthcoming *A Handbook to Luck*. She is also the editor of *Cubanisimo: The Vintage Book of Contemporary Cuban Literature*. Garcia has been a Guggenheim Fellow and the recipient of an NEA grant and a Whiting Writers' Award. She lives in California with her daughter, Pilar.

Falling Sky

Hue, Vietnam
(1982)

Si and his mother had been in Hue for three days and the heat was growing more oppressive by the hour. It was the middle of August and the monsoon brought fresh sheets of dark rain from beyond the Truong Son Mountains. There was talk among the foot jugglers that a typhoon could hit any day. Three years ago, their tent had been plucked from its moorings and a new tightrope walker was unceremoniously blown off to sea. Si listened to their fears with disinterest.

He was on summer vacation and traveling with his mother's circus. Outside of Saigon, the people of Hue gave his mother her warmest welcome, not like those stiffs in Hanoi who applauded politely at best, even when her tigers jumped through triple hoops of fire. At first, Si had been eager to join his mother. During the school year, Ma didn't permit him to accompany the circus and so he stayed in Saigon in the care of an aging, ill-tempered ex-clown. But Si quickly grew tired of the road: the twice daily performances, the watered-down sugarcane juice, the audience's predictable gasps.

His mother didn't want him dirtying his hands either, and this had exposed him to charges of being a spoiled half-breed brat. His spotless clothes and trimmed fingernails only made matters worse. While the circus workers struck down the tents or handled a recalcitrant elephant, Si read his books. "You'll be a scholar," Ma told him again and again until Si believed her. It was true that studying came easily to him, especially mathematics. Problems seemed to solve themselves, the numbers lining up like so many prancing horses.

It was the circus's first Saturday night in Hue and the crowd was large and raucous. Si recognized a few faces from previous shows, mostly men who'd approached his mother after her performances, inviting her to dinner or for a swim at the beach. After the initial formality, they sought a more familiar tone that she didn't appreciate. Ma spurned the men, who skulked away as submissively as her tigers, only to return again for the next show. Si was grateful, at least, that his mother's steady lover, that idiot strongman, was absent from the tour on account of his wrenched back.

The music started frenetically and off-key, as usual. The tent darkened and a searchlight lurched this way and that, exciting the crowd, until it rested on the most beautiful of the trapeze artists high on a platform. Yi-Yi was Chinese and taller than any man in the circus. She wore a red-sequined leotard and white lace-up boots with stars sewn at the ankles.

How often Si had dreamed of unlacing those boots, of caressing Yi-Yi's sweet feet. Every time he thought of this—in the toilet or beneath his mosquito net—his penis grew so hard it no longer seemed a part of him. In her presence, Si merely stared at Yi-Yi, feeling acutely his own ungainliness. He'd heard other performers talking about the glamorous trapeze artist. One of the plate spinners, who'd professed to having spent the night with her, said that "she was built for a man." Si had no idea what that meant, but the other men had laughed.

Yi-Yi balanced a handstand on the solo trapeze then swung down for a double somersault, grabbing the padded wrists of her catcher at the far end of the tent. The audience applauded wildly. She bowed then pulled a handkerchief from her bodice and blindfolded herself. On her back swing, Yi-Yi added a complicated body twist. As a finale, she hung from the *corde lisse* and did an endless dental spin. Si grew dizzy trying to count the number of turns, a hundred at least.

The twirling reminded him of how certain planes fell out of the sky in a whirlpool of metal and flame. Long ago, Ma had told him that his father had died like that, in a crash in the central jungle. His remains, she'd insisted, had never been found. But Si knew she was lying. The faint blue vein pulsing in her temple gave her away. Si understood that his mother lied to protect him, so he tried to leave her in peace. Sometimes, though, he couldn't help asking more questions.

It'd taken him until last year to learn his father's name— Domingo Chen—and that he was a musician. His mother told him that Domingo meant Sunday in Spanish and so Si decided to save everything significant for that day. Then he discovered that his father had been born in Cuba and had Chinese and African blood. So what, Si wondered, did that make him?

His father had left behind two books from the army library at Ma's apartment: a collection of cowboy stories, and another on classic airplanes. When Si was five, his mother had scraped together money for a Vietnamese-English dictionary. Si had spent his childhood painstakingly translating the books, as if everything he'd needed to know was encrypted on its pages. Sometimes he imagined his father riding a horse through "purple miles of pine, a world of serene undulations, a great sweet country of silence." Other times he saw him as a World War II fighter pilot shooting down German ace General Adolf Galland in his Messerschmitt 109.

The clowns had taken over the ring with their ridiculous antics. The lachrymose one was walking the Russian bear, Masha—a recent gift from the Moscow circus—as if it were a pedigreed dog. Masha also roller-skated, rode a bicycle, played several musical instruments (including the flute and the lithophone), and crossed the tightrope balancing a tiny, flowered umbrella. The bear's arrival last spring had caused a furor among the performers, who'd feared that they'd be upstaged. Even the monkeys and geese were skittish around the creature. The head animal trainer was thoroughly charmed by the bear, and so Masha stayed.

Lately, Si had been having the same nightmare. In it, a flock of geese circled his bed, creating an updraft that sucked him up, naked and screaming, to the clouds. The dream frightened Si so much that he found himself checking the sky above his tent before settling down for the night. But everywhere they traveled that hot sticky summer, nothing but the usual stars filled the heavens.

In Saigon, Si and his mother lived near the airport and the regular drone of departing planes metered his afternoons. He had no friends except for Le Thuy, a girl as shy and bookish as himself. She, too, dreamed of leaving Vietnam. After all, what was left for them here? A future selling fish broth amid the rubble of the streets? Le Thuy's favorite uncle, a physicist, had fled the country at the end of the war and now owned a donut shop in Los Angeles with two Cambodians. Le Thuy wanted to join him when she was old enough and open a little bookshop next to his place.

Si had different dreams. First he wanted to find his father, wherever he was, and listen to him play his Cuban drums. Then he wanted to go to engineering school in America and build an airplane that would never fall out of the sky. He'd spent years analyzing take-offs and landings, not just of the planes he could see from a distance at the airport but of every manner of bird, local and migratory, in the lakes and parks of the city. His goal was to make a plane that could land as precisely as an osprey on a flimsy perch.

The Nguyen brothers took over the center ring, tossing a pair of huge ceramic urns to each other with their stockinged feet. Soon they proceeded to foot-juggle a black lacquered table ornately set for tea. Si found it amusing that the brothers could catch anything with their feet but were downright clumsy with their hands. The regular jugglers—who could keep double-bladed axes and burning torches flying while riding their unicycles—were constantly jeering at them. But of what practical use, Si thought, were any of their skills?

Earlier in the day, he'd gone with one of the clowns to visit the Forbidden Purple City, where Tu Duc's tomb was nestled among frangipani trees and a grove of pines. The emperor had ruled in the last century and lived a life of unimaginable luxury. At every meal, the guide told them, fifty chefs had prepared fifty dishes served by fifty servants and Tu Duc's tea was made with dewdrops collected from the leaves of his lotus plants. He'd kept one hundred and four wives and countless concubines, but none of them ever produced an heir. Only eunuchs had been permitted in the inner sanctum where the concubines lived.

Si had difficulty imagining himself with one girl, much less an entire palace filled with beauties. Two years ago, he'd come home from school with a stomachache and found his mother and the wrestler together in bed. He'd watched as the wrestler moved over Ma with a steady precision, as if he were hammering a nail in the wall. Si had gone to the park for the rest of the day and vomited in the lake. Afterward, he'd felt his mother's love to be a more precarious thing.

The ringmaster announced the next act with exaggerated fanfare. The man irritated Si to no end. On duty or off, the ringmaster spoke at top volume. "Pass me the noodles!" he'd holler with drama at a simple common-pot supper. He snored and shat loud enough for an entire army. A half dozen horses with fancy bridles galloped into the ring with acrobats on their backs. The performers, dressed in glittering silver, somersaulted from horse to horse with impressive synchronicity. Finally, they sprang onto the back of a speckled stallion and formed a three-tiered pyramid.

Tomorrow, his mother had promised, they'd hire a boat, just the two of them, and cruise along the Perfume River. Si doubted this would happen. In Hoi An, they'd taken a cyclo together to the coast but Ma's fans had engulfed them, demanding her autograph. Si had stormed off and carved his name deep into the trunk of a palm tree. One day, he vowed, he'd lead a life free of his mother's annoying fame. Such thoughts made him feel guilty. Why, he might've ended up like one of those poor boys selling coconuts at the beach!

"You're a good son," Ma murmured each time Si massaged her tired feet. If only she knew all the terrible things he was thinking. His mother liked to talk more than she listened, and she never asked him anything of significance. Besides, what difference did his feelings make? He understood that his mother lived for him. But whom did he live for?

M a's was the best and final act. The tent went pitch-black and a loud clanking announced the arrival of the tigers' wheeled cage. *One-two-three*, Si slowly counted before the tigers growled in unison, right on cue. The audience shrieked with fear. Then the lights blared brightly and his mother appeared, golden and glorious, her whip held high in the air. The crowd roared their welcome: "Tham Thanh Lan! Tham Thanh Lan!" Ma bowed gracefully, not too low.

Snap! Snap! The tigers fell into line, ready to do her bidding. Si watched his mother's tigers executing their intricate choreography. How did their lives differ from his? What if, for once, their true nature emerged? What if his did? Would this kill Ma? Night after night she bullied the tigers into performing unnatural acts, like dancing a Viennese waltz. Night after night she stuck her pretty, determined head into their mouths until only the coiled bun at the nape of her neck showed.

In the middle of her performance, Ma caught his eye. She smiled at Si from between two wrestling tigers, but he didn't smile back. *What I teach you, son, is not from books but from my suffering.* Last week Si had stolen her peacock brooch, a foreign gift from a wealthy suitor in Bien Hoa. He fancied that one day it would buy his freedom, although it was probably no more than rhinestones and painted gold. Si ate a handful of salted nuts and scrutinized his mother from head to toe. There was a small tear in Ma's flesh-colored fishnet stockings, barely visible behind her left knee. Who else would have noticed this but him?

"Falling Sky" started out as the last chapter to my third novel, Monkey Hunting. *But even as I was writing it, I suspected that it would have a life apart from the rest of the book. The voice of Si, a mixed-race boy—part Afro-Cuban, Chinese, and Vietnamese—spoke to a future beyond the imagination of his ancestors. Through him, I try to capture something of what the future may look like for all of us. My own daughter—part Cuban, Japanese, Guatemalan, and Russian Jew—inspired me to begin to explore the world of multi-hyphenated identities.*

GLEN LOWRY

Wayde Compton

Wayde Compton wrote *49th Parallel Psalm* and *Performance Bond*; the former was short-listed for the Dorothy Livesay Prize. He edited *Bluesprint: Black British Columbian Literature and Orature*. With Jason de Couto, he is one half of The Contact Zone Crew, a turntable-poetry performance duo. His biological parents were a black and white couple who gave him to Family Services after he was born, and in an unusually symmetrical twist of fate, he was adopted and raised by a black and white couple. He lives in Vancouver, British Columbia, and teaches English literature and composition at Coquitlam College.

The Non-Babylonians

I

K elly and Erika stood a little into the street, looking east and west for a cab. Riel knelt on the sidewalk in front of a newspaper box, straining to read the front page of *The New Albion Observer*. It was a late-August morning, not especially bright yet, but he wore his wraparound sunglasses anyway. What was left of the MDMA made his pupils as open as oceans, and everyone knew it was dangerous to trip in the sunshine with eyes widely dilated: UV rays or some such stealthy evil. Kelly and Erika sported their own shades, looking insectlike in the post-dawn. Riel could hardly make out what he was looking at: the text voyaged from the page in the box, out through scratched Plexiglas, through his cheap plastic black panes, and finally into his amphetamine-buggered retinas. He was more or less hugging the box, kneeling there, the tip of his nose almost touching its window, studying the clouded copy like it was the Pentateuch. He was also hiding; the girls would catch a cab quicker this way. They'd flag one, get home, draw the shades, and figure out what to do about the come-down. But now the newspaper's headline and story pointillistically assembled itself in his head: container ship, female stowaway, uncertain origin, language, detained, exact. He searched his pockets for quarters with no success.

Kelly tugged at his collar. Get up, let's go, we got a cab.

He asked her for a quarter, but she was pulling him. He yanked at the box's handle, yanked again.

Get in the goddamn cab, Riel!

He yanked on the handle once more and it opened. He took the newspaper and boarded the yellow sedan, where the wide-eyed driver watched him uncertainly in the rearview mirror, his left hand hovering, ready to go for something beneath his seat.

Just drive, Riel growled. Fuck. I'm not going to *eat* you, I'm— But Kelly cut him off by reciting their address. The driver hesitated, then pulled out onto Davie Street, making a small show of sighing reluctance.

Back at the apartment, they all collapsed upon the living room chesterfield. Riel flattened the *Observer* out on the coffee table and just looked at it, not even trying to actually read. Kelly put the situation at hand into words: We're coming down, so now what?

Phone Frances, Erika answered flatly.

Riel felt a twitch of despair. His body wanted sleep. But that, he knew, would be impossible for hours yet. Another pass would delay the inevitable crash. Erika already had her cell phone ajar, was talking tersely to their fourth roommate.

While they waited for Frances to get there, Erika flicked on some cartoons and sat in front of the television. Kelly got out her crayons and notebooks and sat in front of the coffee table, going for the primary colors. Riel watched her doodle inconsolably and fiercely, and he watched the blue wash of the TV's light shift across Erika's face. The blinds were shut but didn't quite fit the window; the light in the room was checkered. He tottered over to the CD player and put on some Roni Size, so Erika killed the volume on the TV, her eyes never quite deviating from their fix upon the animated golems on the screen. Riel looked at Kelly and felt something near desire. She was grinding her jaw, chewing on nothing. Her mouth cycled with rhythm and without sound.

By the time Frances finally arrived, Riel had been on his back on the chesterfield for an hour straight trying to sleep, struggling to stop his eyes from popping open involuntarily every other minute. The girls had been getting up, sitting down, getting up, and looking out the window over and over.

How was the party? Frances said, breezing in. You still fucked up?

Not quite, Erika said, sniffling.

Frances sat next to Riel, who had jerkily righted himself at her arrival. Louis, Louis, she said to him, setting down her infamous briefcase beside the *Observer*. You're lookin' rough.

She never called him by his proper name, and Riel never corrected him. He could only assume, as everyone did, that he was named after the Métis revolutionary, but why, exactly, Riel did not know—his father had vacated his life without ever explaining the odd christening. (He knew three things about his father: he was black, he was from San Francisco, and he was long gone.) As far as Riel knew, he had no Native ancestry, and all his mother could say about his name was that Riel's father had convinced her during her pregnancy that it sounded "musical." Frances, a proud urban Cree, found it amusing that a non-Native carried such a meaningful name for no real reason. She was polite enough not to make fun of him for it directly, but she made her skepticism of the great man's misinvocation known by referring to her roommate as Louis, Louis, sometimes even singing the Kingsmen's melody as she called him out.

You know, Frances, I think maybe the best thing is that I just tough it out and go to sleep, he said.

Kelly blanched at the suggestion, and opened her mouth as if to speak, but only sighed in quiet agony.

No, no, Erika said, we're going to hit it again. Summer's almost over, and when school starts we're going to get straight. That means we have to do as much drugs as we can *now*. That's just how it is.

That and you fucking called me all the way here, eh? Frances snorted.

We want *more*, Kelly sputtered impatiently. Riel does too. She glared at him.

Frances fiddled with the combination lock on her case, covering one hand with the other to thwart their sight lines. Riel, who was beside her, watched her hands, but Frances glanced at him sideways, warily. He looked across the room. The case snapped open and she said, What do you need? I've got it all. I just saw Victoria last night.

Who's Victoria?

Not a *who*, a *where*. My connection from Victoria was in town last night. They got a laboratory over there. I'm so hooked-up now, it isn't even funny. Up, down, and all around.

After some haggling, Frances poured out three short rails of meth onto the Roni Size sleeve. Intraurban rails at best, Riel thought, if "rails" they were: ALRT shit, for sure, and definitely no John A. MacDonald, sea-to-sea, CPR rails. But beggars aren't choosers, and they were taking Frances's dope on credit. Ostensibly, she was responsible for a quarter of the rent, but they always chiseled the payment out of her in drugs before the first of each month, an overdraft Frances carefully kept track of. Riel couldn't recall a single month of the last six that they hadn't ended up owing her money rather than expecting it from her on rent day.

Riel was spent, and his body was crying out for mercy and rest, but he said, What the fuck? as a kind of grace, and hoovered up the acrid powder anyway. He felt like a rag doll one minute, but three minutes later he was standing up, feverishly hunting around for more drum 'n' bass.

Summer *is* almost over, Kelly said plaintively, her head back to catch the nasal drip. Let's go to English Bay. I want to put my feet in the ocean.

Go? Riel grunted.

Let's walk! Erika squealed with sudden enthusiasm.

Frances laughed. You're insane. You're going to walk to the West End? It's like five kilometers, you freaks.

Riel put on his shoes and started lacing them up. Kelly and Erika watched him, then did the same, and they all put on their sunglasses and started for the door.

Frances, who only dipped into her own supply on days of the month that were prime numbers (or so went the myth she was known by), put her briefcase at the end of the chesterfield, where Riel had just been, and laid her head upon it. Riel had seen her sleep like this many times, protecting her livelihood, he knew, from them, which only mildly offended him. But it amazed him that she could sleep with a four-cornered piece of luggage for a pillow. Frances's day ended there, but Riel's continued sleeplessly out on the sidewalks and all the way to the Pacific where he, his girlfriend, and her best friend stood knee-deep in a greedy tide. They savored the last days of the first summer of the next one thousand years with hallucinations of motion in the peripheries of their sleep-deprived eyes. Riel would turn to look and there would be nothing there but that which was there. Chasing his own optic nerve. Sneaking up on a mirror.

II

The next day, Riel awoke and extricated himself from Kelly's unconscious embrace. Erika was on the other side of her, sleeping too, still wearing her runners. He noticed that he too was still in his shoes, and there was sand in the sheets. He sneered at himself, and got up, scratched, stretched, and wretched twice. There was nothing in his stomach, so nothing came up. He went to the living room. No Frances. He looked out the window. It was sickeningly hot and bright out.

After washing up and eating four pieces of unbuttered toast and a bowl of ice cream, he looked in on the girls. They were still asleep, and he envied them, but nevertheless he perched himself on the chesterfield and picked up the newspaper he had placed there a day earlier. The article that had attracted him returned to memory. He cradled his head in his hands and read.

Mystery Migrant Found in Shipping Container

VANCOUVER—Thursday, 23 August 2001—Longshoremen unloading a container ship yesterday at a Vancouver terminal were shocked to discover a single female stowaway of uncertain origin amongst the usual cargo.

While offloading a container at Centerm, workers noticed the sound of a human voice coming from inside. They immediately broke the lock, opened the container, and notified the Vancouver Police Department. The standard 20' x 8' x 8'6" container had been converted into improvised living quarters, complete with a portable toilet, a supply of water and food, blankets, a battery-powered lamp, and small breathing holes drilled through the walls.

The woman emerged gesturing frantically and speaking in a language none of the workers could identify. The container has been confiscated by the VPD and the woman is currently being detained at their headquarters, where Citizenship and Immigration officers are interviewing her to determine her identity.

A spokesman for the VPD called the stowaway "cooperative, vociferous, but unintelligible." He confirmed that they were uncertain about the woman's exact origin. The ship itself—*The Wing Span*—was initially loaded at the Kwai Chung Container Port in Hong Kong.

Longshoremen interviewed on site disagreed about the woman's appearance, one saying she was "probably Asian," but another commenting that she looked "Arabic." One worker, who is fluent in two dialects, said he did not recognize her language as Chinese.

Riel reread the article, then spoke its headline aloud to himself. Wanting to know the story's development, he went down the apartment stairs and up the street to a café, grabbing a house copy of the day's *Observer*. He ordered a cup and settled in.

Two summers earlier hundreds of Chinese nationals had arrived on the coast illegally, packed onto rickety fishing vessels, and then too Riel had watched a media circus develop around their incarceration and deportation. That was the same year Riel had first read *The Autobiography of Malcolm X* and *Soul on Ice*, books that had stirred and changed him. When he had noticed that everyone in his family, and everyone else he knew in Port Corbus, was angrily unanimous about wanting the refugees sent home, he saw, for the first time, a cohesion among them he had never before fathomed. Everyone in his family was white; everyone he knew in Port Corbus was white. On the issue of illegal aliens, at least, all the people in Riel's life thought alike. He developed a sympathy for the Fujian migrants. Could he help them somehow? Should he write a letter to the *Observer* supporting them? What would el-Hajj Malik el-Shabazz do? Riel read everything he could find about racism in Port Corbus's small library. Then he narrowed his hip-hop consumption down to only the wisest artists: The Coup, Dead Prez, and MC Kaaba. He reevaluated his position that Bob Marley was something to do with the hippies who sold pot on Patourel Beach in the summer, and he bought every CD from *Catch a Fire* to *Confrontation*, poring over Marley's lifetime of lyrics year-to-year as if they were one long book. Armed with a new political outlook, he challenged his teachers and wrote all his essays about racism. His grades improved. He cared about the essays he wrote, which counted for more than he had imagined to teachers in a resource economy–based town with a high dropout rate. Riel had begun high school indifferently, but at the end was surprised to find himself accepted at his second choice of universities in the Lower Mainland. His mother and stepfather were pleased with his success, but dubious about his new stridency, which was, of course, the key to everything. That he was snorting his student loans and attending few of his classes was a turn he hadn't anticipated, a turn that his family knew nothing about. He would hide this carefully when his parents came down for a visit the week after next.

But here, in the pages of the *Observer*, was a case of illegal immigration far more strange than those of 1999. It was now Day Two of the story, and, as he had expected, the *Observer* was all over it. The Mystery Migrant was still in custody, and surprisingly, they still hadn't determined anything about her: they could not be certain of her port of origin, nor even identify the language she was speaking. The authorities refused to speculate to the media, but there were already letters and an editorial about the case. The letters were all shrill, and mainly had her as some sort of terrorist or spy: what economic refugee could afford to send herself in such relative individual comfort? One of the letters called for her to be sent home immediately, saying that "she should be stuffed back in the container they found her in, locked up, and sent back to Hong Kong with 'return to sender' painted on the side." Riel chuckled darkly. They wanted her sent back and they didn't even know where she was from. There had been no photograph in yesterday's paper, but this article was accompanied by a shot of the woman sitting in the back of a police cruiser. A streak of white—glare from the window reflecting the camera's flash—bisected her face, but Riel could still see, examining her features, why there was confusion about her race. She looked, as they'd said, maybe Asian, maybe Middle Eastern. It was hard to tell. Riel himself was used to being misrecognized. He traced her face in the photograph with his finger. Maybe Asian, maybe Middle Eastern. There is such a thing as both too, he knew.

He put the newspaper down and finished his coffee. As Erika had pointed out, summer was nearing its end and the start of school was looming. The coming semester would be make-or-break because Riel was on academic probation. The apartment, friends, clubs, and drugs had eclipsed everything else somehow. What he loved about Kelly was how she drenched herself in bright colors and plastic accessories, like she was wearing toys rather than clothes. She was quirky, in a steely sort of way. She had those multicolored refrigerator door magnets that were letters of the alphabet, and with them she'd spelled out *this is the house of yes* on the white surface; beneath that, Erika had added *there is no should*: the apartment's constitution and sole amendment. But he was fucking up school. If he flunked out, he had no alternative plan. Erika tended to shut down this sort of talk by saying, Twenty-year-olds are supposed to fuck up. That's our job. But Riel was worried. The girls were middle-class kids of university-educated parents, and seemed certain that everything would eventually work out no matter how lost they got. Riel, however, suspected that he had just this one shot. If he fanned on it, he'd be feeding timber into a table saw in Port Corbus for the rest of his life.

Riel took the newspaper and walked back to the apartment. Inside, the girls were up and moping about, abstractedly tidying up. Nobody spoke, and the three roommates moved as if the others weren't there. Riel went to his bedroom and pulled a box cutter out of his desk, slicing the photograph of the Mystery Migrant out of the *Observer*, scratching up the hard cover of a textbook as he did so. He pinned the picture to the wall above and behind his computer, next to the photo of his other hero, MC Kaaba.

Kaaba was better than Tupac, better than any other rapper, Riel felt, though much lesser known. Kaaba wrote lyrics that were a mixture of conspiracy theory, Rastafarian cosmology, and Koranic exegesis based on the Nation of Islam splinter group that Kaaba's parents had raised him in, the Khufu Initiative. Indeed, part of what attracted Riel to Kaaba's music was the connection he felt he had with the rapper because they both grew up in families belonging to weird religious minorities. Riel's mother had remarried and converted to her second husband's faith, so at age eleven Riel had been baptized in his stepfather's church, the New Occidental Jerusalem Church of the Peripatetic Christ, Quadrinitist. Riel's stepfather, Walker, had helped to found the church in Port Corbus in the sixties with several other American draft dodgers who had come to BC during the Vietnam War. (Riel's mother seemed serially attracted to American exiles.) The church had begun as a hippie-oriented, LSD-soaked affair, but over the years had stripped down to a hard core of Jesus freaks eventually pious enough to renounce drugs, free love, and tie-dye. Riel once had read a critique of the church on the internet that referred to it as "a hippie revision of Pentecostal evangelism, created out of expatriate nostalgia." He'd quit the church when he was fifteen.

Riel sat and stared at the two photographs, of MC Kaaba and the Mystery Migrant, side by side on the smoke-colored wall, then he shifted the mouse so his computer would wake up. He opened a program and stared at its gray-framed whiteness, thinking about writing. He stared and breathed until the screen saver finally blipped back on, scrolling words that he himself had input seventeen months earlier. The square of glass said to him BY ANY MEANS NECESSARY . . . GET OUT OF PORT CORBUS.

III

It was Friday and Riel had attended every class of the semester so far, it being only the first unfruitful week. Coming home from campus, he entered the apartment and encountered Frances doling out crank to an autumn-spring couple, some geezer and his young boyfriend. Riel's student loan had been deposited into his account earlier in the week, so he got in line. But the two guys didn't leave when they'd bought their stuff, they made themselves at home, doing bumps off Riel's textbooks without asking. This was happening more often: he'd come home and Frances would be entertaining; there'd be a strange kid asleep in the bathtub, some pale girl rooting through the fridge for food. Riel worried that his CDs were going to get scammed this way, or his computer. But he didn't feel like he had a lot to say about it because the place was really Kelly and Erika's. He'd moved in by default, just by crashing there so regularly. Then Frances offered to pay a quarter of the rent so she could use the place to crash or deal when she was in the neighbourhood. They presumed she had another, real home elsewhere. It was users' economics: Kelly and Erika were getting thrifty, looking for ways to spend less on rent, more on drugs. He eyed the skinny hustler who was fondling his copy of *36 Chambers.* Frances produced a small vial from her "files," and she and Riel traded. Riel pocketed the stuff for later. I was gonna make some tea, she said, and ambled off to the kitchen.

In his and Kelly's room, Riel sat at his desk and looked at his computer, then at the wall above and beyond it. He looked into the black and white eyes of the Mystery Migrant. He had followed the *Observer*'s coverage of her faithfully, but after only three days, they'd dropped the story. During the last two weeks he'd bought copies and scanned the pages for signs of her, but nothing. They had not gotten any closer to identifying her origins. The only thing further they'd learned was that the woman's bags had been full of X rays, which turned out to be of various parts of her own body. There were speculations of illegal organ donation, but oddly, the X rays included all parts of her, head to toe. He didn't understand how the story could have died when nothing had been resolved.

That evening, Kelly and Erika cajoled him into going out. It was dumb, Riel knew, because his parents were visiting in the morning, but it was Friday and he had Frances's speed and government money in his pocket. The girls bought theirs from Frances, who was trying to nap before the evening's work. He resolved to quit the club at a reasonable hour, and be ready to welcome his mother and Walker in the morning with at least a few hours of sleep behind him.

The three set out for The Base. They did half their speed in the washroom and danced till closing, then took a cab to Microphone Check, the doorman's after-hours suggestion. They weren't given an address, but rather just a block, and were told to walk up and down the street until they were spotted and directed in. They did so, getting out of the cab and starting up the street. A guy in a long black coat and fingerless gloves was standing in a doorway eyeing them. He pointed at a building across the street. One-two, one-two, he said, referring to the address above a dark glass door.

Inside they heard the muffled thump-thump-thump-thump of house music coming from above. From behind a desk, a wiry drag queen took their money, forbid in-out privileges, and said, looking at Riel, No tough-guy stuff. You're in a good mood, right? Here to have fun? and Riel nodded. They went down a corridor and up an elevator, eventually finding themselves in a large dividerless office floor full of music, lights, and dancing youth. The DJ was at the back wall and there were speakers in all four corners. The three threw their gear against the wall and claimed a stretch of floor, dancing. When he felt the meth flagging a little, Riel decided to do the second half, so he excused himself, following people who looked like-minded. They led him to an unlighted room at the far end of the floor with a hot-water heater in it and dark figures sitting round the edges intermittently sparking up lighters and talking indistinctly. The music was less pervasive here. The only flat surface was some sort of locker, but others were huddled round it, shaking out various powders onto its surface and snorting them up through rolled-up twenties and fifties. A space cleared across from a young woman, her head bowed over a compact mirror, her dark hair long. He arranged a neat line. When he lifted his head, the crystal was gone, and he stuffed the bill back in his front pocket, pinching his nose to keep the powder in. Across from him, the dark-haired woman lifted her face up from her compact, and pinched her nose in just the same way. He connected with her dark watery eyes.

You.

The woman, startled, stared back at him.

You were in the paper. I read about you.

She half smiled: yes. But she was aiming herself at the door.

He breathed, the amphetamines blazing trails through his blood. She was dressed much like Kelly and Erika; her accent was local. He either had the wrong person or the *Observer* had had the wrong story.

I was following you. You're the Mystery Migrant. I was, like, cheering for you. I rooted for the Fujian migrants too, in '99. He was looking for recognition in her eyes. You *are* you, aren't you?

She laughed. The chorus of Bics singed their shadows.

It was a performance. I'm an artist.

Riel winced. It was a hoax? The migrant thing was a hoax?

Not a hoax. She made a gesture like she was holding a large ball in front of her face with both hands. Art.

Art?

I had myself shipped in that container, intending to get caught. No passport, no ID on me. They had no idea who I was or what I was doing, and I wanted to see what stories would be developed about me, you know, how expectations would shape their perceptions. The stories in the newspaper: I'm writing about them now. The letters from the public were really interesting, don't you think?

Riel felt like running, but he stayed put. But you don't have an accent.

She laughed again. I was born in Canada. Wouldn't have done it unless. They were dying to deport me, although they couldn't figure out where to. But I'm Canadian, so all they can really do is charge me with mischief. I'll get fined, that's about it. I've got a court date. But I had a grant, and I factored a fine into the cost of the performance.

But what language—?

It wasn't a language. I was saying all the phonemes in the phrase "Tower of Babel" over and over again, jumbling them up as randomly as I could. Her smile was wide now. Eventually I fucked it up and the Citizenship and Immigration guy figured it out. It was exhausting trying to keep that up, actually.

Why didn't the *Observer* expose you? They just, like, dropped the story.

They're embarrassed about being duped, I think.

His mind burned. A mental prairie fire. I'm a student. But this, what you're saying, this is something else. He wanted to convey the importance of the moment for him, but the air was moving about liquidly, too quickly, too thickly. I'd like to talk more about it another time, when I'm not tweaking, he admitted.

She took a flyer from her purse. She wrote *Versajna* on the back of it, and her phone number below. He ripped the flyer in half and scribbled his name and number for her too.

Riel turned to go. Kelly was in the doorway, watching him, and he went to her. Versajna passed them and joined the crowd.

Who was that? Kelly said tightly.

You know that refugee I was telling you about, the one in the shipping container? That clipping I've got above my desk? It's her! Only she isn't a refugee, she's a performance artist. Isn't that wild?

Are you obsessed with her or something? Kelly hissed, and she turned away. Riel watched her go. Then he understood that he was supposed to chase her, so he did.

IV

Monday evening, Riel's parents dropped him off at the apartment after their last dinner in Vancouver before going home to Port Corbus. All weekend he'd managed to spend time with them out, doing touristy things in the city, but now Riel could not avoid inviting them up for tea, where they surreptitiously inspected his living conditions. He introduced them to Kelly and Erika, who were on their way out, as his roommates. Frances was asleep in the living room, so Riel and his parents crowded into the small kitchen. After a time, there was a knock at the door, which Frances answered, and three guys wearing black velour track suits came in. Frances peeked into the kitchen at Riel and his parents, and then led the velour-bedecked trio into the washroom, shutting the door behind them. Riel's parents exchanged glances, so he explained that the guys were helping her fix the baseboard. They emerged from the washroom shortly after, the three leaving, and Frances returning to the living room wordlessly. His parents finally excused themselves. They were staying with friends, and had to get a good night's sleep before the long drive home.

After they left, Riel phoned Versajna. They talked about her performance, which she called *The Non-Babylonian*; they talked about university and her occupation, which she described as mailing herself places in spectacularly illegal ways, and she laughed at this. He wanted to know something, but he'd been similarly interrogated all his life, so he held back as long as he could, finally wording it, Where does your name come from?

Where does it "come from"?

I mean, what's your ethnicity?

Ah. He could hear that her words came through a grin: I can't say. I'm still performing, you see. A piece that overlaps with the last one. I haven't answered that particular question for two years and four months now. I'm keeping a journal of all the ways I've been asked, all the responses to my noncooperation, and every speculation.

If you're going to write about what I say, then I don't think I'll say anything.

Too late.

They traded words for three hours.

As soon as he hung up the phone, it rang.

Hello?

I'm not going to let you break your mother's heart.

What?

You think I'm some kind of idiot? Walker said. I know what's going in that place of yours.

Where's Mum? Let me talk to her.

She's asleep. You're screwing up in school, right? You're on drugs, I'm sure.

You don't know anything.

But you are.

If you rang me up just to tell me a bunch of shit that you think you know, then you've achieved that. Mission accomplished. See you later.

You should come back to Port Corbus. Take some time off, straighten out.

Not happening.

I was exactly in your shoes when I was your age. You need some time to get your head together.

Something smacked into the living room window. Riel

looked up. A bird had flown into it, he supposed. He reached over and switched off the light. Look, Walker, I'm just starting the new semester. I'm not going north now, so forget it.

There was silence, except for a little of Walker's breathing on the other end of the receiver, then another thump against the window, and then the click of Walker hanging up.

Riel went to the window and looked out. Two young guys were on the sidewalk below, one of them holding his sneaker in his hand like he was going to shot-put it up at the window again. Riel unlatched and lifted the window, leaned out, and shouted, What the fuck?

Yo, is the Indian chick home? This the spot? Your line was busy, yo.

Riel scowled at them. She's out. He scribbled her cell phone digits on the pad beside the phone and tore the page out, spanned his arm out into the weather, and let the note fall. One of the two tweakers reached up for it with both hands, looking, Riel thought, somewhat like Willem Defoe in *Platoon* when he gets blasted to shit by the NVA. The little piece of paper floated down erratically, and Riel felt for a moment like Galileo dropping a feather to measure the velocity of plummeting bodies in motion. Or whatever the fuck it was he had done to make the church burn him at the stake. Or was that Jeanne d'Arc?

Riel was dreaming of birds. He was watching them light on the leaves of an enormous red tree, each taking a place on a single leaf, and the sun was behind the tree, and it shone through the leaves. There appeared a lumberjack in gold, and he was driving a stone ax into the base of the tree over and over, but the birds would not fly. Inside the dream, Riel could see a close-up image of one birdless leaf, the sun making a glow of red come from it, and the ax made a terrible knocking noise, and then Riel saw that he was looking at the sun through the inside of his eyelids. It was morning. There was knocking, real knocking, and he opened his eyes: the sound of knuckles on the wood of their front door. Muffled shouting. His name being called. Kelly was beside him. Who the hell is that? she said, squinting and stretching.

Riel got out of the bed and sat at the edge. There was more knocking and someone was shouting out there. Ok! he croaked back, and he gathered himself and walked into the hallway.

He was reaching for the doorknob when he heard the voice on the other side.

Open up! You're coming with us, Riel! We know exactly what's going on in this apartment! Get up and get your things! We're driving back to Port Corbus, and you're coming with us!

He stepped back, as if the door had suddenly burst into flames. There was no judas eye in it, but he pictured Walker's blowsy face on the other side nevertheless.

Open the door! I know what's going on here! This is a place of sin!

Riel put the heel of his hand to his forehead. Fuck off! Take your preachy bullshit and just fuck off!

Kelly, Erika, and Frances, awakened by all the noise, congregated in the hallway. That your dad? said Kelly, but she didn't wait for an answer, and left for the kitchen, putting on the kettle. Erika went to the living room. Frances wandered about groggily, like she was searching for something.

Stepfather and stepson argued through the closed door.

Drunkenness, revellings, and such like: they which do such things shall not inherit the kingdom of God!

Behold, a beam is in thine own eye, you fucking hippy redneck!

Oh snap, Erika said. She was sitting on the living room floor with the TV going. Oh my God, you've got to look at this.

Open up! You think it's heaven now, but there'll be weeping and wailing and gnashing of teeth later!

Frances was beside Riel now, no longer searching. Where's my case?

Your case?

Walker started kicking the door on the other side.

Frances grabbed Riel's arm. My *stash*. Where's my fucking *stash*?

There'll be weeping—

How am I supposed to know? You sleep on it, don't you?

—and wailing—

It's gone. You saw the combo on my case. I *saw* you *see* it.

—and gnashing of teeth!

Riel stepped backward and through the bathroom door, closing and locking it in front of him. Immediately, Frances began pounding on *that* door, and cussing him out through it. It was almost syncopated, her pounding and Walker's kicking beyond on the landing.

Riel sat on the edge of the bathtub and put his head in his hands. Frances was shouting about having brothers who'd done time in Matsqui, brothers she was going to phone who would come down here and kick his head in. Then she was quiet for a bit. Now she and Kelly were arguing. He faintly heard Walker's preaching two doors removed, but he could no longer discern the words.

Riel looked at the bathroom window. It was wide open. Outside, it was a fair Tuesday morning. He looked out, then leaned out, observed the alley below. He climbed out the window feet first, and let himself drop onto the blacktop. Frances's briefcase was on the ground at his feet, leaning against the wall, ripped open, and empty. He looked up at the window, then at the case, then up the alley. He was wearing sweatpants and a T-shirt, no shoes. He started walking.

He circled around to Fraser Street. It was just slipping into the post—rush hour lull. A half block down, in front of the apartment, he saw Walker's SUV parked and his mother sitting inside it. He was too far away to note the expression on her face. She was rubbing her forehead. Maybe she was brushing her hair.

He crossed the street. The corner market, where he sometimes shopped, was open and empty. Tameem let Riel use the phone for free, and asked why he had no shoes, pointing down at his feet. Riel shrugged. How else can I be sure that the ground is really there? Tameem frowned and returned his attention to his small portable radio. Voices spoke of attacks on New York and Washington. While the phone was ringing, Riel asked, Attacks? But then Verŝajna picked up on the other end.

Outside, he took a seat at the bus stop and waited. He watched his mother in the SUV half a block up, unaware of him as she stared forward and south. When the bus came, Riel told the driver that he had no money because he had been robbed. He pointed at his bare feet. They even took my shoes, he said. The sloe-eyed driver shrugged. Such a morning, he allowed heavily in a type of English that gently rolled its r's. Riel took a seat in the back.

On his way to Verŝajna's, he decided he was free. He was commuting to the future. He imagined he would not recover his things from the apartment. He imagined he would not complete the semester. He imagined he would neither return nor repent nor weep nor wail. It was the end of everything. *Fin de siècle. Das Ende der Geschichte. E pur si muove.* Riel spoke to himself out loud there in the backseat, but the driver gunned it just as he opened his mouth. The engine sounded so that none of the dozen strangers sitting and standing around him made out his words. There was no manifest reason to repeat.

I come from a family of dockers. My father was a longshoreman for more than three decades before retiring, and my brother is a foreman; I paid for most of my English B.A. by working on the waterfront doing general labor

and night watch. This is partly why I was hired in 2001 to do research for Stan Douglas and Michael Turner's installation film Journey into Fear, *which involved analyzing the history of containerized shipping, and inspired me to think of its metaphorical value. Themes of global migration, nationalism, race, class, religion, and the War on/of Terror, as well as the recent proliferation of methamphetamine in my home province, all converge in "The Non-Babylonians." In this story, I compare the experience of racialization to hoax and myth, and elements both actual and imagined are juxtaposed: Vancouver and the fictional town of Port Corbus; Tupac Shakur and the fictional MC Kaaba, the narrator's idol; the Nation of Islam and a supposed splinter group; and so forth.*

Marina Budhos

Marina Budhos is half Indo-Caribbean and half Jewish, and the author of two novels, *House of Waiting* and *The Professor of Light*; a nonfiction book, *Remix: Conversations with Immigrant Teenagers*; and numerous articles and stories. She has been a recipient of a Rona Jaffe Award for Women Writers, was a Fulbright Scholar to India, and is currently an assistant professor of English at William Paterson University. Her first young adult novel, *Ask Me No Questions*, will be published in 2006.

Hollywood

It began for us with her hair. One afternoon my mother came home with the worst hairdo I'd ever seen. She'd had it dyed and permed, only something went wrong. Her curls had kinked into an orangey, frizzy mass, accenting the freckles on her face. When she came downstairs for supper, my father took one look at her and let out a loud laugh, declaring in his West Indian accent, "You look like a mushroom gone been pickled!" Bursting into tears, my mother ran upstairs and locked herself in the bathroom.

After, I could hear them making up on the front porch, but there was something different in her voice, a firmness I'd never heard before. "It's got to change," she kept insisting. "I just can't take it anymore."

I paid no attention to what she was saying, since my mother's longstanding unhappiness was simply a matter of course in our lives, dating back to 1959, when, as a shy orthodox girl from the Bronx, she impetuously eloped with a West Indian student she'd met two months before at the City College library. I guess she imagined fleeing her insular Jewish world for an exotic life with verandas and coconut palm trees. Instead, she got pregnant and had to quit college while my father quit his studies and became an ordinary schoolteacher. Over the years he'd make promises about taking a sabbatical in Trinidad or living with West Indian cousins in England, but neither ever materialized.

Now it was 1973, the year my braces came off and hot pants were in. I wore a retainer and liked to rub my tongue over my new, straightened teeth. No more did my father grudgingly drive us to Jamaica Estates for our weekly appointment on his way to his night job. Jamaica Estates sat on the north side of Hillside Avenue, the dividing line of Queens, a division made all the more explicit by not only the stone walls which encircled these large, suburban houses and their well-tended lawns, but the decreasing presence of white faces if you kept on south to downtown Jamaica. As something in between and not especially rich, we had always shopped in the discount department stores of Jamaica, unlike my friends from school who went to suburban malls and bought fall coats that cost the entire sum of my wardrobe.

Because of the elevated track, downtown was like a long dark hole, brightened only by squares of flashing light as a train passed overhead. On the bus home, as I flipped through my teen magazines, I fantasized that when we switched buses in the dingy Jamaica Terminal, some movie director would step out of the crowds and insist I audition for him in Hollywood.

Of course this never happened, and the wait for the second

bus stretched dreary and long. Stuck in my throat was a desire to tell my mother all about my plans to flee to California where I would become a light-haired, button-nosed actress in a TV sitcom about some terribly clever family with a big new kitchen and a sheepdog. But as we waited with the other tired mothers and children holding bundles from Woolworth's, I sensed that something here, more than anything, reinforced what it was that was wrong with the picture of our life, so I kept my mouth shut.

A few weeks after the hairdo fiasco, my mother sat me down on the couch. The red of her hair had deepened so it wasn't nearly as awful, but the curls were as wild and frizzy as ever.

"I want you to know that things are going to be a little different this summer," she explained. "I won't be home as much."

"Where are you going?"

She took a deep breath and sighed. I hated when her face got like this, turning into a stiff, tragic mask, as if it might crack apart along two lines that ran down the sides of her mouth. "I'm going back to school."

"Oh," I said, turning away to gaze out the window. This didn't seem like such a big deal.

"You're going to have to help out, you know," she said.

"Why me?" I asked.

"It's a very hard thing to go back after so much time," she explained.

"Everyone thinks my life was difficult because I married your father," she went on. "But what's worse is facing myself, all that ambition I gave up on." Then she added, "After all, I've taken care of you all these years; now it's time you helped me."

I hunched down resentfully in the pillows. "What about my new bike?" I asked in annoyance. "You and Daddy promised."

Her face splintered into angry lines. "Is that all you have to say?"

When I didn't reply, she jerked up from the couch, declaring, "Well, I can see you're a lot less grown up than I thought, Jamila." Then she went into the kitchen to start dinner.

T he warm weather came and now when I strolled down the
street in my summer clothes, I could sense something different light up in the eyes of boys I'd known all my life. Evenings,
they leaped out from between cars, flinging balloons swollen
with water, so they could see our new breasts and nipples poking
through our soaked T-shirts. Adolpho, a chubby boy one year
younger than me, taunted me to come lie on his Sealy Posturepedic mattress. "What's so special about a stupid mattress?" I
yelled, and his friends would guffaw.

One of my friends was Rachel Myerson, a girl who lived
across the street. Her mother, Frances, was the speculation of
much neighborhood talk, for she teased her hair into a platinum
blonde pile. My mother thought Frances scandalously negligent,
since she often took off on Club Med vacations and left Rachel
and her brother Louis alone.

Frances also didn't mind the neighborhood kids drinking
and smoking or playing loud music in her apartment, which is
where we always went after wandering around the streets. One
hot night I went into Rachel's kitchen for some soda to find Louis
leaning against a refrigerator. Louis was the responsible type my
mother always commended; he had hard, firm muscles from lifting weights and worked summers delivering groceries. But contrary to my mother's opinions, I'd always found Louis to be a
self-righteous bore. One time he'd cornered me in the bathroom
with an electric razor, boasting that he'd begun shaving at the age
of twelve. Not knowing what to say, I took the razor from him and
switched it on, pretending to run the buzzing, circular blades
against my own chin.

"Excuse me," I said now.

"Nope," he said.

I rolled my eyes in the appropriate manner. "Cut it out."

"No, you cut it out." He nodded in the direction of Rachel's bedroom, where Adolpho was belting along with Led Zeppelin. "What are you hanging out with those losers for?" he asked. "Why don't you go on a date with me?"

I looked at him, surprised. I wasn't even sure I knew what a date was.

"Don't you want to kiss me?" he asked.

"I don't know," I replied.

"I'll take you out," he offered. "Treat you nice."

"You're stuck-up," I mentioned.

"So what?" he asked, fixing his clear blue eyes level with my breasts. "There a law against that?"

The next morning Mom came down the stairs dressed in a new pantsuit and declared it was high time Dad taught her how to drive, like he'd been promising for years. Reluctantly, he agreed, and I sat on the curb to watch them. They got in the car. Mom sat in the driver's seat with her nose pushed close to the windshield, clutching the wheel with both hands, as if it was a pillow she meant to throw at Dad. The car lurched and stopped and rolled a few inches. They made it as far as the end of the block before the car stopped altogether. I heard the car door slam, then my mother came striding up the block, tears rolling down her face, mascara smeared. My father parked the car and came up to me with a sheepish look on his face.

"What happened?" I asked.

"Damn if I know," he sighed. His West Indian accent seemed impenetrable all of a sudden. "What a fuss that silly woman kick up. Every time I say put your foot on the gas, she hit the brake." He shook his head slowly, as if my mother was as alien to him as I had lately become to her. "So emotional she can be."

As we began strolling toward the house, he remarked, "Don't be making too much noise, Jamila. She on the warpath as it is."

I followed him inside, not especially pleased at this bit of advice. "What about my bicycle?" I asked when we were in hearing distance of my mother. She was in the kitchen starting dinner, a ruffled apron girding her hips. Without turning around, she warned, "Don't drag me into this."

My father's dark face lit up with the same guilty smile as when my mother stormed out of the car. Often when things got bad between them, he feigned a loss of memory. "Did I say that?" he asked.

I stamped my foot. "Daddy."

"Did I?" he repeated to my mother's back.

My mother whirled around, holding a cleaver in her hand.

"Don't play your games, Reginald," she said. "A promise is a promise. At least that's the way I was raised." As her voice rose with accusations, my lungs seemed to swell with her rage toward my father. "She's your daughter, you understand? I'm not going to stand here while you do your Caribbean sweet talk on a little girl." The cleaver rapped loudly on the wooden board. "First it was teaching me how to drive and now this. How cruel you can be."

Then she went on in her clipped, precise voice about the usual, awful crimes he had committed, all of which seemed the fault of Trinidad, which to her had become a source of hopeless deceits and singsong lies. I never knew what it was I should feel about this image of my father, especially when I looked in a mirror and saw how much I looked like him; my skin the same nut-brown color. Even my name came from down there—Jamila was the name of his mother, who sewed money in the hems of my father's trousers when he left Port of Spain for New York.

Now, my father sank down helplessly on the couch and I stood there, sick to my stomach, not sure whether to leave or stay, or even who I was madder at—him for forgetting my bicycle or her for making it into a big scene—such that I was forgotten altogether.

It was finally agreed that my father's checks would first go for driving school for my mother, her two courses at Queens College, and a bike for me. At breakfast one morning my father leaned in and asked me, "So, big girl, you know what kind of bicycle you want?"

"You bet," I replied. I did know the exact bike I wanted. It was a Raleigh ten-speed, boy's style, maroon. Somehow, everything rested on the purchase of this bicycle: I could see myself released from my neighborhood which I now knew by heart, pieces of different lives flying past, houses like the one my orthodontist lived in and faces that were not so weary as those I saw on buses with my mother.

That Saturday, when we went to Buddy's Bike Shop, the instant we walked through the glass doors I could sense the salesmen—really boys not much older than me—snapping to attention, a buzz in the air. A tall guy with a ponytail led me into the showroom where he showed me a brown Tour de France. "What about the Raleigh?" I asked in disappointment.

Glancing once over his shoulder, the salesman leaned in, whispering, "I'll tell you a secret. It really was the same bike." Then he squeezed my hand. Thrilled, I agreed to buy the Tour de France on the spot.

As it turned out, the bicycle was not the same as a Raleigh. It was heavier for one thing, and the gears made a clacking noise each time I shifted. But it was mine and my days seemed to burst wide open. Now, if I got bored of the water balloon games or lingering around the park benches with my girlfriends in hopes some boys would come by, I took off on my bike, riding to every park in Queens. I even fantasized about riding through the Lincoln Tunnel to Route 80, clear across America to reach the dry, golden reaches of Hollywood where I planned to make an impressive speech at the doorstep of some famous TV producer, pleading for a part on one of his shows.

One hot afternoon I parked my bike on a high, grassy knoll overlooking a handball court in Forest Park. Boys with beautiful, shirtless backs gleaming in the sunlight slammed handballs against a wall, while a group of girls stretched out on the hood of a souped-up car as if it were a beach blanket. I knew that these girls, who smeared their mouths with bright lipstick and tied their blouses in a suggestive knot between their breasts, were not much older than me, but I didn't know how it was done—how I might cross that distance between them and me.

A ball rolled a few feet away from me. "Over here!" someone called. I picked up the ball, and as I tugged my elbow back and saw their faces lift, I had a sudden intimation of what they really were staring at: the hem of my halter top lifting; my bare, brown stomach.

"Ooh baby," one of the boys called, smacking his lips. "You are my milk chocolate sundae. Lemme have a lick."

I threw the ball with a jerk, turning away in shame, skin burning. Then I leaped on my bicycle and skidded down the hill, pedaling fast, down Woodhaven Boulevard, toward the skyscrapers rising in a dirty haze on the horizon. I was determined to ride through the Lincoln Tunnel to Route 80 and onward.

I rode and rode, until I was so thirsty I had to pull into a supermarket parking lot to buy a Coke. When I sat down on a curb to drink it, my tears had dried, but my nerves were still thrumming at the thought of the long, frightening ride ahead. I had sixteen dollars and fifty-two cents in my pocket.

Just as I was getting on my bicycle again, a beige-colored car with a sign on its roof rolled forward, honking at me. I steered out of its way but the horn still blew. "Jamila!" someone called.

I didn't recognize her at first with makeup and long earrings glimmering in the sun, but it was my mother all right, strapped behind a steering wheel. "What are you doing here?" she asked me.

"What are *you* doing?" I asked back. I didn't know whether to feel relieved or angry at finding her here. Her lipstick was on straight for a change.

"We're learning turns," she said happily. "And I went on a highway today! Can you believe it, Jamila! Your Bronx mom driving on a *highway*."

"Great," I mumbled. Suddenly, I wanted to tear open the car door and tell her everything, all about what the boys had been saying to me, and how I was running away to California. But the instructor kept glancing at his watch. "The time, Mrs. Lukhoo," he complained, saying the "oo" part of our name like "ewh."

My mother flicked on the turn signal. "You'll get back before dark, okay honey?" she said. "There are chops in the skillet."

I saw her foot lift from the accelerator pedal and the car eased away from me, jerkily, taking a turn too wide.

W hen I got in the door, the phone was ringing. It was Louis.

"So?" Louis said.

"So what?"

"You gonna go on a date with me or what?"

My heart speeded up, remembering the girls and boys in the park; the shame and awkwardness they had made me feel. "I don't know."

"OK, I can take a hint."

"No, wait!" I hesitated, hearing his breathing on the other end. "I'll go. But we really have to *go* somewhere. Not hang around."

"No kidding, genius."

We had agreed to meet that Friday night at seven o'clock on the corner, and at exactly two minutes after seven Louis came striding up the street in new jeans that made his gait wooden and stiff. "Hey, smart girl," he greeted me, brushing my cheek, and I noticed a faint rash tinged his jaw from shaving too hard.

We took the bus to Adventurers Inn amusement park, where the air was close and fishy smelling from the nearby East River and the lights from the Whitestone Bridge washed the sky a dirty pink. Louis insisted we ride only the safe rides like the Spider and Funhouse, and when he helped me down from the little cars his grip around my waist was firm like a father's, but I didn't like it.

In the arcade he made us a punched medallion that read "Louis and Jamila 4-Ever." Then we got back on the bus and he took my hand. Embarrassed, I turned my face away to watch the streets rolling by. His fingers began to stroke the back of my hand. A hot flush spread from my face to my ears.

"You know what your problem is?" he asked.

"What?"

"You need a boyfriend to look after you."

The windowpane rattled cold against my cheek. I had no idea what he meant.

"You're very pretty," he continued, patting me on the knee. "Nice and tan and thin."

"What am I supposed to say to that?"

"Jeez," he said and made a blowing noise through his teeth. "It was just a compliment."

"OK. So now what do I do?"

He smiled and tapped his jaw with a finger. "Why don't you give me a little kiss?"

Pursing my lips together, I shut my eyes and leaned forward. In my mind I could picture the rough stubble on his cheek and wondered if it would scratch like my father's. Just then, the bus took a wide turn, and I went heaving into Louis's lap, banging into his chin. The bridge of my nose throbbed. "Man oh man," he groaned, covering the side of his face with a hand. "You don't have to *throw* yourself at me."

Our next date was to be a whole day at Rockaway Beach. Saturday morning I shaved my legs for the first time, put on my bikini, and stood admiring myself in the mirror. From riding my bicycle so much, my calves were ropy with muscles and when I ran my hand along my scarred knees, I flushed with vanity, amazed at how smooth my skin was.

The bus ride was one and a half hours, during which Louis entertained me with light bulb jokes. "How many mothers does it take to screw in a light bulb?" he asked. "How many?" I replied.

Louis answered: "That's all right, I'll sit in the dark." I laughed so hard, Louis leaned in tight, our thighs and arms bumping and sticking. He whispered, "Now, how many dykes does it take to screw in a light bulb?"

"What's a dyke?" I asked.

Louis's mouth shut and he straightened in his seat. "You're not so smart, after all."

When we unpacked at the beach, I suddenly found myself unable to take off my T-shirt, afraid he would notice my breasts and make a big fuss about them.

"You look great," Louis kept saying. "But what's with the T-shirt?"

"Later," I grumbled. "Don't bother me now."

I couldn't help it. Louis lay too close to me, so I could feel his breath on my skin. All I wanted to do was cover myself from the hot, blinding sun. We didn't talk much, but watched girls and boys walk by in their wet, clingy bathing suits.

I really wanted to swim, but instead sat with my knees pressed against my chest. Louis ran his hand along my knee. "Ooh ooh," he said. "So smooth."

Suddenly I jumped up and bolted off across the sand and went racing toward the water. I'd never been to Rockaway Beach before and this ocean was dirty, floating with Styrofoam cups and cigarette butts. The waves were hardly waves at all, only small rolls slapping gently in my face, and when I floated on my back, I saw the beach was a narrow strip of sand with too many people. Louis waved.

It occurred to me that if I didn't go back soon, Louis might come into the water and swim up from below and try to kiss me. Worse yet, he might try to pull off my shirt. I imagined the two of us, bobbing in the dirty water, the paler moons of my breasts sliding from their cups, his mouth opening in laughter.

I left the water then and trudged back up the slope of sand, dripping like a dog on our blanket. Louis was busy applying suntan lotion to his broad, muscular chest and arms. He squinted up at me and a slow, cocky smile drifted over his face. For a second I thought everything was going to be all right and I would be able to relax and take off my T-shirt.

"You know what you look like with that wet T-shirt?"

"What?"

"A wet pretzel!" Louis was so amused with himself, lotion went dribbling down his arm.

"You are gross," I said, and thumped down on the blanket.

O ur afternoon was hardly a success, not only because Louis failed to get a kiss from me, but later, as we ate French fries and his toes inched up my newly shaved calf, he winked and I failed to wink back. Or, at least I tried, but had trouble doing so—both eyes would shut at once. "Jeez," he laughed. "You really are a klutz."

After we got off the bus, we stood in the middle of the street, hot asphalt burning through our rubber thongs. When Louis leaned toward me, I shut my eyes, readying myself for the kiss.

"See you," he whispered instead.

I opened my eyes, and there I stood in a windshield's warped, tinted glass: bedraggled hair slicked against a small head, T-shirt clinging to a skinny brown torso. I looked exactly like a wet pretzel.

No one was home, so I went upstairs to the bathroom, unpeeling my bathing suit from my sun-sore limbs, sand scattering to the tile floor. After a long, hot shower during which I shaved my legs again, I stood on the turned-down toilet seat and carefully examined my body's profile. For some reason, I was terribly worried that the new, round protuberances of my breasts should not exceed that of my backside. I looked myself up and down, down and up. To my relief, things appeared to be equitably balanced.

Then I put on my mother's silk robe and crawled under the cool sheets in my parents' bed with a grilled cheese sandwich, and the TV on. About an hour later I looked up to see my mother standing in the doorway. When she saw the dirty dishes on the bed, she let out an outraged shout. "Who said you could eat in bed?"

Before I could answer, she was in the bathroom, yelling some more. "Get over here, young lady!"

I hurried over to find her clutching the remains of my afternoon: my T-shirt and still damp bikini, straps dangling through her fingers. "If you think I'm going to pick up after you, you have another thing coming," she went on. "That's over. Do you hear me? Those days are *over*!"

My face went hot. "I don't care!" I suddenly screamed, "I don't care about your stupid school or your stupid lessons. I *hope* you fail!"

My mother's face froze. We stared at one another, she with her terrible tragic mask, me with her robe melting off my arms. Then she thrust the damp things at me, slammed the door, and I was left staring at the bikini in my hands. On the other side of the door I could hear the faucet taps creak, then one of the most familiar sounds to me: my mother weeping, as she often did, thinking I couldn't hear her with the water on.

That night I sat in my room, trying to get up the nerve to call Louis. Across the street, his bedroom window floated like a sugar cube in the black liquid air. It wasn't that I especially wanted to speak to him, but I wanted something, *anything*, to release me from what seemed like the worst of conditions: my mother fuming downstairs with metal clips pinned to her hair, restlessly flicking through a newspaper. After Dad got home, he came into my room and tried to explain I had especially hurt her feelings because, after all these years of getting up the nerve to go back, she had just received a C on her first paper. "What do I care," I said, flopping onto my stomach.

Now I could hear their low, tense voices, and I could tell that a fight was going to start and it was all my fault for shaving my legs and wearing her robe and yelling back at her. I picked up the receiver, dialed, and listened to it ring. Suddenly Louis's voice was on the other end, curious, full of swagger, and when I didn't answer, he turned belligerent. "Is this one of Rachel's little creeps?" he asked. I slammed down the receiver.

I couldn't sleep. Either my breasts hurt when I lay on them or the covers got tangled around my waist. I still tasted salt in the stiff tangles of my hair and when I pressed my lips to my shoulders, the skin was warm and tight. I tried to imagine what it would be like to have a boy kiss that skin. In theory it seemed nice. But after a while these fantasies made my stomach hurt, for they got mixed up with the image of my mother and father on the other side of the wall in that terrible cell of their history: he, with his brown, angry shoulders hunched against her; she, on the other side of the bed, her aging body slack with disappointment.

Around eight o'clock I got up and positioned myself by the window since Louis had a summer job at a grocery store. At eight-thirty his door swung open and I saw him stride out in the gray morning air, a grin tilting across his sunburned face. Only after I caught sight of him was I able to fall asleep.

I still rode but with less ambition. Sometimes I went down Woodhaven Boulevard, hoping, yet not hoping, to run into my mother again. I made sure not to go too far because I wanted to pedal down the street at four-thirty, when I knew Louis might be coming back from work. Usually I wound up circling the same old streets. I was stuck in wanting his attention, having him confirm that although I failed to cross the distance that afternoon at the beach, I had not really failed. I'd even forgotten how much I disliked Louis. But the new light which brightened inside me each time I passed Adolpho and the others now seemed concentrated in the promise of one boy.

A few weeks later I was turning the bike into a leafy pool of shadows when I heard someone shout out behind me.

"Hey! Hey pretzel!"

I squinted. From across the street I could see the blunt silhouette of Louis leaning against a car. He waved. Ribs pounding, I slowly steered my bike toward him. The ratchet noise of shifting gears clicked loud in my ears and I was squeezing the brake handles when I saw what I hadn't seen before—in the sideview mirror, a slim hand, a silver ring winking in sunlight—then I realized there was a girl in the car, a beautiful girl like on TV with straight blonde hair, but by this time it was too late and my wheel jolted over the curb onto Louis's sneaker as I went crashing into him.

We fell with a clatter to the ground, all metal and grease, his sweaty arms springing back from my chest in surprise. I could hear the girl shriek as Louis jumped up from the ground, swearing. "Jesus Christ!" he shouted. "You are such a goddamn klutz!"

I still lay under the bicycle, leg half on, half off the curb, the greasy weight of gears sunk in my calf.

"She's hurt, Louis," the girl said. Louis and the girl lifted the bike from me. My leg began to twitch, and it was all I could do not to cry, so I fixed my eyes on the wispy threads of her cutoffs curving over gently perfect thighs.

"Can you get up?" Louis asked.

When I tried to stand, a fiery pain shot up the arch of my foot and exploded in my kneecap. I stumbled, blood bubbling out of a slash in my leg. The girl stepped back in disgust.

"You need a ride home," she said, gesturing to her car.

"Don't bother," Louis said, nodding in the direction of my apartment.

"She's a neighborhood kid." He tapped his shoulder. "Lean on me," he instructed. I resisted, so he grabbed my hand and wound it around his shoulder. "Lean!" he yelled.

Looking down, I saw the blood had soaked through my sock.

Slowly I leaned into that firmness I wanted no part of weeks ago. When we reached the curb I forced myself to twist around. There the girl stood with her beautiful hair and arms lit up by dappled sun. My bicycle lay like a felled log on the ground.

T he break was a sideways fracture, which meant I had to wear a cast from the knee down. Every morning I sat on a lounge chair, magazines spread around me, drinking Tab. Out of boredom, I painted my toenails and sometimes hobbled into the cool environs of my parents' bedroom and dialed strangers' numbers. "If you can tell me how many miles it is from Santa Monica to Beverly Hills you can win a new Sony television!" I yelled.

"Um, ah," they said.

"Bzzt, too late, you slow cluck," I said and hung up.

Louis and Barbara came by to visit me now and then. Oh yes, that was her name. *Barbara.* She drove a silvery Datsun 280Z and remained very friendly to me after that day. Barbara was already a senior in high school and a champion swimmer. Once she even suggested that when I got better we could all go to the beach together. I didn't answer. Louis reddened and stared at his knuckles between his knees. I knew he would never admit to Barbara that he had taken a dumb klutzy kid like me on a date.

As they got up to leave a few minutes later, he pulled in close, put his hand on my knee, and whispered, "No hard feelings, right, Pretzel?" I nodded.

"I still think you need some guy to take care of you, though." Turning away, the spot where he had touched me sprang like an anger through my body.

July wore on, and afternoons I grew tired of sitting on the lounge chair, scratching my leg with a bent hanger, listening to the churning exhaust of the air conditioner. When my mother came home from driving lessons she often brought me presents. A Lady Bic shaver. *Teen Beat* magazine and glass bead earrings just like hers. I let Adolpho scribble all sorts of stupid things on my cast leg. *Baby I miss you so, the Sealy Posturepedic mattress is lonely.*

The second week in August we went back to the doctor's. When the sawed-off cast split open on the examining table and I saw my withered calf wracked with cuts, a toothy scar where the gears got me, I wanted to scream out loud. But I didn't.

Then he went behind a door. I heard the rattle of metal, and he reemerged, holding an aluminum cane in one hand. I let out a shriek.

"It's just for a month," he explained.

"Honey, please," my mother said. Her hands didn't know where to touch me.

But I couldn't stop the sounds coming out of my throat. I felt so ugly, my wrists two hard bones as I pressed them against my lids. "I want to ride," I sobbed. "I want to be on TV."

But no one understood what I was trying to say, and I pushed my mother away, for it felt as if all my words were being swallowed up in that dark, confusing struggle between us.

After we got home, my father went to school and my mother came outside, dressed in a new purple pantsuit for her driving lesson. Her mascara had smudged, which made me wonder if she had been crying in the bathroom. I instantly felt guilty. "Why can't you stay home?" I asked instead.

My mother shook her head, her long glass earrings dangling on her neck. "Why don't you invite that nice boy Louis over?"

I turned my face away. "He's a bore."

Her arms wound around me, her perfume winey and strong.

"Sometimes I don't know what to say to you, Jamila," she whispered. "But things will change. They *are* changing. That's what's so hard about this time."

I didn't answer, and she kissed me on the cheek and began walking away. Even from here I could see her crazy hair mushrooming red and wild, as if it had caught on fire from the late afternoon sun. Raising myself up, I used my cane to limp toward the street. I so wanted to go with her. But I knew that from here on, I would be left to follow her in my mind, often in anger, the two of us mysteriously aligned. I imagined myself as her: getting off the bus in the El-darkened streets, trudging into the parking lot of the driving school. Then she would slide behind the wheel next to her instructor, start the ignition, and nose into the street, slow and cautious at first, but with time, more and more confident of where it was we were going.

"Hollywood" was one of those stories that slipped out almost effortlessly, once I heard the first sentence. I think because it's the kind of story that, unbeknownst to me, was brewing for a long time. Some of it was straight autobiography—the date, the taunts of the neighborhood kids, even the type of bicycle. But the key was setting it in one summer, in the '70s, where—for the narrator— so much came to a head about herself, her background, and her parents. I grew up in a community where, in the '60s, many mixed-race families found a wonderful oasis for raising their kids. We felt very comfortable since most of us had some kind of unusual mixing in our background. Our parents were often the pioneers—the ones who had braved a lot to be together. But by the '70s, as we were all turning into teenagers, a lot of confusions and social disintegration were swirling around us. That's why the setting of the '70s was also important to me—it's about the end of a certain kind of dream, where, in my world, so many marriages and hopes were cracking apart.

Mamle Kabu

Mamle Kabu is half Ghanaian and half German. She is just starting out as a writer and will have another short story, "The End of Skill," published in the *Anthology of New African Writers* in 2006. She grew up in Ghana but studied in the U.K. for ten years. She currently lives in Accra, Ghana, and works as a research consultant in development issues.

Human Mathematics

Folake's shoes were what made my first memory of her so vivid. She had not yet received her uniform but she was already wearing the sensible footwear that would go with it—hideous things that could only possibly have looked at home on the feet of a middle-aged filing clerk in the dusty, male-dominated offices of an accounting firm or insurance company. It was like meeting myself two years before.

The shoes conformed perfectly to school regulations: "Comfortable, low-heeled, black lace-ups." Wide enough in front for each toe to wriggle around in perfect freedom without encumbering its neighbor. Broad, square heels giving the feet a solid, steady base. Generously cut uppers lacing high and providing excellent support. Yes, they were as sensible as shoes could be. Yet it was an inevitable irony that they would be sadly out of place among the actual shoes that Ridgefield girls wore— shoes with flimsy heels, a few inches of token lace, and above all, pointed "winkle picker" snouts that promised a future of corns and hammertoes.

It was not only Folake's shoes, however, that conjured up my old self; it was her clothes too. There was an awkward formality about them, at odds with her youth, which showed a compliance with regulations and a respect for authority at the expense of fashion and fifteen-year-old female frivolity.

With my two years' experience I knew that such deportment, even in a new girl, could elicit nothing but scorn and ridicule from most of her schoolmates. However, I recognized in her the fresh West African arrival I had once been. We might not be from the same country, but the air of respect and sobriety with which she presented herself was as familiar and intelligible to me as a common language. And from that perspective, it was also completely appropriate.

I knew instinctively that in her first weeks at Ridgefield, Folake would marvel at the tone in which some of her classmates addressed their teachers, thinking "I'd like to see her talk to a teacher in Nigeria like that." In my first term, I had often imagined transporting the more irritating among my classmates to my old school in Ghana where you dared not address even the older pupils in such tones and where bad behavior was punished not by order marks and detentions, but by stinging lashes administered by the sports teacher in the headmaster's office.

The Folake of a year later predictably wore different shoes and had stopped fantasizing about sending cheeky British schoolgirls to West Africa to learn the true meaning of discipline. Like me she had learned to appreciate the intellectual pleasure of freer communication with one's teachers. However, coming from a society in which respect for seniority was deeply ingrained and rigorously enforced, she enjoyed this as a privilege, not a right, and thus never took advantage of it. The teachers and house staff appreciated this in her as they always had in me.

Indeed, Folake and I were often compared with each other because we had several things in common beyond our West African blood.

There were other Nigerian girls in the school, but none were both in Folake's year and in her boarding house, as I was. There were also a few girls from other West African countries and a handful from Eastern and Southern Africa. In addition, there was a strong representation from Asia. In fact, although not officially international, Ridgefield had a strong foreign contingent. There were different degrees of foreignness, however. There were the fresh arrivals from abroad, and then there were the ones who looked foreign but had spent much, most, or all of their lives in England.

The one other Ghanaian girl in the school, Stella Amissah-Smith, fell into this latter category. She had been in the school since the earliest level and had spent all of her life in England. I had been quite excited to meet her at first, but somehow we had never formed a real friendship. My social circle was a veritable league of nations, while hers comprised almost exclusively British girls. The two circles simply did not intersect. Once we both understood that, we maintained a neutral distance from each other.

In these divergent social constellations there was another important difference between us, which, incidentally, also distinguished Folake from me. Strictly speaking and certainly in biological terms, I was only half African. My other half was German, European, Caucasian—white. This distinction, which in purely racial terms might have bracketed Folake and Stella together and placed me outside their subset, did not, in reality, constitute any common ground for the two of them. In fact, the distance between them was even greater than that between Stella and me. On a line with three equidistant points, I would have been the midpoint with the two of them at either extreme. Midpoint was the natural position for me.

The subtle complexities of this situation demonstrated the inefficiency of color as a lowest common denominator for human mathematics. Fortunately for me, I had realized early in life that the ability of color labels to seem hopelessly superficial at best and ridiculously inaccurate at worst, was, like the tip of the proverbial iceberg, the very indication that a dense, hulking mass lurked beneath.

Strangely enough, growing up in Ghana as a visibly brown child, I had been labeled "white." Yet I had metamorphosed into a "black" the first time I traveled to a white country. However, like the chameleon, another creature of distinct in-betweens, I had already learned that it was I who had to make the adjustment, not my surroundings.

In my years at Ridgefield Girls' the ease with which I moved between the colors of my spectrum was as involuntary as the changes in my accent. When I spoke to Folake, her Nigerian accent teased out and propped up my languishing Ghanaian one. When I spoke to the teachers and the British girls, their clipped tones braced and nurtured my burgeoning British accent.

Some of my classmates had teased me about my Ghanaian English in my first year at the school. What seemed to stand out most was intonation. This had caused some embarrassment in my first week when Sarah, a girl who sat next to me in class, had been unable to understand my request to borrow an eraser. The problem was that I pronounced the word with a heavy stress on the first rather than the second syllable. Sarah had obviously never been asked for an "ee-raser" before and wasn't sure what to make of my request. After a few efforts to make myself understood, I realized we were drawing attention to ourselves and tried to put her off, but it was too late.

"What's the matter over there?" asked the teacher.

"Oh, nothing," we chorused. I was anxious for the fuss to die down, and Sarah was sensitive to that. But the teacher genuinely wanted to help because I was the new girl.

"Did you need something, Claudia?" she persisted gently.

"Well, I was just trying to borrow an ee-raser," I mumbled, hot with shame and cold with dread.

"Oh, you mean an eraser," she said straight away. Apparently it was not the first time she had heard it pronounced that way. Her correction had been completely involuntary and was not mocking or patronizing. I was grateful for that but still had to endure the snickers of my classmates.

Although embarrassing for me, the incident had been a genuine misunderstanding on Sarah's part. She was not one of the girls who made fun of my accent. In fact, she later became one of my closest British friends. In my first year at Ridgefield, which I had entered at the third form level, we had sat next to each other in our classroom preceding assembly every morning.

In the fourth form we were in the same dormitory together with four other girls. We were not close in the way best friends were, but we liked each other and had an easy familiarity that came from being thrown together in several settings within the school environment. She sometimes teased me good naturedly by calling me "Ee-raser." My interactions with her, as with the other white girls, generally featured the more Caucasian me.

My Caucasian identity, thus far in my life, had consisted of looking different, being "white" in a black home country, knowing European foods, having an ear for my mother's favorite classical composers. It was being dropped at parties long before they began and collected long before they ended because we were operating by European time in Africa. It was calling my grandparents, even the Ghanaian ones, "Oma" and "Opa."

Thus it was that I was more easily accepted, warmed up to by the white girls, safer territory for them than the pure African girls from Africa. The same situation pertained in reverse. In Folake's first year at Ridgefield I could sense that she was grateful to me for stopping at her downstairs dormitory on the way to breakfast. She had an amicable but still slightly stiff relationship with her dormitory mates and was more at ease with me. She probably sensed that she could be more herself in the few minutes of our walk than for the rest of the day. This was despite the presence of my best friend, Mira. Perhaps Mira's being Indian and strongly accented made Folake comfortable too.

In the fifth form we outgrew large dormitories and earned the privilege of double rooms. Although we were not given a choice of roommates, there was some effort to pair well-known sets of friends and I was happy to discover that I was placed with Mira. Next door were Stella Amissah-Smith and her best friend, Jenny James. Those who were not part of an obvious friendship were randomly paired. And that was how Folake and Sarah became roommates.

There seemed no immediate problem with this pairing. The two had known each other for a year and had often been in my company at the same time in the common areas. However, we had not advanced very far into the term when undercurrents of tension began to hum. Although I had initially been pleased that I could see two friends at the same time, I quickly discovered that I did not feel comfortable when they were both present.

For the first time I became conscious of the switches in my accent. What was normally an automatic, involuntarily transition became a linguistic quandary. As often happens when switching rapidly between languages, elements from one linguistic set soon started to jump into the other like nerve impulses firing out of control. The result was not the smooth, natural blend of the two that I effortlessly used with Mira. It was a jarring, clumsy combination that made me feel awkward like a tuneful songbird that had unexpectedly produced a squawk. Under these tensions conversations dwindled to pleasantries and flat jokes until I found myself looking for an exit.

I started to question myself—my very being and my own genuineness. I did not like feeling awkward and fake, and did not understand why I should feel that way in their room when I never did otherwise. Was it false and deceitful to be black with a black friend and white with a white one? And to be yet a third, perhaps "brown," person with friends who were neither black nor white? Did it make me two- or even three-faced? If it did, could I help it?

For a while I avoided Sarah and Folake, trying to make the echoes go away. Deep down, I knew they were with me to stay, but at least I could quiet them by staying in as neutral territory as possible. In a school like Ridgefield, however, this was not easy and my concerns returned with renewed vigor on the day of the row.

I was always grateful to have missed the main action of that fight. In theory, it had little to do with me anyway. Yinka and Alison were not even in my year. They were younger, and at that stage of our lives and in our highly structured school environment, a year's age difference was worth as much as a decade's in later life. However, both girls were in my house. It was natural for quarrels to break out once in a while in that populous, hormone-charged atmosphere. They usually affected only the two girls involved and perhaps their closest friends. But this one was different. This one became a fight between black and white.

One of the girls had been talking on the phone while the other was listening to a radio program. One had complained that the other was being too noisy, but neither was prepared to compromise. In the end, both radio and telephone were forgotten while they screamed at each other in the corridor. It was never firmly established which of them had first brought color into it, but the myriad versions of "you white girls don't respect anybody" and "go back to your country if you don't like the way we are" that later flew around the school clearly indicated the direction the quarrel had taken.

What disturbed me most was the divisive aftermath of the conflict. There was a tacit need for everyone to take a stance. I feigned a senior's indifference to the immature carryings-on of the juniors, but Mira was not fooled. At lunchtime Stella and Jenny joined our table. I longed to hear Stella's opinion on the topic but did not want to ask her. So I almost dropped my fork when I heard Mira say in a bantering tone: "Hey, so you two are flouting the new rule of segregation, are you?"

"Nothing to do with me," said Stella with a dismissive shrug.

"Pathetic," said Jenny as she passed the ketchup. "I wish they'd grow up."

Stella squirted the ketchup all over her chips and dug into them with gusto. I could see that the topic had already vacated her mind, and I envied her detachment. I was quiet on the way back to classes, and when Mira said, "You don't have to take sides you know, Claudia," I pretended to be brooding over my upcoming mathematics lesson.

But Folake would not allow me to forget the incident. She knew Yinka and her family from Nigeria and was outraged on their behalf.

"Do you know what that small girl said to her?" she fumed when she came to our room that evening. "She told her that she couldn't even speak English properly and then she and her white friends imitated her accent and laughed. Ah! How I wish I could take the lot of them to Nigeria, just for one day. They would smell pepper!"

My African blood boiled up. "Couldn't speak English properly?" I shouted, "Can she speak Yoruba? Why didn't they ask her how many languages she can speak? Someone who can speak only one language, insulting a person who can speak three or four! Chia! They feel so superior, but they don't know that in Africa even the children speak two or three languages."

With every sentence my voice grew louder, faster, and more Ghanaian. Mira shot me a look of mingled awe and amusement. As the conversation heated up she kept up with us by waggling her head from side to side in that uniquely Indian way, that blend of a nod and a shake which looks like no but means yes.

Folake invited us back to her room to share some Nigerian food her aunt had brought on the weekend. Mira was tactful enough to know that Folake really wanted to be alone with me, to bathe in the surging African tide. And indeed, it seemed like an appropriate moment to do such a thing, almost like drinking a toast to the renaissance of our African unity, our enlistment in the war against the insolence of spoiled white girls.

I watched Folake mix the gari and water with that deft grace with which Africans handle food. I was already being transported back to Ghana, even before I caught the pungent, mouthwatering aroma of the salt fish stew. She had warmed it on the little stove in the upstairs kitchen and beamed with pride as she brought it in.

"It's my favorite," she said, spooning it over the moist mounds of gari in the two plates. With eager anticipation I watched the steaming orange rivulets of palm oil trickle over the white sides of the gari like lava from a volcano. We settled on her bed, plates in our laps, relishing the saltiness and the added pleasure that eating with one's fingers always seems to impart to a meal. The unique flavor of the palm oil, the coarsely chopped slivers of onion so characteristic of a West African stew, and the fiery tang of the chili pepper were like old friends found again.

"Ah! Ah! Ah! Tell your auntie I said her stew is toooooo sweet!" I sniffed, sinuses streaming and eyes watering from the pepper. Folake smiled at my African turn of phrase, understanding the compliment. She asked if my mother ever prepared food like that. "Not anymore," I said. "She made the effort when we were in Ghana. But as for the salt fish . . ." I laughed and she nodded knowingly.

"Yes, the smell! As for that one, the oyibos can't stand it."

"Hmm, you know already! How she hated it! She didn't want that fish in the house at all! I used to ask her how she could complain about it when she loved eating those moldy, stinking cheeses. Kai! I could never bring that stuff close to my mouth."

Folake heartily agreed and as we marveled over this gastronomic puzzle, the door opened and Sarah walked in.

Astonishment registered on her face as she saw me seated cross-legged on Folake's bed, plate balanced in my lap, oily orange fingers halfway to my mouth. I could tell at once that the greatest shock had been to discover that the loud African voice chatting and laughing with Folake did not belong to one of her Nigerian friends, but to me.

"Hi, Sarah!" I said too quickly and too brightly.

"Hello, Claudia," she said in a voice which could easily have continued, "pleased to meet you." The shock had been so great that she could not hide her discomfort. She had entered her own room to find herself in alien territory.

"You're invited," I said, unable to think of anything else to say.

"Invited?" she echoed, shaking her head in irritated confusion. "Invited to what?" I pointed at the food.

"No thanks," she said. She was polite enough not to put into words what her eyes said, which was, "How can you eat something that smells like that?" Instead she said, "I was just coming to get my glasses." She grabbed them from her night table and, without further ado, fled the smell of salt fish and the two aliens sitting in the African den that had once been her room. There was an uncomfortable silence that Folake broke with, "My friend, as for dis one she no fit chop am!"

"No, you're right of course. She doesn't know how to eat it," I replied, using a Ghanaian expression that had always infuriated my mother. "What do you mean you don't know how to eat it?" she would say. "Just put it in your mouth, chew it, and swallow it!" But Africans knew what it meant. Sarah could no more have eaten that food than performed a Yoruba dance on the spot.

I giggled at the expression because the memory of my mother's indignation always made it amusing to me. Folake giggled at her own use of broken English. Some tension was released, and I started to feel sorry for Sarah and a little disloyal.

"I hope we didn't offend her," I said.

"Ah-ah! Why should she be offended?" asked Folake. "We didn't do anything wrong. This is also my room."

"Yes, of course, I know," I said hastily. "But I think we made her uncomfortable. She's such a nice girl," I added lamely.

"Well, you may find her nice but you don't have to live with her."

"I just don't know why two people as nice as you and her can't get on," I said with some exasperation, finally giving voice and life to that delicate topic.

"Claudia, please! That girl looks down on me because I'm a Nigerian. She doesn't like my music because it's too 'noisy,' she doesn't like the smell of my food—you saw her just now, didn't you, turning up her nose at it. She doesn't like my African friends coming to the room. She thinks she's better than me just because she's oyibo. And she always wants the window open when it's freezing cold. I can't even feel comfortable in my own room because of her. Ah-ah!"

"Folake, Sarah is not like that. Honestly. She's not one of those girls who looks down on people just because they are black. I've known her longer than you, you know. I mean, she's always been perfectly nice to me."

"Yes, but you aren't really black are you? I mean, you can also be an oyibo when you want to. She doesn't see you as a black. That's why she's so nice to you. As far as she's concerned, you're one of them."

I was not happy with the turn the conversation was taking. I felt somehow offended without being sure exactly which part of what she had said had upset me. I was not even sure if the offensive part had been explicitly stated or implied. Or whether it just hung there between the lines, with or without the intent of the speaker. I also felt that familiar sense of unease that always pervaded me when the issue of taking sides, of being "one of them or one of us" was so bluntly articulated. What I was sure about was that I was no longer comfortable in that room.

I finished my food a little too quickly and told Folake I was sleepy. She had already sensed that the mood was spoiled and did not make it any more awkward for me. That was one of the reasons I liked her: she was sensitive and intuitive. I knew she would not have said what she had if I had not brought up a delicate topic. I had only myself to blame.

After that incident I renewed my resolve to stay in neutral territory. However, as if the cosmos itself had determined to make me face up to my own duality, things came to a head a mere fortnight later. It is amazing how an event of barely a minute's duration can generate hours, even days of discussion, then years of reflection. Yet a minute was probably all it took from the moment Sarah placed the wastepaper bin on Folake's bed until we burst into their room to find a handprint emblazoned on her cheek. Five fingers, long and graceful, stamped beautifully in scarlet on a background white with shock. I had always envied Folake's elegant fingers.

They were locked in a thrashing embrace, clawing, tearing, swaying dangerously. As Mira and I pried them apart, Stella and Jenny came running down the corridor from their room.

"What the—oh my God!" gasped Jenny.

"She hit me, she hit me!" Sarah screamed, as if it weren't evident. Folake stood there with a face like thunder, looking as if she would like to slap her again. I looked from one to the other, lost for words. Mira pulled Sarah away, sat her down on her own bed, and put her arms around her. Sarah collapsed into sobs, ruining the perfect contrast as the red of outrage and humiliation spread all over her face and neck.

The doorway was crowded now as more girls arrived to see what all the noise was about. In her fury Folake addressed us all as one.

"That bitch put the dustbin on my bed!"

Where Sarah's feelings seemed to be composed of equal parts anger, fear, and humiliation, Folake's consisted of pure, unadulterated rage.

"How dare you?" she spat in Sarah's direction, making the word "dare" sound like an explosion. As all eyes turned to Sarah, she wailed: "I didn't even realize what I was doing, I was just trying to sweep the floor."

"Oh please!" snorted Folake. "You knew exactly what you were doing, you wanted to insult me. To tell me I am no better than rubbish." The more impassioned she became, the more Nigerian she sounded.

Realizing the futility of talking to her, Sarah addressed herself to the rest of us. "I always lift up the bin when I'm sweeping—sometimes I put it on the table, sometimes on my own bed, it doesn't really matter. I just wasn't thinking when I put it on her bed. I wasn't trying to insult her. I don't know why she has to be so touchy." And she started crying again.

At that moment the housemistress arrived at the scene. She took in Sarah's weeping distress and Folake's icy fury in a glance. Aware that she might not obtain a clear picture of events from either of them, she allowed Jenny and Stella to acquaint her with the basic facts before ordering all of us back to our rooms. Before we left I went up to each of them briefly.

"Sorry, Sweetheart," I said patting Sarah's shoulder awkwardly. "You'll be fine. Can I get you anything in town?" It was harder to look at Folake, her unrepentant rage more daunting to face than tearful misery. So I just said, "Let's talk about it later, OK?"

Out of the corner of my eye I saw Stella watching me with an amused expression and as we walked down the corridor, she said with a smirk, "Poor old Claudia, always trying to be everyone's friend." The sting of that well-timed remark lasted for years, but over time, my resentment mellowed into something bordering on pity for her.

After speaking to the two girls, the housemistress telephoned their homes and asked for them to be collected from school. They returned on Monday, Sarah with her mother and Folake with her aunt who served as her guardian in England. After a long meeting in the headmistress's office it was decided that Folake, as the primary aggressor, should be suspended for the rest of the term. This would also neatly postpone the need to solve the accommodation problem for the two of them until the next term. Since the Christmas holidays were little more than a week away, it was not such a long sentence, however it did mean that it was Folake's last day of school until the new year.

Sarah was punished with a detention for engaging in a fight. She was furious as she felt she had only been defending herself, but as she later recounted, the headmistress said she should have walked away and reported the situation immediately. Both girls were reminded in the crispest terms that fighting was unseemly, unladylike, and utterly forbidden at Ridgefield.

I had little chance to discuss events with Folake before she left that day or indeed to do much beyond saying good-bye and wishing her a Merry Christmas. Although I spent some time with her while she packed her things, we could not talk properly in front of her aunt. Only when her aunt carried the bags downstairs did she hug me.

Perhaps she read in my eyes that I felt let down, that I wanted to ask her why she had done it—why had she lived up to their stereotypes?—for she said in a rush: "Claudia, I'm not usually a violent person, you know that. But she really offended me and it was the last straw. I can't put up with that sort of thing anymore. I have my dignity too. I know she's your friend too, and I'm sorry you're . . . caught in the middle, but it's OK, you don't have to take sides."

Folake was put in a different boarding house the following term. Several of her Nigerian friends were there so she fit in easily and became even more a part of their set than she had been before. These changes, combined with our increased workload as we prepared for our examinations, facilitated a natural loosening of our relationship. Mira and I still chatted with her whenever we sat together in the dining hall, but things were never quite the same as they had been before the fight.

Ten years after we left Ridgefield I received a telephone call from Mira.

"You'll never guess who called me this morning, Claudia!"

It was Folake. She had stayed in touch with Mira longer than with me, but it was still at least six years since Mira had heard from her.

"She's married now and guess what, she's just had a baby, a boy!"

I was delighted and full of questions. Apparently Folake had married an Englishman whom she had met at university and was now settled in England for the long term. I could not imagine my old schoolmate as a married woman and with a baby! A little mixed baby, brown—like me.

"She wants to get back in touch with you, Claudia. I gave her your number, I knew it would be OK with you. It is, isn't it?" To my surprise, I felt tears in my eyes, and I think she heard them in my voice although it was just for an instant.

"Of course, Mira! Of course it's OK."

"I told her we'd come and see the baby. Can you imagine seeing Folake again!" And we started reminiscing about her, what a character she was, the fun we had had together, her irresistible "Ah-ah!" that we couldn't wait to hear again. As I giggled like a schoolgirl I felt a slight lightening of a burden I had carried for years.

"I can't wait, Mira, it'll be so great!" She giggled in turn, rolling back ten years with that girlish sound, and although we were on the phone, I could just see her, waggling her head from side to side.

As a child I found nothing strange about having one black parent and one white. It seemed as natural a divergence as the fact that one was male and the other female. Being yet another color myself seemed equally unremarkable. But definition comes from others, and it gradually seeped into my consciousness that I was assigned the identity of the parent who was foreign—the white one. Later, when I lived in Europe, I realized that the same

rule applied, and my racial identity reversed from white to black. Mastering the balancing act of contradictory racial identities in the knowledge that those imposing them are often unaware of their very existence is a demanding task in and of itself. Even more difficult, however, is the task of defining one-self. "Human Mathematics" is the story of a mixed-race person forced into self-evaluation by simultaneous loyalties to friends who match her different racial sides. It is a reflective piece on a journey of self-analysis, which I could not fully recognize or comprehend at the time I began it. During this journey I was sometimes assailed by guilt and self-doubt, but I arrived, finally, at a secure acceptance of my racial identity for precisely what it is—mixed.

Neela Vaswani

Neela Vaswani is half Indian (Sindhi) and half Irish (County Kerry). She is the author of *Where the Long Grass Bends*, a collection of short stories. Her work has appeared in the *O. Henry Prize Stories*, *Shenandoah*, and *The Cimarron Review*, among other publications. She is a Ph.D. candidate at the University of Maryland and teaches in the brief-residency M.F.A. in Writing program at Spalding University. She lives in New York City.

Bing-Chen

I t's too long," his mother said. "You look like a crazy bird."

His hair, brown, lank, was tufting around his ears.

"My girl's in Chinatown. Gives a good cut. Pretty, too. You could get me a newspaper; there was a flood near Gualin."

"It's fine," he said.

"Sticking up all over. Like a bird."

"Let's talk about something else."

"So much grey—you're starting to look like me."

"I'll go, I'll go. I'll get a haircut. What's the name of the paper?"

She twirled her brush, ground the ink.

"Just use a pen."

"David. You can wait a few minutes."

He watched her hands, the knuckles fat and crippled. She put the brush to paper, her strokes lean; the two black characters shiny.

"Show it to the vendor," she said. "You won't even have to open your mouth."

He took the subway to Grand Street, his mother's directions and the name of the newspaper in his pocket. A heat welled from the sidewalk. He eased through the crowds to a produce stall selling cabbages, spiny leechees, winter melon. His mouth watered when he saw the pomegranates.

To avoid a huddle of tourists, he walked in the street. He passed stalls crammed with wind chimes, wicker birdcages, calculators, dolls with motorized, wagging heads, black cloth shoes with tin buckles, then consulted his mother's directions. *Get off subway. Go south and east. Second right. Chicken store on corner.*

There, plucked and hanging in the window. Four of them, with talons, and glazed, blue eyes. Chickens had dangerous feet. On the plate, in pieces, they seemed harmless. He turned right.

It was an alley, not a street, and it smelled of fish. Laundry flapped from the fire escapes. A woman in a white shirt leaned from a window, smoking a cigarette.

He could still buy the newspaper and go home.

But it was hot. His hair felt sticky. He might as well get it cut.

The door swung open, inward. His mother's girl. She was Chinese, of course. With dyed-blonde hair and square, pink-painted nails. She said, "*Ni hao ma.*"

He shook his head.

She laughed. "OK. Come in," and pulled him through the door.

"You're third. I have two other customers. Prom day."

She led him from a dark foyer to a wide, square room. On a couch was a woman filing her nails. David sat down. The nail file rasped, rasped.

There was only one counter, one mirror, one chair. Pictures of cats and Tom Cruise were taped in neat rows around the mirror. The girl stood in front of it, scissors in hand, and snipped at the ends of her blonde hair. She wore a pink tennis dress and white high heels. There were Band-Aids across the backs of her ankles.

The woman rose from the couch and disappeared through a red-beaded partition. She left the nail file.

"Bye, Ma." The girl raked her fingers through her hair and peered at her roots in the mirror.

"You Chinese, Mister?"

"Half," he said.

There was a knock at the door. The girl dunked the scissors in a container filled with Windex-colored fluid and black combs.

"Who's Chinese? Ma or Da?"

"My mother," David said. "My father was American. German."

The girl laughed, "My mother washes hair, my father works at bank," and walked with light taps to the door.

A brunette and a red-haired girl stood glowing in the stairwell light. Both girls held transparent, plastic bags. The brunette went through the red beads for a hair-washing. She had curly hair, tight, thick curls, hair that grew out, not down. Her body curved with the softness of porn stars, a good shape over nice bones. As the red beads clicked around her, she lifted her shoulders and cringed.

The other girl was hard-faced and deeply tanned. She moved the nail file and sat down on the couch with David. "So, Ming," she said, "do you want to hear about my dress?"

"OK, sure."

"I got it at Bloomie's. It's black organdy with a trim of pearls. Strapless. My mother says it looks perfect with my red hair."

"Nice," Ming said, but her lips stuck to her teeth, dry and false. The girl waved her mother's check between her fingers, its amount line blank. When Ming did not walk over to collect it, the girl dropped it on the floor next to the couch.

To David she said, "Me and Marcy come to Chinatown just for Ming. My mom discovered her last year. Our cleaning lady comes here, too. She's so cheap, it's scary. Ming, I mean, not our maid."

What a voice. Husky, like she'd been smoking twenty years longer than she'd been alive. David picked up the magazine lying between them and cleared his throat. The hard-faced girl used her pinkie to clean lipstick from the corners of her mouth.

H ow you want it?" Ming asked Marcy as the girl parted the beads and entered the room, a towel draped over her shoulders, her hair wet and heavy around her face. She held out a magazine picture of a model with gleaming, pin-straight hair. Ming snatched it away and jammed the picture into the side of the mirror. She pumped a bar at the bottom of the chair, raising it a few inches.

First, Ming combed Marcy's hair, yanking her head back-ward with each stroke. Then she removed a spiked brush and hair dryer from a hook at the side of the counter and tilted the girl's face upward, scrutinizing her. Sighing, Ming pointed the hair dryer at the picture in the mirror. "No good," she said. "We do my way." Marcy started to protest, then leaned back in the chair.

Scowling, Ming pulled at Marcy's hair. She used some purple goop, then sprayed something from a plastic bottle. Except for an almost imperceptible twitch of the eyelids, Marcy was still. David felt sorry for her. She wanted a different self, but her hair-dresser wouldn't allow it.

He watched Ming rotating around the girl. At times Marcy's hair looked awful, stuck with metal pins and plastic clips, but when Ming released a section from its confines, it fluttered down elegantly. Ming worked fast, her mouth set and determined, blonde hair swinging. Her black roots spread from the crown of her head in a star shape.

The sweetness of hairspray made David drowsy. He closed his eyes, daydreaming about the hard-faced girl. He pictured her stepping carefully into her strapless black dress, afraid to muss her hair. Her shoulders were freckled. He saw her sitting stiffly in a chair, looking at a clock.

M arcy was hugging Ming. Her hair was beautiful, still curly, but twisted into long, smooth spirals. She smiled at David. "God Bless America," he said, and whistled.

Ming held up a hand mirror so Marcy could see the back of her hair. The hard-faced girl sat on the couch, legs crossed, licking the tips of her fingers and turning the pages of a magazine. She would be a paradigm First Lady, polished and brisk, MADE IN THE USA labels sewn into her blazers, a compact and travel-size tissues in her purse. When it was her turn to be coiffed, she allowed Ming to swathe her in a plastic apron that snapped shut at the neck like a bib. She looked directly at herself in the mirror, sure of how she would turn out.

David wondered how he appeared to the prom girls. Did they think he was old? Did they know he was Chinese? He had said only three words—for all they knew, he could be fresh off the boat. But no, his shoes and pants were obviously American. And he had no accent. His brown hair graying on the sides; his brown eyes deep and gathered. Epicanthic folds, his ex-girlfriend, Kerry, a med student, had said.

Sometimes people could not tell he was Chinese; other times it was all they saw. It had always been like that. He suddenly wished he could have the constancy and assurance of Ming and the prom girls. Made of one thing, they knew who they were. So young, and they already knew.

His mother had liked Kerry. They still kept in touch, sent holiday cards: *Kerry is starting a private practice; she's married; they had a boy.*

W hen the prom girls left, Ming stood in front of David; "You're uneven on the sides," she tugged on her blonde hair. "I'll fix it. No problem."

Heels tapping forcefully, she led him behind the red beads into a small room. By a filmy window he saw a sink with a scooped neckrest. Shampoos and dyes stacked the shelves above the sink. An olive green hat with a peaked brim hung on the wall. It looked like a Communist cap. To the left of it was a narrow staircase. He saw a pile of folded towels on the bottom step.

When he settled his neck and head in the sink, he was practically lying down. He was surprised when Ming began washing his hair, but he did not ask about her mother.

Vigorously, she scrubbed his head. Her long nails scratched at his scalp, hurting and tickling. David closed his eyes and let her clean him, relaxing as she cradled his head with one hand and rinsed the back of his neck with the other. A breeze from a fan moved the beaded partition. It clicked softly.

He thought of the painting above his mother's bed. As a child, he had liked to look up at it. A snowcapped mountain, deep in wispy clouds. Shan Shui, mountain and water landscape—his mother had told him. One day, he realized there was a man in the picture standing with a staff at the base of the mountain. It made him feel strange to think he had looked at the painting for years without ever noticing the tiny figure.

Bing-Chen, Bing-Chen? he could hear his mother calling him. By his name, his Chinese name. She only called him David if she was mad at him—or his father. Sometimes she called him Little Rat. As he had left her apartment earlier in the day she had said, gently: "Things will get better. It's your year, Little Rat."

The smell of peanuts and red-bean paste filled the room. From upstairs, he heard a sizzling, then smelled chicken. Ming was leaving. He should follow her.

She held up her hand, "Stay there. You need more time."

He lay back in the chair, his head resting in the curved sink. The smells here were familiar, homey. His mother cooked chicken with bok choy and straw mushrooms. He looked at the exposed pipes hanging above his head.

Yellow. Laney Carson, his prom date, had worn a yellow dress. He had bought her an orchid.

He remembered the shock on Laney's face when he introduced his mother. "I didn't know you were Japanese," she said. She had blinked.

"Sorry," he answered.

What a stupid thing to say. Sorry. He hadn't even corrected her.

O K. It's time," Ming said, and led him to the counter. She stepped on a pedal, lowering the chair. This part was always uncomfortable. He didn't know where to look—in the mirror, at the wall? Maybe he should close his eyes.

Ming circled him, tilting his head up and down. She combed his hair forward, then parted it down the middle, drawing her finger up the line of his scalp. Snipping and sighing, muttering and tugging, she moved around him. His hair was black with wetness. She did not seem to be cutting much, just, somehow, shaping.

Switching on the hair dryer, Ming feathered her fingers through David's hair. He closed his eyes and thought of his mother sitting in the same place, the same chair. Her gnarled hands in her lap. Ming was her girl. They probably chatted the entire time, telling stories and jokes.

He didn't want to talk. He wanted to sit there, under the warm stream of air and Ming's light, soft hands.

T he hair dryer stopped whirring. David opened his eyes. His hair was dry, jet black and glossy. Ming had dyed it.

It hung around his face in an oval frame.

"Looks good," she said and grinned. "Thirty bucks."

Scattered around the chair was a pile of shorn hair, rising slightly in the wind of the oscillating fan. His black, Marcy's brown, the hard-faced girl's red, sprinkles of Ming's blonde. The fluffy heap was like an animal. With a push broom, Ming swept the pile to the side of the room. She straightened the magazines and put the hard-faced girl's check on the counter between a can of Aquanet and a statue of Future Buddha, *Mi-lo Fuo*, who predicted the weather and carried a cloth bag of treats for children.

Yes, he had listened. He remembered some things.

His hair was shiny and even on the sides. He looked younger. Like his mother's first cousin. Ming hadn't asked his permission. But the dye-job did look good.

He would get his mother's newspaper and drop it off on his way home. They would have tea, listen to the radio. She would tell him about the flood near Gualin.

Emptying his wallet, David gave Ming forty dollars. "Here," he said. "*Xie-xie*. Thanks."

She lifted a hand in farewell. "*Zai jian*."

In high school, there was a girl whose hair I admired—black, wavy, to the small of her back. One day she came to school with her hair cut short and ragged. I heard she had cut it herself, the night before, after breaking up with her boyfriend. Her hair took on greater meaning for me. It became an expres-

sion of loss, transformation. The power of a haircut to change: that idea stuck with me. Many years later, I was walking on Mott Street in New York City's Chinatown, and I glimpsed a girl with dyed blonde hair standing in an alley. I went home and wrote "Bing-Chen."

To me, the heart of the story is Bing-Chen's identity and how he relates to it. People have always asked me the strange and annoying question: "What are you?" Sometimes people see that I am Indian (but never Irish); sometimes they think I am Lebanese, Mexican, Portuguese (but never Irish). In my youth I longed to have what I mistakenly perceived as the stability of being "one thing." I felt the insipid social pressure, the myth that to be of two cultures is to be somehow confused. To me, Bing-Chen is at a particular phase of selfhood. He is on the verge of being comfortable with his identity as a shifting, fluid negotiation. I wrote the story seven years ago, but I still think of him. I see him, happy, sitting in a lurching subway with his mother. They speak a mix of Mandarin and English, and at the end of a sentence, he laughs.

MALLORY SAMSON

Kien Nguyen

Kien Nguyen was born in Nha Trang, South Vietnam. He left the country in 1985 through the United Nations' Orderly Departure Program. His first book, *The Unwanted*, is a critically acclaimed memoir and deals with the struggle of growing up as an Amerasian under Communist rule. He has also written two novels, *The Tapestries* and *Le Colonial*. He was nominated for the Grinzane Cavour Prize and won the 2005 NCM Pulitzera Prize for ethnic writers. He is now writing his fourth book, *One Hundred Percent American*, about growing up ethnic in America. "The Lost Sparrow" will be included in this novel.

The Lost Sparrow

Out of the darkness a mellow glow spilled down on her. Where was it coming from? Like a full moon it illuminated the corroded bars of her cell and glinted off the only piece of furniture, her metal-framed bed. The air was heavy with tobacco—the scent of her stepfather.

She held her breath, even though she knew it was useless to hide from him. Despite her attempts to block him out, her pores had absorbed him, her hands were black with the dirt from his back, and her face dripped with his sweat. The cage was swaying lazily. She heard it creak—a low rumble with no echo.

A tattered dress clung to her skin. As she sat in isolation on the thin mattress, her mind went back to the cottage where she lived, along with her mother and stepfather and their two children—a mute boy of five and an undernourished girl of three. Both were too tiny for anyone to believe their ages. Their home had a low, worn-out corrugated tin roof with holes as large as coconuts, a single metal bed, two wooden chairs, and a pit in one corner of the dirt floor that they used as a toilet.

It had been thirteen years since her American father had impregnated her mother and returned to his land of rich and plenty, never to be seen or heard from again. She had been forced to call another man *bố*. In the stifling heat she often watched her stepfather sitting on his haunches, chewing on chicken feet and gulping clear rice alcohol from a brown terracotta bowl with a chipped rim. The front of his shirt was stained with the mud of the rice fields. His thin lips, under a reddish mustache slick with chicken fat, smacked with delight, while his slits of eyes darted at her from beneath thick, blue-black brows.

She would never tell him that she and her half-brother and half-sister went without food while he feasted on chicken feet and rice wine. She would just sit against a bedpost, saying nothing, clutching her siblings while her mother roasted a few sparrows over an earthen kiln. She had caught the little birds earlier that day. The smell of singed feathers was enticing, and she was mesmerized by the fire that licked its tongues around the dark morsels of flesh.

These are young chicks, her mother would say as she turned the spit, and the children inhaled deeply. *They are delicacies only served in fine restaurants*, she added, nodding her head in confirmation. The girl would say nothing as she swallowed her saliva. She knew hunger well, had known its pangs since the day she was born.

She had placed the sparrows' feet in the sun to dry, then strung them together so she could wear them in a necklace. If they really had been young chicks, as her mother claimed, her stepfather would have eaten them. But since they were not, she wore the necklace of sparrows' feet as a sign of her own strength. Feet to walk, so she could take herself away from this place. Feet to nourish her anger, to fill her with power so she could challenge her stepfather. Feet to take her forward and back, so she could retrace her life, to identify the point when everything had gone wrong, hopefully to make it right. Decorating her neck with sparrows' feet didn't make her a savage; it made her a survivor. The birds' talons dug into her skin, constantly reminding her of who she was.

This is one fine looking half-breed, and I've seen many. Her stepfather's mustache rustled, like aging corn tassels. She could feel his fingers stroke her hair. *So blond,* he whispered. *Just like a mermaid.* He lifted her and she screamed.

Be careful, her mother warned. *Don't frighten her! She's the ticket that will take us to America.*

It was raining. The roof of their hut leaked and her mother caught the water in the only cooking pot she had. Her belly was soft and streaked with stretch marks, like a burlap blanket that had served beyond its time. *And you. Stop wailing like a cat in heat. What in hell is wrong with you?* her mother growled. *Be grateful for your father and obey him, make him happy. Look at the others of your kind that were left on the street corners, begging for money, going through trash cans fighting for scraps of food like dogs. You don't know how lucky you are.*

The girl covered her eyes. She knew what her mother was talking about. The idea that she could become one of those cast-off children was enough to make her sick with fear. She knew about the babies who had been abandoned at birth. Periodically those who survived were collected and brought to the orphanages throughout the city. Beyond the tall walls and barbed-wire fences, their woes could still be heard.

Shortly after the fall of Saigon, on a bright day when she was six, her mother had taken her to the city. For most of the journey her mother had wept loudly, until she had collapsed on the tarpaulin-covered floor of the bus with her head buried in her daughter's lap. At last she had gone limp and, the girl suspected, fallen asleep.

A Catholic nun had met them at the door of a decaying building and showed them through the three-story former hospital that housed over five hundred children and only two caretakers. From the top floor the girl had looked over the banister and watched the orphans below, ranging in age from a few days to ten years, trapped in their own filth. Feces had been smeared on the walls, on the floors, and in and around the beds. Many of the children had been naked, their rib cages visible under their taut skin, their faces dirty and wise beyond their years. They'd reminded her of a barrelful of live frogs, hundreds of them stacked on top of each other, that she had seen in the market.

The nun had led them down a hall to a smaller quarter filled with cribs. Each crib had held two or three infants. The nun had hit the bars on the windows with a cane she carried to keep the children away from the guests. *Mrs. Tran,* she'd said to the girl's mother in a low voice. *I cannot take in any more children. I'm sorry if she was your mistake, but as you can see, the orphanage is desperately understaffed. Sister Tam and I are two old women and this place is out of control. I have begged the government to help us, but so far, we haven't heard from them. I cannot—*

Near them, a thin voice had cried out. A child had tried to climb over the bars of the crib, his tiny arms reaching out, his whole being begging to be held. The girl had caught him before he'd fallen and he'd clung to her with all his might. The entire room was starving for affection.

The nun had pulled the child from her, as though peeling a lizard from a wall. Her face had been a collage of dirt and sweat and tears, and her small eyes, behind the thick-rimmed spectacles, had been swollen and red veined. She'd rocked the child on one shoulder.

I'm sorry, she'd said. *You can't pick them up. Once you do, they'll hang on forever.*

The toddler had whimpered. Hope and despair had collided in his eyes. She'd felt as if she were looking in a mirror. Her mother had grabbed her hand and stormed down the stairway, not stopping until they were back at the bus station.

That had been 1975. Now she realized she was worth something—an airplane ticket that would take them to America. The soldier who had caused her mother so much shame was now regarded as a savior. A new law allowed anyone who could prove half heritage with an American to resettle in the new world as a refugee. Her golden hair and hazel eyes would guarantee her flight to freedom, accompanied by her full-blooded Vietnamese family.

Cool, damp air traced her barely formed breasts. When she reopened her eyes, she was inside the cage. Her bed swung, suspended like a hammock. The creaking metal, her stepfather's scent, the dark universe of her cell, everything she had feared returned with the savagery of an insane hunter. She was trapped, alone, in the emptiness of dead moments.

She shouted, packing her whole being inside that scream. Her cry vanished without an echo. She inhaled and screamed again. And again. Her shouts seemed to make the cell shudder and get smaller. She grabbed the bars and sank to the bottom of her cage. The moonlike pool of light dangled above her, like a thick cloudbank against the surrounding darkness.

Soon, the light seemed to grow hotter and her skin glistened with sweat. It would be nice if it rained, and she could sit in the shade of a banyan tree, like the one she used to frequent near the rice paddies beyond her village. Beneath its thick leaves, she had watched over her brother and sister and taught them to set a trap to catch sparrows. Like the birds, they'd come there to seek the tree's refuge.

Their trap was made from a V-shaped metal bar. Each end was fastened to an elastic inner tube, which in turn was tied to two wooden stakes that were driven into the ground, giving the appearance of a large slingshot. The apparatus was stretched back as far as the children's thin muscles could pull it and held in place by a pin. A string connected the pin to where they hid, behind the rugged tree trunk.

Grains of rice were the bait that lured the unsuspecting birds. At the precise moment, the girl would release the pin. A loud, cold, brief thud would silence the other birds. Then a tiny droplet of blood would splatter on a nearby rock. But in the quiet of a still afternoon, it made an everlasting sound.

She never wavered. Constant, nagging hunger honed her concentration, and she would always release the pin at the right time—except on one occasion. Her target that day had been a male sparrow, but he'd looked different from the others, almost like a finch. The colorful plumage covering the crest of his head had glistened in the sunlight as he stood before her, suspicious and alive. Despite her hesitation, the pin had released itself. What happened next was over in less time than it took to draw a breath. She'd watched a tiny ball of feathers, wings spread and feet jutting, hurtle into the air and then fall to the ground. The sun had beat down on his limp body. The girl could always guess how much damage she had inflicted on her prey by the way it was hit. She'd sat and waited. She'd noticed the tip of the sparrow's wing shudder; but from the distance, it might have been from the wind.

The other children had crept forward. She'd moved ahead of them. Her bare feet had felt the hot sand. The smallest bird she'd ever seen lay crumpled in the dirt. All color seemed to have drained from him. One of his black eyes had blinked, looking up at her. The whitish yellow stripes drawn back from the sides of his beak indicated that he was still a fledgling. She'd picked him up. His grip on her finger had been unsteady.

She'd reached for the crude bamboo cage, made of woven twigs, that the children used to carry their catch home, in case a stunned bird should awaken and try to escape. Opening the door, she'd placed him on the bottom of the cage, turning her face to avoid his penetrating stare. When she'd slid the little gate shut, its snapping sound had jolted the bird from his stupor. He hopped to his feet, one wing hanging much lower than the other—a clear sign of a broken bone. His excitement had grown as he'd found himself trapped, and he'd begun poking his head through the bamboo bars, over and over, quickening his pace as his efforts proved to be vain.

She'd held the cage in her palms and sat on the dirt. For several minutes she hadn't moved, while her brother and sister hovered by her side, watching the wild bird hammer his head through the slits until his beak bled. Could a creature so small understand the futility of its actions? she'd wondered. He'd never give up trying. A metal bowl of water near him had gleamed in the sunlight, and she had had to squint to look at the sparrow. With the sun directly on top of them, his plumage had seemed to be on fire as he'd sagged to the bottom of the cage, furled his uninjured wing to his chest, and expired.

The last thing she recalled was the way the sparrow had stared at her with his half-shut eyes. In his gaze she'd seen her own hopelessness, each time she was pinned under her stepfather. His lust, like the sting of a strap, was a crescendo of pain that she must bear alone, in the darkness.

Each time it happened, she became paralyzed. She closed her eyes, yet she saw everything, her body steeping in his breath, her mind retreating, going mad with the urge to flee. When daylight came, her shame and her fear were too much to bear. The happiness on other children's faces taunted her, for she would never regain her innocence. She paced the schoolyard, shivering, trying to shake off his imprint. Loneliness enfolded her, and darkness made a void in her chest as cold and empty as death.

Dead, dead, she tried to fix upon the possibility of death as an escape from her tormentor, and yet she yearned to live, to twirl in the glorious sunlight, embracing herself with her twiglike arms.

The road that led to the freeway that led to another city waited for her, full of promise. But terror pulled her back, and she was still inside the cage, in a false universe that spread to infinity. She tried to look beyond the dim, glimmering light into the thick blackness around her. From it came a powerful stir that touched something deep inside her. The creaking of her cell grew louder as it seemed to contract. Rusted metal bars ground against each other and sent sparks flying into the air.

She explored the jail looking for an escape. Gripping the metal bars, she poked her head through them. She searched a long time, putting all her efforts into this quest, hoping to find a secret door that would release her. She flew from one bar to another like the sparrow, trying to squeeze through the open spaces, feeling the welded joints, licking the drops of condensation, tasting the rusted metal. Thinking back to her science classes, she tried to learn from the patterns of corrosion, the way the paint peeled, the smell of the rust, and the dampness of the cool, humid air. This was her time and her life, and everything in this cage had become a part of her. She inched along the cell, touching, sniffing, talking to herself, examining, her pulse beating the rhythm of the squeaking, until she came back to her starting point. She clung to the bars, out of breath. Her face bled, her nails were caked with filth, and her tongue was chapped from the rust. Exhausted, she crumbled onto the floor.

She was afraid to shut her eyes again, to sleep. With her eyes closed she would see only the darkness. She would no longer be real. There would be just a void, silent and unending. Eventually she might become part of it, but never voluntarily. She would go on poking through the metal bars, searching for an escape from this dreadful place. Her mind might deteriorate with the incessant repetition, but she would keep trying to figure out the things that made up this world.

Listen to your mother. You don't want to upset me, your new father. His breath brushed against the nape of her neck.

No words could ever describe her fear of him. She had

learned to go to bed with a knife hidden under her pillow, but she was never able to bring herself to reach for it. His weight crushed her into small pieces, one, two, three, four, countless times being penetrated, mangled, killed, hundreds of invasions, hundreds of deaths. He was a monstrous creature above her, laughing and panting and sweating. One night, instead of waiting for him to retreat, she had plunged out into the dark night, her hand clutching her necklace of sparrow feet. The wind howled as she ran down the street, her bare feet striking the ground, the ugly discharge dripping down her legs. The village was asleep, dreaming behind closed doors. She strewed the fragments of her broken self along the road, leaving a path of sparrows' feet that fell from the string of her talisman.

Behind the tree, reality was different. From there she could see the whole village. She used to stare down the long winding road to the end of the hill, where certain women would come outside and sit under the awning of a shop that sold rice wine. When their feigned laughter caught the attention of the local rickshaw drivers, the women would bare their breasts, driving the men mad with passion. In the shameless display of human flesh, the women's faces and expressions were too far away to be distinct, yet she could see the sores on their bodies. Sometimes the wives of the rickshaw drivers would run down the hill in a pack and throw rocks at the brazen women. A fight would break out for a few minutes. The prostitutes were like a disease waiting to contaminate everyone.

The banyan tree spread its powerful branches, solid and quiet and ancient, a pillar that connected the earth to the heavens, a safe haven for all the lost sparrows. She found the tree without looking for it. Her feet straddled its roots as she talked to it, her thin limbs wrapped around its rough bark, seeking comfort. If only she could be one with the tree, then she would be no longer afraid.

Under the branches she adjusted her torn dress and tried to smooth her hair, the golden strands that set her apart from the rest. She felt the tree whisper its wisdom, telling her what it had seen, in the beginning, when a Vietnamese village girl had allowed an American soldier to mount her in exchange for a carton of cigarettes. She pictured their wordless struggle of hurried pleasure amid the mad war, the stray bullets felling the buffalos, the birth, her birth, the way her golden hair first felt the soil when she was released into this world.

When her mother found her, deep in the shadow of the tree, she had found her voice to ask, *Where were you when I cried for you? My new father is now the father of my unborn child.*

Liar, liar. Her mother's unexpected, exploding anger silenced her. The girl's cheeks burned with vengeful slaps. She was dragged home by the hair. *You filthy liar. How could one so young come up with such lies? I don't believe you. Not my Thien. He's a good man.* Slap. Slap. Her mother shoved her to the floor of the hut. *You want to act like a whore? I'll sell you to that brothel down the road.* She saw herself among the bare-breasted women. The sores would sparkle on her skin like jewelry. *Damnable whore.* She tried to rise. The room blurred and she swayed. She tasted blood in her mouth. Her knees were scraped, her elbows bruised. Slap. Slap. Her stepfather arose from his drunkenness. She looked at him in growing horror, knowing things before they happened.

How could you do this to me? her mother screamed at him. *We have big plans. Now you're ruining everything. How are we going to explain this to the American officials? They'll never let us in.*

The grimace on her stepfather's face deepened. His reddish mustache quivered. *Such lies*, he said. Chaos everywhere. The sparrows flying blindly. The gigantic tree, silent—hardly a witness. And the moon. And night. All had changed their melodies. With the back of his hand he slapped her so hard she sailed through the air and landed in her cage. She howled, remembering his lust. Looking down at her from above, he kicked her repeatedly in her stomach, then switched position to stomp on her head . . .

She stood under the pool of light. All she had learned was

that she was alone, from the moment she took her first breath, inhale, exhale. When she breathed, she remembered, and she saw herself moving through a world that could not see her, people who had become blind, among the lost sparrows that couldn't defend themselves. Somehow she was alive, trapped inside herself, in a darkness that had no end, watching shadows, with an unknown source of light overhead, his odor everywhere, as she experienced fear, horror, and madness over and over again.

The cage shook. Creaking sounds reverberated as the bars vibrated. The light above her reddened, like a bucket of burning oil ready to pour down on her. The black heavy shadow that had been lurking around her reached forward. It gripped her metal cage and ripped it apart as if it were made of bamboo. Flocks of sparrows streamed from her open palms. She looked down and saw herself, lying in a hospital bed perfectly still. She stared at the hateful black figures surrounding her bed, shadows that resembled her mother and her stepfather as if they were fragments of her memory. She flew past them, and the scenery in front of her changed—the banyan tree was now a bright torch in a world filled with tall buildings. She flew alone. Where she was going, they were not allowed.

When I was about six or seven years old, just before the fall of Saigon, I was introduced to Chim Hót Trong Lồng, *a novella written by a well-known South Vietnamese writer, Nhật Tiến. Translated, the title means "When a songbird sings in a cage." It's a diary of a little girl who was born by a Vietnamese prostitute and a foreigner. She was left in a strict boarding school run by Catholic nuns, in which parents could only visit on Sundays. On that day the girl would dress in her best clothes and wait outside at the gate, most of the time in vain as her mother rarely made an appearance. At the end, her mother died of tuberculosis, leaving her behind to an uncertain world.*

As I was growing up, this story affected me a great deal because I, too, have a Vietnamese mother and an American father whom I've never met. And I, too, was sent to a similar school. Students were allowed to see their parents only on Sundays. As a little child, I knew what that waiting was like. And I developed an invisible but everlasting bond with the author, whom I'd never met.

In the resort town where I lived, there were many children born to unknown American fathers. After the Communist takeover in 1975, many of them were abandoned and destined to live off the street, labeled as children of the dust. Even those who lived in homes led a poor existence because of the new regime's cruelty and intolerance. My story, "The Lost Sparrow," was inspired by such a girl I once knew. She was a beautiful, angelic child of eight when the rumor of her stepfather raping her first surfaced. To profess his innocence, this man beat her daily, claiming to the neighborhood how he couldn't have committed such a crime since he hated her so vehemently. Eventually her mother sold her to a local brothel. On my way to school, I would see her sitting among adult women, all waiting for customers. When the girl saw me walk by, she would never look up. Years passed and she contracted a sexually transmitted disease. I left my town for America and never learned her fate. I can only assume.

In writing "The Lost Sparrow," I wanted to give an ending to those lost innocents I witnessed. As for me, I married the daughter of the man who wrote Chim Hót Trong Lồng. On my wedding day, he whispered to me, "From now on, you can rest assured you have a father." And I have called him Dad, ever since.

Danzy Senna

Danzy Senna is the author of two novels, *Caucasia* and *Symptomatic*. She is a recipient of a Whiting Writers Award, a *Los Angeles Times* Best Book of the Year Award, a Book-of-the-Month Club Stephen Crane Award for First Fiction, and the Alex Award from the American Library Association.

Triad

I. Cherries in Winter

Laura smells what's happening under the table, but she doesn't say anything. It doesn't seem appropriate to mention, given the circumstances. Nobody else says a word either. They just eat their food in silence. A new one floats up, and Laura tries to hold her breath as she takes another bite of turkey. It's more difficult than she imagined, to eat without breathing.

Laura's mother died yesterday. She died quietly, all drugged up, in a white room surrounded by black nurses. It was a planned death, like a planned pregnancy. Everybody had plenty of time to mourn before the official end actually came. Relatives from both sides have come to town for the funeral tomorrow, and the aura at the table now is one of suppressed relief and impatience for the ceremony to be over.

The last time Laura saw her mother was two weeks ago, in the hospice in New Haven. Her breasts were gone and she wore a bandana over her head so that she looked like a young boy. So pale, she looked almost see-through. She drifted in and out of awareness, but when she was awake, all she could talk about were cherries: the blood red of them, the sweetness of them, the coolness of them, the sensation of the pit rolling over her tongue. Laura went everywhere that cold gray day looking for cherries, but they were out of season and when she came back to the hospice her mother was not talking about cherries anymore. Her eyes were closed and it was time for Laura to catch the train back to campus.

A new smell wafts up from under the table. It's unbelievable that such a small dog could make such a big impact on the world. Laura holds a napkin over her mouth and eyes the other guests. They scrape at their plates unhappily.

"Pass the gravy, Laura," her father says, nodding his big head toward the bowl. Her father looks fatter than he did two weeks ago. The weight sits on his chest where it's supposed to be most deadly. She hands him the gravy.

Aunt Mabel made all the food. She and Gus drove from Syracuse this morning with a whole trunk-load of steamy Tupperware containers.

"Have you chosen a major?" Uncle Gus asks her from across the table.

"Fine arts."

"Better than crude arts." Uncle Gus snorts with laughter after he says it.

Laura just nods and takes another sip of wine.

Through the window above Gus's head, she can see it has begun to snow. Soft flakes drift down and make a home on the branches of the apple tree where she used to sit, hiding from the world. She went there for many reasons, but the one she remembers most is her father. Once, it was her runny nose that made him angry. He couldn't stand the sight of it. He saw it as evidence of stupidity. He came after her one day, holding a car key wrapped in toilet paper. He wanted to pick her nose, but he didn't want to use his actual finger so he'd made this prosthesis. Laura shrieked and sobbed and squirmed out of his grip, and made it up that apple tree before he could catch her.

Now that Laura was an adult, her nose-running had turned into chronic nasal congestion, sinusitis, as it were. A wan vegetarian in her dormitory at school suggested that she might be allergic to wheat and dairy. Last month she'd stopped eating both and her nose was now a clear and easy passageway. She thinks that if her nose were still blocked she wouldn't be able to smell the stench under the table. Another one floats up just then, a real doozy. Aunt Mabel coughs into her napkin.

"Jesus fucking Christ," her father says, rising. His chair falls to the floor behind him. "Where is that damn dog?"

He reaches under the table and she hears the yelp of Atticus, being dragged out from his hiding place. Atticus is old, nearly toothless. He was her mother's dog, a replacement baby for when Laura got too old to hold. Her mother used to take that dog everywhere. Now he sleeps almost all the time. Her father grips the dog by the scruff and belts him once, twice, across his rump. The dog scurries away whimpering, his tail between his legs.

Her father picks up his fallen chair, looks down at the table, daring anybody to say a word.

Uncle Gus snorts with laughter. "I thought it was you all that time, Bob."

Aunt Mabel laughs a little and everybody goes back to their food.

Except Laura. She stares out the window, where the snow is falling harder. When she was a kid, Laura used to play a game at dinner. She would imagine that she was a passerby on the street out front, somebody who just happened to glance in through their picture window at this dinner scene. She would imagine herself and her family through that stranger's eyes: a red-faced and bearded fat man at the head of the table, a slightly haggard wife serving food from the kitchen, a pudgy girl with braces feeding scraps to the dog under the table. Would they see this scene and think, Happy Family? The American Dream? Or would they notice the details: the swiftness with which the father belted back his glasses of scotch? And the way his voice grew louder and more slurred with each course? Would they know just from looking that some nights after dinner, his rage ended with that small mother bloody and bruised and weeping? On those nights, Laura would lie in the dark holding her pillow and praying to some faceless Sunday school God that her mother not die tonight. Because she always believed her mother would die a bloody death at her father's hand. She never guessed her mother's death would come from the inside out—a pedestrian passing of the most common and blameless variety.

L aura lies in the dark of her bedroom staring at the embers of her teenaged self. A poster of Harrison Ford still hangs above her bed, another one of Jennifer Beals from *Flashdance* beside her dresser mirror. Her stomach makes unhappy sounds. Aunt Mabel's turkey isn't sitting well with her, but somehow she drifts off to sleep.

She wakes sometime later in the darkness to the sound of beeping garbage trucks outside.

Her mother looked almost beautiful in that hospice bed, androgynous and tiny, translucent. The last thing she said to Laura: "What I wouldn't do for a nice cold bowl of cherries."

Laura gets up and goes to the bathroom off the hall with the puffy pink toilet seat that makes a sighing noise when she sits down on it. It's only four-thirty A.M. She heads back to her room but instead of getting back into bed she dresses in the dark, then goes outside and sits in her father's Chevy, letting it warm up before she rolls slowly out of the driveway.

Connecticut is an embalmed state. The houses sit like taxidermy, animals stuffed and hung, their marble eyes watching her as she cruises past. The Star Market is open. She doesn't know if it's been open all night or if it has just now opened for the morning. The only other person she sees as she moves through the aisles is a man behind a table. Over him hangs a sign that says ENSURE: COMPLETE BALANCED NUTRITION FOR A HEALTHIER YOU. Behind him is a sculpture of bottles with the same words on them. When she moves past, he holds up a Dixie cup with white fluid in it. It reminds her of the hospital, the fluids that flowed in and out of her mother. "Would you like to try Ensure?" She shakes her head and moves on toward the produce department.

The fruit is piled neatly, identical apples and identical pears, not a mark on their waxy skins.

There are cherries too, imported in the winter from Peru. The sign says 5.99/LB. She fills a bag until it can't hold any more.

Outside, the parking lot is still empty, but the sky has begun to brighten. She sits in the Chevy with the motor running, eating the cherries. They don't taste very sweet. They are dry rubbery things, and after a few tries she sets them on the seat next to her.

When her mother came home that afternoon so many years ago, she found Laura perched in the tree, still hiding from her father. Her mother put her hands on her hips and laughed at the sight of her daughter. "Is that a monkey up there?" she called up. "Come on down, Sweetie Pie, I need your help."

That same evening, Laura sat at the kitchen table and snapped green beans and watched her mother move around, cooking dinner and humming to the sound of Billie Holiday on the radio. Or, no. Maybe it was Johnny Cash. She isn't sure. And as she thinks about it, she isn't sure about any of the details. She can't remember what her mother was wearing, whether she was thin or fat, how she wore her hair, in a bun or down around her face. She can't remember what she looked like before the illness. Hard as she tries, she can't conjure up her face. It's slipping away already. And she knows there will come a day when she won't miss her mother anymore—a day when she only misses the feeling of missing. But she's not quite there yet. She still feels something of the dead hovering inside her. It lives for a moment in her chest, misshapen and bruised as a backyard fruit. She closes her eyes and lets it hang inside her. Then it falls away, too heavy to hold. She starts up the engine and heads on toward home.

2. Peaches in Winter

Yvette smells what's happening under the table, but she doesn't say anything. It doesn't seem appropriate to mention, given the circumstances. Nobody else says a word either. They just eat their food in silence. A new one floats up, and Yvette tries to hold her breath as she takes another bite of turkey. It's more difficult than she imagined, to eat without breathing.

Yvette's mother died yesterday. She died quietly, all drugged up, in a white room surrounded by a bevy of island nurses. It was a planned death, like a planned pregnancy. Everybody had plenty of time to mourn before the official end actually came. Relatives from both sides have come to town for the funeral tomorrow, and the aura at the table now is one of suppressed relief and impatience for the ceremony to be over.

The last time Yvette saw her mother was two weeks ago in the hospice in New Haven. Her breasts were gone and she wore a bandana over her head so that she looked like a young boy. Her skin seemed to grow darker the closer she got to the other side, as if she was turning to wood before Yvette's very eyes. She drifted in and out of awareness, but when she was awake, all she could talk about were peaches: the swirling blush of them, the sweetness of them, the coolness of them, the final sensation of the pit against her tongue. Yvette went all around New Haven that cold gray day looking for peaches, but they were out of season and when she came back to the hospice her mother was not talking about peaches anymore. Her eyes were closed and it was time to catch the train back to campus.

A new smell wafts up from under the table. It's unbelievable that such a small dog could make such a big impact on the world. Yvette holds a napkin over her mouth and eyes the other guests. They scrape at their plates unhappily.

"Pass the gravy, Yvette," her father says, nodding his big head toward the bowl. Her father looks fatter than he did two weeks ago. The weight sits on his chest where it's supposed to be most deadly. She hands him the gravy.

Aunt Grace made all the food. She and Byron drove all the way up from the city this morning with a whole trunk-load of steamy Tupperware containers.

"Have you chosen a major?" Uncle Byron asks her from across the table.

"Fine arts."

"Better than crude arts." Byron snorts with laughter after he says it.

Yvette just nods and takes another sip of wine.

Through the window above Byron's head, she can see it has begun to snow. Soft flakes drift down and make a home on the branches of the apple tree where she used to sit, hiding from the world. She went there for many reasons, but the one she remembers most is her father. Once, it was her runny nose that made him angry. He couldn't stand the sight of it. He saw it as evidence of stupidity. He came after her one day, holding a car key wrapped in toilet paper. He wanted to pick her nose, but he didn't want to use his actual finger so he'd made this prosthesis. Yvette shrieked and sobbed and squirmed out of his grip, and made it up that apple tree before he could catch her.

Now that Yvette was an adult, her nose-running had turned into chronic nasal congestion, sinusitis, as it were. A wan vegetarian in her dormitory at school suggested that she might be allergic to wheat and dairy. Last month she'd stopped eating both and her nose was now a clear and easy passageway. She thinks that if her nose were still blocked she wouldn't be able to smell the stench under the table. Another one floats up just then, a real doozy. Aunt Grace coughs into her napkin.

"Jesus fucking Christ," her father says, rising. His chair falls to the floor behind him. "Where is that damn dog?"

He reaches under the table and she hears the yelp of Rex being dragged out from his hiding place. Rex is old, nearly toothless. He was her mother's dog, a replacement baby for when Yvette got too old to hold. Her mother used to take that dog everywhere. Now he sleeps almost all the time. Her father grips the dog by the scruff and belts him once, twice, across his rump. The dog scurries away whimpering, his tail between his legs.

Her father picks up his fallen chair, looks down at the table, daring anybody to say a word.

Byron snorts with laughter. "I thought it was you all that time, James."

Aunt Grace chuckles a little and everybody goes back to their food.

Except Yvette. She stares out the window, where the snow is falling harder. When she was a kid, Yvette used to play a game at dinner. She would imagine she was a passerby on the street out front, somebody who just happened to glance in through their picture window at this dinner scene, and she would imagine her family through that stranger's eyes: a bespectacled light-skinned man with a goatee, a slim, nervous, brown-skinned woman serving food, a pudgy preteen girl in cornrows feeding scraps to the dog under the table. Would they see this scene and think, Happy Family? The American Dream? Would they see this scene as evidence of progress? Would they think, how wonderful, a black family living in this neighborhood? Or would they understand that the father, the good doctor, wore two faces? A healer by day could become cruel by night, wounding with the scotch flowing through his veins. Would they know just from looking that some nights after dinner, his tirades ended with her mother weeping at his invectives, wishing aloud that she were dead? On those nights, Yvette would lie in the dark holding her pillow and praying to some faceless preacher God that her mother not take her own life. Because in her heart, she always believed her mother would die at her own hand. She never guessed her mother's death would come from the inside out—a pedestrian death of the most common and blameless variety.

Y vette lies in the dark of her bedroom staring at the embers of her teenaged self. A poster of Michael Jackson still hangs above her bed, another one of Jennifer Beals from *Flashdance* beside her dresser mirror. Her stomach makes unhappy sounds. Grace's turkey isn't sitting well with her, but somehow she drifts off to sleep.

She wakes sometime later in the darkness to the sound of beeping garbage trucks outside.

Her mother looked almost beautiful in that hospice bed, androgynous and tiny, like a dark, fragile doll imported from a distant land. The last thing she said to Yvette: "What I wouldn't do for a peach."

Yvette gets up and goes to the bathroom off the hall with the puffy pink toilet seat that makes a sighing noise when she sits down on it. It's only four-thirty A.M. She heads back to her room, but instead of getting into bed she dresses in the dark, then goes outside and sits in her father's Chevy, letting it warm up before she rolls slowly out of the driveway.

Connecticut is an embalmed state. The houses sit like taxidermy, animals stuffed and hung, their marble eyes watching her as she cruises past. The Star Market is open. She doesn't know if it's been open all night or if it has just now opened for the morning. The only other person she sees as she moves through the aisles is a man sitting behind a table. The sign over his head SAYS ENSURE: COMPLETE BALANCED NUTRITION FOR A HEALTHIER YOU.

Behind him is a sculpture of bottles with the same words on them. When she moves past, he holds up a Dixie cup with white fluid in it. "Would you like to try Ensure?" She takes the cup and sips from it. The drink tastes like chalk. It reminds her of the hospice, the fluids that flowed in and out of her mother in her last year. She hands it back, wipes her lip, and moves on toward the produce department.

The fruit is piled neatly, identical apples and identical pears, not a mark on their waxy skins.

There are peaches too, imported in the winter from Peru. The sign says $2.99/LB. She fills a bag with five of the heaviest, ripest ones she can find.

Outside, the parking lot is still empty, but the sky has begun to brighten. She sits in the Chevy with the motor running holding a peach. It's perfectly round and perfectly soft, but when she takes a bite, it doesn't taste sweet. It is a mealy, tasteless thing, and after a few nibbles she sets it on the seat next to her.

When her mother came home that afternoon so many years ago, she found Yvette in the tree, still hiding from her father. Her mother put her hands on her hips and laughed at the sight of her daughter. "Is that a monkey I see up there?" she called up. "Come on down, Sugar Pie, I need your help."

That same evening, Yvette sat at the kitchen table and snapped green beans and watched her mother move around, cooking dinner and humming to the sound of Billie Holiday on the radio. Or, no. Maybe it was Johnny Cash. She isn't sure. And as she thinks about it, she isn't sure about any of the details. She can't remember what her mother was wearing, whether she was thin or fat, how she wore her hair, in an Afro or braids. She can't remember what she looked like before the illness. Hard as she tries, she can't conjure up her face. It's slipping away already. And she knows there will come a day when she won't miss her mother anymore—a day when she only misses the feeling of missing. But she's not quite there yet. She still feels something of the dead hovering inside her. It lives for a moment in her chest, misshapen and bruised as a backyard fruit. She closes her eyes and lets it hang inside her. Then it falls away, too heavy to hold. She starts up the engine and heads on toward home.

3. Plums in Winter

Soledad smells what's happening under the table, but she doesn't say anything. It doesn't seem appropriate to mention, given the circumstances. Nobody else says a word either. They just eat their food in silence. A new one floats up, and Soledad tries to hold her breath as she takes another bite of turkey. It's more difficult than she imagined, to eat without breathing.

Soledad's mother died yesterday. She died quietly, all drugged up, in a white room surrounded by stern-faced nurses. It was a planned death, like a planned pregnancy. Everybody had plenty of time to mourn before the official end actually came. Relatives from both sides have come to town for the funeral tomorrow, and the aura at the table now is one of suppressed relief and impatience for the ceremony to be over.

The last time Soledad saw her mother was two weeks ago, in the hospice in New Haven. Her breasts were gone and she wore a bandana over her head so that she looked like a young boy. Her green eyes had the frosted sheen of sea glass as she writhed under the hospital sheets. She drifted in and out of awareness, but when she was awake, all she could talk about were plums: their blue-red skin, the sweet messiness of their juice, their coolness, the final sensation of the pit against her tongue. She talked about how there was no other word to describe the color of a plum than the word for the thing itself. *Plum.* And wasn't that remarkable? Soledad went all around New Haven that cold gray day looking for plums, but they were out of season and when she came back to the hospice her mother was not talking about plums anymore. Her eyes were closed and it was time to catch the train back to campus.

A new smell wafts up from under the table. It's unbelievable that such a small dog could make such a big impact on the world. Soledad holds a napkin over her mouth and eyes the other guests. They scrape at their plates unhappily.

"Pass the gravy, Soledad," her father says, nodding his big head toward the bowl. Her father looks fatter than he did two weeks ago. The weight sits on his chest where it's supposed to be most deadly. She hands him the gravy.

Aunt Rose made all the food. She and Uncle Izzy drove down from Boston this morning with a whole trunk-load of steamy Tupperware containers.

"Have you chosen a major?" Izzy asks her from across the table.

"Fine arts."

"Better than crude arts." Izzy snorts with laughter after he says it.

Soledad just nods and takes another sip of wine.

Through the window above Izzy's head, she can see it has begun to snow. Soft flakes drift down and make a home on the branches of the apple tree where she used to sit, hiding from the world. She went there for many reasons, but the one she remembers most is her father. His temper. Once, it was her runny nose that made him angry. He saw her runny nose as evidence of stupidity. He couldn't stand looking at it. He came after her one day, holding a car key wrapped in toilet paper. He wanted to pick her nose, but he didn't want to use his actual finger so he'd made this prosthesis. Soledad shrieked and sobbed and squirmed out of his grip, and made it up that apple tree before he could grab her.

Now that Soledad was an adult, her nose-running had turned into chronic nasal congestion, sinusitis, as it were. A wan vegetarian in her dormitory at school suggested that she might be allergic to wheat and dairy. Last month she'd stopped eating both and her nose was now a clear and easy passageway. She thinks that if her nose were still blocked she wouldn't be able to smell the stench under the table. Another one floats up just then, a real doozy, followed by the dog's satisfied lip-smacking. Aunt Rose coughs into her napkin.

"Jesus fucking Christ," her father says, standing. His chair falls to the floor behind him. "Where's that damn dog?"

He reaches under the table and she hears the yelp of Blue being dragged out from his hiding place. He was her mother's dog, a replacement baby for when Soledad got too old to hold. Her mother took Blue everywhere with her when he was a puppy. Now Blue is old, nearly toothless. He sleeps almost all the time. Her father grips the dog by the scruff and belts him once, twice, across his rump. The dog scurries away whimpering, his tail between his legs.

Her father picks up his fallen chair, looks down at the table, daring anybody to say a word.

Izzy snorts with laughter. "I thought it was you all that time, Melvin."

Aunt Rose chuckles a little and everybody goes back to their food.

Except Soledad. She stares out the window, where the snow is falling harder. When she was a kid, Soledad used to play a game at dinner. She would imagine she was a passerby on the street out front, somebody who just happened to glance in through their picture window at this dinner scene, and she would imagine her family through that stranger's eyes: a portly black man at the head of the table, a zaftig red-haired woman in a peasant blouse serving food from the kitchen, a surly teenaged girl with corkscrew curls feeding scraps to the dog under the table. Would they see this scene and think, Happy Family? The American Dream? Would they even understand that this was a family? People got confused sometimes. They made up complicated explanations for the family—the man must be foreign, the woman must have adopted the kid from Brazil—rather than going with the obvious. Would they guess that the good professor liked to bellow when he was drunk? Would they guess that the good professor, with all his Poitier dreams, had a problem with his temper? Would they see that the mother wore makeup sometimes to hide her bruises? Not only would they guess it, but they would assume it. And so the girl, the corkscrew-curls girl, always smiled hard and wide on picture day, so wide her jaw hurt a little, hoping that her smile could save them all from the assumptions. Behind the smile, she always believed back then that her mother would die at her father's hand. But her father went to a meeting one day in the basement of a church and got sober a year later; and eventually, the hitting disappeared along with that bottle of scotch. And somehow her parents stayed together, started to look a little alike. And in the end, her mother's death came from the inside out—a pedestrian passing of the most common and blameless variety.

L ater, Soledad lies in the dark of her bedroom staring at the embers of her teenaged self. A poster of Public Enemy still hangs above her bed, another one of Jennifer Beals from *Flashdance* beside her dresser mirror. Her stomach makes unhappy sounds. Aunt Rose's turkey isn't sitting well with her, but somehow she drifts off to sleep.

She wakes sometime later in the darkness to the sound of beeping garbage trucks outside.

Her mother looked almost beautiful in that hospice bed, androgynous and finally thin, the girl-woman a thousand diets had failed to make her. The last thing she said to Soledad: "What I wouldn't do for a nice cold plum."

Soledad gets up and goes to the bathroom off the hall with the puffy pink toilet seat that makes a sighing noise when she sits down on it. It's only four-thirty A.M. She heads back to her room, but instead of getting into bed she dresses in the dark, then goes outside and sits in her father's Chevy, letting it warm up before she rolls slowly out of the driveway.

Connecticut is an embalmed state. The houses sit like taxidermy, animals stuffed and hung, their marble eyes watching her as she cruises past. The Star Market is open. She doesn't know if it's been open all night or if it's just now opened for the morning. The only other person she sees as she moves through the aisles is a man sitting behind a table. The sign over his head says ENSURE: COMPLETE BALANCED NUTRITION FOR A HEALTHIER YOU. Behind him is a sculpture of bottles with the same words on them. When she moves past, he holds up a Dixie cup with white fluid in it. "Would you like to try Ensure?" She stares into the cup, always tempted by free lunches, but it reminds her of the hospice, the opposite of plums. She shakes her head and moves on toward the produce department.

The fruit is piled neatly, identical apples and identical pears, not a mark on their waxy skins.

There are plums too, imported in the winter from Peru. The sign says 3.99/LB. They are mostly hard, the gold of their youth still showing under the purple. She fills a bag with six of the ripest she can find.

Outside the parking lot is still empty, but the sky has begun to brighten. She sits in the Chevy with the motor running, eating a plum. It doesn't taste sweet or messy. It is a hard, clean, bitter thing, and after a few tries she sets it on the seat next to her.

When her mother came home that afternoon so many years ago, she found Soledad in the tree, still hiding from her father. Her mother put her hands on her hips and laughed at the sight of her daughter. "Is that a monkey up there?" she called up. "Come on down, Babe, I need your help."

That same evening, Soledad sat at the kitchen table and snapped green beans and watched her mother move around, cooking dinner and humming to the sound of Billie Holiday on the radio. Or, no. Maybe it was Johnny Cash. She isn't sure. And as she thinks about it, she isn't sure about any of the details. She can't remember what her mother was wearing, whether she was thin or fat, how she wore her hair back then, in a braid down her back or frizzed up and wild around her face. She can't remember what she looked like before the illness. Hard as she tries, she can't conjure up her face. It's slipping away already. And she knows there will come a day when she won't miss her mother anymore—a day when she only misses the feeling of missing. But she's not quite there yet. She still feels something of the dead hovering inside her. It lives for a moment in her chest, misshapen and bruised as a backyard fruit. She closes her eyes and lets it hang inside her. Then it falls away, too heavy to hold. She starts up the engine and heads on toward home.

"Triad" is three versions of the same story. In each one, the race of the protagonist changes, along with certain details. For each girl, the emotional experience of losing her mother is nearly identical. It is only from the perspective of the outsider, the reader, the watcher, the passerby on the street, that the story splits apart into three separate narratives. I wanted to explore the tension between the internal invisible self of a character, and the external self projected onto her by the world. I suppose this story also reflects my ambivalence about the categorizations imposed on writers of color. We are expected to offer up authentic representations of our group, to serve up culture as neatly as platters at an ethnic food fair. Stay true to your race, stay true to your experience, write what you know *goes the mantra. But why would any writer choose to contract when she could expand instead?*

Credits